THE MAGICIAN'S TAL

THE MAGICIAN'S TALE

DAVID HUNT

Hodder & Stoughton

Readers interested in learning about achromatopsia are urged to
contact Ms. Frances Futterman; The Achromatopsia Network;
P.O. Box 214; Berkeley, CA. 94701-0214; USA.

Copyright © 1997 David Hunt

First published in the USA in 1997 by G P Putnam's Sons
First published in Great Britain in 1997 by Hodder and Stoughton
A division of Hodder Headline PLC

The right of David Hunt to be identified as the Author of
the Work has been asserted by him in accordance with the
Copyright, Designs and Patents Act 1988.

10 9 8 7 6 5 4 3 2 1

British Library Cataloguing in Publication Data

Hunt, David
The magician's tale
1. English fiction – 20th century
I. Title
823.9'14 [F]

ISBN 0 340 68891 2

Typeset by Palimpsest Book Production Limited,
Polmont, Stirlingshire
Printed and bound in Great Britain by
Clays Ltd, St Ives plc

Hodder and Stoughton
A division of Hodder Headline PLC
338 Euston Road
London NW1 3BH

THE ILLUSION

This illusion is performed out of doors, often in a dusty field. The magician works inside a circle surrounded by spectators, assisted by a young girl, his obedient daughter.

Near the end of his show, the magician suddenly and unexpectedly takes hold of the girl, pulls a dagger from beneath his cloak and slits her throat.

Blood spurts, spattering their smocks and sometimes the clothing of spectators nearby.

The magician stuffs the body of the girl into a bulb basket he has used throughout the show. Once she is inside, he covers the basket with a cloth, and mutters incantations.

Removing the cloth he shows the audience that the basket is empty, the body of the girl gone.

Just then the spectators hear a shout from beyond the circle. They turn to see the girl gaily running through the crowd into the magician's waiting arms.

– J.M. Frost, *Strange & Extraordinary Feats of Indian Magic* (1888)

ONE

THE SUN IS ABOUT to set. I check myself in the mirror – glowing eyes, dark brows, small triangular face, medium-length dark hair parted on the side. I brush down some wisps so they fall across my forehead, then dress to go out – black T-shirt, jeans, black leather jacket, sneakers, Contax camera around my neck.

I wear black to blend in. My hope is that by dressing dark and with my face half concealed by my hair, I can slink along the streets, barely seen, covertly stealing images.

I pause at my living-room window. Dusk is magic time, the sky still faintly lit. Street lamps are on and lights glow from windows, making the city look mysterious and serene. The view's so spectacular it's hard to tear myself away: North Beach, Telegraph Hill, the Bay Bridge sharply defined, all still, silent, glowing behind the glass.

I move to my telescope, set the cross-hairs on a penthouse terrace just below Coit Tower. The image is so clear I feel I can touch it if I reach out. Garden chairs, pots overflowing with geraniums, sliding glass doors leading to an art-filled living room behind. No lights on inside. The Judge must be working late. I know him well. I have no lover now.

I take another moment to savour the view. I'd like to stay, watch the sky turn black, perhaps wait until the lights come on in that living room across the valley. But it's time to go out; I have an appointment with a friend.

It's chilly tonight. I turn the collar of my jacket up, peer around. A cable car is poised at the top of Lombard. Tourists disembark to descend the famous crooked street. I enter the park in front of my building, named for George Sterling, poet of the city. He composed some good lines, was eloquent on the fog, wrote 'its touch is kind', described San Francisco as this 'cool gray city of love'. He also wrote: 'At the end of our streets are stars.' Not bad. Unfortunately, Sterling was no Carl Sandburg, but then San Francisco isn't a 'City of the Big Shoulders' either.

I pause by the Alice Marble Tennis Courts, turn to look back at my building, slender in the dusk. I make out lights in some of the apartments and the glow of a Japanese paper lantern in mine. I shrug, cross the park, look for the young bearded homeless guy who sometimes sleeps amidst the bushes. Failing to find him, I take the stairs that descend the steep western slope of Russian Hill.

Polk Street: it's quiet, residential at its upper end, but as I stride south it takes on a different character. Apartment buildings give way to stores and restaurants, then, slowly, block by block, to sleaze.

Around California Street they begin to appear – the crazed, the addicts, the dispossessed. Sad, sick, broken, they perch on the sidewalk beside signs and cups, or slouch within doorways against glossy garbage bags filled with their possessions.

I pass a cavernous old movie-house, a trio of junk shops, a metaphysical bookstore, cheap Chinese restaurants, funky hotels and saloons, sleazy erotic boutiques and adult film rental joints. The strip here, called – sometimes affectionately, more often disparagingly – Polk Gulch, intersects with alleys bearing the names of beautiful trees: Fern, Hemlock, Myrtle, Olive, Willow.

In these passageways I observe young men poised alone against the sides of buildings, others lingering in small groups, twos and threes. There's a glow about them, a force-field of energy. Hustlers of different races, objects of desire, they stand still, silent, awaiting clients.

I've been roaming this neighborhood since the beginning of the summer, always at night, always armed with my Contax. Those first weeks I didn't take pictures, preferring simply to look, explore, make my presence known. As I picked out probable subjects, they, too, began to notice me. Spotting my camera, they gave me a name, Bug, short for Shutterbug. I disliked it but pretended I didn't, since a street-name here connotes acceptance.

'Hey! It's Bug. She's on the street.' Word flashes down the Gulch as if by semaphore.

Some also note my affliction.

'You blind, girl?' a scrawny, tattooed kid bellowed at me yesterday as I staggered along on one of my rare daylight excursions. 'What's with the shades, Bug? Drugged out?' Then, when I ignored him: 'Think you're a fuckin' star?'

I know better than to respond to taunts, a lesson I learned painfully on school playgrounds years ago. But to those who become my friends, I cheerfully reveal my handicap.

I'm an achromat, which means I'm completely colorblind.

The correct name for the malady is autosomal recessive achromatopsia. It's rare; I doubt there are five thousand of us in the US. I lack cone function in my retinas and thus cannot see colors. My visual acuity is poor, though better than most complete achromats. My biggest problem is photophobia, the reason that in daylight I must wear heavy, dark red wrap-around shades. Outside, on a brilliant sun-filled San Francisco afternoon, the rods in my eyes become saturated, the world goes white, I become lost in a dazzling blizzard – a sensation, I'm told, close to what vision normals experience as snowblindness.

But there are advantages. One is aesthetic – seeing the world uniquely in terms of gray tones instead of hues. Another is good night vision. In darkness, I like to think, I can see like a cat.

I'm searching for Tim. He called this afternoon, said he needed to talk. There was urgency in his voice, perhaps even fear. I offered to meet him at once, but he said he had to see someone first. We agreed to meet at his spot on Hemlock Alley at 7:00 p.m., then go up to the Richmond for dinner since he didn't think he'd feel like hanging around the Gulch.

It's 7:10 now and I see no sign of him as I occupy his niche beside the dumpster. The brick wall behind me, against which I've photographed him many times, is thickly layered with graffiti – names, symbols, dates, obscenities – most fading, a few freshly applied. I wait as the traffic thins out on Polk, but few passersby peer down the alley. It's still too early for the chickenhawks.

Tim and I met when I started taking pictures here. Of all the street people I've come to know these last months, he's the only one I think of as a real friend. He doesn't know it yet but he's also on his way to becoming the central actor in my project. All my best shots frame him – alone, surrounded by others, or on the periphery of a group. As for the formal portraits, his are the strongest. It's his eyes, I think, so large and luminous, and the fine shape of his chin and jaw, that make the camera love him. He's got the cheekbones of a Greek god, the unruly hair of a savage. Whether pouting in his niche against the graffiti-scarred wall or posing bare to the waist on

Angel Island with the city gleaming white behind, he emerges as a splendid modern *ephebe* – urban warrior, heroic, fragile, seductive. Yes, the camera loves him. The photographer loves him too.

7:30, getting cold, not a typical October night. *Where are you, Tim?*

He claims he's twenty but barely looks seventeen, perfect disproof of the adage that a life of vice will mark your face. His unsullied beauty is his capital. Creamy of skin, fair of cheek, he's the eternal adolescent of his clients' dreams. He tells me he intends to work the street a few more years, save his money and retire. He pauses, then confides he's already got fifty thousand dollars stashed. When I stare at him in disbelief, he shows me the smile of a sphinx. Surely if you have that much, I tell him, it's time to quit right now?

Gently he shakes his head. 'Not yet, Kay. I still enjoy it. The people . . .' He laughs. 'Well, most of them. The adventure too, not knowing what'll happen, who I'll meet. It's like an addiction – the money, being desired so much people pay big-time just to touch me. And it's fun playing diamond-in-the-rough.' He shows me his sweetest grin. 'Or rhinestone, as the case may be.'

Clever boy!

Yet even as I'm appalled by his casual disregard for my warnings – that sooner or later he'll fall into the clutches of a sociopath or be infected with HIV – I'm still beguiled by his glamour. Street-hustler as psychic explorer – that has emerged as my theme. In my pictures I want to capture the lives of those who, by offering their bodies to danger and to lust, risk all, and by so doing achieve a kind of stature.

'So,' I ask him, 'when you retire what will you do?'

'Live the good life,' he says softly. He's got it all figured out. He'll move down to Mexico, a town called San Miguel de Allende. Already, he tells me, he's picked out the house.

'Yo! You there! You for sale?'

It's Tim's friend, Crawford, a lean, blond Minnesotan hunk who somehow manages to maintain a permanent tan.

Crawf beams. 'You look really hot there, Bug. If I had some bucks I'd buy you in a flash.'

Hustler's banter . . . yet to be thirty-five and female and told one is attractive in a milieu where maleness and youth are the sole components of allure – I'm flattered.

'Waiting for Tim,' I tell him.

'Saw him last night. Not since.'

'If you do, tell him I'm here, okay?'

Crawf nods, smiles, tells me again how hot I look, then saunters off like a panther.

In fact, I've discovered, hustlers sometimes do purchase one another's services. Tim says it's fun to play the john once in a while, and that he's always flattered when another street kid wants to pay him for sex. When that happens, he tells me, street etiquette requires he approach the kid a few days later and reciprocate.

It's a quarter to eight and I'm getting impatient. I've never known Tim to be late. I decide to cruise the Gulch a while, then check back. I slide over to the intersection, turn the corner, become part of the stream.

Silver-haired businessmen hauling briefcases, sweaty evening joggers in Lycra work-out suits, frugal shoppers, doting couples, apprehensive tourists – we all run the gauntlet here, never certain what the street people will do.

An old Asian lady, Mao-era haircut and crazed eyes, gesticulates angrily toward my camera. Stepping toward a store-front to avoid her, I nearly trip over a street vender in swami position presiding over a display of flashlight batteries and tattered paperbacks.

'Watch it, Bub!'

Is he mispronouncing my street-name, or does he think I'm a guy? No matter, I hurry on.

Nearly everyone here under twenty-five displays a piercing. I note ringed eyebrows, lips, tacked tongues. If this is what they show, I wonder what baubles must dangle beneath their clothes?

I'm fascinated by the hustling scene, though it was fear and revulsion that originally drew me. Last spring, Maddy Yamada, my photography coach, suggested I get out of the studio, go into the street, start photographing what I feared. Struck by her advice, I realized that for years I'd feared the Gulch . . . and so decided to take it on.

At first I didn't know what I was after. It's easy and glib to document commercial sex. But on the Gulch, I became aware those early weeks, there were more interesting images to be captured. Meeting hustlers, I discovered unexpected qualities: gentleness, courage, love of adventure, even a desire to heal, which gave the lie to the view that those who sell their bodies must be desperate or hold themselves cheap.

With Maddy's help, her critiques of my proof sheets, I began to sharpen my vision. It wasn't, I understood, just the hustlers I should shoot, but the reactions to them in other strollers' eyes. Not just apprehension or fear . . . also cunning, avarice, lust. So, I asked myself, who here really are the stalkers and who the prey? And I thought: Perhaps with my camera I'll find out.

I spot Knob at the corner of Polk and Bush. He's talking to a middle-aged bald guy in a cashmere turtleneck. Knob's nearly thirty, old for the Gulch, sports a goatee, has close-cropped hair and a husky fire-plug build. Tonight he wears tight jeans, dark T-shirt, leather vest. Occasionally, I've heard, he'll do a session himself, but more often he acts as broker, negotiating deals for kids whom chickenhawks, fearful of jailbait, are too timid to approach.

Knob gestures, Baldy nods, the conversation appears intense. Then Baldy thrusts something into Knob's hand and moves away, casting down his eyes as I approach.

'Knob!'

'Bug!' Knob furtively sticks whatever into his pocket. I figure I've been witness to a drug deal.

'Negotiating?'

Knob sneers. 'Cheap guy. Too cheap to close.'

'What'd he want?'

'The usual.' Knob turns away. He's wary of me, thinks I'm a do-gooder, perhaps even an undercover cop.

I change the subject: 'Seen Tim?'

He shakes his head.

'Well, if you do—'

He makes an imaginary pistol with his hand, aims it at me, squeezes off a shot and winks.

8:15. Tim's more than an hour late. I'm worried – he's never stood me up before. I go to a pay phone outside the Wing Mai, call up my answering machine. No messages. Perhaps he lucked into a score. He couldn't have forgotten; his tone was too urgent. I feel something's wrong, but can't wait longer. I'm cold and hungry. I decide to get something to eat.

Two blocks south there's a Korean barbecue place I like, but tonight the smell out of the Wing Mai is good. I peer through the window, spot Alyson sitting with Doreen. The tables are linoleum and the lighting's fluorescent which hurts my eyes, but the girls are fun. I slip on a pair of shades, enter, present myself.

'Hey, Bug!' Doreen gestures me to a chair. 'We'll have a real girlie dinner now.'

They're pecking with chopsticks at a whole cooked bass. I summon the waiter, order a bowl of hot and sour soup. As usual Alyson and Doreen are dressed hot. They have slim figures, nice breasts, wear make-up. In most ways they're more femme than I am.

'How're tricks?' I ask.

Doreen moans. 'You want war stories?' She's the more ironic of the two. She and Alyson refer to one another as 'mates', room together, ply the same trade. I've been in their room at The Hampshire Arms – one huge bed, dirty windows, over-stuffed closets, jumbles of clothes on the chairs. They rarely take clients home, prefer to perform out, or, as a last resort, in cars. The clients don't mistake them for women. She-males, girls-with-cocks, are what they want.

'There was this john two nights ago . . .'

'Monday, Doreen,' Alyson corrects.

'Whatever. It was a *scene*.'

She describes an equestrian scenario they performed in a grand house on Tiburon Island: pony saddles, reins, horse tails, the works.

'See, we're supposed to be mares,' Alyson explains.

'The props were pretty good.'

'The john was the "stallion"?'

They smile, exchange a look.

'More like a gelding,' Doreen retorts.

Such stories fascinate me. I'm full of questions. Was it apparent that the Tiburon man had enacted the scene before, or did he strike them as a novice? And where did he get all those elaborate props?

My queries confuse them. They're not interested in the hows. It's the experience they savor, entering a client's madness, his fantasy.

'Actually, he was fine,' Alyson concedes.

'If you like dead horse meat,' Doreen adds.

Alyson breaks up. We share a sweet cooked banana dish for dessert. I ask if they've seen Tim.

'Yeah, yesterday,' Doreen says. 'He had attitude.'

'How do you mean?'

'Like he was on the warpath or something. He pranced.'

Alyson laughs. 'That's what we did Monday – oh, Lord, we pranced! Till our tails switched up and down. "Not side to side," the john kept saying. Should have seen him, Bug – he was practically in tears. "You're not flicking flies off your rumps, girls. You're horny horsies!" Eventually we got it right, made him happy.'

10:00 p.m. I decide to go home. I'd like to stay, perhaps take a few pictures, but because of the cold there's little going on. Also I'm feeling low. I thought Tim needed me, that confidences would be received. I was looking forward to playing the role of stand-in mom, since, until now, he and I have been mostly an older sister/kid brother routine. He's rarely spoken of his family, mentioning only that they live back East and are estranged except for an outcast gay uncle in New York. Tim is decent, loyal, soft-spoken. I'm sure there's an explanation, but I can't help but feel stood-up.

As I walk toward the Bay, I recognize a sports car, a silver Mercedes SL 600, patrolling Polk. The driver guns his engine. He's a hawk, I know, one of the rich ones who often hang around. The car's flamboyant but the occupant thinks he's invisible in darkness behind the glass.

One little-known fact about us colorblind: we can see through most camouflage. In World War II we were used as bombardiers, and many of us are good at spotting birds and snakes whose coloring conceals. The reason, of course, is that we're not distracted by color, concentrating instead on tonal values and shapes. So I'm able to make out the man in the Mercedes, not clearly but well enough to recognize him. It's Baldy, the guy I saw talking earlier with Knob.

Then, as he drives by, gunning his engine again to show off his power, I catch a glimpse of his profile and from that understand more: I've not only seen him before, I've surreptitiously photographed him several times. I didn't recognize him at first because he wasn't wearing his toupee.

I shiver as I climb the Chestnut Street steps. It's windy on Russian Hill. Too late now to venture safely across Sterling Park, so I follow Chestnut, turn right on Hyde, pass the crooked block of Lombard on my way up to Greenwich beside the cable-car tracks and the endless cable that rumbles beneath the street.

My building's at the crest. Constructed in the 1920s, slim and elegant, it offers some of the city's finest views. The rent's high, I sacrifice to live here but have never regretted it. If by some fluke I should someday strike it rich, I'll probably buy a few things but I won't move.

I let myself in through the gilded grille door, step into the elevator cab, push the button for the ninth floor. For me it's early. I adore the night; no photophobia, colors mean little, I don't feel caged-in and my vision's at its best. I needn't blink, rarely have to squint. Horizons are limitless. It's a world of grays, a world I can roam and understand.

I enter my flat, go to the living room window. The whole city lies before me like a bejeweled carpet spread across the hills. The high-rises of the financial district glow against the inky sky. The Bay Bridge appears delicate. Coit Tower, illuminated, is a pillar of power sprouting from the peak of Telegraph Hill. Some say it resembles a giant nozzle, but I always see a phallus. The water in the Bay looks like roiling oil. Oakland, a distant galaxy, twinkles in the East.

I move to my telescope still aimed at the penthouse. Now the living-room lights over there are on.

So tell me, Judge, what are you doing tonight? Reading a brief, meditating over Justice, or perhaps bedding down some girl, young, slim and petite, the way you like?

I spend half an hour gazing through the telescope, swinging it slowly across the city. Strange how the windows lit up night after night are usually the same.

There's something comforting in this. I like checking on windows I know, seeing familiar furniture, lamps, flickering TVs . . . familiar people too, like the night-gowned lady on Leavenworth who putters endlessly in her kitchen, or the long-haired guy in the high-rise on Green who performs slow *tai chi* exercises on his terrace late at night. They're like friends, these stay-at-homes. I respect their privacy; I'm not looking to catch them in their undies. When I do stumble upon an intimate event, I usually turn my telescope away. It's not that I'm so high-principled; with a camera in hand I'm a mad-dog voyeur. But San Francisco is a city replete with telescopes, and, since we must live together here, we observe a certain code.

The lens in the light-house tower on Alcatraz revolves. High-masted ships, tied down at the Hyde Street Pier, creak on gently lapping waves. On the street a car passes in low gear emitting an expensive growl. Is it Baldy in his Mercedes, unable to score, grinding out his frustration on the hill?

I'm seized by dread. I must have closed my eyes, fallen asleep on the couch. I wake up suddenly, terrified. Did I hear something in the distance – a scream, a wail?

I listen attentively. A sound is missing. It takes me several seconds to understand: the rumble of the Hyde Street cable; they turn it off around 2:00 a.m. So . . . it was silence that woke me up. I stretch, stand, go to my telescope, frame the Judge's penthouse once again. Now the windows are dark, the roof limned by moonlight. San Francisco is asleep.

I move to my bedroom, pull down the black-out shades, take off my clothes, slip naked beneath my sheets. I want to dream tonight, perhaps even dream in color. To do this once is my longest-held desire. To really understand what people mean when they call something blue or green, to see tomatoes as red instead of black, to see the sun as yellow instead of a shade off-white, to understand the true meaning of such expressions as 'I'm feeling blue this morning'; 'He's yellow, a coward'; 'I'm green with envy'; 'Look at that red-hot mama dance!' How I wish!

The shrill ring of the phone cuts through my dream. I awaken with a start, grasp for the receiver, knock the apparatus to the floor.

I fumble for it, bring the hand-set to my ear.

'Bug?'

'Yeah?'

I hear sniffling. 'It's me, Crawf.'

'Crawf! Jesus, what time is it? What's going on?'

'Tim,' he says. 'You were waiting for him.'

I check my watch. It's 7:00 a.m. 'What're you telling me? That he just showed up?'

A long pause. 'He's gone, Bug.'

I'm silent. Then I start to tremble.

'You know that old black guy, Rory, the one sells empty soda cans?' I know who he means. 'He was messing around an hour ago, going through this dumpster on Willow. Found these parts, you know – body parts. Got spooked, called the cops.' I hold my breath. 'They came right over, dug around, found a head.' *No!* 'It's Tim. He's dead, man.' Crawf is sobbing now. 'Someone wasted him . . . then cut him up.'

I THROW ON LAST night's clothes, pull on sneakers, grab my camera and a heavy set of shades. I don't own a car; can't get a licence because of the achromatopsia. For a moment I think about phoning for a cab, then decide to go on foot. I know that if I move fast I can get over to Polk and Willow in ten minutes.

At the door I expect to be hit by harsh morning light, but soupy fog has settled over Russian Hill. The light's subdued, the tones muted, so I hang my shades around my neck and take off bare-eyed across Sterling Park.

Sorrowful fog horns resound from the Bay. I take the steps two at a time, then, on Larkin, begin to jog causing my camera to bounce against my chest. I turn right at the Chinese Church, descend to Polk, then run flat out.

Few people about. Most stores are shut. Grocery trucks are making early deliveries. Half-awake people blinking at newspapers sprawl at the tables in front of Starbucks. A lithe young woman in black sweat pants races past; except for a sports bra she's bare above the waist.

The fog's less thick here, I start picking up glare. I slow to fit on my wrap-arounds. Once on the Gulch I notice a change in mood. The trash is out, the sidewalks are littered, but instead of the usual morning energy, I sense despair. Homeless men and women, reclining in doorways, peer out with haunted eyes.

I spot the patrol cars three blocks up, parked at angles, lamps whirling on their roofs. I know the lamps are red but they appear dark to me, revolving beams of charcoal light.

Crawf, in white T-shirt and jeans, sits slumped on the curb, head cradled in his arms. I settle beside him, put my arm around his shoulder. He turns to me, sobs against my jacket.

I wipe away his tears. He's freshly shaved and his long blond hair smells of coconut shampoo.

'Thanks for calling me, Crawf.'

'You two were tight. Lucky I kept your card.'

Gently I push back his head. I want to look into his eyes. 'Tell me what happened.'

Crawf blinks. 'Some john, I guess. One of the bad ones. Must've been.'

That much I already figured out.

'How come you're sure it's Tim?'

'Rory said so. And that old bag-lady, Marge. Tim used to give her money. She went up to the cops, made them show her.'

'That's what I'm going to do.'

I stand, uncap my lens, approach a mustachioed cop standing in the intersection of the alley. His hands are linked behind his back. He rocks back rhythmically on his heels.

'Pardon me.' He turns slowly. Just as he notices my camera I squeeze off a shot.

'What're you doing?'

'Taking pictures.'

He puts out his hand. 'Press Pass?'

'Don't need one. This is a public street.'

'This is a crime scene, ma'am.'

I sweeten my tone. 'I hear the victim was a friend. I want to see him, make sure.'

He stares at me. Confused by my shades perhaps he wonders if I'm a druggie. 'Stay here. I'll check with the detective.'

He stoops under a band of tape suspended between saw-horse barriers, approaches a frizzy-haired man in a rumpled suit. They confer, Frizzy-hair turns to me, beckons. I cross the crime-scene line.

'I'm Detective Shanley,' he says. 'Who're you?'

'Kay Farrow.'

'You knew the victim?'

'I think so. I hope not.'

'Yeah . . .' He gazes at me. 'Why the shades?'

I touch them lightly. 'Photophobia.' His smile's slightly crooked. He looks about forty. In a few years he'll have a turkey gobbler neck.

'But you can see all right?'

'Depending on the lighting, yes.'

'This isn't going to be a pretty sight,' he warns.

'I've seen plenty of ugly things.'

'Oh, have you now?' He guides me toward the coroner's van.

'My dad was a cop,' I tell him.

He stops, peers at me. 'Farrow . . . there was this Jack Farrow.' I nod.

'Jack Farrow's daughter. I'll be damned.' He gazes at me. 'How *is* old Jack?'

'Happy,' I say. 'Retired.'

'Now how 'bout that!'

At the van he takes my arm. 'Like I said, Kay – this is going to be rough.'

I remove my shades, raise my camera to defend my eyes. I've been coping like this for years. By interposing a lens I stylize reality and by so doing shield myself from pain.

I want to shoot even as the coroner's assistant starts to lift the cloth. I'm too horrified. Seeing no body shape, I feel my knees go weak.

The hair, as always, is wild and beautiful, the over-size eyes still gorgeous. There's a terrible wound in what's left of his neck. His expression spells bewilderment. I turn to Shanley. He's holding a handkerchief to his face.

'Well?'

'His name's Timothy Lovsey,' I tell him. 'On the street they call him Rain.'

I start to take pictures.

'What the hell!' Shanley grabs at my camera. I evade him, squeeze off three more frames.

'I've been photographing him for months,' I explain. 'These'll be the last shots.'

I lower the camera. He gazes at me.

'You can't take pictures anytime you feel like it.'

'I think I can.'

He shrugs. 'Tell me about Timothy. What did he do? Did he have family? Where did he live?'

'Where's the rest of him?' I demand.

'We got his arms and legs. Haven't located his torso yet.'

I glare at him. 'You better fucking well find it!'

'Look, lady.' Now he's pissed too.

'Don't "look lady" me.' I take a step back. 'Scrounge around,

Shanley. There're plenty of dumpsters. He used to stand by the one on Hemlock. I'd start there if I were you.'

'We already checked that one,' Shanley says. 'Come on, Kay, help me out.'

I shake my forefinger at him. Shanley peers at me like I'm a loon. I hand him my card. 'Call me when you find the rest of him,' I tell him. 'Then maybe I'll help.'

I stalk off, turn, take a final photograph. I want to capture the hideous, lonely, sorrowful end, what it's like when you're beautiful as a Greek god and end up beheaded, your head tossed in a rusty dumpster on an alley littered with discarded condoms off Polk Gulch.

I grab hold of Crawf, pull him into a coffee shop – not a yuppie place with gleaming machines but a hole-in-the-wall called Roy's where the counterman's got a cough and there're stale doughnuts and wedges of pie displayed on tiers in a plastic vitrine.

'You're sweating,' Crawf says. He picks up a napkin, wipes my forehead. 'Shaking too.'

'I feel bad,' I tell him, 'like I'm going to puke.'

The counterman gives me water. I drain the glass, motion for a refill.

Crawf slurps his coffee. 'Glad I didn't look. Couldn't take it. I got a really weak stomach.'

'Who was he seeing, Crawf?'

'Johns? I don't know. Maybe someone new.'

'He told you that?'

'No, but he seemed different last couple days.'

'Different how?'

Crawf shrugs. 'Like he was angry about something.' He wipes his mouth. 'I'm getting out of here, Bug. Just made up my mind. Going down to LA, stay with my brother. Don't think I'll be back.'

'It's no better down there,' I warn him.

'I know. But I'm not going to work the street. I'll sign up for acting classes like I always wanted. If I work hard maybe I can make it. What do you think?'

'Maybe, sure.'

So many of them, I know, share this fantasy, remember it when they get scared or fed up. A few even end up in triple-X films . . . if they have the skill to orgasm on demand.

Tim only wanted to retire. I think about what he told me. Did he really have fifty thousand saved? If so, could he have been killed for it? Where would he have kept it? In a bank? Not likely.

I grab Crawf's arm. 'Let's check his place.'

Crawf doesn't like the idea but changes his mind when I point out there might be something there he can use.

'I always liked his bomber jacket,' he says. Then, appalled at himself, he brings his hand up to his mouth.

Tim's studio is in a tenement building on Mission south of Market. The neighborhood's no treat: a needle-exchange parlor on the corner, a tough leather bar called The Tool Box from which an odor of disinfectant permeates the morning air. But the building itself isn't bad; the stairwell graffiti's been erased. I smell cat piss and roach spray and am pleased by the sound of Verdi. Someone in the building's playing an old Callas record, loud.

Tim kept his spare key in the hall molding above the fire-extinguisher. I'm too short to reach it, but Crawf lunges, brings it down. He tells me he played basketball in high school.

I hesitate. What if there's someone inside? Crawf must have the same thought for he's poised to run. I meet his eyes then knock loud. No response. I insert the key.

The room's empty, sparse, neat as a pin. Tim repainted it a month ago, also installed new vinyl tiles in the bathroom. I start to take pictures. I want to document his nest, which certainly doesn't appear inhabited by a man with fifty thousand dollars saved.

No phone; he used the pay phone on the corner. No stereo, just a Walkman on the dresser beside a stack of neatly folded underwear. On the floor his futon, his sleeping bag rolled and tied on top. A trestle desk supports a steam iron, a guide to Mexico and a Spanish language workbook spread open awaiting study. I turn to the walls: a *Body Heat* poster, and, opposite, a dozen prints of portraits I took of him taped to the plaster. His ravishing, large eyes meet mine. I lower my camera. My anger dissolves. I perch on his bedroll and start to bawl.

Crawf opens the closet. Six ironed denim shirts on hangers, four pressed pairs of jeans. Sneakers, shoes and boots aligned. No cowboy belt or bomber jacket. Maybe he was wearing them when . . . I choke up.

'Too weird,' Crawf says. Suddenly he looks frail. 'I don't know, Bug – maybe we shouldn't've come.'

'You're right. It was a lousy idea. Let's get out of here now.'

Crawf nods; he can't wait. I lock the door and pocket the key. If Shanley finds the torso maybe I'll give it to him. On the stairs, opera music still pouring down, I work to compose my face.

We cut back through the Tenderloin, past malodorous curry joints protected by grilled roller screens, past a Laotian grocery and a pitiful store-front dental clinic. A woman in thigh-high boots, a regular, is out early strutting her stuff. There may be colors on these streets, but everything looks gray to me.

The Gulch is busy, cars and buses jammed up, pedestrians marching briskly to work. Some regulars are out, people who normally don't eat breakfast till afternoon. Word's spread. I see faces creased with fear: *Who's going to get it next?*

Lots of cops, but I don't see Shanley, only uniformed people climbing around dumpsters and emptying bins. A sharp-looking female cop expedites traffic at the intersection of Sutter and Polk.

I'm sick at heart, my eyes hurt, my friend was killed. At first I loved him for his beauty, later for his gentleness. Now I realize I knew him hardly at all.

'I'm going home,' I mutter to Crawf. He nods, probably glad to be rid of me. 'Catch you later.' Then I remember. 'Good luck in LA.'

'I'll send you a postcard,' he says.

To get away from the traffic and noise I take California over to Larkin, a residential street. I walk slowly. I want to remember Tim as he was, erase the image of his separated head. That he's gone, is dead, cuts too deep. That he was mutilated makes the loss too cruel.

Who else cared for him beside Crawf, myself and a few others on the Gulch? There was a girl he once mentioned, said he wanted to get us together. He'd told her about me, he said, and she was anxious to meet me too. He was sure I'd want to photograph her. I remember the way he smiled when I asked him why.

Then there was Uncle David in New York. Tim mentioned him a couple of times. I try to concentrate, remember his last name. I should call him so he can pass word to Tim's folks.

There's still fog on Russian Hill. Strange how this city has so many micro-climates, the banana-belt that cuts across Noe Valley, the chilly mists of Seacliff, the bitter-cold summer mornings on Pacific Heights. When there's an earthquake the Marina district, built on landfill, turns to jelly, while on the shale-rock hills we feel the tremors less. It can rain furiously in San Francisco, while the sun bakes Berkeley dry. Sometimes the fog clings to the Bay, other times to the peaks.

I spot Shanley standing in front of my building. He's conferring with a woman, taller than me, with short dark slick gelled hair. I approach warily. Shanley introduces us. She's a detective, Hillary Lentz. 'People call me Hilly,' she says cheerfully, extending her hand.

I look hard at Shanley. 'Found the rest of him?'

'Not yet.'

'I told you – come see me when you do.'

He's annoyed. 'Christ's sake, Kay, wasn't us cut him up. We're doing all we can.'

Hilly joins in. 'If we're going to find the guy who did this every hour counts. Give us a break. This is someone you cared about, right?'

A good argument, so I relent, invite them upstairs. In the elevator Shanley asks if I have photos of Tim. I tell him I have hundreds. He asks if he can borrow one.

'What for?'

'Posters. We'll plaster the Gulch, ask for leads.'

'No one there'll talk to you.'

'They will if they think about it. The person who did this could easily do the same to them,' Hilly says.

Suddenly I remember how decent cops can be, how a job one would think would harden people often has the opposite effect. Dad was a softy, still is. I decide to trust them. I unlock my apartment door.

'Why keep it so dark? You gotta have great views,' Hilly says.

'Sunlight hurts my eyes and the views are just as good at night.'

They peer around. Hilly studies my decor. 'No colors except the books,' she observes. 'Nice effect.'

'It's not an effect. I wanted it that way. I'm colorblind.'

They stare at me. Shanley muses: 'Colorblind photographer. Interesting . . .'

'I shoot in black and white,' I tell him. 'You're thinking: "I thought only boys were colorblind".'

'Actually— ?' Shanley says.

'That's not colorblindness, that's red-green confusion. The inheritance pattern's different. Anything else you want to know?'

'No need to get hostile.'

'Guys!' Hilly shows her palms. 'We got a homicide to deal with. How 'bout we work on that?'

I take them into my office, converted from the second bedroom, open a drawer of my flat-file, pull out a box of prints. I show them only the formal portraits, not the more intimate shots. 'Good-looking kid,' Shanley comments.

'You liked him a lot,' Hilly says.

'You can tell?'

'Definitely.' She picks up my Angel Island portrait. 'The way you photograph him here – it shows.'

It feels good to hear her say that. For the first time since Crawf woke me, I think maybe I can handle this.

'This street name, Rain,' Shanley asks, 'what's that all about?'

'Just a name. He had this kind of . . . I don't know . . . inner sorrow, I guess.'

'Poetic,' Hilly says. 'Who gives out these names?'

'Someone starts it, and if you don't act offended others pick it up.'

'Yours, we hear, is Bug,' Shanley says.

'Great detective work. You investigating him or me?'

We go back to the living room. They want to know what Tim did. I gaze at them. Are they putting me on?

'He was a hustler.'

'So we heard. How did you two get involved?'

'Involved how?'

'However,' Shanley says.

I gaze at him. There's meanness there. Hilly, on the other hand, seems decent enough. Good cop/bad cop. I turn to her.

'When I started shooting on the Gulch, Tim Lovsey was one of the first people I met. We liked each other, started hanging out. I saw him maybe four, five times a week. Whenever I was up there, we'd have coffee or a drink. He called me yesterday, said there was something important he wanted to talk about. We agreed to meet at seven. I waited on Hemlock for over an hour. When he didn't show, I checked around. No one had seen him since the day before.'

'What was on his mind?'

'He didn't say. I could be wrong, but I think he sounded scared.'

'You think—?'

'—there's a connection? Sure, otherwise I wouldn't be telling you this.'

'What else can you tell us?'

Hilly, I observe, is taking notes.

'Not much. Couple weeks ago he told me he had fifty thousand stashed. You might want to look into that.' Shanley nods. 'What was that wound in his neck?'

'He was shot before he was beheaded.'

'That's how he was killed?'

'Probably. Think it could've been a john?'

'I'd say that's a good possibility, wouldn't you?'

I stand. I've had enough of them. I give them the Angel Island print, which they like because Tim looks sexy in it and that'll draw attention to their posters. I promise to think hard and come up with his uncle's name. Finally I give them his address and hand Shanley the key. I don't mention that Crawf and I were just there.

'Let me know when you find the rest of him,' I tell them at the door.

'Sure. Any particular reason?'

'I want to arrange a funeral.'

I'm sitting in my office, shades down, studying photos I took of Tim. It's my way to recall him, honor his memory.

Suddenly I'm angry. He knew what he did was dangerous. At least twice we discussed the risks he took each time he went home with a stranger. I lectured him: sex workers are targets; the encounters are anonymous, giving confidence to johns who feel sadistic fury toward figures in their pasts. When the sex worker is chosen to represent that figure, he or she can end up the victim of a murderous rage.

I told him how often I'd read about slain prostitutes and about the series of homicides in Britain where the killer picked up his victims in gay bars.

Tim nodded. He knew about all that. It's dangerous too, he reminded me, to cross the street.

That was the only time I blew up at him. 'Are you looking to get killed?'

He smiled at me, his special tender way. 'You don't understand, Kay. Most of my johns are sweet. I tune into the vibes. When they're bad, I pass.'

'How can you tell?'

He shrugged. 'You're on the street a while you get a sixth sense for stuff like that.'

I stare at a photo I took of him juggling rubber balls on the ferry boat to Sausalito. He wears a tanktop and shorts, and his hair is mussed. I remember the day well, a Sunday. On the spur of the moment we decided to cross over for lunch. The water was choppy, the ferry left a churning trail, kites flew over Alcatraz, the Bay was filled with sailboats sharply bent to catch the wind.

There were kids on board and as we approached Sausalito Tim entertained them with his juggling act. He was terrific, kept four balls going. Later I asked him where he learned to do it. He said he ran away with a circus when he was ten.

He was joking of course, but he did have off-beat and engaging skills, was facile with close-up magic, pulling coins out of ears then making them disappear. He could stick a knife down his throat, and, he told me, knew how to charm a snake.

He wanted me to know he had a past, even as he refused to reveal it. Enjoying his mystifications I played along, figuring sooner or later he'd tell me the story of his life.

I open the box that contains the nudes. I can hardly bear to look at them. Why, I wonder now, didn't we have sex? He considered himself bisexual, told me he'd had girl friends and said he'd enjoy accommodating women if there were female takers for what he had to offer.

'There are,' I assured him. 'I see older women with young hunks all the time.'

'Gigolos,' he said with contempt. 'I'm a hustler.'

'Is that better?'

'Freer.' He seemed certain about it. 'No one controls you. You live the way you like. You hustle, make things happen, don't dance for anyone, do your thing.'

It was from such conversations that I developed my notion of hustlers as free spirits and psychic explorers. A flawed perception perhaps, a romanticized view of a sordid way of life. But that was where my pictures led me. My eyes were my guide. I shot what I felt.

The phone rings. It's Shanley. He's calling on his cellular from Tim's apartment.

'Who else has keys?' he demands.

'Why?'

'Someone's been in here that's why,' he says angrily. 'Place is ransacked. Everything's fucking upside down.'

I cry a little, then pace like a caged beast, then put on my shades and pull up the blinds and stare out at the city smothered in late morning fog. Low-pitched horns moan from the Bay. A naval hospital ship, heading for Oakland, slips between the Embarcadero and Treasure Island. The ship is white, ghostly, and bears a huge cross which I know is red but which appears black to me.

I'm torn between grief and anger, and my anger, I fear, is gaining the upper hand. My mother shot herself when I was twenty, stuck my father's spare gun in her mouth then pulled the trigger like a cop. That happened fifteen years ago and I still feel anger more than pain. I think anger's a way to hold on to someone who's died; if I can feel angry enough, my memory of the person won't fade.

Noon, I'm trying to center myself. I keep thinking about Shanley's call. Between the time Crawf and I were at Tim's and the time Shanley got there, barely an hour passed. By then a lot of people found out what had happened. Any one of them could have broken in.

Except . . . Shanley didn't say there'd been a break-in; he asked who else had a key. So it must have been someone Tim trusted, or the person who killed him . . . since he would have had his own key with him when he died.

David Jeffrey – Uncle David's name suddenly flies into my mind. He's in the entertainment business, lives in Manhattan, was the only member of Tim's family who didn't disown him, rather took him in, helped him come to terms with his sexuality. It was Uncle David who loaned him money to move out to San Francisco. He doesn't know that Tim became a hustler, thinks he's working here as a waiter. He also doesn't know where he lives since Tim, moving often, keeps a private mailbox at one of those wrap-it/ship-it stores in the Castro.

I pick up my phone, dial New York City information. There're two

David Jeffreys, three people listed as D. Jeffrey, and, using alternate spellings, half a dozen more David and D Jefreys and Geoffreys. I take down the numbers even as I know I won't place the calls. Too many names, too many times I'll have to ask: 'Are you Tim Lovsey's uncle?' Better to let Shanley do that. But then, I remember, I don't really want to talk to Shanley anymore.

I go into my darkroom, process a couple of undeveloped rolls, mechanical work that keeps me busy. After I hang up the rolls to dry, I retrieve a negative strip from my safe – the one that contains my favorite of the Angel Island shots. I place the strip on my lightbox, examine it with a magnifying glass. Seeing Tim this way, with the blacks and whites reversed, fills me with a mellow sorrow. I feel this negative, being the piece of film upon which light he reflected actually fell, contains more of his essence than prints made from it.

Colorblindness, which I once viewed as a curse, has turned out to be a gift enabling me to see the world differently than others. People think they understand colorblindness: 'Oh, must be like looking at black and white movies all day long.' Perhaps it is. I have no idea. The concept of 'gray' as a color doesn't mean anything to me either. I see black and white and shades in between, 'a world cast in lead', as Greta Benning, my favorite high school art teacher, used to say. 'Consider taking up drawing or etching, Kay,' she advised. I tried both. All my life I wanted to be an artist, I just wasn't sure what kind.

When I started at the San Francisco Art Institute, it was with the intention of becoming a sculptor. Since sculpture materials are generally monochromatic, color perception isn't vital to success.

Everything was going fairly well, when, my second year, I took a course in studio photography. Within a week I knew I'd found my medium. My dad, responding to my enthusiasm, gave me his camera, an early model Nikon. I started carrying it with me, shooting everything that interested me, often also using it as a telescope to see things when the rods of my retinas got saturated by brilliant light.

A camera around my neck didn't look nearly as odd as the handheld monocular most achromats carry. Soon it became a part of me – my tool, limb and shield. Since I couldn't see very well in daylight, my camera became my eyes; later, looking at my photographs, I was able to see what I had 'seen'.

Since I graduated from art school I've worked as a photojournalist for an alternative newspaper, a portraitist, and, for five years, a studio and location fashion photographer. I've covered sports, rock concerts, political campaigns; photographed politicians, writers, dogs; shot spreads for *Details*, *GQ* and *Elle*.

Three years ago I went cold turkey on commercial work, determined to devote myself full-time to personal projects. I'd always wanted to be a fine art photographer. Finally, with a little money saved, I decided to take the shot.

I've been fortunate. Last year I published a book, *Transgressions*, the best of two years' worth of pictures in which I used black-and-white studio fashion lighting techniques to glamorize and thus counter-document the pain of battered women. The idea was to show the pride of women, who, though beaten in body, were unbowed in spirit. Reviews were good though sales were not. The high priestesses of political correctness called me traitor.

The controversy helped get my pictures shown in New York. I exhibit and sell locally through the Zeitgeist Gallery. Having turned art photographer I earn a lot less than when I did fashion work, but I get by, and, most important, feel fulfilled.

My Polk Gulch project is different than *Transgressions*, not executed in the studio, but, in accordance with Maddy Yamada's advice, entirely on the street. The working title is *Exposures*. Again I'm looking to glamorize what most people regard as sordid, but this time my technique is different: whatever glamor accrues to my hustler-models comes from within, not from lighting and directed poses. And the glamor portraits are only half my project; the other half is my documentation of transactions of the flesh. I've amassed hundreds of grainy images, shot candidly with available illumination at night, of my heroes interacting with johns, meeting, negotiating, driving off. The best of these, the ones I intend to use, catch the looks on the faces of hustler and john as their eyes meet, they inspect one another and forge the deals that lead to intimate acts unseen.

3 p.m. The fog has lifted. I put on my shades, grab my gym bag and walk down to Cow Hollow for aikido class. The dojo, Marina Aikido, is situated above a store on the corner of Laguna and Lombard, one of the most heavily traveled streets in the city. The instructor, a black

woman named Rita Reese, is tough, sinewy, a former marine. Not many mystical Zen-like utterances from her; she's more contemporary woman warrior than classic sensei.

I change quickly, then move out to the floor to stretch and practice katas. Today our class has nine women, three men. There are a couple of high school girls, several women in their thirties, and Justine, a lithe middle-aged woman with gray bangs, an advanced student with whom I often work out. I'm one of the smallest in the group: five feet four, 114 pounds. I make no claims to being a star martial artist. I attend because I love the beauty of aikido, the clarity, the concentration, the spiritual practice. My efforts to achieve mastery make me feel powerful. And, too, I enjoy the exercise.

'You're not concentrating, Kay. Claim your space! Blend your energy!'

Rita, so elegant in her *hakama*, the split floor-length black skirt that, being a black belt, she's entitled to wear, is a caring instructor. But today I'm not in the mood to blend my energy; I've come here to release it.

We pair off for freestyle practice. Justine and I face one another. We bow to show respect, that we hold no anger, that it isn't hostility that drives us, but love of sport and art.

Suddenly I attack. Justine grabs my arm, turns, throws me down. I don't fall well. It hurts when I hit the mat. Aikido is not only beautiful, it can also be very painful. Today I welcome the pain. I want to fall hard, again, again and still again, want to leave class sweaty and sore.

Again I attack. Again Justine throws me. Her moves are circular, balletic, her throws nearly effortless. Rita, I see, is watching us. Up from the mat, I check myself in the mirror. I look, I think, like a rag doll, broken and spent.

By the end of practice, my jacket's drenched with my sweat, my hips and shoulders are bruised. After we bow, Justine embraces me.

'Next time I'll attack, you'll apply techniques,' she promises.

Rita approaches shaking her head, causing her braided corn rows to flick. I'm breathing hard. She brushes something out of my hair. 'You're a punching bag today, girlfriend,' she says.

I nod.

She stares into my eyes. 'I've seen you do much better. You seem vulnerable. Don't forget, Kay, on the mat all secrets are exposed.'

I stare back at her, tears pulsing from my eyes. 'I lost someone close,' I blurt.

Suddenly she hugs me. 'Oh, Kay! I'm so sorry!'

I won't let this go, I decide, as I walk back up the hill. The light is dazzling; I blink even though I'm wearing heavy shades. *You can't kill someone I care about then chop him up and throw the pieces away like trash and get away with it.*

Questions flood in: Who *was* Tim? Did he have enemies? Where did he learn to juggle and do close-up magic? Who's his Uncle David? Who's the mysterious girl he wanted me to meet? What did he want to talk about yesterday? Did he really have fifty thousand stashed? Who turned over his flat?

I want to know all these things because he was my friend and because, I've just decided, his life and death will be the subject of *Exposures*. I'll change my concept. The book will no longer be about Gulch hustlers among whom he will be a featured player. It will be entirely about him, how he lived and died. I already have the pictures. What I need now is the story.

THREE

TONIGHT BEFORE VENTURING OUT I wait till magic time is over, until the failing light drains away the colors from the city, colors I know are there but cannot see. Then I enter the nightscape.

This evening Polk Street is the same yet different, crawling with cops, patrol cars parked on every block. No dealers are out, few street people. The human flotsam has retreated to the alleys of the Tenderloin. With the law so visible the habitués deem the Gulch unsafe.

At the corner of Polk and Bush, I pause to examine a poster stapled to a power pole. It's my portrait of Tim, beautiful and bare-chested, the city gleaming behind. The image is mine, but the light values are not – the contrast has been pushed. Tim's skin has gone swarthy making him appear a sunburnt soldier rather than an androgynous *ephebe*.

The caption below is straightforward enough:

TIMOTHY LOVSEY (A.K.A. 'Rain') WAS FOUND MUR-
DERED THURSDAY NIGHT, HIS BODY LEFT IN A DUMP-
STER ON WILLOW ALLEY. TIMOTHY FREQUENTED THE
POLK GULCH AREA. ANYONE WITH INFORMATION
REGARDING THIS VICTIM'S DEATH AND/OR RECENT
CONTACTS IS ASKED TO NOTIFY DETECTIVES SHANLEY
AND/OR LENTZ, 270–7111. ANONYMITY GUARANTEED.

I stand back, take a shot of the poster. Suddenly I feel a presence behind.

'Not bad, huh?'

I turn. It's Hilly, wearing dark slacks and black leather blouson jacket much like mine.

'Sorry, forgot to give you photo credit,' she says.

I smile, ask if she and Shanley have gotten any calls.

She shakes her head. 'We've only had these up since five. Took all afternoon to get them made.' She grins. 'The mills of the gods grind slowly at SFPD.'

'You haven't found the rest of him?'

Again she shakes her head. 'I promised I'd call when we do. I meant it.'

I turn from her, peer south down Polk. Something in her gaze makes me nervous. Also I don't want her to see my eyes.

'Shanley told me Tim's studio was messed.'

'Yeah, like the shit hit the fan.'

'Tim was neat. He didn't have much stuff.'

'Whatever he had was tossed. Futon and bedroll slit, goose down churning in the air.'

'Money?'

'If there was it's long gone now.'

I turn back to her. 'What do you think about the mutilation?'

Her eyes are steady on mine. 'It's a goddamn' shame.'

'Ever seen anything like it?'

'No, but Shanley has. I've only been in Homicide since January. Before that worked sex crimes seven years.'

'Isn't this a sex crime, Hilly?'

'Don't know that yet.'

I understand what she's saying: that without Tim's torso they can't be sure.

'We're having a little problem,' she says. 'We need information, that's why we put up posters. But soon as we put them up, people rip them down. Doesn't help the cause.'

I'm not surprised. Posters are bad for business. Life goes on; there are livings to be made.

'Is that why the cops are around?'

'They're more like, you know, a presence.'

'Here today, gone tomorrow?'

She shrugs. 'There's a great big city to patrol.'

'And who cares about a murdered hustler, right?'

She stares at me, offended. 'You don't think we care?'

'I'm keeping an open mind.'

'Got any suggestions?'

'*Me?*'

'Sure, why not?'

Our eyes meet. Is she coming on to me? I check her ring finger for a wedding band. 'Here's one suggestion – get the uniforms off the street. You want to cover the Gulch, do it in plainclothes, otherwise none of the hustlers'll work and none of the johns'll come around.'

'Good idea. Thanks.' She looks at me. 'Do you live with someone . . . have a boyfriend?'

'Not at the moment, no.'

We walk a block in silence. There's traffic but not the cruising kind. I tell her a little about my project. I don't mention the hundreds of shots I've taken of johns.

'I care about people,' she says. I wait for the other shoe to drop. 'I didn't know this kid so I can't care about him as much as you. But I do care, I want you to know that.' She stops, peers into my eyes, shows me her sincerity. 'Shanley and me – we've got a heavy case load, but I'm not letting this one go. We won't solve it picking up fibers and prints. The only way's with faces, descriptions we can tie to names. We need informants with good information. Otherwise—' She shrugs.

'I understand.'

She smiles slightly. 'I'm a lesbian. Better you hear it from me than hear it around.'

'That's fine.'

'Anonymous consensual sex doesn't bother me. As for sex for money – seems like a reasonable exchange. But hurting and killing because it gets somebody off – no, Kay, this dyke won't stand for that.' She relaxes. 'I saw your book last year, liked it, even stopped by the gallery to see the originals. Beaten-up women – in Sex Crimes they were my stock-in-trade. Took Polaroids of them all the time. Not like your stuff. In mine they looked,' she shakes her head, 'kinda wretched. The way they looked in yours, even with the bruises and black eyes, I don't know – they seemed like movie stars almost. Which got me thinking.' She smiles broadly. 'Enough flattery for tonight?'

'Actually,' I tell her, 'I can never get enough.'

She laughs. 'Don't know what your angle is on this hustling scene, but you've got contacts here.' I nod. 'Maybe you'll pick something up.'

'I don't know,' I tell her. 'I'll check around.'

She squeezes my hand. 'Thanks!' She turns, strides off.

I wander down to O'Farrell, then over to Larkin. Some of the Gulch action has moved here. I see several female streetwalkers but no hustlers. I recognize Silky, a mid-thirties black woman with huge lips, corn rows and a swagger.

I approach. 'Where're the guys?'

She gives a twirl with her thumb. 'Freaked out tonight, child. Try Van Ness.'

I take Myrtle Alley over to Van Ness, walking quickly, spooked by the lack of people lingering against the walls. Van Ness, an avenue with a center strip, doubles here as US 101, a major route that cuts through the city.

At the corner I look both ways. Cars and trucks speed by, the sidewalks are deserted. I start toward City Center, then catch a glimpse of a familiar form turning into Olive. I pick up my pace, follow him into the alley.

'Knob!'

It's him, I'm sure, though he speeds up, keeps his head down and doesn't turn.

'It's me – Bug!' I yell after him then start to run. He sidesteps into the portal of a garage. When I reach him, I'm out of breath.

'Fuck you want?' he demands. His expression is surly.

'Tim and me were tight. What d'you know?'

'Fuck ask me?'

'You know the Gulch, Knob. Cops think the killer's a john.'

He sniffs then makes a gesture as if to push me back. He wants to intimidate me. I hold my ground. He's four inches taller and eighty pounds heavier; he could knock me over with a swat. In his eyes I see the calculation of a ferret.

'What's the problem?' I ask.

'Don't like cops.'

'I'm not a cop.'

'So you say.'

We glare at one another. 'I'm a photographer, Knob. Ever seen me without a camera?'

'Taking pictures – that's what a cop would do.'

'*Why?*'

'Catch people.'

'What kind of people?'

'People with stuff to hide.'

'What kind of stuff?'

'Married guys, like that. Who they are, where they live.'

'Like Baldy from last night?'

'Who?'

I find his dumb act pathetic. 'The bald guy in the Mercedes,' I explain. 'The one you were talking to, the one who wanted chicken and wouldn't close.'

'Don't know what you're talking about.'

'Guy flaunts a car like that he's asking to be noticed. Not that difficult to check out a license plate.'

Knob narrows his eyes. 'Fuck you want?'

'I want to know who's violent, who could've done this to Tim. I'm not a cop, but I'm going to start working with them if his friends here don't cooperate.'

'I don't know nothin'.'

I soften my tone: 'You liked him. I know you did.' I lie: 'And he liked you.'

Knob considers that. He's not big on human sentiment. I press him a little more.

'You're slinking around now because you're scared. And you're right. What they did to Tim, they could do to you, to anyone.'

'Who says it's a "they"?'

For the first time he surprises me. 'Okay, suppose it's one guy – does that make any difference?'

'What do you mean?'

'Built-in risk, isn't it? Risk of the trade. Stop one there's always another, right?' I pause. 'Or were you—?' Suddenly I think I understand what's on his mind. 'You're not planning on taking care of this yourself?'

He snorts, pushes me. This time I yield. The push is real, not a gesture as before.

'Tell me?' I plead as I stumble back.

'Outa my way,' he says roughly. He shoves me again hard. I fall to the pavement. He walks away.

My knees are scraped. They smart as they rub against my jeans. If I hadn't needed to protect my camera I'd have used my hands to break the fall. My knees can take it; my Contax can't.

This is the first time I've been hit since coming to the Gulch.

I'm more shocked than hurt. Now the security I've felt here gives way to apprehension. It's been my illusion, I realize, that this place has grace. Yes, I've witnessed moments of unexpected gentleness, but basically, I know, the Gulch is a jungle.

I pick myself up. Knob is gone. At least he didn't kick me then stand around and gloat. I remember a book by a gonzo journalist who hung out with a motor-cycle gang. He thought he'd become one of them. The day they turned on him and stomped him he learned he wasn't.

Suddenly I feel a need to take pictures. But what is there to shoot? I stride back to Polk, start blasting away at the cops. Then I stop. These shots won't get me anywhere. If Tim is to be the subject of *Exposures*, I should capture the grief of his friends.

I go into Walgreen's Pharmacy, purchase bandages and disinfectant, then limp my way over to The Hampshire Arms. The hotel, now seedy, has seen better days. Squares of the marble lobby floor are broken and the rough stucco walls are dark with soot. I approach the desk. A young man with bad skin is reading a comic book. He doesn't look up.

'Doreen in?'

He scratches a pimple. 'Who?'

'Doreen . . . of Alyson and Doreen.'

'Room 314.'

I find the house phone, call upstairs.

They're both in, too broken-hearted, Doreen tells me, to play the street.

'Can I come up?'

'Sure,' she says, slurring her words. 'Just give us a couple minutes to straighten the joint.' I dress my wounded knees in the lobby, then take the elevator to three. I think it's more like straighten themselves, since, when Doreen opens the door, I find the joint in its usual disarray. The gals are wearing unisex underwear, not the frilly kind I'd expect.

Doreen glances at me then at herself in the mirror. She isn't wearing make-up and her wig's askew.

'Hell with it!' she says, pulling it off. Her head, I see, is shaved. Her hands shake as she flings the wig across the room. Alyson immediately follows suit. Her head is shaved as well.

'Don't feel all that girlie tonight,' Doreen explains, voice a half octave lower. The floor is cluttered with high-heeled shoes and boots, the air pungent with stale cigarette smoke, cosmetics and gin.

'Night like this you just want to sit home and cry,' Alyson says.

The two of them plop down together on the bed. I take a chair, perching atop a pile of wrinkled tutus and lingerie.

'I'm here to take your pictures,' I announce.

At first they're against it, don't like the notion of being photographed unmasked. But it doesn't take long to convince them.

'When you show real feelings,' I tell them, 'dress-up doesn't matter.'

For the first few shots they assume mock-feminine poses, then they give it up. As I shoot they continue to drink straight gin, no tonic or vermouth, gulping it down like stevedores. There comes a point when I stop viewing them as she-males and begin to see them as they are: a couple of slim young skinheads who happen to have tits, getting plastered because a friend's been killed.

'Tell me about bad johns,' I ask, framing Doreen against the mess in the closet.

'What'd you wanna know?' she asks.

'How bad does it get?'

Alyson lets out with a hoot. 'Dearie, you got no idea!'

'They stink, some of them. You'd think they'd clean up for a date.'

'They call you names – "bitch", "slut", like that.'

'Not that we mind. It's a validation really.'

'Then there're the sickies.' They glance at one another, clink glasses, toss back great gulps.

'Some like to beat up on you. Spanking's all right – but they gotta pay extra. A few'll get carried away. Couple times I've come home with a black eye.'

'When that happens, what do you do?' I'm shooting now from the floor, framing them against the stained and ragged wallpaper.

'You get out of there, honey. Fast as you can. A john out of control – that can lead to real injury.'

'I had one last spring.' Alyson falls back on the bed. 'Good looking, middle-aged, computer exec type. Married, lived down the peninsula somewhere. We had a few dates. He seemed nice enough. Brought me flowers, talked about earrings. Told me he liked male pussy, that was his kink.'

Doreen hands Alyson a lit cigarette. Alyson props herself on an elbow, takes a long drag then exhales in a stream.

'One night he gets loaded. We're in this motel room on Lombard. Suddenly he starts bashing me around. We're all – us! women! – we're all whores, he says. He hates us, *all* of us. I feel his rage. I'm scared. I know I gotta get out before he busts me up. I try to calm him. "Hey, George, it's me, Alyson. I'm a she-male, remember. All this is make-believe." I'm taking a chance; these guys want to forget you're a boy. But I do it anyway, meantime wipe away my make-up and peel off my wig. So there we are, two guys commiserating over what sluts women are, how they ought to be like – now he's getting really vicious – exterminated! Eviscerated! Finally he gets up to take a piss. That's when I make my break. I shake all the way home in the cab. I never saw old Georgie again.'

'Probably too scared to show his face,' Doreen says. 'Guy like that, we pass the word. No one else'll touch him.'

'I figure he burned his bridges down in San Jose, that's why he started coming here. Now he's probably playing in Santa Cruz. Sooner or later he'll break some girl's arm or kill her. Guys like that only get worse. We release something in them. After that . . . well, you know the saying: You can't squeeze the paste back into the tube.'

By midnight Doreen and Alyson are dead drunk and I've shot out two 36-frame rolls. I leave them snoring away head to toe upon the bed.

On Polk the cops are gone. There's hardly a person on the street. My knees are fine now; bandaged, I walk well. I check the saloons. Most are empty. The Werewolf is closed and so is The Shillelagh.

It's strange to walk here with no one about. It's as if this place has died. Perhaps this will be Tim's memorial – a single night of silence on the Gulch.

I wander up to the Jerry's All-Night Pizza, peer in through the window, notice a couple of regulars: Slick, an albino, and a kid named Remo who barely looks thirteen.

I enter, approach. 'Seen Crawf?' I ask.

'Hear he left town,' Slick says.

I sit. Silence. Have I interrupted a private colloquy? The harsh fluorescent lighting hurts my eyes.

I raise my camera. They tense, then relax as they remember who I am.

'Just a few shots,' I promise. 'I want to catch the gloom and doom.'

Slick stares down at his coffee; Remo sticks out his tongue. Then, after goofing off, he offers me his profile. 'I'm collecting bad john stories,' I tell them, still shooting. 'Got any good ones?' That gets them going.

The first tale is strange. Seems there's a doctor who likes to take kids to his office in Pacific Heights where he subjects them to lengthy physical exams. As he does he whispers degrading things. 'Bet a lot of cocks been down here,' he says, peering into a boy's throat. 'Now bend over and spread those cheeks.' The culminating event is a prolonged inspection with a proctoscope.

'Physical part's not so bad,' Slick says. 'It's the fuckin' humiliation gets you down.'

Slick's nineteen with white hair and stubble above his upper lip. He's scrawny, pale, his eyebrows and eyelashes so faint I can barely make them out. I can't read colors but Tim once told me Slick's irises are pink.

At one time or another he and most of his friends have been hired by the doctor, who, after a couple of exams, loses interest and asks for a steer to someone new. Slick affectionately chucks the point of Remo's chin. 'Wouldn't send you to him, kid. Not even for a cut.'

Remo's got his own story about a black van with blacked-out windows that took him, another young hustler and two teenage girls high into the hills of Marin. The van pulled straight into a garage from which they were taken blind-folded to a basement and told to strip. They entertained a group all night, perhaps a half dozen men and women. They were tickled with feathers, caressed and used, for which they were paid a collective fee of a thousand dollars and deposited, terrified, back on Fisherman's Wharf at dawn.

There's an exuberance in the boys as they recount these adventures that reminds me a little of Tim – the comaraderie of veterans exchanging war stories at a bar.

'That Marin group's sick, the doctor too, but what about the *real* bad guys?' I ask.

They're non-plussed. Then little Remo states the obvious:

'Go with one of them, you don't live to tell the tale.'

*   *   *

Sitting on a high stool in my apartment living room, peering through my telescope, I feel as though I'm in the crow's-nest of a ship. The night is designed for surveillance: vistas long, horizons deep, lamps mere points of light. No blazing walls of sunlight to limit my vision. The night city lies naked to my eye.

I check the Judge's windows, find them dark . . . as are most other residence windows at this hour. I swing the telescope toward the cluster of high-rises downtown; lamps burn in offices for the night cleaning crews.

Swinging north-east I catch the reflection of the moon on the Bay with the lights of El Cerrito flickering beyond. I observe a small but brilliant glow in the Berkeley Hills, perhaps a house on fire. I leave my telescope, go into my office, peer out at the Golden Gate Bridge. They say that when people jump from it they nearly always face the city, perhaps because to face west, the Pacific, would be to renounce the worldly causes of their sorrow.

The eighteenth-century British chemist, John Dalton, was the first scientist properly to describe colorblindness, namely his own. In truth he was a dichromatic protanope, meaning his deficiency was a not uncommon inability to distinguish red from green. Dalton's belief, that all colorblindness was like his, has long been disproved. But convinced of his theory that the fluid in his eyes was tinted blue and thus absorbed red light, he willed one of his eyes to Cambridge University, directing that it be examined after his death.

It was, in 1844, by his friend and doctor, Joseph Ransome, who even peered through it finding the liquid transparent and colorless. To this day the pickled eye remains at Cambridge; Dalton's DNA was extracted from it several years ago. But it's the intimacy of the act, Ransome actually using his close friend's eye as a lens, that comes back to me with poignant force as I pull out the nude photographs of Tim I took just three weeks ago.

Perhaps these pictures of his naked body will tell me something, help me solve the enigma of his death. That, at least, is my hope as I begin to study them, meditating over the vulnerability of his flesh.

I hadn't planned on shooting nudes, though, in retrospect, it seems a natural outgrowth of our work. Our Angel Island session, for instance, when Tim took off his shirt to pose for the portrait now on the posters being ripped off lamp posts on the Gulch. There's something about bare skin that lends intimacy to a photograph, which is probably why one famous photographer is alleged to be so adamant that her subjects strip. Nakedness, after all, is the ultimate physical secret. In our time is there a commodity more precious than celebrity skin?

I was, I confess, aroused on Angel Island, whether by Tim, his body, the sweetness of the air, softness of the lambent light, or, most likely, the whole gestalt. It was a balmy windless autumn day, the waters of the Bay were still, gulls circled and the shoreline grasses were lustrous as pewter.

I often become aroused when work goes well. I love photography, the sense of capture, the sureness that possesses me when I'm getting at something deep. But on that day the arousal was especially intense. I remember wanting to grasp hold of Tim, roll with him in the high grass just above the island shore. I remember feeling certain he noticed my excitement, his only comment on it being a smile. It was as if he acknowledged my condition, but, being the object of desire, left it to me to make the initial move . . . which, on account of pride, I did not do.

A few days later, when I showed him the Angel Island proofs, he was thrilled.

'This is how I want to look!'

'The camera doesn't lie.'

'I wish I could always be so beautiful, Kay.'

'Perhaps you are,' I said.

He softly shook his head. 'Some days are better than others.' He brightened. 'Would you shoot me nude? I'd like to see myself naked through your eyes – beautiful lying eyes.'

I took it that he was suggesting that if the camera doesn't lie, surely the photographer does. In the face of such a challenge how could I resist?

We executed the nudes on a Sunday in my living room, beginning mid-morning, working till late that afternoon. I loaded a second camera with color film, a concession to his wish for color prints. Normally I refuse to shoot color. What's the point since I can't see the hues? But no request of Tim's could be denied. I would shoot with one camera for him, with the other for myself.

I was nervous about the session, looking forward to it too. Since I'd always felt that Tim was holding something back, a nude session could be a way to break through his reserve. Starting back in art school I've shot numerous nudes in my career. Always as a session begins I'm filled with a sense of moral responsibility. This results from my feeling that with my camera I'm all-powerful, while my subject, of whatever gender, is defenseless before my gaze.

I felt this way waiting for Tim, and when he arrived felt his anxiety as well. Yes, he had asked for this, but he couldn't help but feel nervous too.

I was dressed skimpily, in sleeveless jersey and nylon shorts. My feet were bare. I'd turned the living room into a studio, drawn the shades, set up lights, spread a thick black velour curtain down one wall and across the floor. By so doing I'd made a conscious decision to shoot Tim in limbo against deep black. I didn't want to produce Avedon-style pictures in which he'd appear pinned against stark white walls. Rather I was after pictures that would be both luminous and romantic, emphasizing his beauty, imbuing him with glamour.

I started to shoot even as he undressed, since his manner struck me as extremely sensual. When he was naked, I discovered no surprises. Everything was as I'd imagined.

For the first rolls I had him pose against the wall, then lie down while I climbed a ladder and shot him from above. As I focused in on him I became interested in details: the way his arms met his torso, the curve of his ass, his nipples, armpits, genitals, the fuzz of hair on his chest, the musculature of his back when he lay down and extended his arms above his head. He enjoyed posing, rolling around, stretching and twisting, creating abstract forms. He did things with his body that, as I examine the proofs, seem nearly impossible unless he'd been trained as a contortionist.

I'm looking at a shot in which he's standing on his hands. His body, in profile, fills the frame. His legs curl back over him so his feet extend further forward than his head. His face though concentrated is nearly expressionless, as if to show he feels no strain.

In another shot he's leaping, arms up like a volleyball player about to execute a smash. His entire musculature is exposed, his cock has flopped up, his hard abdomen is tautly etched. At the thought of such beauty ruined I start to sob.

As the session continued, I remember now, a glaze of perspiration rose to coat his skin. He began to gleam as if he were oiled, and a fragrance, musky and saline, rose from him, the sweet aroma of his sweat. It wafted to me as I moved about, filling my nostrils, snaking deep into my lungs.

Such intimacy!

It occurs to me now that in a very special way we *were* making love that day, he the model, I the photographer, synchronized, engaged in an elaborate courtship dance. We didn't speak, rather moved slowly in relation to one another, he posing, seeming to know what I wanted, I shooting, picking up on his signals. 'Yes! Kiss me here! Now over here!' his body seemed to say, and the clicks of my shutter were like licks against his flesh.

By the end, I recall, I was sweating myself, my shirt glued to my nipples and back. I remember envying him the freedom of his nudity while wishing I could tear off my own scanty clothes. The truth, of course, is that I wished he would do the tearing.

There came a moment when I actually thought that could happen. We were both poised for it, I'm sure. But the spell was broken when a slight trembling shook the building. Then it was too late, the moment dissolved and the energy lost was not regained.

That night on TV a reporter announced that a mild quake of Richter magnitude 3.2 had struck the city.

We were finished. Tim pulled on his jeans then we lay together on the velour, exhausted from eight hours of work.

He asked how I thought the session had gone.

'I'll know when I see the proofs,' I said.

'Your gut feeling?'

'Great!'

'Can we do it again?'

'Yeah, but not for a while. Too soon and we'll repeat ourselves.'

He nodded. There was at least half a minute of silence, then he told me he had a secret wish.

'I've always wanted to be photographed a certain way,' he said, 'holding a special pose.' I waited for him to explain. He was nervous, I could see, perhaps even ashamed.

'Tell me,' I urged.

He stared at the ceiling. He didn't want me to see his eyes.

'Saint Sebastian,' he murmured in a confessional whisper. 'You know who I mean?'

'The saint tied to the tree with arrows in his chest?'

'Stomach too . . .'

'You want to pose like that?'

He nodded, then rolled on to his side.

I was familiar with the eroticization of the Saint Sebastian image in the work of the Japanese writer, Yukio Mishima, and the British filmmaker, Derek Jarman. 'Yes, we could set that up,' I told him, 'perhaps in a quiet corner of Golden Gate Park. Tie you to a tree beneath a shaft of sunlight, then glue the arrows on.' I let my hand graze his bare stomach. 'Do you identify with martyrdom, Tim?'

While he thought about that, I stood and began to unload my cameras.

'Guess so,' he said softly, 'since it turns me on.'

I glanced at him. 'Then we'll do it,' I promised, 'and you'll find out if it's the image that excites you, or playing the part.'

I took the rolls to my darkroom. When I returned he was fully dressed. He helped me dismantle my lights, roll up the velour, put my living room back in order, then I changed and we walked down to North Beach for pizza.

Looking at the nudes now, I see decent enough studies but nothing that strikes me as powerful. That's always the problem when you work a well-mined field, and, God knows, the human nude, male and female, is well mined. Still in these shots I see Tim's body whole, the body with which he made his living.

All those years when I was afraid of Polk Gulch, avoided it, and, when obliged to cross it, strode through it as quickly as I could, it wasn't the atmosphere, buildings or even the people that frightened me, it was what they *did*.

What kind of people, I'd ask myself, rent out their bodies to strangers? And who *are* these strangers who feel they have the right to rent the body of a person they don't care about or even know? It was to answer these questions, give face to these people, that I started to explore with my camera.

When I started I had no idea how I'd feel towards them, whether I'd like them or despise them. All I knew was that I wanted to expand something within myself, overcome my fear, enlarge my sympathy for those who are reviled.

Tim more than anyone showed me the way. Through him I learned to see hustlers as fragile beings with the same yearnings as myself. I also came to understand that their bartering of their bodies was in principle not so different from the transactions between athletes and their fans. In the latter case the ticket holder has bought permission to gaze, in the former he has paid to touch.

I pick up a photograph in which Tim is facing away, posed like a Greek sculpture of a youth. With his head turned his body becomes idealized, a body beautiful – open, accessible, voluptuous. Again I feel desire for him, and, as I do, am filled with regret. So many things held me back – fear of disease, ruining our friendship, being inept with such an experienced lover. Fear most of all of letting myself go.

These, of course, are selfish thoughts, considering the terrible wounds inflicted upon him. Perhaps if we had made it, everything would have been different. He would have given up his trade, he would have lived.

FOUR

I'M STANDING IN MUD on a ridge in Wildcat Canyon Regional Park, Hilly Lentz on one side of me, a Contra Costa County deputy on the other. Shanley, cell phone in hand, stands ten paces ahead. Below us, about a hundred feet, in an area of scrub demarcated by police tape, a number of County and SFPD criminalists are combing the brush. It was here today at dawn, deep in a thicket, that a hiker spotted a male torso.

It's 8:00 a.m., a raw, chilly morning. A slow steady rain has been falling for over an hour. I'm wearing a black slicker and boots, the cops are in ponchos, Hilly and Shanley wear nylon rain jackets with hoods, SFPD printed in large block letters on their backs. I hear the crackle of field radios as the criminalists communicate below. Through the surrounding mist I make out El Cerrito. San Francisco, a few miles across the Bay, is obscured by fog.

Two men from the coroner's office lug a lumpy dark rubber bag up the hill. In it is the torso which may or may not be Tim's. It's two days since I looked at the shots from our nude session, studied the curves of his body, the texture of his skin. I have not been called here to ID him; the Medical Examiner will do that by matching the cuts on the limbs. They also have my Angel Island photograph which shows the freckles on his chest. Still I have come. Hilly called me as she promised and now I am here, standing on the muddy ground, camera in my hands, a witness.

Click! I shoot a long shot of the advancing men. *Click!Click!* I shoot them again as they move closer. The images will not be clear, and that's good, I think, for my feelings on this ridge are not clear either. They're dark, they concern bloodshed and carnage, and blood for me is always black.

Shanley is walking toward the men.

'How's it look?'

The older of the two wears a watch cap. He grumbles, 'Rain's messing everything up.'

His younger colleague nods. He's gawky, bare-headed, with stick-out ears.

'Animals've been at him,' he says. He gives a little tug to the sack.

'What kind?' Shanley asks.

'Dogs maybe. There're a couple wild packs around. Maybe a mountain lion. There's one killed a lady here last spring.'

I remember the story; it was on TV. The woman was walking a trail bike. The mountain lion, waiting in a tree, leapt upon her back.

Suddenly I feel sick. I think I understand Shanley's question. He wants to be sure the person who did the butchering didn't engage in a little cannibalism first.

I start down the hill. Shanley calls after me.

'Where're you going?'

'Take some pictures,' I reply without looking back.

'No, you're not. No!' His voice is stern.

I ignore him.

'Halt!' he yells. I halt. 'You can't enter a crime scene. Restricted area down there.'

'I'll stay outside the tape, how's that?'

Hilly has reached me. She takes my arm. 'Better come back up, Kay,' she says. 'Otherwise he'll make you leave.'

She escorts me up the hill, then goes to Shanley. They confer. Shanley, I'm certain, wants me taken home; Hilly is arguing that I be handled with care.

They're wrong, I'm not traumatized. Horrified: yes. Angry: absolutely! But I'm not in the least disoriented. I know exactly what I'm doing: collecting material for *Exposures*.

The rain starts falling harder. I watch as the crew spreads plastic sheets to protect the crime scene from the elements. Is this the killing ground, the place where the body was dismembered? Has the earth here been consecrated by Tim's blood? I take another shot so I can find this place again, revisit it when the cops are finished, leave flowers, light candles, sit and watch them burn down to pools of wax. Perhaps I will leave some kind of marker too. I'm sure that the torso in the sack is his.

*   *   *

Noon. Back in San Francisco. The rain's stopped, the fog's burning off, but on Russian Hill it's still thick. Hilly has just informed me by phone that the Medical Examiner has matched the Wildcat Canyon torso to the arms, legs and head from the Willow dumpster.

'It's your friend,' she says. 'At least now he can be buried whole.'

I phone my father, tell him I need to see him.

'Love to visit with you, darlin',' he says. 'Shall we wait till after dark?'

No, I tell him, right away.

He's surprised but doesn't ask me why. We agree to meet for lunch at the Tai Yuet, a *dim sum* place on upper Geary.

As I arrive by bus I see him entering. He's wearing the same shapeless heavy wool sweater he's worn for years. Soft grey locks of hair curl over his ears. I race toward the restaurant door, reach it just in time to grab him from behind, press my face against his back.

'Dad . . .'

He turns, hugs me hard, then kisses my forehead. As always in his mighty arms, I feel safe.

The Tai Yuet is filled mostly with Chinese, convivial groups seated at large round tables. Our table is small, square, set against the wall. The waitresses stroll about offering delicacies from trays. Dad speaks some Cantonese from the years he worked Chinatown. The girls giggle when the big guy with the meaty Irish face tells them in their own language he'll have a little of this, a little of that, and could they bring over a flask of rice vinegar, please?

'Grand to see you, Kay.'

His eyes sparkle through his squint. He's sixty-two, his skin is lined, there are bags beneath his eyes. Still, he's handsome. I think he looks like a character actor, the kind that play old-timers in Westerns. You know the type – they crouch around the campfire at night sadly recalling the way things were, grieving over the end of the open range.

I marvel at his gentle manner. Since he retired from SFPD and started City Stone Ground, a bread bakery two blocks away, he's become increasingly sweet and self-effacing.

'You look pretty relaxed,' I tell him.

'Morning's over. That's the hard part of the day. Actually, I feel good,' he says. 'Cop work never felt right.'

'Took you long enough to discover it.'

'Yeah, well, some lessons are hard to learn.'

He sets down his chopsticks, peers into my eyes.

'There's a sadness about you, Kay.'

A waitress offers a bamboo steamer containing dumplings. He mumbles 'No, thanks' in Cantonese without taking his eyes off mine.

I tell him about Tim. Till now he's only had the vaguest notion of my project. I know it disturbs him to learn I've been hanging out in such a squalid milieu, but I detect nothing judgmental, rather a deepening sympathy as he gently shakes his head, swallows and exhales. When I get to the dismemberment he despairs.

'Gotta be a copycat,' he murmurs.

'What if it isn't?'

'Gotta be. Too many years.'

He wants to know about Tim's torso, whether and how it was marked.

'Hilly didn't say anything about that.'

'Did you ask her?'

I shake my head. 'If there're marks, what would they mean?'

'If they're the same, I'd say they'd mean a lot.'

He stops eating. When I offer him a shrimp dumpling, he shakes his head.

'Tell me about it,' I urge.

'What?'

'The T case.'

He groans. 'That's a sorrowful ugly story.'

'You're a terrific storyteller. You used to tell me great bedtime stories.' I'm remembering how much I loved the one about the little girl who couldn't see colors but could read people's minds.

'That was to help you sleep, darlin'.'

'Now help me understand.'

'Oh, Jesus,' he groans, 'it seems so long ago . . .'

There were six T-case victims, he recounts, five homicides plus Robbie Sipple, the first in '76, the last, Sipple, in '81, one a year in between. After Sipple they stopped. They were called the T killings because only the torsos were found – no heads or limbs as with Tim. The victims were young males and four were never identified. No fingerprints, no dental work, and in those days DNA matching didn't exist. It was a fluke that even one beside Sipple was IDed;

he'd been missing, his parents had filed a report, he'd recently had a gall bladder operation and the surgeon recognized the scar.

'He was gay, promiscuous.' Dad says 'gay' blandly, but he's of the generation that can't pronounce the word without an involuntary wince. 'We learned he hit the baths every night. We assumed the others were like that too, kids who'd drifted here, gay life-style capital. But without heads or hands we couldn't ID them.'

The five torsos showed certain traits in common. They were from lean, hard, gym-toned bodies; they were all caucasian; they'd been sodomized; their blood had been drained; their skin had been washed; they'd been left in public places (the Presidio, Point Lobos, Mount Davidson, Twin Peaks, Golden Gate Park) where they were certain to be found. That was one odd thing: that they hadn't been buried or disposed of like the limbs and heads. The other odd thing was the tattoos.

'We told the papers there were marks. We never got more specific. They were always on the back, on three victims the right shoulder area, on two the butt.'

Dad pours tea into his cup, brings it to his lips, blows on it, sips.

'The tattoos weren't elaborate, the work was fair at best. We had tattooists in. They estimated the work on each took approximately three to four hours. The designs were abstract. There wasn't a picture of anything, just these curves and lines. The tattooists thought they looked like tribal markings, but they couldn't identify the tribe. We brought in an anthropologist. She said that they looked vaguely South Pacific Island. She couldn't ID them either.'

'Were there colors?' I ask.

'The ink used was black.'

Well, I think, *that's something.*

The case was never solved. Hundreds were interviewed: tattooists professional and prison-trained, surgeons, butchers, known homosexual sadists. There were many leads, all checked out, all dead-ends. Then the killings stopped as abruptly as they began. It was one of those weird unsolved San Francisco cases, like the Zodiac killings, but in the T case there were no taunting letters to the press. The killer remained quiet . . . as if his cutting and tattoos said it all. There was something terribly cold and cruel in Torsos that struck everyone who worked it.

'It was only once that we got even partway close. That was when I was involved.'

Dad pours another cup of tea, holds it in his hands to warm them. This is the bad part of the story, I know, the part that changed his life.

'It was spring '81. I was working the Haight, foot patrol, feeling burnt-out. I was thinking a lot those days about what to do when I retired, mulling my dream of setting up a bakery, producing and selling first-rate bread. It was around eight p.m. I was on Waller when I got the call – disturbance on Frederick just two blocks away. There's a hill there, you know, pretty steep. So I huff and puff my way up to this smallish Victorian on Frederick, and there's a middle-aged lady standing on the stoop, the room behind her lit like a Christmas tree.

'She lets me in. She's fairly panicked. Tells me she owns the house, rents out the basement and a flat upstairs. It's the basement tenant's got her worried. He's new, been there just a couple weeks. Around seven she heard strange sounds from his room, and, a few minutes before, a scream. Too scared to go down and check, she dialed 911.

'I listen hard. I can't hear anything. That tells me whatever was happening is probably over . . . and maybe it was just the TV turned on loud, a horror film, cop show, something like that. Still I go down by the outside steps and rap on the door. No answer, but I hear something faint inside like maybe an animal scratching at the wall. I turn the handle and the door opens, no lock, not even firmly shut. There's this young caucasian male lying in the middle of the floor, wrists bound behind his back, tied to his ankles too. He's helpless, hog-tied, buck-naked except for this hood he's wearing, a full head black leather hood, kind you see in some of the gay leather stores, what they call a discipline helmet, bondage hood, whatever. And he's moving a little but not too much, and I get the impression maybe his air's cut off.

'I rush over to him, start working on the hood straps. His body's sticky. I yell to the landlady to call for an ambulance. Hell of a time getting that hood off. All those straps and zippers – it was practically sealed to his face. Finally I yank it. This gag thing comes out with it. There's vomit inside and if he's breathing I can't hear it. But he's got a pulse so I cut the ropes, turn him over and start the old artificial respiration, pinching his nose, breathing into his lungs. He starts gurgling. By this time the medics have come. I step back. They give him oxygen.'

Dad brings up his napkin, wipes his brow. It's easy for me to imagine him ministering to the kid in that basement, bringing him back to life. It's the way I like to think of him, a hero.

'After I get off him I look around. I tell you, Kay – this was one shabby pad. No bed, just a ratty couch with broken springs. No closet, just a pile of clothes in the corner. Airplane size lav with rusty metal shower stall. Beaten-up black and white TV. Basically no possessions of value . . . and that makes me curious, because that hood he was wearing, it wasn't cheap.

'Lots of people in the basement now. Medics, other cops working the Haight, a sergeant from a command unit happened to be in the neighborhood. Lots of confusion too. "Who is this kid?" "Is he okay?" "He sure didn't tie himself up like that!" "Hey, what's this? Looks like some kind of ink."

'They cart the kid out, ambulance him over to Cal Med on Parnassus, then the rest of us start poking around. "Hey, look at this – amyl nitrate!" "Wow! A syringe! Think he injected himself?" We're handling everything, passing it around, nobody thinking this has anything to do with the T case. I mean, how could it? No one's been killed, no one's been cut up, there's no torso, nothing to connect it.

'It's only the next day we find out different. The kid's name is Robbie Sipple, he's nineteen, he works as a stock clerk in a pagan goods store on Ashbury, moved to the city from Dallas just a month before. Seems he took the afternoon off, was lingering in a gay bar when a handsome thirtyish guy picked him up. Robbie brings the guy home, they screw their brains out, then Robbie takes a little nap. When he wakes up he finds himself bound and gagged with the guy lying next to him whispering weird stuff into his ear – how's he's going to kill him, take his body to a house where he'll cut it up, then leave the pieces in various places around town. Robbie'll just disappear, the guy whispers, no one'll know he's dead 'cause there won't be any trace of him. And now, before he does all that, he's going to put some neat little decorations on Robbie's butt.

'The tattooing was about to start when somehow, terrified, Robbie spat out his gag and let out with a scream. Right away the guy wrestled the bondage helmet over his head and bound him in it so he couldn't make another sound. There was a tiny hole in the hood, to let in just enough air so he wouldn't suffocate. Robbie couldn't hear anything, couldn't see, move, could barely squirm, didn't know if the guy was still there or not. So he started to panic. Just as he passed out, certain he was going to die, I came in and pulled the helmet off.'

Dad gets the check, pays, we leave the restaurant, start walking over to the bakery. The sun's shining so I put on shades. I like walking with Dad on the street.

'You get the picture, Kay. We got someone who was literally in the hands of the T killer, who barely escaped. We got someone who saw him, can describe him, work with a police sketch artist. We also got evidence, stuff that belonged to the killer: the hood, the tattoo ink, a syringe. There may even be fingerprints in the kid's apartment. In short, we got the mother lode. Except—'

Dad stops to greet a customer, a woman carrying a City Stone Ground bag. She compliments him on his bread and courteous Russian refugee staff.

'—except,' Dad continues, 'all that good luck suddenly turns to shit. Robbie Sipple dies. Right there in the friggin' hospital! He gets out of bed, stands, takes a deep breath and drops to the floor. Naturally they autopsy him. He's got some kind of congenital heart disease. You hear about these cases – high-school kid plays basketball, suddenly keels over, he's gone. Problem was young Robbie hadn't given us a description yet. Just two words: "handsome" and "thirtyish".

'And there was another problem too, a very big problem. That hood I pulled off him, the ink, the syringe – no one can find them. They're not in Robbie's apartment, not in the police property room. They're gone. Vanished. Thin air!' Dad snaps his fingers. *Click!* 'Like that!'

We're standing in front of City Stone Ground. I smell the aroma of the bread. It reminds me of weekends during my childhood when Dad baked for us, trying out brands of flour, sources of spring water, new shapes, baking stones, leavenings. He was a magician with components: flour, yeast, water, salt. Our house was filled with the sweet warm fragrances of his *pain au levain*, round sour-dough loaves, baguettes. Bread-making, which started as his hobby, soon became his obsession. He was striving toward something pure and impeccable – a perfect loaf with a shattering crust. He loved working with his hands. He'd talk about kneading, how good it made him feel. Once, when I asked him why he liked bread-making so much, he meditated on my question. 'A good loaf doesn't lie,' he finally said.

Dad shakes his head. He's getting to the bad part now, the part that happened after they found the evidence was gone. 'Everyone who was there that night – me, the other cops, the sergeant – we're called into a meeting with Inspector Jonathan Topper Hale, lead detective on the T case, so-called city's smartest cop. We go over it with him again and again. No one can explain the loss. We all remember seeing the evidence, handling it, but everyone says he handed it off to someone else. Bottom line: no one took responsibility, secured it, bagged it, initialed and sealed the bag. But then no one had any inkling it related to a capital case. Conclusion: we must have left it in the flat, but the flat wasn't sealed. So what happened to it? Hale starts bearing down. "Don't you remember? What are you – assholes? You left the stuff there like fuckin' idiots?"'

There's a gloss of sweat on Dad's forehead as he relives the humiliation. 'The top forensics team in the city went into that basement. They dusted, vacuumed, crawled around the floor with their friggin' microscopes. They found lots of prints, all sorts of hairs, but nothing they could convincingly tie to the guy who told Robbie Sipple he'd kill him and cut him up.

'You remember what happened. The IA investigation, which was supposed to stay internal, except somehow it got leaked. The articles that came out, the way they made us look. Then the editorials, so sarcastic – the tax payers of the city actually *paid* people to bungle a crime-scene that contained the only T-case evidence ever discovered.

'The sergeant, Wainy Waincroft, was demoted straightaway to patrolman. He quit. I was reassigned to a dead-end desk job. Everyone who was there that night was disciplined. They wanted to stigmatize us, make examples of us . . . and they did.'

Dad wipes away the sweat.

'It hit me hard, your mother worse. You remember how she got. She couldn't take the stress, got so bad she couldn't bear to leave the house. I passed it on to her, I guess. Didn't mean to. You know that. But it just pushed her deeper into her depression. Then, what she did, Kay, I guess you could say it goes back to that night . . . though I think she was so ill she'd have probably done it anyway even if they'd promoted me, named me friggin' Commander of Patrol.'

He spreads his hands.

'That's the story. Maybe now you wish you hadn't asked. How's it feel to know your old man could've been famous, the guy who cracked the T case? In law enforcement, if you're lucky, you get a chance like that once in a career. I got it and blew it . . . and here I am.' He smiles. 'In that way at least, I like to think, it was the best thing could've happened.'

He pulls me to him, kisses my forehead then the top of my head. I tell him I want to photograph him. He's delighted, dodges into the bakery, swiftly changes into whites, plops on a baker's hat, grabs a flat wooden peel, steps back out.

I pose him in front of City Stone Ground, the big window through which the huge brick oven can be seen. He beams at my lens, a dusting of flour on his cheek, a gentle smile on his lips. I fire at him twice. *Click!Click!* I catch him, as in an August Sander study: the quintessential Happy Baker.

Everyone needs a coach. Mine is Maddy, also my friend, mentor, guru. I pay her for private coaching which does not mean I go to her for lessons in technique. She simply looks at my work, discusses it with me, critiques it, coaches me on how best to achieve my goals. Her insights are smart, penetrating, sometimes merciless. I've learned more from her about photography than from any teacher I've ever had.

She lives on Alhambra in the Marina, a flat area of Art Deco period homes and apartment buildings that abuts the Bay. She's seventy now, stopped taking photographs years ago, but the walls of her flat are covered with framed prints of her work, astonishing pictures taken on city streets, some dense with life, others soft, moody, underpopulated, all poignant, full of feeling and wondrous San Francisco light. Also hanging here are many fine portraits of local artists and writers, and the famous pictures she took of GIs during the Korean War, some of the darkest, most intense combat war photographs ever shot. Don't look to Maddy's work for still-lives, whimsy, charm or arty 'decisive moments'. She's mistress of the direct, unblinking gaze; the gaze that, in her words, probes, strips, reveals.

She greets me with a hug. A tall, thin, fragile white-haired woman, almost gaunt, she's visibly aged this past year. There're rumors she's ill, but she'll allow no discussion of her health. And even if Maddy has faded physically, her eyes are as keen as ever. People who interview her never fail to mention them. One journalist described 'eyes so sharp you feel they should be registered as dangerous weapons'.

We sit in her living room. Expecting me, she has thoughtfully lowered the blinds in advance.

'You're troubled, Kay.' Her eyes probe mine.

How well she knows me. I tell her about Tim.

'Terrible, terrible . . .' She takes my hand. 'My heart aches for you, dear.'

She retires to her kitchen to make tea. When she's gone I look about. A snapshot of Maddy with her late husband, Harry Yamada, sits on the lamp table beside my chair. The picture was taken aboard an ocean liner sometime in 1951. They stand at the railing, young, beautiful and in love, arms about one another, staring into the lens. Behind them the port of Yokohama glitters in the dawn. Maddy is on her way to Korea for the first time to cover the war for *Life*.

When she returns, I spread out the nudes of Tim. She fills my cup, examines them, then turns her attention to my proof sheets. It's proof sheets, she believes, that tell her most – how I work, what I was trying to do, where I made decisions good and bad.

'I'm unhappy with them,' I tell her.

'You shouldn't be,' she says. 'There're some strong images here.'

'Not strong enough.'

She shakes her head. 'You're wrong, Kay. I think you feel that way because all that's left of him is on film, and for you now that's not enough.'

Perhaps she's right.

'If these were just snaps,' she goes on, 'it would be a different story. But these are photographs and we don't make photographs of people to substitute for their presence. What you've brought me is a project, a session with a nude model. You're exploring him, exploring your relation to him by studying his face and body. You're even, in a way, making love to him . . . as you always do when you care about a subject. The caring here is strong, Kay. Very strong. These aren't abstract nudes. Oh, sure, a few times you yield to the impulse to make designs. But really these are portraits of a very beautiful young man who happens to be unclothed. Interesting work. Significant. There's real power here. Something tense, thrilling.'

She sits back. I'm grateful. Even if she's being kind, she has helped me understand what I did. Yes, that afternoon we took the nudes was a time of mutual exploration, perhaps as much of me by him as of him by me. There was magic between us, magic Maddy says I captured, magic I have no right now to deny. I thank her, we stand, embrace and then I leave. Walking home I consider how lucky I am to have her for a friend.

I call Hilly. The jerk who answers her line says she isn't there. As soon as I give my name, Shanley picks up.

'What can we do for you today?'

'Were there marks?' I ask.

'Huh?'

'On Tim's torso – marks, tattoos?'

'What kinda question's that?'

'You're saying there were?'

'I'm not saying anything. I'm asking you a question.'

'I helped you. It's your turn now.'

'Turn to do *what*?'

'What do you think?'

'Look, Kay, maybe I'm missing something here. I'm a cop, you're a civilian. You came forward, as you rightly should. Now you wanna play detective, do it on some other guy's case. Not on mine. Got it?' He hangs up.

It's twilight. I'm walking in North Beach . . . among tourists, stockbrokers, young people in love, sailors, Asian immigrants, commercial travelers seeking companionship, addicts, alcoholics, people nostalgic for the beat period, self-styled San Francisco poets.

I'm thinking about none of that, thinking instead about color-blindness and the many misunderstandings that surround it. The most common is that only boys suffer from it and that they inherit it from their mothers. In fact, the defective gene that produces most color deficiencies, such as red-green confusion, *is* far more likely to affect males and *is* carried by the mother on the X-chromosome. If a female child's mother is a carrier and her father is color deficient, both her X-chromosomes may carry the defect and thus cause her to suffer from the malady.

However, this inheritance pattern does not apply to autosomal recessive achromatopsia. In my case, and that of other achromats, there's usually no family history of the defect and males and females are equally affected. Furthermore, if I have children I won't pass the defect on except in the unlikely event I mate with another achromat or carrier. All of which is to say that my colorblindness can't be definitively attributed to either my mom or my dad.

Why, in this cosmopolitan environment, am I thinking about inheritance patterns, chromosomes, defective genes? Because I have the chilling feeling that Dad, my closest relative on this earth, who speaks so passionately about honesty and how a good loaf of bread doesn't lie, was less than fully truthful about his involvement in the T case when he recounted it to me over lunch.

At home I search not the heavens but the city with my telescope, seeking answers in dim doorways, parked cars, lit-up rooms. San Francisco, they say, belongs to everyone – not just to its residents but also to all the visitors who travel here and see and come to love this place. City on the Bay, Queen of the Pacific Coast, Luminous City, Jewel of the West. It is also City of Vertigo, of Lust, of Meretricious Charms. Conan Doyle called it a 'dream city' with the 'glamour of literature'. John Steinbeck wrote of it as a 'gold and white acropolis rising wave on wave against the blue of the Pacific sky'. My favorite description is Oscar Wilde's: 'It's an odd thing, but anyone who disappears is said to be seen in San Francisco. It must be a delightful city and possess all the attractions of the next world.'

Tonight the Judge is home: I see lights and movement through the French doors that open to his terrace. I wait patiently for him to show himself. Five minutes, ten, fifteen . . . my eyes grow weary. I pick up a fashion magazine, examine glossy black and white photographs of slick-haired, sleek-bodied young men and women modeling underwear. When I peer again through my telescope I'm rewarded by an appearance. The Judge leans upon his terrace balcony looking west toward me.

Does he remember that I live here across the valley? Does it occur to him that just now I may be looking straight into his eyes?

FIVE

I'M STANDING IN A small crowd just outside the vault-like doors of the Main Library, due to open at 9:00 a.m. With me are the usual suspects – early birds, scholars, nerds, as well as homeless residents of the Civic Center encampment who need to use the toilets.

Behind us, across the plaza, the dome of City Hall reflects the sun. Through the library doors we can see people moving inside. They don't acknowledge us, don't give a glance as they officiously prepare for us, the sweaty horde, hovering with growing impatience for the opening.

A Chinese intellectual, briefcase and wire-rims, checks his watch and stamps his foot.

'Always late!'

'Op-en! Op-en!' A young trouble-maker with a mohawk starts the chant. Others join in. A black guard approaches the doors, stares out nervously. 'Op-en! Op-en!'

Finally, at 9:07, the great doors are unbolted. We of the sweaty horde surge inside.

I'm sitting in the periodicals room before a large black microfilm reader unspooling a reel of the *San Francisco Examiner* vintage 1981. The T case is a recurring motif that year, as is the name Jonathan Topper Hale, the oft-quoted SFPD inspector, who promises the public that he and his 'crack team' of investigators are 'doing everything humanly possible' to solve 'these horrific and hitherto intractable crimes'.

Persons having knowledge of the quarry, defined as 'probably a white male in his thirties who may have a meat-packing or medical background, with a possible additional interest in tattoos and/or tattooing' are urged to phone the T CASE HOTLINE, where all tips, whether attributed or anonymous, will be promptly checked out.

'Interest in tattoos and/or tattooing' – clever that, I think. Not a word about the application of tattoos to the torsos, leaving the reader to surmise that the victims were chosen on account of tattoos already on their bodies. Yet the phrase is sufficiently enticing that if someone actually did know a person capable of both butchering and tattooing, he/she would still be likely to phone said information in. Above several of the articles appear pictures of Inspector Hale: late-forties, brooding, authoritative, canny eyes, black hair, thick eyebrows, matching black mustache. His visage announces: *I am one serious cop*.

But the more I read about Hale, the more I get a sense he isn't all that popular with colleagues. 'Sure, he's a great policeman,' one unnamed Department source tells the *Examiner*, 'but he has this weakness – a craving for personal publicity.'

Others, speaking of Hale's brilliance, also mention his arrogance. Inspector Hale, I come to learn, is no shrinking violet. But he has his defenders. Over a period of nine weeks three letters appear in the LETTERS TO THE EDITOR column praising 'this outstanding law enforcement officer' for his 'brilliant performance' and 'unselfish devotion to duty'. One writer goes so far as to define the inspector as 'perhaps the finest of San Francisco's finest, the closest thing we've got here to a cop's cop'.

On 12 May 1981 a scandal erupts diverting attention from the T case investigation, which, in any event, is going nowhere fast. An astute *Examiner* reporter, one Jim Steele, noticing that the three letters praising Hale were written on the same typewriter, checks out the letter writers' names and finds they're fake. Increasingly suspicious, he secures a document typed by Hale on a machine in his office and has it matched by a typewriter expert to the typing on the letters.

Hale, of course, denies any knowledge of the forgeries, but voluntarily resigns 'for the good of the Department'. His moral breakdown is attributed by unnamed sources to everything from 'worked-related stress' to a 'warped sense of humor'. Hale's attorney, Denis Roquelle, speaks of 'the immense tragedy that has overtaken this exemplary officer who is pilloried now because his brilliance has long aroused the envy of the gutless wonders who staff the upper echelons of SFPD'.

I gaze at a picture of Hale as he leaves the Hall of Justice for the last time. Proud, unrepentant, features set into a crooked grin, he projects himself as a man above the fray and the petty jealousies that have brought him down.

There is more. I make my way through reels from the *Chronicle* as well as the *Examiner*, sniffing around the untidy corners of the case, avoiding coverage of the Robbie Sipple incident, circling it, saving it for last . . . and not because I think it'll taste so very good. Rather I'm apprehensive it will tell me things I'd rather not know. Except that I *do* want to know those things.

Stop diddling, Kay. Confront your demons!

T VICTIM DROPS DEAD IN HOSPITAL AS 'DUMMY' COPS MISLAY EVIDENCE

The story is as brutal as the headline. The excoriated 'dummies' are individually named: Patrolmen Jack L. Farrow; William D. Hayes; Enrico S. Puccio; Luis Cruz Vasquez and Sergeant Lucius D. Waincroft. Adjectives and nouns flow fast and thick: pathetic, inept, irresponsible, incompetent, dolts, dunces, bunglers, chumps, buffoons.

I wince as I read the accompanying articles. It's hard not to think of these men as dolts. Hardest of all is to imagine Dad among them, casually handling evidence then abandoning the basement apartment without securing it. One minute he's a hero saving Robbie Sipple's life, the next he's Prince of Fools.

I can't buy it. I ask myself why. Because Dad is the most exacting man I know, rigorously correct, even compulsive in matters having to do with property, finances, relationships and procedures concerning everything from automobile maintenance to the making of exotic breads. He pays his bills the day he receives them, figures his taxes to the penny, promptly repays loans, conscientiously returns borrowed possessions, keeps his doors locked, his papers in order, teaches me, his child, the virtues of truthfulness and reliability. 'The most important thing about a person is personal integrity,' he teaches. 'In fact,' he adds, 'it's the *only* thing.'

Am I to believe that this man who never misplaced anything, never left his house or car door unlocked, never read a set of instructions he didn't follow, never in twenty years as a cop fouled or in any way tainted a crime-scene, could be party to such bungling? I cannot.

Which leaves me again with the thought that the story he told me yesterday wasn't straight. That something else happened that night at Robbie Sipple's. That Dad, alone or in complicity with others, obstructed justice. That at the very least he had knowledge of such obstruction and for some reason, which I cannot comprehend, preferred to suffer the indignity of being called a dummy rather than tell the truth.

Methodically I photocopy every relevant page of microfilm, not at all certain why I bother. No solid connection yet between Tim's dismemberment and the old T case, but, because of Tim, I've stumbled back into a mystery that for years I put out of mind.

Just before I return the reels to the desk, I search out Mom's obit. There is none, only a death notice:

> Farrow, Carlotta Ryan – Passed away San Francisco, 9 October 1981, age 43. Beloved wife of Jack L. Farrow, loving mother of Kay R. Farrow, cherished sister of Tom Ryan and Arlene Ryan O'Neill. She leaves behind feelings of joy and love that touched all she met, including her nieces, nephews and numerous students at Marina Middle School to whom she taught music through the years. Friends may visit Friday, from 1 to 5 p.m., at Terry Sullivan Mortuary. Funeral arrangements are private.

Emerging from the library on to Civic Center Plaza I enter an arena of blinding light. Quickly I slip on shades, but even then the brilliance is nearly unendurable. As I squint and blink my way across the Plaza, I feel tears forming in my eyes – whether on account of photophobia or recalling my mother's death I cannot be sure.

From home I phone the *Examiner*, ask to speak to someone on the crime desk.

'That'd be City,' the operator says. She connects me to a Jason Lubow, who identifies himself as a police reporter. I complain that the killing of Timothy Lovsey has barely gotten notice.

'That Polk Gulch thing?'

'That's the one.'

'We ran it.'

'Six lines.'

'We'll run more when there're developments.'

'Like what?' I ask.

'Arrest. Explanation. Something that wraps it up.'

'Otherwise it's just another hustler homicide, right?'

'You said it, lady. Not me. But a Gulch hustler – you know, those things happen. Doesn't make for the most sympathetic victim in town.'

'What about a tie-in to the T case?'

'What's that?'

Lubow never heard of it; he's only been in San Francisco six years. As I fill him in, I hear the clicking of computer keys. When I'm done he tells me he'll check it out.

'If you don't mind my asking,' he asks, 'who am I speaking with?'

'A concerned citizen,' I tell him and hang up.

An hour later I get a call from Hilly Lentz. There's traffic in the background, so loud I can barely hear her.

'Where are you?'

'Pay phone. You never got this call, understand?'

'What's going on?'

'Shanley's crapping in his pants.'

'Something I did?'

'Your little query about tattoos.'

'So tell me – *are* there tattoos?'

Her wordless breathing is my confirmation.

'What's the big secret?' I ask.

Again she doesn't respond, instead gives me her address.

'I'll be home by six,' she says. 'Drop by at seven and we'll talk.'

She lives on Collingwood near 20th in the Castro. It's a nice Edwardian, renovated and well kept-up. A guy with a buzz cut, Dalmatian on a leash, emerges as I mount the stoop.

'Need help?' he asks with the demeanor of a landlord.

'Looking for Hilly.'

He laughs. 'House cop, third floor.'

I nod, kneel to meet the dog. I like Dalmatians, they're black and white. But now this one starts nosing at my groin.

'Oscar! *Oscar!*' Buzz Cut yanks at the leash, pets his pooch, grins. 'He's heavy into crotch worship, dear. Can you blame him?'

'Well, who should I blame?' I ask.

Hilly's waiting for me in her doorway dressed in a grungy grey SFPD

T-shirt and baggy sweats. She laughs when I describe the encounter on the stoop.

'If Oscar takes after Jerry he's into just about everything,' she says.

She shows me around. The flat is spacious, but messy like a grad student's – living room, eat-in kitchen, bedroom, bath. An aerobics class schedule and police duty roster are taped to the refrigerator door. In the half-open closet I catch sight of black leather motor-cycle gear. I glance into the bedroom, notice a pair of handcuffs dangling from a bedpost.

'Standard cop issue.' Hilly giggles. 'Fantasy facilitator device.'

Back in the living room she clears off a place for me on a couch, opens two cans of beer. Just as she hands me one a cat leaps into my lap. 'Meet Puddy. She's an old thing Puddy is. If she bothers you, just brush her away.'

I stroke the cat. 'What's going on, Hilly?'

She grins. 'Shanley says to kiss you off.'

'Because I asked about tattoos?'

She gives a weak smile. 'I gotta be careful what I say.'

'Hey, you invited me here.' To set her at ease I disarm myself by placing my camera on the floor. 'If we're not going to talk freely, what's the point?'

She exhales.

'Why *did* you invite me?'

'I like you. You care. Few people do.'

A shallow observation, but I let it pass. 'Tim Lovsey was my friend.'

She nods. 'I know. But it's more than that. Your dad was a cop. That makes you part of the family . . . if you know what I mean?'

Dysfunctional family, I think.

'Do you know anything about my dad?'

She takes a swig of beer. 'Shanley does, says he was involved in the old T case.'

'That's right. Yesterday we had lunch. It was the first time I heard his version. I was in art school at the time so I never got a fix on it. Now I'm starting to. What's the connection? The tattoos the same?'

I gaze into her eyes. I can't be certain but I think they're blue. I don't know why that matters. Blue, brown, hazel – eyes to me are either light or dark.

'One thing you might be interested in – Med Examiner says Tim tested negative for HIV.'

I sink back into the couch. I feel relieved. He told me he was negative, got tested regularly, but a side of me wasn't sure. Perhaps if I had been I'd have made a move on him on Angel Island that idyllic afternoon.

'The tattoos?' I ask.

'No tattoos,' she says.

'Then why— ?'

'He was marked.'

I push Puddy off, sit straight. '*How?*'

She tightens her lips. 'Police business. I'll get shit-canned if I say more.' I wait her out, knowing she wants to tell me. 'There was painting,' she says finally, 'black oil-based paint on his back. Abstract shapes, curves, what the Med Examiner calls arabesques. Like the old case, but crudely done. And something else. A number. Seven. Like the T killer was starting up again from where he left off in '81.'

She lets out her breath. She's crossed the line; too late now to turn back.

'Personally I don't think that's possible,' she says. 'It's been too long. Why would he stop so long then resume? And a few other things. Paint instead of tattoos. That suggests this person doesn't have tattooing skills. Also the limbs and head – leaving them for us, making it possible to ID the victim. Finally, why dump them so near the place where Tim hung out? Why do that . . . then leave the torso the other side of the Bay?'

She's trying to sound dispassionate but the vibrato in her voice gives her away. Listening, I feel we're talking about stuff that has no connection to real life.

'Maybe the heads and limbs of the earlier victims were left in dumpsters too,' I say. 'Those times the trash was hauled. This time a homeless guy happened to be hunting empty soda cans.'

She shrugs. 'Could be.'

'Butchering's a skill as much as tattooing. Isn't it a big coincidence to have two butchers?'

'Definitely.' She peers at me. 'What about the fifteen-year gap?'

'Maybe the killer was in prison.'

'That's Shanley's theory. He's checking it out.' She smiles craftily as if we're playing a mind-game. 'What else?'

'The need to kill quieted down. Then something triggered it again.'

'Department shrink suggested that.' She shakes her head. 'Sounds like detective story crap to me.'

'How do *you* explain it then?'

'Without discounting any of the above, my hunch is a copycat. No great breakthrough, true. But it's what I think.'

'My dad's theory too.'

'The question is, why.' Again the crafty smile. 'Someone who knows a lot about the T case . . . but not everything. That's the key. How come he knows certain things closely held at the time, yet doesn't know other things the top investigators knew? He has a source. Find the source and maybe we'll find him. That's the theory I'll be working on.'

She stands, suggests we go out, grab some food. I watch as she goes to a mirror, checks the gel on her hair then slips on a leather vest.

As we walk toward Castro she nudges me in the ribs.

'I shouldn't be seen with you, but we don't have to worry around here.'

There are plenty of gay SFPD cops, she tells me. And the proportion of lesbians to straight women may even be greater than the proportion of gays among the men. Which is why, she confides, she moved to San Francisco. She's from LA, member of a law enforcement family. Her father and two of her uncles are cops, one brother's with the Secret Service, the other with the FBI.

'Don't know why they went Fed. To best the old man, I guess. In a family like ours you'd think I'd be the black sheep. But both brothers are proud of me. Like: "Sis is great!" As for Pop – he's a little less enthusiastic. I guess he wishes his only daughter were straight.'

A pair of stout diesels approach, sporting engineer's boots and Oakland As caps backwards on their heads.

'Hey, Hilly!'

'Dina! Jude!'

They eye me slyly as they pass.

Hilly smiles. 'They think we're on a date.'

'They can think what they like.'

'Right!'

I'm not sure how I feel about these undertones. I think I find them amusing. What interests me is why Hilly is extending herself. What does she want from me anyway?

I like the Castro, its parade of purpose and flamboyance, tanktops and tattoos, tight asses, pert tits, piercings, muscles, leather, flesh. Some call it a ghetto, but for me it's a vital portion of the city, alive with young men and women steamy with sexual energy. I believe it's that energy and the freedom it implies that ultimately enrages the bigots. I don't think they hate gay people for what they do in bed; what they can't stand is how much they enjoy it.

Hilly leads me to a solid wooden door. A discreet brass plaque identifies it as The Duchess. The moment Hilly opens it we confront a wall of sound – loud talk, laughter, heavy metal music. It's dark, but I can see the place is crowded with women. I smell beer, cooking oil, cologne, cigarette smoke, sweat.

'What do you think?' Hilly asks. 'They give great grilled tofu.'

'It's not the clientele,' I assure her, surveying the crush. 'Just looks like it might be hard to talk.'

'So true . . . and so sad!' She beams. She wants to be agreeable. 'I know another joint, quieter . . . around the corner.'

She leads me to the kind of nondescript coffee shop you'd expect to find near a bus terminal. The patrons are quiet, the booths are upholstered in plastic. Perhaps it survives as a refuge from the funky dives around.

'No tofu here,' Hilly says, 'but they make good salads.'

When the waitress comes we both order low-fat Caesars. After she moves away Hilly and I stare at one another. Hilly smiles first.

'Shanley told you to kiss me off,' I say. 'So why'd you call me?'

'Aren't you glad?'

'Sure. But what d'you say we cut the crap?'

'Fine.' She turns serious. 'I don't like Shanley. We're supposed to be partners. He treats me like an underling. He's homophobic too.'

'File a complaint. Isn't that what people do?'

She narrows her eyes. 'I've been waiting a long time for a case like this. Now that I've lucked into it, I'm not about to let it go.'

I stare at her.

'Don't get it, do you?'

'I'm trying,' I say.

'Solve it and I'll never take shit again. Not from Shanley or any of the other assholes down on Bryant Street. I'll be queen of the heap, one of a handful of cops who get written up, ones the public knows and trusts. If I stay in law enforcement I can go to the top. If I decide to get out it's an easy move over to politics.' She licks her lips. 'Cops dream of stumbling into a case like this. It's cop heaven . . . and now I'm at the door.'

I'm amazed by her outburst. This isn't good cop Hilly talking now, this is one tough, ambitious woman.

'I still don't—'

'Why you? Because you knew the victim. Shanley thinks you've given all you got. I think you've got more to spill.'

I think about my photos of johns. *But she couldn't know about them.*

'Did you speak to any of Tim's friends?'

'They're not keen to talk to cops.'

Her eyes twinkle. 'Think they'd make an exception?'

'Because you're gay? No. You're still the law.'

She shrugs. 'You're the one who called Lubow, right?' I shrug in turn. 'Jason Lubow. The *Examiner.* He says it was a woman who wouldn't give her name. Anyhow he won't write anything. Shanley's got him in his pocket. He's persuaded Lubow to cooperate.'

'Why're you telling me all this, Hilly?'

'I want press coverage too. You can help me with that.'

'Why should I?'

'You're pissed, Kay. I saw it in your eyes the other night. Your buddy was mutilated. You want this solved as much as me . . . and you know I'm on the right track.'

'Pissed' seems a bland word for how I feel, but maybe Hilly, lost in her ambition, can't identify with my raging sorrow. Anyhow it doesn't matter if she reads me right; what's important is that I read her.

'I might be willing to help,' I tell her, 'but it can't be a one-way street.'

The wily smile again. 'Tell me what you want?'

'Photographs.'

'Of what?'

'Tim's body, head, limbs, torso, the marks too, and photos of the crime-scenes, Willow and Wildcat Canyon.'

'Why?'

'For a book I'm doing documenting his life.'

She ponders. 'What about copyright?'

'Police pictures are public property. Anyway, I won't use them the way they were shot. I'll blow up details, collage them, create something new.'

'Interesting . . . hmmm . . . I think I could manage that. A few prints here and there won't be missed.'

'There's more.'

She smiles. 'I figured. What?'

'Anything in the T-case file on my dad.'

She laughs. 'Don't want much, do you?'

'Would that be so hard to get?'

'If it's in an IA report it'd be damn' near impossible.'

'Suppose it's in his personnel file?'

'Retired cop? I never asked for anything like that. Don't know if I can.'

'Of course you can, Hilly.' I bear down. 'You've already got your justification. You're looking for the new killer's source – who knew what, who's the leak. To investigate you'll need to read the files of everyone involved – from Inspector Jonathan Topper Hale right down to Patrolman Jack L. Farrow.'

I reach for the tab. Hilly mildly protests, but allows me to pick it up. She's worked a long hard day; she's tired. Our little mind game's worn her down, but it's invigorated me.

She walks me to the Muni stop at Market and Castro. We agree to think things over and let each other know. She gives me her home phone number, urges me to call whenever I like. As we wait for the bus she tries to lighten up.

'Ever make love with a woman, Kay?'

I look at her. 'Now how did I know you'd get around to that?'

She's amused. 'Doesn't seem to make you uncomfortable.'

'I'm sex-positive,' I tell her. 'Can't be otherwise and spend time on the Gulch.'

''Suppose not . . .' She seems disappointed. The truth is I never have slept with a woman, but I don't feel like answering her question. She's shown me a lot of herself tonight, some of it unattractive: a willingness to manipulate, to forge temporary alliances, anger, ambition, greed for success. As nice as it might be to reciprocate, I decide to follow one of Rita Reese's favorite aikido maxims: *Never let your opponent see all of your face.*

'Can I take your picture, Hilly?'

She turns a little to the side, demure. But I've already got my

Contax up. *Click!* Then, as she reverts to her cocky self, I hit her again twice: *Click!Click!*

'You clever lynx!' She grins.

The bus is coming.

''Night.'

''Night, Kay.'

She waves as I jump aboard.

Too early to go home. I get off at Market and Polk, walk through City Center Plaza to the Gulch. This is my first expedition since my run-in with Knob. It's been four nights. I'm curious to see if things have changed.

On my way I think about Tim. He could have made a different life for himself if he'd settled in the Castro, found a decent job, met someone he liked and settled down. Perhaps that's what he had planned for his retirement. But then it occurs to me he did have a connection to the Castro: he kept a private mailbox there.

The first thing I notice on the Gulch is that things are back to normal. The dealers are out, the hustlers are at their stations, the street people – AIDS victims, homeless people, freaks, drugged-out adolescents – are clustered on the usual corners outside the sex stores and saloons. The second thing I notice is that there're no more Timothy Lovsey posters on the posts. Every single one has been torn down. So much for Shanley's hope of soliciting information. So much too for the first street exhibition of my photographs.

I spot Knob ahead at the corner of Fern conferring with his two favorite pretty boys, the ones I think of as his acolytes. As I approach I detach the lens from my Contax, button it up inside one jacket pocket, the camera body inside the other. Knob and I have some unfinished business. *Never advance with weakness*, Rita says.

He notices me coming, pretends he doesn't. Does he really think I'll just pass by? Disputes on the Gulch tend to get resolved. But then I'm only a girl.

Aikido is a defensive art. Before I took it up I studied karate. One step past Knob I wheel around, kick out at his stomach, then straight-arm the side of his head. As he struggles to keep balance, I smash him in the head again. As he goes down I kick at his knees, then sweep him to the ground.

He writhes on the sidewalk. There's blood on his face. His acolytes stand over him. They gape.

'That's for skinning my knees,' I tell him. 'We can end it here or carry it on. Your choice, Knob. But if you want a second round, get ready to be hurt.'

He stares up at me with a mixture of surprise and respect. He wipes away the blood.

'I been feeling bad about shoving you, Bug. Guess we're even now.' He shows me a shit-eating grin. 'You sure know how to punch.'

My first inclination is to extend my hand, but I'm wary of a feint. I nod, give him a shit-eating grin of my own, then leave it to the acolytes to lift him and clean him up.

Varoom! Varoom! Between Bush and Pine I hear the roar of a car in low gear. Looking around I spot the same Mercedes SL 600 I saw cruising the night I thought Tim stood me up. I can't see the driver through the reflecting glass, but I know it's the same bald chickenhawk. Quickly I unbutton my pockets, snap together my camera, take aim at the license plate and shoot. Just then the car swerves abruptly into Sacramento Street, then races up into Pacific Heights.

No sign of Crawf; perhaps he really did go down to LA. I don't see any more cops than usual. The Shillelagh is back in business. Passing The Werewolf I spot Slick standing at the bar. Deep in conversation with the bartender, his albino complexion makes him prominent in the dark room of shadowy men. On the next block I come across Alyson lingering in the doorway of The Snafu. We greet each other. Her lipstick's messy, her wig bedraggled. I ask after Doreen.

'On a date,' Alyson confides.

We chat a while. I smell gin on her breath. She confirms that Crawf left town.

'Cops been around?' I ask.

She shakes her head. 'Just the first couple of nights. They don't care, you know. To them, dearie, we're all trash. Just trash.'

I spend a few minutes peering through my telescope: no lights on in the Judge's penthouse and nothing else interesting to be seen. Since there's still film in my camera, I set up lights and a tripod, prepare to take self-portraits. I pose against the nightscape to the east, stare into my lens as honestly as I can. Rapidly I whip off the rest of the roll.

Whap!Whap!Whap!Whap!Whap!

I'm still wired; no way I can sleep. I take the exposed roll into the darkroom for processing. Nothing like darkroom work to quiet the mind.

I'm pleased with my results. The shots at Wildcat Canyon are appropriately moody, not surprising with all the mist and rain. The portraits of Dad are as I imagined they'd be, pictures of a solid, honest man. My second last shot of Hilly, catching her special mix of self-centered brashness and vulnerability, is superb.

As for Baldy's license plate, it's barely legible, very small due to my wide-angle lens and blurry since he'd already started to drive away. But with a magnifying glass I can make out the first three digits. Enough to trace him, I think, since there aren't that many twelve-cylinder Mercedes coupés around.

As for my self-portraits, I'm unimpressed. I look all right, I guess, but there's something vacant in my face, my eyes appear flat as if I'm in a daze. In a sense, I know, I am. The events of the last week have taken their toll. I seem to have entered a dreamworld where people speak without emotion of dismembered torsos, limbs and heads. I look at my self-portraits and long to see myself as fierce. I wish like a tourist I'd handed my camera to a passerby on Polk. Then I could see how I looked when I knocked down Knob.

When Carl Sandburg wrote: 'The fog comes on little cat feet', he was writing of Chicago, 'Hog Butcher for the World'. Here in San Francisco the fog has its own manner of approach, sometimes bounding through the Golden Gate like a panther leaping through a hoop, fierce, growling, ready to scrape and flay at everything within. This is the consequence of a sharp collision between very cold, deep Pacific Ocean water and hot Central Valley air that creates then draws off mist . . . resulting in our famous teeth-chattering San Francisco summers.

It's mid-autumn now, normally fog-free, but there have been sporadic anomalies in our climate. Today the fog is a thick gray syrup. Since fog is a lot easier on my eyes than brilliant light, I decide to venture out.

I'm armed with my Contax and a list of seven private mailbox service stores in the Castro, copied from the Yellow Pages. My mission: to discover Tim's box, and, by so doing, discover . . . I'm-not-really-sure. My method: systematically to visit each store and show the proprietor Tim's picture. However, on the Van Ness Avenue bus, I think up another approach, less methodical but a lot more fun. I'll try to put myself in Tim's shoes and psych-out the place that would have appealed to him most.

My first stop, on Sanchez off Market, is a dreary, narrow store stuffed between a barbershop and auto parts shop. *He wouldn't have liked it here*, I decide, and move along to the next. This is a modern well-lit full-service place on Castro, offering fax, photocopying, key-cutting, the works. I don't like it, no achromat would – fluorescent light hurts our eyes. I decide Tim wouldn't like it either: too antiseptic, not welcoming enough. But the third place, on 18th between Castro and Hartford, seems a likely bet. There's just something about it, including the folksy name, MAIL FROM HOME. I think: *This could be the one*. I enter. A clean-shaven body-builder type in a tanktop greets me with a smile. There's a stuffed teddy bear on the counter, a studded cockring secured around one leg. Yes, I think, this is just the sort of kinky place Tim would have liked.

I introduce myself to the reception-person. His name is Gordon; he has a moon face and beautiful white teeth.

'I have a friend I think rents here. I know this is kind of weird, but would you be willing to look at his picture?'

Gordon nods, sizing me up. I'm hoping he takes me for a friendly butch.

I show him the Angel Island portrait, not from the poster but a print I made myself.

'Sure, I know him,' Gordon says. 'Box 475.'

I nod solemnly. 'Well . . . he's dead.'

Gordon is stricken. 'Oh, wow! Man! Was it— ?'

He means AIDS. I shake my head. I show him the tiny clipping from the *Chronicle*.

He reads it. 'This is terrible,' he says. 'Maybe even worse than . . . you know.'

'Uh-uh,' I say, 'nothing's worse.'

I tell him I want to close down Tim's box and arrange for his mail to be forwarded. I offer two months' additional rent and whatever Gordon needs for forwarding. As he considers my request, I try to preempt his misgivings.

'Look,' I tell him, 'I don't have court papers. I don't even have a death certificate yet. But I was his best friend. His family disowned him. They think he deserved what he got. So, do you think you could forget the formalities this time?'

He studies me a moment, takes down my name and address, then goes to the back of Tim's box, pulls out the contents, hands them to me, promises to forward whatever else comes in. When I try to compensate him for this gracious act, he gently waves my money away.

Back on the street, I can't believe my luck. I walk over to Castro, find a cafe, fetch a cup of cappuccino, carry it outside to a table, sit down and examine Tim's mail. There are three items. The first is a postcard bearing a postmark from Florence, Italy. The front shows Michelangelo's David. On the back is a scrawled message:

> *Thinking of you*, Gorgeous One, *missing your silken . . . ha!*
> *Quite a little threesome we had, yes? David (see reverse) is*
> almost *as good-looking as you, but, alas, is stone! I shall be back*
> *in Baghdad this fall ready for* heated *pleasures. Till then,*
> GO, most *fondly and devotedly,*
>
> *Jerome*

Second is a letter from attorney J. F. Judd strongly urging Mr Lovsey to settle his long-overdue account of $1250 for services rendered in connection with his 5 July arrest for loitering and solicitation. Unless prompt payment is received, the letter threatens, Mr Judd will have no choice but to take legal action. Third is a letter bearing a return address in New York. The sender has only affixed one name: deGeoffroy. Something about it strikes a note. It takes me a moment to make the connection. Of course! deGeoffroy – not Jeffrey or Geoffrey. The letter must be from Uncle David.

I stir my cappuccino, take a sip, wipe my spoon and use it to slit the envelope. There's a fresh hundred-dollar bill inside and a letter written in ink on a single sheet of creamy paper:

> *Dear Boy!*
> *How kind of you to write. It has been a very long time, but I*
> *have not forgotten you or A. I know (and so must you both)*
> *that I never shall.*
>   *We shared most precious times, the three of us. And then it*
> *ended – Poof! – as in a puff of smoke. My fault entirely. Be*
> *assured I never blamed either one of you. Sometimes it takes a*

great, indeed an enormous, loss to shock one into appreciating how very fortunate one has been. Sometimes, it seems to me, those cataclysmic events took place only yesterday.

I try to understand why you have sought contact after so many years. May I take your note and the good news that you are happy and well as a sign of . . . forgiveness?

I barely know San Francisco, have been there only twice. I do know it's a pretty place. How wise of you to have chosen beauty!

Please don't worry. I shall not attempt to trace you. I know better than to press myself unwanted. But if one day you should express a desire to see me again, be assured my bags are already packed.

Please, if convenient, keep me apprised of things and tell me that A. too is well and safe. I hold you both most dearly in my heart.

With great affection,
David deG

My hands are shaking. Whatever does this mean? Sure doesn't sound like the cuddly Uncle David I heard about. More like a tragic and passionate lover, I think, one who did a wrong and in turn was wronged. But who is A? What *did* they do? And exactly how many years ago is 'so many'?

The fog is lifting. Starting to blink, I slip on my shades and head for the bus stop on Market. There's a side of me that wants to phone Mr deGeoffroy at once, tell him what's happened. Another side is reluctant to get involved in a relationship which appears to have been so disturbed. But if Tim has family, they have a right to know he's dead. And I have many questions.

Manhattan directory assistance lists only one deGeoffroy. I take down the number, dial.

My opening is awkward. I introduce myself as Tim's friend. Tim, I say, always referred to Mr deGeoffroy as 'Uncle David'. Babbling on, I detect impatience on the other end.

'Is something wrong?' he asks.

'Well—' Tongue-tied, I wish I'd rehearsed.

'Yes,' he says, 'something's terribly, terribly wrong.'

The voice is cultured, with a British inflection. But not truly

British, I decide. More stagey, like the learned theatrical-English of an actor.

'Explain yourself at once!' he demands.

'He's dead,' I whisper. A gasp, a long pause and then a sob, followed by a wail. Not knowing what to say, I stay quiet.

'I should ask you how this happened, I suppose. But I'm not sure I want to know just now. Or is this a trick, a canny little hoax cooked up by that naughty lad?' Dead silence, as if he's holding his breath. 'Say that it is. Please say it is!'

'No, not a hoax,' I tell him. 'Sadly not.'

'Yes . . . sadly,' he murmurs, 'I believe you. I don't know you, but I believe you are sincere. It would be too cruel to be otherwise.'

He is weeping vigorously now. I wonder how long I can bear witness to his grief. Then I start to cry myself. It just comes out of me in a way it hasn't till now. Delayed reaction – or is it because at last I've found someone with whom I can share my heartache, someone who also loved Tim, who truly cares? It's so strange what we're doing, total strangers sobbing together on a transcontinental call. But it feels real to me and also right. Everything else has been so crazy, so why not this?

'Forgive me,' he says, choking back his tears. 'I seem to have started a chain reaction.' I imagine him smiling as he says it. 'Now please tell me about the other. How is she?'

'I don't know who you mean.'

'You don't know her?' He sounds surprised.

'Who?'

Silence, then: 'Perhaps another day. Forgive me, my dear, for asking again for your name. This time I shall write it down, your number too. I'll call you back tonight, if that's all right? I do want to talk more, but if you'll forgive me, not just now. Now I must try and – how do they say it these days? – begin to process my pain.'

After putting down the phone I sit still for several minutes. I'm moved and also mystified. *Who is this man?* And who is the one he calls both 'the other' and 'she'? Is it 'A' referred to in his letter?

I take an early aikido class. Rita puts us through our *katas* and then tough drills. We line up facing her, then we each attack with all our might. She turns, deflects, compliments, criticizes. When it's my turn she slams me hard into the mat. The pain is sudden, harsh. I cry out. Feeling betrayed, I'm furious and scream at her: 'Why me?'

Rita laughs softly as she helps me up. 'Why *not* you?' she asks.

Later she pairs me with a big guy, Tom, 6'3", 220 lbs, long slick black hair, wiry chest hair curling out of his *gi* jacket. Tom's a novice. He can't believe he's been assigned to practice with a petite woman.

Rita whispers: 'Nice stud muffin, huh?'

I shrug.

'Show him what we're about,' she says. Somehow Rita knows when a student needs to let off steam. She's my instructor, has instructed me to teach Tom about centrifugal force. I have no choice, I must do as sensei commands.

The first time I throw him, he hits the mat with a thud. In aikido the cliché is apt: the heavier they are, the faster they attack, the harder they will fall. He springs up, smiles to show me he doesn't mind, we bow to one another, then immediately I throw him down again. This time he doesn't get up so fast and his smile isn't so sweet. Since I have nothing against him, I imagine that he's Knob, and re-live the glorious moments of my payback. I toy with him a little, then dump him hard. Rita helps him up, brushes him off. We bow to one another. His eyes show pain.

After class, to show there are no hard feelings, I invite him for coffee on Chestnut. He tells me he's an actor. He wants to know why Rita over-matched him.

'She wants you to understand size and strength can be a disadvantage,' I tell him, 'that aikido's about blending energy, not just applying techniques.'

'I already knew that.'

'Yeah . . . but did you *feel* it?'

He gazes at me, rubs his shoulder. 'Now I do,' he says.

David deGeoffroy phones back a little after six. The first thing he asks is whether he's caught me at a bad time.

'Not at all,' I assure him. 'I've been waiting for your call.'

This time his tone is different. He sounds charming, almost merry. He's inquisitive, wants to know all about me – my age, what I do, how I knew Tim, how and when we met?

On the latter point I'm cautious. Not knowing how Tim has presented himself, I don't say a word about hustling, turning tricks or johns. I simply say I've been photographing him, employing him as a model. After a while, when I feel I've revealed enough, I try to turn the conversation around.

'It's your turn,' I say. 'I know you're in show business. What exactly do you do?'

He seems amused. 'I thought you knew. I'm the Magician.'

The Magician! I didn't know there was a 'the Magician' in Tim's life.

'The one who taught him to make coins disappear?'

'That . . . and a few other things.' He pauses. 'May I ask you a favor? I'd love to see some recent photos.'

I promise to FedEx several in the morning. 'What about the rest of the family?' I ask.

Another pause. 'There's no one left.'

'Just yourself?'

'In a manner of speaking,' he says.

We banter on. He insists I call him David; in turn I request he call me Kay. Soon we're 'Daviding' and 'Kaying' each other like long-lost friends, a weird sort of intimacy since we've only just met telephonically over a tragic loss. When I tell him Tim's San Francisco friends called him Rain, I can almost feel David glow.

'I like that. Name suits him. He was always a bit moody. But so sweet, so very sweet.' He pauses. 'It's been so long since I've seen him, so many years. The silence, you know, the awful roaring silence. Then, out of the sky, like a bolt, comes his note. I have it here. I want to read it to you.' He clears his throat. '"I'm well, happy, working as a waiter, trying to make ends meet and make sense out of life and all that happened. My juggling's gotten rusty but my close-up work's still pretty good. If you get this let me know. Tim."'

He's ready now, he tells me, to hear how Tim was killed. I decide to give it to him straight.

'Shot in the throat. Cops don't know by whom. And this is the bad part – mutilated afterwards.'

A very long silence this time. 'Cut up, you mean?'

But how does he know that? 'You sound as if . . . like you expected it?'

'I don't know quite what I expected,' he says. 'It occurred to me, that's all – that it would be of a piece, so to speak.'

I don't know what he's talking about, and there's something detached in his tone that makes me mad.

'Well, you seem to have processed your pain quite nicely.'

'Please don't think poorly of me, Kay.'

There's nothing I can rejoin to that, especially as his response is so mild.

'There are things to be arranged,' I tell him. 'Tim's burial, cremation, whatever. What do you want me to do?'

'I never thought about it. Cremation, I suppose.'

'Out here?'

'He was happy there, wasn't he? Why don't you make arrangements and let me know? Keep it simple, dignified.' He asks me to choose a funeral home, have them call him. He'll put it all on his credit card. 'When everything's ready, let me know and I'll fly out. Then we'll meet . . . and really talk.'

I prepare myself a salad, devour it, then eat an apple, then another. I stare out the window for a while, then telephone Dad to ask if he can run a license plate.

'Can't do it myself,' he says, 'but Rusty'll do it if I ask.' Rusty Quinn is his old partner, still on the force.

I give him the first three digits from Baldy's plate, then the make and model of the car.

'What's this for, Kay? If you don't mind my asking.' I tell him. 'Why not turn this over to Shanley. It's his job?'

'Because Shanley's kissed me off and there's probably no connection anyway.'

Dad mulls that over. 'Cops aren't supposed to run license plates for private parties. It's a pretty big favor to ask.'

'Fine, Dad,' I tell him, 'I'll hire an investigator. Just thought—'

'I'll take care of it,' he says.

Feeling cooped up, tired of looking out the window, I walk down the other side of Russian Hill into North Beach. I always like walking here, charmed by the neighborhood, the Old World coffee houses populated by a mix of Italians, bohemians and tourists, the flourishing pizza parlors emitting wonderful aromas, the funky street life, and the small, almost quaint district of raunchy live-action sex shows. There's something harmless about North Beach, put-on and theatrical, a far cry from the desperation and danger I feel on the other side of the hill. Life on the Gulch is sour, the flesh market there for real. On North Beach it's more like a dating game, like play.

I wander, peering into cafes, then spend an hour browsing at City

Lights Bookstore. I glance through the latest photography books, see work I respect but nothing that challenges my eye. What about my own project? Will *Exposures* expand people's vision? I compose a subtitle: 'Life & Death of a Street-Hustler'. Will anyone buy it? Will anyone care? I must think they will, otherwise my work is useless.

I turn on Greenwich Street, ascend Telegraph Hill. I rarely walk here during daylight; I like the neighborhood but feel awkward blinking my way around. And there's something else: nostalgia. The Judge lives up here. I used to visit him often, arriving even before the sun had set, so anxious was I for his company. Nowadays I watch over Telegraph from my perch on Russian. To actually walk here seems like a trespass.

Greenwich dead-ends at Grant Street, but there are steps for pedestrians that lead up to Kearny, and from there it's just a few paces to the building I know so well.

It smells sweet up here, there's the fragrance of wild fennel and nightblooming shrubs mixed with the resin scent of the Monterey cypresses that compose the woods around Coit Tower. I'm so accustomed to viewing this place from a great distance through a lens that I'm surprised by the intimacy this sweet aroma conveys. Suddenly I feel heady. My pulse starts to race. It's been a while, but I recognize the sensation. I know I must leave; the feeling's too intense. I turn and run back down the hill, skidding and nearly falling on the incline.

SIX

HAVING NEVER ARRANGED A cremation before, I call Sullivan's, the mortuary that took care of my mother. I speak to Randy Sullivan, grandson of the founder, explain the situation and the fact that Timothy Lovsey's body is in pieces. Randy, grasping the problem, instructs me how to get the parts released. He quotes me a price with an additional option of a boat trip to scatter the ashes at sea.

'Will you want some kind of service?' he asks.

I tell him no, nothing formal, that most likely some friends will gather, say a few words, and leave it at that.

'Sounds like just what the deceased would have wished for,' Randy says.

After I hang up I wonder why he put it that way, since he obviously has no knowledge of the deceased or his preferences.

I phone Shanley. He listens politely as I tell him I've contacted David deGeoffroy in New York, that Sullivan's will be taking care of the body, and that I want to wind up Tim's affairs, including termination of his lease and removal of personal effects from his studio.

Shanley's helpful. Clearly he prefers me as supplicant to the angry shutter-happy female he's been dealing with. I even detect a smidgin of warmth in his voice as he asks how I'm holding up.

'Pretty good,' I tell him, 'considering the circumstances.'

'Glad to hear it. Hilly and I were talking about you just this morning. We think you've been great. Let me know if there's anything I can do, not just on this – on anything at the Hall of Justice. I don't claim to swing a lot of weight, but there're plenty of folks here owe me favors.'

Is this the kiss-off Hilly told me about? Is this how cops handle it these days, so nice, polite, eager to assist? If I get a Health

Department citation for improper disposal of photochemicals, will Shanley get it fixed?

Dad's busy time starts at 4 in the morning and tapers off after 10. These are the hours when he and his Russian emigré helpers bake the loaves, deliver them to stores and restaurants and sell the main part of the day's production to walk-ins. Dad has one of those numbered-tag dispensers on the counter so customers know whose turn it is. He likes calling out the numbers, looking the customer in the eye, fulfilling the order with dispatch. Fine bread is his joy, good service is his pride. City Stone Ground, he wants you to know, is no kind of hippie joint.

I arrive at 11, watch him through the window. As always in his white apron he appears the Happy Baker. I don't know where this tendency of mine comes from, this need to turn people into archetypes. The Solemn Judge, the Happy Baker and now the Enigmatic Magician.

'Dad!'

'Hey, darlin'!'

He grasps me in his arms, enveloping me in a cloud of flour and yeast. As a girl I could never get enough of his hugs. To this day they take me back to a time when I knew I'd always be protected by his strength.

'Got the info for you,' he whispers. He holds me back. 'Bull's-eye, I think.'

Arm across my shoulder, he leads me into his office off the baking floor. From his desk, neatly stacked with folders, bills, purchase orders, receipts, he extracts a slip of paper. 'Rusty ran the plate. When he called this morning he sounded impressed.' He hands me the slip. 'Take a look.'

The first digits of the plate number and the car make and model are matched with a name: Marcus P. Crane. Something familiar there; I've read about this person but can't remember where or who he is.

'Address mean anything to you?' Dad asks.

It's in the 2600 block on Broadway, one of the fancy parts of Pacific Heights.

'Marcus Crane. Think about it,' he coaxes.

'I'm thinking. Give me a hint.'

'Read the society columns?'

'Not if I can help it.'

'If you did you'd know Crane is the husband of a local legend.'

'Sarah Lashaw?'

Dad winks. 'You got it, darlin'! She of the fabulous parties and the violet eyes.'

I don't have to remind him I can't see violet. He knows my weakness better than anyone. But for years, like most everyone in town, I have heard about Mrs Lashaw's eyes, their haunting beauty.

'She married Crane ten years ago,' Dad says. 'He's hubby number three . . . or is it four?' I'm surprised Dad knows this; evidently he *does* follow society. 'Crane's a dud like the others. The difference is he's got better manners. Old San Francisco family. Holds down some kind of half-ass job in finance. Does what she tells him, holds her chair, hitches the clasp on those egg-sized emeralds she wears.'

Now it starts coming back: Sarah Lashaw's violet eyes and the deep green emerald necklace she wears to complement them. The stones may not actually be egg-sized. More like quail's eggs, I think.

'Is Crane bald?'

Dad shrugs. 'Don't know. But from what I hear Lashaw is one very tough lady. Best not to mess with 'em, darlin' – not unless you got 'em by the hairs.'

At the Main Library I use the microfilm reader to look up references to Marcus Crane. The photos show him with a full head of hair, but his features match those of Baldy. There are many mentions but little of substance. Seems aside from being Sarah Lashaw's husband, he's known more for affability than accomplishments.

Mrs Lashaw is another story. Reading about her one would conclude she's some kind of social goddess: grand-scale entertainments, masquerade balls on behalf of this or that worthy cause, impeccable taste, meticulously decorated homes, an apparently limitless fortune. But as I read more, what comes through is a portrait of a demanding woman, spoiled and suffused with a sense of her own entitlement.

Using the periodical index, I retrieve articles from back issues of *House & Garden*, *Town & Country* and *Architectural Digest*. Mrs Lashaw, I discover, is indeed a handsome middle-aged woman whose natural good looks are bolstered by her lavish surroundings.

Vases of fresh cut flowers fill her rooms. Fine contemporary art adorns her walls. Studying pictures of the calculated interiors of her various homes, I note a horror of empty space . . . as if the filling of the rooms, their overflowing, will somehow mollify the emptiness within.

She is, moreover, an accomplished equestrienne. Astride her favorite gelding, Folly, in helmet, jodpurs and hacking jacket, she beams at the camera, a long thin dressage whip dangling carelessly from her hand. Another spread shows her and Crane picnicking with friends on the vast expanse of lawn before their Napa Valley house. The goodies (recipes courteously provided) are packed in English wicker baskets, while the picnickers recline on oriental carpets spread upon the grass.

Do I sound envious? I hope not, for everything in Mrs Lashaw's ethos is the opposite of mine. She embraces the ornate while I'm drawn to the austere; she fancies gilt while I prefer black; she likes couture while I slop around in jeans. But, I remind myself, it's not she who is the object of my scrutiny, rather her suave and stylish husband whom I've seen cruising the Gulch attempting to rent underage male flesh.

From the Main Library I walk to Pacific Heights, our most posh quarter, though there are those who would argue for the enclaves at the tops of Nob and Russian Hills. Stately mansions, meticulously renovated Victorians, vast Art Deco apartment houses. Personally I find this neighborhood boring: few contrasts, everything smooth and groomed, svelte women, perfectly behaved children, nannies with European accents pushing heirloom baby carriages. The foreign consulates are here, as well as numerous small apartment buildings with molded escutcheons above the doors. Hedge walls, lookouts, tile and slate roofs. I pass the baroque marble palace of a famous romance novelist whose diamonds are said to rival Lashaw's emeralds.

Mounting the greensward of Alta Plaza I break a sweat. A pair of fortyish in-shape women in fashionable togs are battling it out on one of the tennis courts. Long rallies and cutting strokes – from a distance theirs appears a friendly match. But up close I hear pants and grunts, glimpse the steely eyes of fierce competitors.

From the crest of the hill I can see the whole southern portion of the city. The huge antenna on North Peak breaks the pewter sky. There are sunbathers on the slopes, people training dogs, kids playing ball. To the north is Cow Hollow and the mercurial Bay. The sun beats down; the branches are serene. A perfect afternoon in our golden City by the Bay.

Crossing Divisadero I ask myself what I'm doing here, what I expect to find. I uncap my Contax preparing for action . . . though I expect to do nothing more than quickly view Lashaw & Crane's San Francisco home. The houses here are huge. This is an area of mansions with grounds, not the stuck together townhouses of Eastern Pacific Heights. Two turreted Victorians, a Mediterranean villa, a timbered Tudor, a mansard-roofed Norman – the 2600 block of Broadway is a wonderland of retro architectural fantasies.

The Lashaw house lies behind an iron fence of sharp pointed bars and flamboyant double-swing gates. Surrounded by shrubs and trees, it's not easy to make out its style. It's probably my achromatopsia that's got me confused, causing shapes and textures to blend, which, to a vision-normal, would be differentiated by color.

I walk along the fence gazing through the bars, not the least concerned whether I'm observed. I catch sight of an Asian gardener working with clippers on hands and knees. Though only fifty feet away, he's so intent on his work he doesn't see me.

I press up against the grate, poke my camera through, snap off three or four shots. Because my Contax is a view-finder model and not a reflex, it throws off little sound. Through it I can make out large leaded windows and a great wooden door set back within a recessed entrance. I move a few feet, peer through my viewfinder again, see that the entrance ceiling is actually a groin vault. Then, noticing that the tops of the windows are arched, I recognize the architectural style. The Lashaw house, faux-ecclesiastic, is built like a rectory, a manse suitable for a prince of the church. I walk to the end of the property, take another shot, then slowly pace back, peering in all the while. Just as I pass the main gate, I hear a mechanical sound. The gate doors start swinging out. Then I hear a familiar growl.

Varoom! Varoom!

As I turn to the street, I bring my camera to my eye. A Mercedes SL 600 is hovering just twenty feet away, convertible top down, driver sporting full head of air-blown hair.

Varoom! Varoom!

Mr Crane is impatient; the gates are opening too slowly for one so important as himself.

Without thinking I start taking his picture, walking backwards along the side of his car. I can smell the oily heat of the engine, the finely painted metal hood baking beneath the sun. *Whap! Whap! Whap! Whap!* I'm out in the street now, taking three-quarters back views, and, although the gates are now fully open, Mr Crane is not driving in, rather he is turning in his seat giving me the eye as I move around the back of his vehicle, through the cloud of its exhaust, and approach him again from the driver's side.

Whap! Whap! Whap! Whap!

This is fun! Reveling in my outrageous conduct, I feel the same surge as when I throw down an opponent in aikido class.

'Excuse me! Miss!' *Finally the chickenhawk squawks!* He whips off his dark glasses, perhaps expecting me to do the same. I disappoint him. Then I'm surprised. He's beaming, showing me the face of a bon vivant.

'Ah, sorry – paparazzo at work! Or should I say "paparazza"?' He grins.

'You got it!' I stick my camera in for a close-up. *Whap!* I notice faint adolescent acne scars on his cheeks.

'Why me?' His voice is calm, polite.

'Why *not* you, Mr Crane?'

He nods, amused, guns his engine. *Varoom! Varoom!* Then he tilts his head to expose his profile. He's preening for me! I can't believe it.

'My best side,' he says, grinning again.

'Thanks. I need good clear shots.'

'I had no idea people find me so handsome.'

I'm impressed by his sang-froid. This, I realize, is one slick customer. I lower my Contax, peer directly into his eyes. 'The one's I took on Polk weren't all that clear. And of course you weren't wearing that pretty wig.'

He holds the grin, then, for a second, the mask starts to crack. A glimmer of confusion, perhaps humiliation. Does he wonder who I am? A blackmailer out to expose his secret life?

Whap! I take a final shot, then step back. That'll be the good one if I caught him right. He studies me then blinks, as if etching my features on his memory. *Varoom! Varoom!* The car lurches into the safe interior courtyard of his manse leaving black skid marks on the pavement at my feet.

In the echoing lobby of the Hall of Justice I pick up the envelope Shanley has left for me at the reception desk. No note inside, just the key to Tim's studio. From there it's not much of a walk to his building on Mission.

I feel sad as I mount the steps. The cat piss and roach spray smells are the same. This time an aria from *Tosca* wafts sensuously down the stairwell from an upper floor.

On the landing I look around. The fire-extinguisher is in place. As my eyes rise to the molding above, I consider leaping up to see if there's anything there. Quickly I dismiss the idea. I'm too short, and, besides, I already had Crawf fetch Tim's spare key, the one I later gave to Shanley, the one I'm now holding in my hand.

There's police tape on the door. I cut it neatly using the edge of the key, let myself in, softly close the door behind. From Hilly's description, I'm expecting a mess. But that's not what I find. Yes, the room looks different – the floor is covered with loose down from Tim's slit-up sleeping bag, the stuffing of his futon is strewn about. But his clothing and possessions have not been randomly tossed. Rather I detect a certain rigor in their arrangement – underwear in one pile, jeans in another, sweaters in a third. There's something about this sorting that touches and confuses me, something caring, perhaps even loving, I think.

I go to the kitchen, search beneath the sink, find a box of garbage bags, tote several back to the living room and start cleaning up. I throw in the torn futon and bedroll, the perishable food in the refrigerator and all the stuff in the bathroom – toothbrush, razor, shampoo. When I'm done with that I pitch Tim's clothes into two large nylon duffel bags and a backpack I find on the closet shelf.

Back out on the landing the *Tosca* recording seems even louder. I haul the garbage bags downstairs, stick them in one of the trash cans in back, discover some discarded cardboard boxes, carry two of them back up. These I fill with Tim's Walkman, shoes, boots and books. Then I carefully remove my photographs from the wall.

Something's wrong. One of them is missing, the Angel Island shot. Someone, it appears, has carefully removed it. I see marks where the tape previously adhered.

Now everything's packed except the *Body Heat* poster, kitchen utensils, a couple of plates, glasses, a frying pan and the paltry furnishings. Since these items have little value, I decide to leave them for the next tenant. I haul the duffels, backpack and boxes out to the landing, and prepare to relock the door.

I hesitate. I know the cops have searched the studio; I also know they're pros. But still . . . I look up at the molding again.

I go back inside, take Tim's wobbly desk chair, place it against the wall, climb on to it, start running my fingers around the molding that rings the room. This exercise takes a while; after each sweep of my hand I step down, move the chair a few feet, then step up again. I'm about to give it up when my fingers brush against something metallic. I stand on tiptoe, reach up, bring the object down. A key. To what? It's far too big for Tim's box at MAIL FROM HOME, it's clearly not a bank safety deposit box key and it doesn't match the key to his room. But interestingly it's the same size and make. I pocket it and leave.

This time no music in the stairwell as I carry the duffels and boxes down. I hear a door open on an upper floor, then shut after a few seconds as if the person changed his/her mind about going out. It takes me three trips to get everything down to the front hall. I leave the stuff there while I go out to find a phone.

The Tool Box is a gloomy bar. A couple of guys in black T-shirts are playing pool. They and the bartender, a bear in tanktop sporting grotesque tattoos, glance up when I walk in. Determining my gender, they smile to hide their disappointment.

I use the pay phone by the lav to call for a taxi, then start back toward the tenement. A few steps out of The Tool Box I freeze. At the end of the block a person is turning the corner. For an instant I'm certain it's Tim. The hair, bearing, walk, seem the same . . . yet something, too, I know, is wrong. Perhaps it's his height, I think, as I rush up to Grace Street to check. Turning the corner myself I'm suddenly blinded; the late-afternoon sun slams into my eyes. I blink, turn, examine the after-image before it fades. It's not Tim, it's someone shorter, but then of course it has to be since Tim is dead. I recall how, in the months after my mother's death I occasionally thought I saw her on the street. It took me a while to understand that I made this mistake because I wanted to see her so very much.

Waiting for my taxi I think about after-images, a byproduct of achromatopsia. Since they're a coping mechanism, achromats who wear shades from an early age generally don't experience them.

What happens, according to studies I've read, is that very bright light immediately saturates my rods, but the moment I close my eyes the light level fades to a point that my retinas are able to pick up and retain an image of what I 'saw'. The emergence of an after-image is similar to the emergence of a photographic image on a sheet of exposed paper when placed in developer. But unlike the photographic variety an after-image is transitory, lasting only a few seconds, just long enough for me to examine and identify people or objects invisible when I try to see them with open eyes.

When my cab arrives, I load everything in, drive to my building, haul the duffels and boxes into the elevator. I have little storage space in my apartment but Tim's possessions are so meager I find room for them in the back of a closet.

I phone Tim's landlord, Murray Paulus, tell him I've cleaned out the studio, that he's free now to re-rent it. When he mutters something about not being given the customary thirty days' notice, I point out that homicide victims generally don't know their fates in advance.

Paulus is caught short. 'Hadn't thought of that,' he says. 'Guess you're right. Kinda different when the tenant's mortally sick.' His voice brightens. 'I got a deposit, so the hell with it!' He hangs up.

Lord praise you, Mr Paulus!

Attorney J. F. Judd is not so kind. He still wants his $1250.

'Tim died penniless,' I tell him. 'You can't get blood out of a stone.'

'No, but I can go to Small Claims Court and make trouble for his executrix.'

'That's not me,' I tell him. 'I'm just a friend. He didn't leave a will.'

'Intestate and no assets – I've heard that one. Still, someone's gotta pay. I don't work for nothing, not when it's cleaning up after someone's dirty deeds.'

'Just what dirty deed did Tim do?' I ask.

'Took money from an undercover vice cop. The guy hired him to take a blow-job.'

'How'd you get him off?'

'Entrapment, pure and simple.'

'Well, Mr Judd,' I tell him without much regret, 'seems this time you're going to have to eat your fee.'

A little after six I phone Hilly at home.

'Hi ya,' she says cheerily. 'I was going to call you tonight. I got goodies!'

'Great!'

'Not the stuff on your dad – that's going to take a while. But I got a complete set of crime-scene photos. Not bad, huh?'

I'm impressed. I really want those pictures.

'What can I do for you?' I ask.

In the short silence that follows, I imagine the gears meshing within her brain.

'I know a little about you, Kay.'

'Such as?'

'Such as . . . you used to work for that free rag, *Bay Area News*.'

'That's right. Years ago. I was staff photographer.'

'Still connected there?'

'What's on your mind?'

Another pause, more grinding of the gears. When she speaks again her voice is a purr.

'I want a reporter I can trust, someone ambitious who'll protect me as a source. I want someone, preferably female, who wants to win the fuckin' Pulitzer Prize. I want—'

'I know exactly what you want, Hilly. You want what Shanley's got, a reporter in your pocket.'

'You're smart, Kay. You got me figured. So – do you know someone fits the bill?'

'Actually I do. It's a "he". Joel Glickman. You won't find better. And he's already got a Pulitzer.'

I hear her intake of breath. 'Wow! Can you introduce me?'

'Maybe,' I say coolly. 'I'll lay the groundwork. Meanwhile see what you can turn up on my dad.'

The sky's inky now, moonlight touches the roofs. I peer out my window and fiercely resolve I will never stare out and see, as so many do here, a thousand points of . . . slight.

I feel jumpy, don't know why. Perhaps I'm still spooked by that apparition on the street. Also I feel lonely, wish I were sitting someplace busy with a group of friends, a restaurant or bar full of young people drinking, talking, laughing. I miss that kind of fun – which I used to have so often in my twenties. What I miss most, of course, is a lover, someone to hold me and to hold, to hug and lick and kiss. Wistfully I look across the valley. Then I pull on sneakers, grab my Contax and go out.

The night air is warm, surprising in November. A TV weather-person says we're enjoying an Indian Summer. The trees cast sensual velvety lunar shadows on the sidewalk. The Hyde Street cable rumbles steadily beneath the street.

I cross Hyde, pause at the corner, trying to decide which way to go. Down the eastern slope into North Beach where I can lose myself in the joyful anonymous crowds, or down the western side to the Gulch to walk among the wounded and dispossessed?

Tonight it will be the Gulch. But why I am drawn to haunt that street of damnation is a mystery I cannot solve.

I pass the Alice Marble Tennis Courts. The surrounding high steel fence cuts the moonlight into squares. I hear a dog wail in the distance. Looking to the Bay I see a great cruise ship, decks and portholes lit, slipping between Hyde Street Pier and Alcatraz.

Walking on the gravel alley between the trees and benches of Sterling Park, I hear the snapping of a branch. I pause, listen.

'Bug . . .'

A thick voice moans my street-name.

I turn. Just then someone leaps at me from the shrubbery, pushing me so hard I reel into the trunk of a tree. Another, perhaps the one who called to me, straight-arms my shoulder. I fall. Then they are upon me, three of them, I think, three silent males dressed in black, two turning me on to my stomach, holding me down, grinding my face into the dirt, while the third climbs onto my back, pulls some kind of fabric sack over my head, then starts beating at the sides of my face with his fists.

I hear their breathing, sense them gloat, smell their excitement, their bodies, their foul breaths. My camera is trapped beneath me. The metal bites into my breast. I squirm and scream. The fists rain on my ears and cheeks. The gravel of the walkway crushes against my mouth. I taste blood. The beating doesn't last long, perhaps fifteen or twenty seconds, but to me it seems like an eternity.

They get off me. One of them kicks me. The point of his sneaker catches my flank. 'Nosy fuckin' bitch!' I squirm to protect myself.

'Hurt the bitch, make her howl,' orders the thick voice that called to me before. Another kick. I try to howl but can't. The breath's been knocked out of me. I gasp for air.

Then they are on me again, turning me on to my back. I try to look at them, but, head bagged, can see nothing through the cloth.

One of them grasps at my camera, rips it away. Then they run off down the path. I roll and shake and cry. Tearing the bag off my head, a pillowcase, I hear the pat-pat-pat of their receding steps. Silence. I growl, hug myself, snort out my pain. 'Help! Help me!' I cry, but I don't recognize my voice.

He is holding me, a young man, carefully wiping the dirt and blood from my face with a moist cloth. He sits on a park bench; I lie on it with my head in his lap. I look at him and know immediately who he is: the strange homeless youth with the long hair and beard who has been living in the park for months.

'Hospital,' I whisper. My throat is raw.

His huge eyes stare into mine. Perhaps he doesn't understand.

'Get me to . . . hospital,' I whisper again. There's dirt in my mouth. I choke, then try to spit it out.

'Police.'

Fear in his eyes as he shakes his head.

'Doctor.' He nods. 'Hospital.' He shrugs. 'St Francis. Hyde Street. Close.'

Then I pass out.

The handsome black-haired resident standing above me smiles down, the ironic smile of a cynic. There's no pity in his face but lots of curiosity. I'm a case. He's had me X-rayed and scanned. He's seen my insides. His skin is dark, his eyes liquid, lustrous.

'They sure did a job on you,' he says. He speaks with the accent of an Oxford don.

I peer about. The ER walls are white. Medical equipment gleams. The gurney I'm on is narrow and hard. Phones ring. Nurses stride briskly past. Every so often I hear soft chimes followed by softly uttered cryptic announcements on the hospital PA.

I look back up at the resident. He is Indian. A stethoscope is nicely draped about his neck. I read his name off the little bar pinned to his white coat: DR C. PATEL. 'They call me Sasha,' he says. *Sasha*

Patel. Nice name, multi-cultural. I smile. He smiles. He likes me. He tells me I'll be fine.

'Two black eyes, cut and swollen ears and cheeks, contusions, abrasions, two ribs very tender but not-quite cracked. They're going to hurt, those ribs. I wouldn't laugh too much if I were you. Try not to cough either. Better still, don't yawn. You're on morphine now. The Tylox I'll give you may cause a headache. I don't think there's a concussion, but if you feel dizzy or strange, come back right away. Understand?'

'You're not keeping me?'

He smiles, shakes his head. 'I'm sending you home.'

'How did I get here?'

'By taxi. The driver told the nurse some bum bundled you in.'

'That bum, as you call him, cleaned me up. He saved my ass.'

'No,' Dr Patel says taking my hand, 'I cleaned you, I saved your ass.' I look up at him. I wouldn't mind kissing him. The most I can offer now is a grin.

'See, that didn't hurt so much.' He turns serious. 'Who did this to you?'

'Three men.'

'Not a spouse?'

'I don't have a spouse.'

'What did they want?'

'My camera.'

He's a skeptic, Dr Patel is. 'A beating like this just for that?'

'Well, it was a very fine camera,' I tell him, 'and I think there was something else.'

'What?'

'A message, a warning – to stay away.'

'Good God! Why not send a letter?'

'A beating's more emphatic, I think.'

He raises his eyebrows. He's an ironist, I can tell. He's also solicitous. The hospital, he informs me, must report the incident to the cops. He plies me with pain-killers, three kinds, two for fallback in case the side effects of the Tylox are too severe. He tells me I have a good supple body which helped prevent more serious injuries. He tells me I'll feel pain for a few days, but that the more I move about the better. Finally he asks me for a date, Wednesday or Thursday, his evenings off this week. I gently decline. The nurse who escorts me to a cab tells me Dr Patel is a lady's man.

'And we love him for it,' she adds, 'this town being . . . well, you know how it is.'

Back in the sweet cocoon I call home, I take my sore body to bed. I'm lucky. Bones could have been broken, I could have been raped and sodomized. And that may yet happen, I think, for I have no intention of heeding such a tastelessly delivered message. From this point I shall be on guard; I shall not be taken again by surprise. My greatest concern is my camera. I have several spares but my Contax and I were as one. Well, you win a few, lose a few. Better to lose a camera than to end up in traction. Perhaps one day soon I'll buy myself a new one. Till then I'll manage with what I've got.

It takes me four full days to recuperate, and, even then, in the mirror my face looks like shit. Like a boxer's after a brutal fight, I think, but of course I wasn't in a boxing match. I was attacked from behind.

I go out a couple of times, slowly walk a block then return home. The rest of the time I spend in the darkroom, or on the phone, or despairing over my soreness and marveling over my luck.

What, I ask myself, is the worst thing that could happen to me short of premature death? The answer's simple: to lose my vision. Without my eyes, defective though they are, my life would be an empty torment.

My snaps of Marcus Crane are great. I'm thrilled I took the time to unload the roll; better to have lost my camera than these precious images. It's the full sequence that makes them work, me and my camera circling him while he twists to keep me in view, at first unperturbed, debonair, finally breaking as he understands I'm a threat. This, for me, is the beauty of black-and-white vision and photography – the way it can distill the essence of an individual, cut through the mask, reveal the person's core. I see much evil in my final image of Marcus Crane. I shall print the entire sequence in *Exposures*: 'Cornered Chickenhawk'.

Was it Crane who had me beaten? I think so, though it could also have been Knob acting on his own. Anyhow, I know Crane and Knob are pals, that Knob brokers Crane's chicken dinners. I also know Knob hates me, and I'm almost certain he was the one who called out 'Bug . . .' to make me turn. Later, instructing the others to 'hurt the bitch, make her howl', Knob's particular intonation came through. Yes, it was his show, perhaps just payback for dumping him in front of his boys. If Crane was involved it was strictly as paymaster. If so, I think, he probably wasn't Tim's killer, since, in that event, he'd most likely have ordered me killed.

David deGeoffroy is due in tomorrow. We're to meet at his hotel. Sullivan's has everything arranged for a Friday scattering of the ashes. It's up to me to get some of Tim's friends to come along.

Before I do that, however, there's someone I want to find: the strange boy who lives in Sterling Park. Walking with trepidation into the Greenwich Street cul-de-sac, I start searching for the place where I was mauled.

It isn't hard to find. The alley of trees is gorgeous as ever, the gravel has been freshly raked, the resin aroma of Monterey pine perfumes the warm autumn air.

I caress the side of the tree against which I was thrown, then kneel in the dirt. How miserable I was, yet exhilarated too, all my senses alert. During those painful seconds, I believe, my thought processes went dead. It was pure feeling that suffused me: helplessness and terror.

Carefully I lie down in the position in which I was held, then twist and turn allowing the sensations to flow back. I feel weird doing this, but believe it's necessary for my recovery. When I stand up again I feel purged. Nietzsche, I believe, had it right: what does not kill me can only make me stronger.

The youth is standing before me now, not twenty feet away. He has appeared silently out of the shrubbery. He stands still as a statue, his beard so wild it hangs down like a tangle of vines. His huge eyes meet mine, not sharply but in wonderment. He sends me a signal that he has come in peace but that he will feel more comfortable if I don't approach. 'Hi,' I say shyly.

He nods. From our last meeting I know he's not exactly talkative.

'I came here to find you – to thank you,' I tell him. 'You took good care of me. Thanks for putting me in that cab.'

'You were asleep,' he says, voice sonorous. I smile; these are the first words I've heard him speak.

'I guess I passed out. You were kind to me. I live close by. I've seen you many times.'

He nods again, as if to say he has seen me too. I wonder: has he observed me standing naked in my bedroom window at night staring out at the Golden Gate?

'Can I bring you something? Food?' He shakes his head. 'Drink?' Again he declines. I was wrong about him; I thought he'd ask for whiskey. 'Are you sure? Nothing at all?'

He smiles again, sweetly, shakes his head, then withdraws back into the shrubbery like a ghost.

At 9:00 p.m. I prepare to go out. My ribs are still sore, my cheek bones are still bruised, my eyes are still black, but I don't put on makeup to cover my marks. I also make a point of carrying a camera, the old Nikon Dad gave me when I first took up photography. I want this trek up the Gulch to be a statement.

I cheat a little, take the bus as far as Sacramento Street. Since walking's still painful there's no point in strutting if no one's around. Dismounting, I peer about. I don't see anyone I know . . . which is fine since I felt less than stylish stepping off the bus.

On the next corner, California, I run into Slick and Remo. They look closely at me, but don't say anything about my bruises. Still it's clear they've heard what happened. News has spread by Gulch-telegraph. Now word will spread that Bug is back, undaunted by her ordeal . . . with a different camera too, a big black one, twice as big as the old one.

Soon others surround me: Doreen and Alyson, Scott, Silky, Fizz, Toad and Wrench. I tell them about the scattering of Tim's ashes, invite them all to come along. They nod but I doubt any of them will show. It's one thing to regret the murder of a friend, another to engage in public mourning.

'Where's Knob?' I ask innocently, looking around.

Eyes are lowered. Slick says he saw him in The Werewolf. 'Well, remember,' I announce, 'I'm still working on my book. So you'll be seeing me around.'

'You're always welcome here, Bug,' Doreen says.

A chorus of approving nods. Heart thoroughly warmed, I thank them and continue on my way.

Outside The Werewolf, I question my sanity. Yes, I want to show these people class, but I've been injured and am in no condition for a fight. I don't think Knob will pick one in public, but I can't be sure. Still, I know I must complete my mission, so I straighten up and shoulder my way inside.

The Werewolf's a shadowy place, far more frightening to me than The Tool Box. Combination meat rack, gay bar, piss stop for the street, it's a place to trash out, choose a piece of chicken, or just shoot up in the toilets. There are females in here, some of indeterminate genitalia, pre-ops, post-ops, a few girls looking to become boys. This is also a place where elegant pervs and goths come on weekends to slum.

I push my way through the crowd. Brushing against people does no wonders for my bruised ribs. Trying not to wince, I put on a stoic face. I spot Knob over by the wall, hanging out with the acolytes who witnessed his humiliation at my hands. Did they join him in the ambush? If so are they proud to have gone three-on-one against a woman?

'Knob.'

'Bug.'

Our greetings are strained. I nod slightly to the acolytes. They smirk.

'Been looking for you, Knob.'

'Here I am.'

'We're going to have a little ceremony for Tim. Thought maybe you'd like to show, being one of the leaders on the Gulch.'

Knob grins, then guffaws. The acolytes follow suit. Yet the eyes of all three appear uneasy; they don't know what to make of me, what I intend. An unctuous grin. 'Looks like someone roughed you, Bug.'

'Yeah, someone tried to, three of them in fact. Jumped me from behind. Brave boys, very brave.'

'Too bad.' He lowers his eyes to my Nikon. 'Camera's not so nice. Lost the other one, did you?'

I meet his eyes. 'It's not the camera that's important, Knob. It's the film inside. You know – the *evidence*.' I raise Dad's Nikon, trip the shutter. *Whap!* Knob is stunned. *Whap! Whap! Whap!* Finally the steely eyes blink before my gaze.

Enough! I tell myself. *Cut it off.*

And so I do, turning my back, casually shouldering my way out through the smoke to the street. I leave high-pitched squeals of laughter behind, but I don't think they're directed at me.

SEVEN

UNTIL I DISCOVER HIS real name, I think of my park inhabitant neighbor as the Youth. And though he's declined my offer of food and drink, I nonetheless fix him a picnic. I place several containers of prepared tofu, a package of sliced cooked ham, a packet of pretzels, three apples, two bananas and a can of Coke in a square styrofoam carton, which I tie up with ribbon. All this I deliver to the very place where I was sandbagged. No sign of him, but I'm pretty sure he's near watching over his domain. I place the carton on the bench where he cleaned me up, scrawl 'FROM KAY' on top, pirouette and depart.

The Magician: I'm not sure what I expect as I sit in the lobby of the Mark Hopkins Hotel awaiting Uncle David's entrance. We've arranged recognition signals; I'll be dressed in black with a camera around my neck, he'll wear a polka dot ascot. Our rendez-vous is set for 3 p.m. Already he's a quarter hour late.

When finally he appears I'm amused. The man perfectly matches his voice. If ever in the future I need 'a dapper gentleman' for a shoot, I'll seek one as debonair as David deGeoffroy. Tall, ramrod straight, his soft gray hair beautifully cut into overlapping locks, he has a Clark Gable pencil-line mustache, wears the requisite ascot plus matching handkerchief in the breast pocket of his blazer, sports brilliantly polished English shoes, and, to top off the effect, carries an ivory-headed walking stick which he twirls jauntily as he surveys the lobby.

Spotting me, he raises his eyebrows. I smile; he advances.

'My dear Kay – at last!'

He surprises me by bowing and bringing my hand to his lips. Old-world manners. I feel ridiculous standing before him in leather jacket, T-shirt, sneakers and jeans.

Instantly I like him. He's handsome, his grooming's impeccable, his smile engaging. He looks to be in his late forties, but in excellent condition, reminding me of the sleek sort of man my mother used to call 'a racing tout'.

'Shall we stroll?' he asks. Again I notice the theatrical accent. 'Or would you prefer a drink?'

'A walk sounds good.'

As we leave the hotel, he salutes the doorman with his stick.

I guide him around the Pacific-Union Club into Huntington Park. Since it's a dazzling day and I wish to conceal my bruises, I am wearing my darkest wrap-around shades. The dark red lenses activate the rods in my eyes by tricking them into thinking it's night.

When David asks if my eyes are weak, I briefly explain my malady.

'So you don't see colors?'

'None,' I tell him. 'Just the lightness and darkness of things.'

'Must be a bit like experiencing the world in grisaille.'

I'm pleased by this remark which demonstrates a knowledge of art.

'Can you tell what color an object is by the particular shade of gray?'

'Sometimes but not always. To me colors take on different values in different kinds of light.'

That either satisfies him or he's too polite to query further. He compliments me on the portraits I sent of Tim.

'Beautiful pictures, Kay – full of affection. He looks as I'd imagined. I keep seeing glimmers of the boy.'

He stops before a park bench. 'Shall we sit?'

He props his stick against the seat. An elderly Chinese man performs elegant Tai Chi *katas* on the grass.

David touches his finger to his line mustache. 'This may be painful for you, but I'd like you to tell me what happened. Not just the bare bones, but the whole story, ugly though it may be. I know this is a great deal to ask but I'd be most grateful, my dear. I truly would.'

How can I deny him? I nod, then tell him the story, not glossing over the more sordid facts.

He winces as I describe the hustling scene on the Gulch, mutters 'poor boy' beneath his breath. By the time I finish with the gory details of dismemberment, I see tears forming in his eyes.

'Shot in the throat, then cut up! My God! That's so . . .' He brings his hand to his mouth. Like many of his gestures, this one's overwrought, though not, I feel, insincere.

'I'd almost say appropriate,' he adds, 'though it isn't, of course. In no possible way *could* it be.' He turns to me, again touches his mustache. 'You don't know what I'm talking about, do you?'

Over the next several hours, David deGeoffroy and I roam the city, stopping every so often for a restroom visit or for tea. We walk a while, then sit, then get up and walk some more. Our pace is measured. There's a trancelike aspect to the afternoon, the way we move among people in the parks and streets yet seem to exist on a separate plane. My rib cage is sore but I steel myself against pain. I don't want to lose the thread. David's story has everything a good tale should: energy and mystery, passion and regret. Listening, I think of it as the Magician's Tale.

'This, Kay, I confess – straight out of college I was a middling magician, a so-so practitioner of legerdemain. My close-up work was adequate: card tricks, flying coins, cups and balls, sometimes salt and pepper shakers and stubbed-out then reconstructed cigarettes. I was good enough to bum my way around Europe for a couple years working street cafés. Whenever I was broke I'd sit at a table, take my saucer from beneath my cup, place a couple coins in it, then practice tricks as if for myself. Sooner or later someone would ask if he could watch. I'd nod at the saucer, and would resume when he added coins of his own. In two or three hours I could make enough to buy myself a simple dinner and rent a humble room.'

David pauses, flutters his hands. 'Maybe I was better than mediocre. No question, after a while I got slick. My patter was good, movements smooth. Still, I was no master magician, not by any stretch.'

One thing I notice as he talks: his extensive repertory of gestures. Touching his forefinger to his mustache, shooting his cuffs, fluttering then dry-washing his hands – every move seems calculated to divert attention from something else, some devious bit of sleight-of-hand.

'It was only when I returned to New York that I started getting serious. First thing I worked up a persona – top hat, black cape, cane, white gloves, the works. I became,' David winks, 'The Great deGeoffroy.' He laughs. 'No, not my real name. That's Hyman Goldstein, Brooklyn born and bred. My father was a milliner. Later he and my uncle started a company, Novelties Unlimited. Basically they produced low-end powder puffs.'

Offering these background notes, he gives his stick a stylish twirl.

'I ran an advertisement and started to pick up work, kids' birthday parties mostly, affairs such as that. Soon word spread that I was good. It got to the point where I turned engagements down.

'I was making decent money then, spending it too, not just on personal luxuries, though I've always had a taste for the finer things, but most of it on better tricks and lessons in technique. I wanted to become a real magician and that meant constructing an hour-long cabaret act. I wasn't at the grand stage illusion level yet, but would soon be headed that way.

'I took a class with a carnival conjurer, learned juggling, fire-eating, swallowing swords. I wasn't particularly interested in doing these things in public but wanted to master them as a discipline. I also spent a lot on private lessons with a retired vaudeville magician.' David smiles. 'The Great Alexis! He *was* great. He'd come out with a saber dressed like a cossack about to launch a pogrom, then bluff through his act using this marvelous throaty Russky accent. Pretty funny considering his original name was Terry O'Higgins. But he was effective. Good illusionist too. Taught me a lot – the Needle Trick, Chinese Linked Rings, torn newspapers, silks and billiard ball multiplications.

'Slowly, as I mastered these effects, I incorporated them into my routine. Mind you, everything I did was classical magic, nothing novel or extraordinary, nothing people hadn't seen before. That was my problem. I was too ambitious to settle for the standard repertory of tricks. I wanted to show people something new, stand out from the herd.

'It was then that I started doing serious research, hanging out with the old-timers, delving into old books. One day, in the main reading room of the Forty-second Street Library, I came upon a sector of magic I had previously known nothing about – Indian and Malay magic which amazes by means of bizarre, shocking and blood-curdling effects involving such grotesquery as self-lacerations, even the decapitation of small creatures such as fowl. I remember putting down that book, closing my eyes and thinking about what I'd read. And then, as in a vision, I saw myself in a turban with black beard and coppery skin, doing those very things.'

He gives me a glance to measure the effect of his words. *Decapitation*. I wince at the memory of what happened to Tim.

'Sounds awful, Kay, I know, but remember, back then we weren't in the age of the touchy-feely magician, or, for that matter, animal rights. What I wanted was to truly astound people, shock them out of self-satisfied contentment. I'm sure as an artist you can understand. *Epater le bourgeois!* Right?'

He chuckles then kicks out with his well-shod foot – a demonstration, I gather, of a fond desire to put the boot to the middle class.

'Yes, I think in those days I was pretty violent, not on the surface – there I was smooth as glass – but underneath where the raging anger roils. I promise you, I'm not like that anymore. Look at me – I'm a dandy! But peering back eighteen years I see myself as an angry thirty-year-old kid.'

He pauses. 'There was something else. It went like this: if I could not be as great a mentalist as Dunninger, as great an escape artist as Houdini, as great a stage illusionist as Blackstone, then I would become something none of them had been – a violent, flesh-cutting magician-personage, reincarnation of the conjurers who worked the villages of South Asia leaving astonishment, terror, nightmares in their wakes.'

At this point we're sipping green tea in an upstairs Japanese tea-parlor near Fillmore and Bush. The window is open; bitter smells permeate the air. I look at David and see a man lost in a mist of tormented memories. I decide not to interrupt. Better for us both if I simply let him speak. Perhaps he senses my anxiety, for suddenly he smiles.

'Maybe you know this, Kay,' he speaks calmly, 'the true magician's grail, the ultimate act of magic, is an illusion called the Indian Rope Trick.'

I nod.

'No one has ever seen it convincingly performed . . . though huge sums have been offered to anyone who can. Even indoors it presents a series of complex problems: the rope, the child's climb, the fakir's subsequent climb with the sword, the disappearances, the rain of dismembered limbs, the fakir's reappearance, the child's reappearance at the end. In fact the trick can be done reasonably well in a theatre with the help of motorized rope, stage smoke, catwalks, split-second timing and lots of skill. But to mount it in the open air as originally described – there's not a respectable illusionist who thinks that's possible.

'The Rope Trick has always baffled magicians. Most believe it exists only in legend. Still, the deeper I looked into Hindu and Malay magic, a sort of hybrid illusion of my own began to take shape. Mind you, nowhere near as astonishing as the Rope Trick, perhaps more like a poor second cousin. But if it could be done (and I had no doubt it could) it would be a tour de force: shocking, astounding and appalling all at once . . . with the added bonus of a healing finale.'

David sips from his cup, then sits back. Knowing he has me spellbound, he becomes expansive, reveling in his control.

'It took me over a year to work it out, to practice my part of it and devise the rest. And then I began my search for confederates. I consulted theatrical agents, placed advertisements, even sought people out on the street. My confederates, you see, had to possess a certain appearance, and, more difficult, had to be available and willing to obey. You'd think it wouldn't be all that hard to find people happy to work with a magician, earn good wages and experience fascinating travel. But what I wanted my confederates to do was extremely off-putting to those I approached, repulsing them on account of the nature of the performance and because basically what I wanted was to borrow and employ their precious kids.'

Again I feel troubled. Too many of David's words cut close: 'decapitation', 'flesh-cutting' . . . and now the awful phrase from his description of the Rope Trick: 'rain of dismembered limbs'. Jesus! What the hell is he talking about? Who are these children? And if, as I suspect, one of them was Tim, in what awful bloody rites were he and David involved?

We are walking rapidly up Fillmore toward the Washington Street-Broadway crest, past pricey restaurants and boutiques purveying elegant housewares and apparel. David is once again his jaunty self, twirling his stick. The words gush from him, yet now his saga takes on an edge. It's as if in the telling he's reliving the particular moment he's about to describe, the moment when, as he puts it, he first laid eyes on '*them*'.

'I'd been searching for a set of identical female twins. They'd have to be intelligent, possess an innate flair, little show-offs if you will. They'd also have to have extremely pliant bodies as at least one of them would be trained as a contortionist. Finally there was the matter of size: I wanted little kids, small and lean, preferably no older than five or six. That way, if they didn't grow too fast, they could, after training, perform with me for at least four years. According to my plan, when they grew too big, I'd simply replace them with another pair.

'But, as it turned out, *not* so simply. Stage-parents were delighted when I'd ask to see their little darlings, but when they learned the criteria – rigorous training, devotion and discipline, long road trips, dyeing of the skin – they'd become alarmed. And if not by all that, then surely by the nature of the little play their cherished sweethearts would perform. When they understood what was involved they'd turn furious: "What are you – a *monster*? You expect our twins to do something so disgusting as *that*?"'

He lowers his voice. 'It was at a birthday party in Fairfield County that I saw them. A glorious October day. A beautiful house set within a garden bounded by a millpond with classic red horse barn behind. The setting was a fantasy. Wherever you walked you heard the tinkle of water and the crunch of fallen leaves beneath your feet. The party was held outdoors, and it was there that I performed, setting up my table between the pond and the house portico, the children seated before me on the grass.

'The birthday kid, a snooty little thing turning eight, struck me as incredibly spoiled. I remember the obnoxious way her parents showered her with gifts: accessories for her pony, a bridle from Gucci, a saddle specially made by Hermès.

'Bored with her, I looked around. There were twenty-five or thirty children. As usual I tried to choose one or two toward whom I could direct portions of my act. I saw the usual all-American freckle-faced boys, suburban sugar-and-spice type girls. Not an interesting face in the lot, I thought . . . until my eyes alighted on *them*.

'A striking pair, the girl with long blonde hair, the boy with his hair cut short. Because they were differently dressed I took them for brother and sister, not grasping at first that they were twins. You see, it was their eyes, not their twinship, that attracted me – huge, live, sensuous eyes, fascinated and fascinating, boring into mine, eager, greedy for my magic. Powerful eyes. Burning eyes. The kind of rapturous eyes that, when you see them, you know they can devour you alive.'

David stops, turns to me.

'Oh, Kay! The thrill of it! Remember, by that time I'd been

performing for kids for several years. My hunt for suitable twins was more than a year old. Yet never in all that time had I seen anything like these two – their sparkle, mesmerizing beauty. Had I been a pedophile I'd have fallen into lust! As it was, I merely fell in love . . .'

As David again steps out he changes his tone, taking on the part of a cool stalker on the hunt. 'Remember what I was seeking: a pair of six-year-old identical females. A pair of eight-year-old opposite-sex fraternals had never occurred to me. With good reason. I didn't think such a pair could accomplish what I had in mind. But watching this pair as I performed – and I performed by rote that afternoon though not, apparently, to the detriment of my act; afterwards, receiving the congratulations of parents, I was informed several times my show had never been better! – watching them, attentive to them, noting how attentive they were to me, I began to calculate if there was some way I could adapt them to my trick.

'One thing was clear – even if they weren't literally identical, they looked amazingly alike. Eyes, faces, even their heights were the same. I tried to imagine them with duplicate hair-cuts. Then, it seemed to me, they'd be almost perfectly matched. And the matching loose-fitting garments I had in mind would well disguise the difference in gender. What struck me most, apart from their eyes, were the identical expressions on their faces, alertness and also something sorrowful which I felt would boost the trick by arousing spectator sympathy. By the time I'd finished amazing that party of spoiled little brats, I'd concluded that not only could I adapt these two, but that no other pair I would ever find would possibly do for me as well.'

We are at the top of the ridge that runs along Pacific Heights separating it from Cow Hollow below. At one time an area of slaughterhouses, Cow Hollow is now a neighborhood of fine shops, chichi restaurants, real estate brokerages dealing in the city's finer properties. Here we pause, David to gasp at the beauty of the Bay, I to take his picture. As a performer he knows well how to pose. Perhaps later I can seduce him into showing vulnerability. But shooting him now I wonder if the pleasure in his eyes can be accounted for less by the stunning view before us than the memory of his good fortune that golden Connecticut afternoon.

Descending into Cow Hollow, he describes how, after the magic show, he schemed to meet the pair and learn their names. He carried a bunch of THE GREAT deGEOFFROY business cards depicting a little drawing of a magician pulling a rabbit from a hat. He wanted very much to get one of these into their hands, and so began to hand them out to everyone, kids and attending parents alike, finally reaching the coveted glowing twins.

The girl, he understood immediately, was the leader, the boy more shy, submissive to his sister. Even then he knew she would be the one who would learn contortion and thus star in the crucial first portion of the act, while the boy, disguised to look like her, would emerge only for the finale.

Both were full of praise for his performance. Listening, he was struck at once by their intelligence and poise.

'How can we learn to do these tricks?' the girl asked.

David could barely believe his ears. Perhaps, he thought, this is a fateful meeting, one that will forever change three lives. Taking a certain risk, he knelt until his head was level with theirs. He whispered: 'You *will* learn to do them, both of you. I will *teach* you how!'

A risk, of course, because such a statement could be taken as a come-on . . . which, indeed, it was. David didn't see himself as the proverbial bogeyman of the suburbs, the one kids are warned against from the time they're old enough to play alone outside. He would not be the dark stranger with candy canes in hand who would hang around the back of the schoolyard. David deGeoffroy was no kind of kidnapper, merely a talented magician with an ambitious plan. But if ever he were tempted to spirit kids away, it was at the instant he first felt the collective breath of those two on his cheek, saw the sparkle that lit within their eyes as they learned that they too could be taught to mystify, dazzle and astound.

He asked their names. The boy was Timmy, the girl Ariane. When he asked if their parents were around as he would like to meet them, Ariane responded that their parents had passed away in an accident two years before, and that they now lived with their Aunt Molly but a hop, skip and jump down the road.

By this time, nervous about paying them so much attention, David glanced around. No one, he was pleased to discover, seemed even to have noticed. In fact the party had broken up into a mêlée, kids laughing and playing, adults dishing out wedges of birthday cake and globs of multi-colored ice cream. Kneeling between them again, he said: 'If you really want to learn magic, have your aunt give me a call. I'll come out from the city and give you lessons in your home. But remember, whatever I teach must be kept between of us. Magic, you understand, is a *secret* craft.'

And, as at this their eyes enlarged, he knew that he would have them, that he *must*.

He was elated as he drove back to New York. All the portents were right. And in his short exchange with the twins, he had divined a possible weakness: if it was true that both blood parents were deceased, then perhaps Aunt Molly was the kind of surrogate whose feelings were founded more in obligation than parental love.

He sweated out the next few days wondering if she would call. He had decided that if she didn't he would take the initiative himself. However on the fourth day after the party he found a message on his machine from a Mrs Molly Kerrigan responding, she said, to an offer to teach magic which her god-children, Timmy and Ariane Lovsey, had reported he'd made. If in fact his offer was real, she'd appreciate it if he'd be so kind as to call her back.

At the first meeting, wishing to inspire confidence, he dressed like a school teacher in tweed jacket and regimental tie. He also made a point of addressing himself to Aunt Molly, maintaining eye contact with her while throwing occasional soft glances and friendly remarks to the kids, who, eyes glowing, sat together on the rug, arms wrapped about their knees.

It was in the family room of a nondescript split-level that the meeting took place. Aunt Molly offered cookies and coffee, with soft drinks for the twins. She was a good-natured, slightly dishevelled, plump fifty-year-old woman with a head of tight untrained gray curls, who worked as voting registrar in the local Town Hall.

As David spoke about magic, he did not forget that his sole purpose was to sell himself. He was, he wanted to convey, a responsible adult who would not only teach an exotic craft, but also something that would remain with his students all their lives – discipline, commitment to excellence, the rewards of practice, the very things they would learn if they took up a musical instrument.

Molly, he quickly understood, was overwhelmed by the twins. A widow, she had three grown children of her own, one a travel agent, one a bus driver, the youngest just finishing a stint in the Marines. Having exhausted herself bringing up three ordinary kids only to find herself suddenly burdened in middle age with two more, both brilliant, intense, most likely conniving and very difficult to please – David sensed her desperation.

That night a deal was struck: he would come out once a week on Tuesday afternoons to teach magic to the twins for less than a music teacher would have charged, providing props and apparatus at wholesale prices with no profit to himself. By the end of the evening everyone was satisfied, not least of all Timmy and Ariane.

For that first Tuesday, he could barely wait. In the intervening days he worked out a strategy. He would play it absolutely straight for several months, coaching the twins, measuring their abilities, building up trust which, according to his plan, would lead in time to deep complicity. He would turn them into little magicians, and, with the bonding power of magic, make them his allies. He already loved them; if he could make them love him, then nothing, he felt, would be impossible.

The lessons went well. The twins were talented. Ariane was delighted at the prospect of becoming a contortionist, and Timmy soon became skilled at juggling and manipulating coins and cards. During the lessons, which he kept informal, David carefully built their confidence, teaching them how to recoup after a mistake, delighting them with special games by which he tested their talent for theatrics.

They constantly surprised him. They adored deception. And they lacked the most obvious flaw in a child-magician, the desire to flaunt their secrets by revealing them to friends. Ordinarily when children are mystified by a trick, their first query is: 'How did you do that?' From Ariane and Timmy the first question always was: 'Please, David, *teach* us how!'

Confusion, bedazzlement, mystification – the Lovsey twins were natural adepts. They loved waving the wand, rubbing the ring, conjuring spirits from the dark. They reveled in hocus-pocus and abracadabra, liked nothing better than to pull a coin out of an ear or force it up through the surface of a table. Wine that turns to water then back to wine, flying cards, the levitation of balls – David had never seen such quick, deceptive little hands. And being kids they delighted in scatological variations such as pulling colorful scarves out of each other's rear end to the accompaniment of rude noises simulated by their mouths.

But what they liked even more than prestidigitation were the sword-box illusions: the Scimitars of Baghdad, the Decapitated

Princess, the Mismade Lady, the Headless Chinaman in the Mysterious Trunk. These illusions, which David introduced after several months, fascinated them on account of their ability to horrify. He explained the principle: how by severely shocking people one can make them vulnerable to effects which, in a normal state, they would never accept.

It was seven months before he broached to them the special trick. He told them he had invented it uniquely for the three of them, and it was only because they were twins that it could be made to work.

David deGeoffroy and I sit in the great San Francisco bar, Top of the Mark, on the nineteenth floor of the Mark Hopkins Hotel, he nursing a Martini in a perfect conical glass, I refreshing myself with a lemonade. The views here are spectacular, encompassing the city. The sun is low, the mood mellow. I'm underdressed, but David doesn't seem to mind. However, when I remove my shades, he comments on the bruises on my upper cheeks and shiners around my eyes.

'Do you live with someone, Kay?'

'No. And I wasn't battered by a lover. I was jumped the other night, probably because I stuck my camera where it didn't belong.'

'This has something to do with Tim?'

I nod.

'You're a brave girl.'

'Less brave than pissed off. Listen, David, the suspense is killing me. Isn't it getting time for you to, you know— ?'

'Describe the trick?'

'Yep, the trick.'

He nods, takes a careful sip, folds his hands. First, he says, he will describe it from the audience point of view, then explain how it is done.

The illusion is best performed outdoors, preferably in an open field. The Great deGeoffroy is dressed and made up as an Indian fakir – turban, robe, dark skin, black beard and mustache. He is assisted by his daughter, Zamantha, a small, lean, dark-haired girl with flashing dark eyes and coppery skin. She's a spunky little thing, cloaked like an Indian in an immaculate, white pleated smock. Through the performance she acts as a Jill-of-all-trades, handing apparatus to the fakir, juggling balls, performing cartwheels, passing the hat to the assembled crowd. Being eager and affectionate, she quickly wins its collective heart. Thus the crowd is shocked when, near the end of the performance, the fakir suddenly turns on her on account of some minuscule error.

'Idiot! Haven't I taught you *never* to do that?'

Zamantha squeals an apology, but that's not good enough. The fakir is working up to a rage. He slaps Zamantha hard. She cries out, cringes from him in fear. He grabs her by her hair, drags her to the edge of the circle, threatens her with severe punishment, while she begs feverishly for mercy.

'Enough!' The fakir retorts. 'I'll teach you a lesson you won't forget!'

And with that he draws a dagger from beneath his robe, brings it to Zamantha's neck, and, with a single swipe, slashes her fragile throat.

Immediately blood spurts, drenching Zamantha's pristine smock, staining the fakir's robe. A few drops may spatter too on the clothing of people seated nearby. The audience goes into collective shock. Mass confusion! Screams! Blood bubbles from the dying Zamantha's throat.

But despite the chaos the fakir, projecting the confidence he has shown throughout, persuades the audience that no harm has actually been done, meanwhile placing the apparently dead Zamantha into a large bulbous wicker basket which he has employed earlier in other tricks.

He has great difficulty stuffing her inside. The mouth of the basket is narrow and Zamantha is bigger than she looks. When he finally gets her in, he covers the mouth of the basket with a cloth, then, proceeding to calm the audience, changes out of his bloody robe.

Now come the incantations, pronounced in a language no human can understand. However a few choice words of English are interspersed to the effect that the fakir is evoking the Lords Of Darkness to restore to life his beloved daughter, who, due to some terrible flaw of character, he has wrongly killed.

A pause while the fakir allows the suspense to build. The audience holds its collective breath. Can he bring little Zamantha back? She was so sweet, endearing. The fakir swears that if he cannot, he will immediately hang himself before their very eyes.

With a flourish he suddenly tears away the cloth cover from the basket, which he then tilts and revolves so the entire audience can see inside. It's empty! Zamantha's gone, disappeared! And then, just as the audience gasps, they hear the voice of a little girl crying 'Papa! Papa!' from far beyond the circle. Collectively they turn. It's Zamantha, alive and well, in spotless garb, skipping gaily toward them from the distance. The crowd parts to let her through. She runs to her father, throws her arms about him while he in turn hugs her. They kiss, embrace, then take their bows, acknowledging thunderous applause and a rain of coins and bills thrown in appreciation for the fabulous illusion just performed.

David takes another sip of his Martini. 'Now is that a good trick or not?'

'It's good,' I say. In fact, damn' good, I think . . . if not also bloody and cruel.

'By now you've figured it out.'

'I know the part of Zamantha is played by both kids.'

David nods.

'But there's plenty I don't understand.'

He smiles. 'I'll break it down for you, mystification by mystification. First, the slitting of the throat and the explosion of blood. That's done with stage blood, bloody meat entrails and liver. The effect's so repugnant and the audience so shocked that most members turn away. Those who don't can't bear to look too closely.

'Second, the stuffing into the basket: due to the use of the loose-fitting smock, Zamantha appears a good deal larger than she is. I fake it when I appear to have trouble getting her in. There's actually lots of room, but I want the audience to think she barely fits.

'Third, her disappearance: in fact she's in the basket the entire time, even as I rotate it so everyone can see she's not. This is where the contortionist training comes in. The basket interior is lined. Zamantha curls herself inside the lining against the round middle of the container and thus becomes invisible. By the way, when we perform outdoors there's no question of a tunnel. Indoors, to show there's no trap door, we set the basket on a legged stand off the floor.

'Last, the reappearance. The second Zamantha, as you rightly figured out, is played by her twin. With identical garments, haircuts and flashing eyes, plus effeminate gestures in which Timmy's been carefully rehearsed, the audience believes it sees the girl I "killed".

So you see, Kay, once it's explained, like all stage illusions, it's simple
. . . at least in theory.'

He asks if I'll join him for dinner. I accept but suggest I go
home first and change. He pooh-poohs that, insisting I look fine,
pointing out we're in a city known for its informal style. We adjourn
downstairs to the dining room where David orders a bottle of Opus
I to accompany our food. Once settled in and eating he continues
his tale.

'The moment I described the trick, the twins were entranced,
eager to start rehearsals at once. Except that there was some unhap-
piness on Timmy's part, a feeling that he was being shortchanged.
After all, he pointed out, as much to Ariane as myself, *she* would
have most of the fun participating throughout the show, while *he*
would only make an entrance at the end and until then remain
hidden from view.

'Although I hadn't anticipated his objection, I knew at once I'd
have to deal with it. Any anger or jealousy between the twins and
my plan could fall apart. I was trying to think up a solution when
Ariane came up with her own – she and Timmy would each perfect
both parts, Zamantha I and II, then alternate the roles.'

David laughs. 'Think about it. The twins were all of eight years
old at the time, yet already highly assertive. Ariane especially – she
had this disingenuous way of taking charge, consulting Timmy and
myself, yet controlling the dialogue so in the end she'd get her way.
There I was, a mature (or perhaps not-so-mature) adult sometimes
having to approach an eight year old as supplicant. In addition she
constantly took on the role of Timmy's protector, as in this case
with her proposal that they split the Zamantha part.

'Frankly, I was wary. She was the better contortionist, and body
contortion was essential to the trick. I also didn't think Timmy could
sustain the part of a girl. It was one thing to play Zamantha at the
end, quite another to make her believable throughout. But Ariane
had no such qualms. *She* would coach her brother until he could
give a faultless imitation. Meanwhile they'd have fun switching.

'As it turned out she was right. Although to my eyes she was
slightly better as Zamantha I, our audiences were dazzled no matter
which twin played the role.'

By this time David and the twins had grown close. He had won
their confidence; they adored him as a father. Thus he left it to
them to bring Aunt Molly around to the idea that they be allowed

to work with him full-time over the summer. The kids were clever little manipulators; they knew exactly which of their aunt's buttons to push. They had a lot going for them: her pity for them as orphans; an intelligence far superior to hers; a polished heart-breaking manner when making a request; an iron will in pursuit of their goals.

One Tuesday afternoon in May, after David had finished giving his lesson for the week, Aunt Molly sent the twins outdoors to play then invited him into the living room to talk. Would he consider, she asked, taking the twins on for the summer? They so loved magic, he had told her many times that they were talented, they could assist him during performances, and she'd be willing to pay a reasonable fee for his trouble. David said he'd give the matter some thought and get back to her the following day.

When he did he proposed that they draw up a contract regarding the rights and obligations of the parties, necessary protection since he would be taking responsibility for two minor children. As for a fee, none would be required; the twins would earn their keep by assisting at performances. A good deal all around, he said, since they'd have a great summer learning experience and he'd have two charming child confederates with whom to expand his act.

Within a week the contract was signed. The day after school let out, the twins joined him in New York. Thus began a five-year relationship which lasted until they were thirteen years old.

Summer stretched into fall. At that time a new contract was drawn naming David as full-time guardian. A private tutor, a young woman named Beverly Jenkins (David's then-girlfriend, an aspiring magician in her own right), was engaged to keep the twins current on school work, act as sitter and chaperon, and stage-manage the show. Meantime all obligations to Molly Kerrigan were rigorously met – at David's insistence since Ariane and Timmy showed little interest: weekly phone calls, frequent letters, occasional visits home. A fine arrangement by which Aunt Molly was relieved of the stress of bringing up two difficult children, while the Lovsey twins, liberated from a stultifying home-life, were free to discover their natures while seeing the world.

By the end of August the Zamantha Illusion had been thoroughly rehearsed. The three of them performed it publicly for the first time on a carnival ground near Camden, Maine. The show was taut with energy. Audience response was tremendous. Afterwards a vacationing Broadway producer approached to say he'd never seen a magic act so bold.

Thus began years of travel that took the Great deGeoffroy and his little troupe from one end of the country to the other, on to Europe for a two-year tour, then to Australia, New Zealand and Japan. There were other illusions in the act, of course, but the Zamantha was its signature. The posters featured it: a little Indian girl with bleeding throat being stuffed into a basket by a fierce-eyed fakir. The caption read: SEE THE GREAT deGEOFFROY BRING ZAMANTHA BACK TO LIFE. Even professional magicians who understood the mechanics were dazzled by the execution.

It was three years into the relationship, in the midst of their grand European tour, that the first serious difficulties arose. As the twins grew taller, certain modifications were made, but there came a point where the gender difference became too pronounced to be ignored. Timmy's voice began to change and he starting shooting up, while Ariane's hips began to widen and breasts began to bud. A falsetto, elevator shoes and floppy garments could only go so far. As the twins passed their eleventh birthdays it became clear the Zamantha Illusion would have to be dropped.

They worked up new tricks, some quite excellent, including an Indian livestock illusion involving a cobra and a mongoose, a Double Sawing-In-Half Illusion, a Torture Harness Escape and a violent illusion called Pillars Of Fear. But nothing could equal the Zamantha, which depended on the interchangeability of twins. Thus the twins' relationship with David entered a new phase; later, in retrospect, David would call it 'our Baroque'.

Around this time David turned to Beverly Jenkins. In the classic tradition, in which a pretty young woman acts as confederate to an all-powerful magician, David began to center his show on complicated illusions in which he cut her in half and/or made her disappear while Ariane and Timmy were relegated to minor roles, performing flips and cartwheels along the fringes of the stage, juggling balls and swallowing knives while apparatus was hauled in and out. When David was ready to perform a new illusion he'd reappear, and, in an amusing leitmotif, swat at the twins and shoo them off.

This did not go down well with two exceptionally brilliant children who'd grown accustomed to being the center of attention in a blood-curdling, heart-stopping display. Why couldn't David come up with something new for them, something extraordinary, instead of these degrading stunts? But David could not and tried to explain to them why – that their value to the show lay in their ability to appear identical, and, now that they no longer did, a return to a stable home-life was probably in order.

He did not put it so bluntly, but the twins quickly grasped their situation. Since there was no hope of ever again playing in a substitution trick, their future as child magicians was bleak; on the other hand, any humiliation was better than resuming life with tiresome Aunt Molly.

It was Ariane who came up with a solution, albeit a temporary one. She suggested to David that she and Timmy recruit and train a new set of twins.

David was extremely fond of the Lovseys, and he was not without compassion and loyalty, but he recognized that the twins charmed him less as they approached adolescence than they had as graceful young innocents. He also felt responsible for them and a measure of guilt for having used them to further his ambitions. It would soon be time, he knew, to cut them loose, but since Ariane's proposal enabled him to keep them on a while longer, he agreed to set them the task of finding substitute twins without thinking through the fallacy.

It was a ploy, of course, a manipulation; Ariane had no intention of finding a suitable pair. Oh, she turned up twins, several sets of female identicals, and at first things would seem to go well. But then always a problem would arise – insufficient commitment, lack of suppleness, recalcitrance, stupidity, or, Ariane's favorite bugaboo, equivocal parents. Each failed involvement would waste a couple of months. Meantime Ariane and Tim (he no longer cared to be called Timmy) were secretly working up an act of their own – an act so good, fated to become so popular, it would guarantee their position in the troupe.

'It *was* fabulous,' David tells me, as we sip coffee after dinner. By this time the hotel dining room has nearly emptied. 'A mentalist routine, extraordinary because it was performed by kids. Mentalism, you understand, depends upon charisma. A top-notch mentalist has to be bigger than life. So to see a girl twelve years old command a stage entirely by herself – the effect was tremendous. And Ariane brought it off. She had grown that powerful. I was amazed.

'Actually what they did was a classic Second-Sight routine, Ariane blindfolded sitting on a stool in the center of the stage, Timmy roaming the house, asking audience members to show him objects such as watches, jewelry, banknotes and coins. Ariane would then divine what was being shown, describing the objects in great detail. In the case of banknotes she would give the serial numbers, in the case of coins the denominations and dates.

'Such feats are accomplished by a complex set of signals having to do with the first letters of the words the confederate employs to frame his questions to the medium. Questions such as "What does the gentleman have?" or "Tell us what the lady is holding up?" convey detailed information, which is then further refined in regard to color, size, and so on, by such follow-up questions as: "Hurry now!" "Come on, Ariane!" "Surely you see it in your mind's eye!" etc. The codes are complicated. Mastering them requires a major feat of memorization. Yet the twins, by rigorous practice and intense concentration during their routine, could dazzle audiences even more than when I sliced Beverly into sections, recombined them and at the end brought her back, smiling and whole.'

I look closely at David. 'You sound like you were jealous.'

He nods. 'I was! They prepared their act behind my back, sprung it on me as a surprise. It was polished, professional. They were prodigies. I was overwhelmed. Then as soon as they started performing, it created tremendous word-of-mouth. Crowds thronged the theatre. I felt eclipsed.'

David beckons to a waiter, orders a cognac. I settle for a second coffee.

'They had something powerful going. Call it twinship. Their rapport was so finely tuned, their need to stay on the stage so great, that they brought off one of the most demanding of all routines. Yes, I was jealous. I was also proud. It was I, after all, who had trained them, and now was being surpassed.'

Listening I see wonderment in David's eyes, the mixture of pride and envy, amazement and dismay he's just described. The memory of Ariane's power still disturbs him. But where, I interrupt to ask, was Tim in all of this? Was he merely his sister's stooge, or did he acquire power of his own?

'Certainly,' David says, 'he was a fine magician. He had talent and his juggling and sleight-of-hand were better than hers. But she was the one with presence, who radiated authority, so I'd say she was the superior, the one for whom magic was nourishment. Reaching the top in magic, as in music or sports, calls for more than talent. It requires mental toughness, inner strength, a will for power. Ariane had those traits, Timmy didn't. What I grasped, and even feared in her, was a potential to go all the way.'

This kind of self-knowledge came later to David; during the Baroque he was only aware of his unease. There were moments, he remembered, when he considered devoting his life to the twins, stepping down from his role as the Great deGeoffroy to become their full-time manager. He even thought up a new name for Ariane – he'd anoint her the Amazing Amoretto, meaning 'Little Cupid' – not to be confused with the bitter almond-flavored Italian liqueur of similar name. But these were daydreams. David was still too young to renounce his ambitions and become a stepping-stone for a child.

By the time they reached Japan he'd made up his mind: the twins would have to go. But then came something unexpected, news that Aunt Molly, felled by a stroke, had been placed in a nursing home by her grown kids.

David was upset; the twins were not. They pretended to be, engaged in some whimpering, enough to get them by. Seeing through their act, he was appalled by their coldness, wondering if he was now responsible for a pair of minor sociopaths.

'They scared me, really did. Now I understand it was just Ariane. I realize I've been talking all afternoon about them as if they were one person when in fact there were two distinct personalities involved. She was powerful, he was easy-going. She was dominant, he submissive. She was fearless, and, now that I think of it, cool, distant and very strange. He, though similar in many respects, was warmer, more like a normal child. At the time all this happened, remember, they were at the age when kids get, you know,' David smiles, 'sexualized. Hormones raging through their bodies. Hair sprouting up in odd places. Loss of innocence, not that they ever had much of it . . . but they looked as if they did. Now suddenly they were horny, and, if that weren't enough, were turning rebellious. Not on the stage – there they were smooth as country cream. But off-stage they started making demands for what Ariane referred to as their fair share of the earnings. They wanted to stay out late, eat out in restaurants, go dancing, do as they pleased. What could I do with them? Couldn't send them home – there was no longer a home to send them to. Couldn't abandon them to their own devices – they were still far too young. But I couldn't control them anymore. They refused to accept my discipline. It was obvious things couldn't go on this way, that we were headed for a crisis.'

The waiters, restless and forlorn, no longer hide their irritation. David suggests we adjourn to the lobby where, he promises, he will finish up his tale.

'I've barely mentioned Bev. That's a saga in itself. But you should know she was sensitive to what was happening and very affectionate with the twins. She'd been tutoring them for five years, so well that when she took them to an American school in Japan, they tested at an eleventh grade level. She'd grown close to them, was concerned for them . . . and also for me. She didn't think the twins and I were good for each other anymore. We discussed this a lot, agreed a separation was in order. A year or two apart, we felt, would be in the best interests of all concerned. When she came up with the idea of enrolling them in a private boarding school, I agreed this was our only remedy.

'She set out at once to find them a proper school, one that would provide guidance and discipline while still nurturing their creativity. She sent out letters. Catalogues came back. At first the twins were scornful. They'd glance at a catalogue then toss it aside. The school looked like a prison, the teachers looked stupid, the kids looked like nerds. But Bev was patient. Gradually she got them involved. Perhaps there was a decent place somewhere in the world, she said, where they could spend a couple of happy years studying, preparing for college, participating in sports, making friends.

'On this later point Ariane was quite resistant. She got angry whenever we'd suggest she and Tim make friends their own age. "We don't want friends our own age," she'd say. "We've far more in common with adults." And she was right.

'Finally, after months of prodding, we narrowed the choice to three schools. I sent out letters. The first to come back requested grade transcripts and recommendations. That left two. Both were interested. The head of the American School of Tangier wrote of its exceptional drama program, while the principal of The Piñon Valley School in Scottsdale, Arizona, mentioned its progressive policies, and, in view of the twins' unusual background, offered them three-quarters scholarships. Needless to say Piñon Valley was our choice.'

David and I occupy one of those formal furniture groupings that adorn hotel lobbies, a square composed of couches and easy chairs arranged about a low marble table. David, reclining against soft cushions, has dropped his busy mannerisms of the afternoon, flutterings of the hands and touchings of the mustache, the diversionary tactics of a magician. Now he sits still, his voice, previously so theatrical, now sounding weary and also, finally, real.

'We had a lot of fun getting them ready for school,' he says, 'buying them proper clothes, shoes, luggage, heaping them with gifts – cameras, backpacks, tennis rackets, Walkmans, everything we thought prep school kids ought to have. We got them fresh passports, made airline reservations, air-shipped ahead trunks filled with sheets, pillows, blankets and towels. We even sent a crate of magical apparatus so they could amuse and astound their schoolmates.

'The night before their departure, we had a lavish farewell dinner in a private room at the best restaurant in Osaka. Lots of talk, laughter . . . they seemed so happy and relaxed. We reminisced about the last five years, recalling our successes, the great days of the Zamantha Illusion, our many misadventures too. They seemed so normal that night, natural, at ease. When we said goodnight we embraced and kissed. In the morning, at the airport, I found myself shedding tears. I hoped, I told them, in the spring to bring the act back to the States. Then we would see them often. Their last words to me were thanks for everything I'd done, the precious world I'd opened for them, the tricks and life-lessons I'd taught. Then they were off. Bev and I stayed past the take-off, until the great plane disappeared. Then we returned to the city and walked around feeling relieved but also empty, the way I imagine all parents feel the day they first send their kids off into the world.'

David looks down, shakes his head. 'We never saw them again. We know they got to LA. Immigration and customs records confirmed that much. They were to change planes for Phoenix, but they never checked in for their flight. We didn't even know they were missing until two days past the time they were due, when we received a telegram from the school informing us they hadn't arrived. We were worried sick. Could they have been abducted? That didn't seem likely at their age. Perhaps they'd taken a little vacation, gone off on their own for a couple of days. Surely, I thought, they'd turn up. But then I remembered the odd formality of their goodbyes. There was something final about their manner, something in the nature of a permanent farewell. It was then that it occurred to me they'd flown the coop.'

Now another change of demeanor as the chuckle fades and hurt creases David's face. 'Yes, they'd flown, and, more than that, they'd absconded with half my funds.'

Being an itinerant magician, David received his earnings in local currency, either from theatre managers or direct from audiences when he performed outdoors. Since the troupe lived in hotels and ate in restaurants, he paid all expenses out of pocket, converting the surplus into money orders which, from time to time and from wherever he happened to be, he mailed off to his bank in New York. There the savings accumulated in various accounts, adding up after three years abroad to not inconsiderable sums.

In one money market account alone there was fifty thousand dollars. As David later reconstructed the scam, most certainly masterminded by Ariane, the twins prepared a series of documents authorizing the bank to transfer that money to an account they set up at the Tokyo branch of an LA bank. The documents, which he later saw, bore his actual signature. The twins had tricked him into writing it by a classic sleight-of-hand substitution with a school parental permission form. Since the documents were in order, the signature correct and the transfer bank-to-bank, David's New York bank obliged. Having moved the money to Japan, the twins intercepted the confirmation letter, withdrew the funds in cash, which they took with them on their flight to the States, in the process committing several serious felonies not the least of which was wire fraud.

David moans. 'They only took half my savings – their way, I suppose, of acknowledging all the fine things they thanked me for as they left. A few weeks later we received a postcard from Mexico City, short and sweet. I remember it well: "Dear David & Bev, We're happy, healthy and safe. Sorry about the $, but what else could we do? We figure we earned it and you can easily make more . . . which we cannot. We miss you both. Love, A & T."' David looks at me. 'Can you imagine?' He shakes his head. '*They were just thirteen years old.*'

On my way home in a taxi, my mind whirls. I'm amazed by what I've heard. I could have stayed on at the Mark Hopkins to talk all night; David as much as asked me to. But after eight hours of non-stop listening I was too exhausted. Also I needed time to assimilate his story.

I now understand many things – how Tim learned to juggle and do card tricks; the identity of the person David called 'the other' and 'she' and referred to as 'A' in his letter. I wonder: is Ariane still around? Is she the mysterious girl Tim wanted me to photograph? Is she the person I momentarily mistook for him on the street the day I cleaned out his flat?

For that matter, was the fifty thousand he told me he'd saved the same fifty he and Ariane ripped off? Finally, what if anything does all this have to do with the way Tim was killed?

Downstairs, in the lobby of my building, I find the same styrofoam box, ribbon neatly retied, that I left for the Youth in Sterling Park. Inside I find the ham and Coke untouched, and a 'Dear Kay' note, signed 'Drake', hand-written in large round letters thanking me for the provisions. So . . . now I know my homeless savior's name and that he's a vegetarian who prefers organic food. *Only in San Francisco*, I think. I resolve to leave a fresh package for him soon.

The blinking light on my answering machine greets me as I open my door. I rewind the tape, find two messages, one from Hilly saying she's got what I want, the other from Dr Sasha Patel expressing concern over my health and inquiring whether I'm free to go out with him Saturday night.

After a shower, dressed only in my robe, I spend half an hour with my telescope snooping around. Lights are on in the Judge's penthouse. I think I see people moving behind the glass doors. Perhaps he's hosting a dinner party, one of those intimate candlelit affairs for six he likes so much. Good talk, good wine, a rich French stew, followed by salad accompanied by a cheese soufflé, with fresh ripe fruit for dessert. Among the guests perhaps the dance critic from the *Chronicle*, the stunning Assistant US Attorney who argued so brilliantly before him the week before, his old law school roommate and charming wife, and the Judge's latest Special Friend, who works at the Butterfield & Butterfield auction house and has the body of a swimsuit model.

Flickering light illuminates the table. The talk turns mellow as the candles burn down. Talk of art and theatre, the latest production at Berkeley Rep, the mayoral race, the future of the Presidio and such as that. Even as I watch, four of the guests rise to leave. Air is kissed, bodies are hugged, then a long lingering farewell at the door. Finally the Judge and Special Friend are left alone. He turns to her, reaches out with his arms. Their faces draw close. Their glistening lips are about to touch . . .

Savagely I jerk my telescope away. It takes me a moment to realize I've actually seen none of this, have been looking through the eyepiece with closed eyes indulging in a fantasy.

Just as I fall asleep I'm struck by a thought: could Tim's androgyny, which I found so engaging, so attractive, be accounted for by the fact that in the Zamantha Illusion he played a girl?

EIGHT

ONLY FOUR OF US attend the scattering of Tim's ashes: Doreen and Alyson in full drag, David deGeoffroy and myself. It's a sour morning, the sea fog hangs like a canopy above the Bay. Once through the Golden Gate and in open sea the water turns rough, we shiver beneath the metallic sky, the boat isn't large, we're all uncomfortable and Alyson looks as if she'll maybe puke.

We do the job quickly, David holding out the urn, allowing the ashes to be caught by the wind . . . which blows them north toward the Marin headlands. Chrysopylae was the original name given to these Straits in 1846, Greek for Golden Gate, an attempt to mirror Chrysoceras or Golden Horn, the Byzantine name for the harbor of Constantinople. *Chrysopylae*: I love the sound of that word, mutter it several times to myself as the ashes spin into the air. Once they're gone, we return to San Francisco, David pays off the captain, we find a cab at the wharf, drop the girls at The Hampshire Arms, then drive on to my building on Russian Hill.

The purpose is for David to pick up Tim's belongings, but upstairs he looks so sad, I play good hostess and offer him a glass of Chardonnay.

'Beautiful place you got here, Kay,' he says, despite the fact that fog obscures the views. 'And I like your black and white decor. Austere.' He peers at me. 'A bit like you.'

I haul out Tim's stuff. We sit on the floor and go through it. David smiles at the clothes. 'Hard to imagine him so tall.' He holds up Tim's Walkman. 'I wonder – is this the one I bought him in Japan?'

There's something maudlin about him today. The dandified clothing's the same, but the manner is not. He's moody, disturbed. The mawkishness, I decide, is a cover-up.

Casually I pick up my camera, start taking pictures. David performs for me, makes a few faces, then, giving up control, resumes his examination of Tim's things. He thinks, quite wrongly, that I'll stop. He can't imagine I'd want to continue photographing him unposed. How poorly he understands. I want to find the vulnerable person hiding behind the double subterfuge, the imperious magician and the grief-stricken 'uncle'. I want the truth.

'Quite the little shutterbug, aren't we, dear?' he enunciates in a brittle, irritated tone. Then, when I make no motion to stop: 'Click-click-click! You know, dear, it does get boring after a while.'

I pause. He looks up at me. *Whap! Whap!*

'Will you please fucking stop it!'

'I won't,' I tell him. 'This is how I see.'

He spreads his arms, relents. 'Sorry, Kay. Just edgy today, I guess.'

'Not because of Tim. You've known for a week he's dead. There's something else. What?'

'It's her,' he says. 'She's nearby. I feel it.'

'Ariane?'

He nods.

'They could have split up. He never told me about her, didn't mention her to you in his note.'

He looks at the array of possessions. 'Something missing here. Where's his passport, his address book?'

David's right. 'Maybe the cops have it. I'll check.'

He listens as I phone Shanley. After I shrug and hang up, he shakes his head. 'I still think she's around.'

'For all you know she's married with kids in Kalamazoo. Or beating the bushes as an itinerant magician.'

'She's definitely not doing professional magic. That I've already checked.'

I study him as he sits on my floor surrounded by Tim's jeans, shirts, boots. 'She was the one you loved,' I say.

'I loved them both.'

'But her most.' I take another shot. *Whap!* 'There's more to it, isn't there?'

He lowers his eyes. He can't bring himself to confess.

'They didn't just up and leave because you were sending them off to school. *Did they*, David? There was something else.'

He stands. He wants to leave. I've no intention of letting him go. If there's more, I mean to find out what it is.

'Better tell me, David. You'll feel a lot better if you do.'

He sits down again amidst the scattered clothing. 'Please, no more pictures,' he begs.

I set down my camera. He's silent. I sit beside him, prepared to listen.

'Yes, I loved her,' he admits. 'Very much. I—' He shakes his head. 'She felt my desire. She was so powerful, seductive. She came on to me. I couldn't resist.' He pauses. 'I'm still ashamed.'

'How long did this go on?'

'Couple of months. We started just before the end.'

'Did Tim know?'

'Probably. They confided everything. Also they planned their escape so well. The stealing, fraud – later, when I learned the dates, I realized they started on it shortly after she and I—' He shuts his eyes. 'They probably figured that gave them the right, and . . . well . . . maybe it did. I never brought charges. It never occurred to me. I thought I'd wait them out, be patient and sooner or later they'd come back. I made it easy for them, returned to New York, opened a mail-order magic house, took out ads in all the magic journals and magazines. A couple of years ago I started running a personal ad: INFO WANTED ON ZAMANTHA ILLUSION. I figured since magic was in their blood eventually they'd see it, then they'd call or write. And so finally Tim did. Too late. He never got my reply.'

David interpreted Tim's note as a test to determine if David was searching for them to get his money back. They had to know that much before they risked a call. And Tim, being less emotionally involved, was the logical one to make the overture. The bland tone of his note was effective and sly.

'"Working as a waiter, trying to make ends meet" – his way of telling me the money was long gone and he was working at an honest job. The hundred dollars I sent back was my way of telling him money wouldn't be an issue. I figured we'd write back and forth for a time, send each other these kinds of messages. Eventually, I hoped, he'd trust me enough to call. Then, perhaps, he'd allow me to see him, see them both.'

He shrugs, not, I understand, to dismiss the possibility, but the way a man might shrug when a great opportunity has been lost.

'She's here. I'm certain. She may have seen us yesterday while we walked.'

'If that's true why didn't she contact the cops, take responsibility for his body?'

Again David shrugs, turns his palms to the ceiling. 'I just don't know,' he says.

He takes only Tim's Walkman, leaves the rest of the stuff with me to give away. After he goes, to check out of his hotel and catch his plane, I ask myself why I didn't tell him that Tim had spoken to me about a girl he knew, who, for reasons never explained, I would very much want to photograph. Or the apparition I saw near the corner of Mission and Grace the day I cleaned out his studio. Or the mysterious person who entered with a key and tossed the studio between Crawf's and my visit and Shanley's. Or the fifty thousand dollars Tim claimed he'd saved. Or about his dream of retiring to San Miguel de Allende – since the postcard from the twins had been mailed from Mexico City.

Why did I deprive him of so many clues which might have given him hope? Should I call him tomorrow, confide? Having been so candid with me, hasn't he earned my confidence?

The truth, I decide, is that I still don't trust him, feel there's more to his story, yet another layer he didn't reveal. And I'm out for bigger game than a reunion with a girl whose life David so radically bent. I want to complete *Exposures*, and to do that I must discover who killed my friend.

The *Bay Area News*, being an alternative newspaper, is appropriately situated in a cutting edge neighborhood – on Folsom in SoMa, surrounded by other alternative enterprises: a used record store called Psychosis, an erotic boutique called Marquis de Suede, a dance club called ATF (Alcohol, Tobacco & Firearms), famous for its orgiastic fetishwear blow-outs where the dress code is strictly enforced. There are stores that specialize in furniture of the 1950s, photographers' studios, numerous pubs including the infamous adjoining BoyBar and GirlBar (never the twain shall meet), and a half dozen basement and storefront avant-garde theatres.

The *News* takes up the top floor of a four-story warehouse. There are only two ways up, freight elevator or fire stairs. I take the stairs.

I came to work here straight out of the Art Institute willing to shoot most anything in return for pay. The wages were lousy, barely enough to get me by. I ended up sharing a ratty Edwardian on Cole Street with three *News* colleagues. But the work was fun, we were young, high-spirited, priding ourselves on breaking stories the mainstream press wouldn't touch. Even more we enjoyed smashing taboos, inserting obscene words into articles, praising alternative rock bands with names like Genitorture, and, for the hell of it, kicking The Establishment in the butt.

Memories flood back as I mount the stairs. The stairwell walls are embellished with graffiti – a scrawled one-liner 'Camille Paglia is smarter than Gloria Steinem', an obscene reference to Kierkegaard, a DYKES ON BIKES poster adorning the landing. The blended pizza-and-pot aroma is also the same. I remember attacking these stairs with unprocessed film, trying to beat impossible deadlines. 'Kay! Get over to the Clift. Mick Jagger's checking out'; 'Joey! Drive Kay round to the back of the Hall of Justice, we need a shot of the Trailside Killer in manacles.'

Most of my old newsroom colleagues have long since moved on. Because the *News* is the sort of place that burns you out, it's nearly impossible to work here past the age of thirty. But there are a few who've made the paper their home. One is Joel Glickman. He originally came out from Brooklyn for the Summer Of Love, lived on the Haight, balled and grooved. He joined the *News* at its founding years before I arrived, and is still here a dozen after I left. In the meantime he's won a Pulitzer for his exposé of corruption in the City Assessor's Office. Since then he's received numerous offers, including one to be San Francisco bureau chief for *Time*. But Joel is happy at the *News*. Here he can do what he wants. He's even paid a decent middle-class wage, probably the only reporter on the paper who is.

The spiky-haired receptionist peers at me. 'How may I help you?' she asks.

'Kay Farrow to see Joel Glickman.'

Her squint grows intense. 'Is Joel expecting you?' I nod. In my day they weren't nearly so protective.

Joel's office is a cubicle, but he's got a window. Even if the glass is streaked, that's a sign of status. His desk is piled with papers, his walls covered with old cartoons. His Pulitzer certificate, cheaply framed, hangs cockeyed to show how little he expects you to be impressed. Joel, now balding, drooping mustache and goatee tinged with grey, beams up at me through what look to be the same steel-frame grannies he was wearing when we met.

'Hey, kiddo! You look great!'

I pull off my shades, flaunt my shiners. 'Little beaten-up, that's all.'

His forehead furrows. 'Serious?'

'Not as bad as it looks.'

I tell him I was jumped, and that the reason's probably connected to the purpose of my visit.

'So what's the reason, kiddo?'

I shrug the question off. 'Still got good sources in the cops?'

'A few,' he says. 'Most are afraid to talk to me.'

'Afraid you won't protect them?'

He smiles. 'They figure I'm being watched.'

'Are you, Joel?'

He laughs. 'Imagine how much it would cost and how paltry the pickings?'

He's right. It would be exceedingly unprofitable, not to mention illegal, to keep Joel under permanent surveillance.

'I may have a new cop source for you,' I tell him. 'She's working on something hot and ready to leak.'

'Interesting. What does she want?'

'Her name in lights – when it's over.'

'Corruption?' Joel licks his lips.

'No, so don't salivate. But it's a good story. I'm working on it myself.'

We go around the corner to The Transcendental Café, where, in my youth, I wasted more hours than I like to recall. The walls here have been laboriously papered with old Tarot cards. The resident swami sits at the window table staring goggle-eyed into his crystal ball.

We order herbal tea, then I tell Joel my story. I leave out the background stuff I got from David, but am frank about my own interest and Dad's involvement in the old T case.

'I remember Torsos,' he says when I finish. 'Particularly that wacko inspector – what's-his-name? – Hale, the one wrote all those lovely letters of self-praise. City's "Top Cop" they called him. But there was something rotten in the cotton.'

Joel's smart. He knows there's more to the equation. 'Okay,

you're setting me up with Hilly. So tell me, kiddo – what do *you* get out of all of this?'

'She's getting me some information out of police files.'

'That's illegal.' I nod. 'She must want this bad.'

'She does. Because she's a woman, because she's a lesbian and because the guy she works with treats her like shit. Her partner's got his own reporter by the way.'

'Who?'

'Lubow at the *Examiner*.'

'Good man.'

'But no Joel Glickman.'

'No.' He grins. 'Surely not.' He studies me. His eyes grow serious. He turns slightly so the light glints off his grannies. 'This information – it wouldn't be *personnel* information, would it?' I nod. 'About your dad?' I nod again. 'Want to tell me more?'

I hesitate . . . then decide to spill. Joel, after all, is like family. 'Remember, years ago, I told you how my mom shot herself?' He nods. 'That was the same year Dad took abuse for the lost T-case evidence. I have this feeling there's a connection there.'

'Fine, suppose there is – why go back to all that pain?'

'I've got to know where I came from, Joel.'

He measures me, nods. 'Just wanted to see how much you care.'

He says he thinks the story's worth pursuing whether it connects to the original T case or not.

'Just the idea,' he says, 'that there's this kid living that way down on Polk Gulch, then he gets killed and nobody cares, and there're forty, fifty other kids doing the same thing, taking the same risk – that's important in itself. I also like the subplot, that there're all these closeted rich guys – lawyers, stockbrokers, whatever – who swoop down in their cars from Pacific Heights and Marin basically to plunder young bodies.' He nods. 'Yeah, I like it a lot.'

We agree to divide it up – he'll pursue it as an investigative piece for the *News* while I'll make it the subject of my book. Meantime we'll pool our information, credit one another in our respective work, and I'll supply Gulch photographs for his piece.

He thinks my calling Hilly at home is a mistake.

'Once I start asking indelicate questions around the Hall of Justice, the bigshots'll figure there's a leak. Hilly'll be suspect. They'll start watching her, maybe even tap her phone.'

'Aren't you being a little paranoid, Joel?'

He shakes his head. 'Uh-uh, kiddo. I've been through this too many times. People who blow whistles tend to get burned. We need a contact code, for her protection as well as ours.'

When he describes what he has in mind the intrigue excites me: calls from phonebooths; alternate safe meeting places designated 'A' and 'B'; chalk marks on a mailbox in the Castro when we want to meet with Hilly or she with us.

'I also want you to buy a micro tape-recorder. From now on tape all important conversations. In a story like this there're always disputes. If you can produce a tape, ninety percent of the time you're off the hook.'

'I'm glad I brought this to you,' I tell him. 'I feel like I've been floundering.'

'I'm glad you brought it to me, too,' he says. 'Just like old times, kiddo, right?'

I walk him back to his office. He shows me pictures of his new live-in love, Kirstin, the Scandinavian Ice-Goddess, showing off in a bikini on Stinson Beach. Also photos of his daughters, one enrolled in a post grad marine biology program at Scripps, the other majoring in English Lit at Cal.

Joel, I suddenly realize, is nearly fifty years old. Before I leave I photograph him at his desk, the mishung Pulitzer above his head. *Whap! Whap!* Another archetype for my collection: the Intrepid Investigative Journalist.

Sasha Patel is not to be denied, his proprietary interest possibly explained by his having viewed my insides via X-rays and scans, not to mention his hands-on acquaintance with my anatomy. I always thought doctors were detached, that clinical fleshly contacts had no power to arouse. Such, apparently, is not the case. After considerable prodding on the phone, I agree to meet him at the Buena Vista tonight after his shift. But I make it clear this will be a one-off, that I'm not in a dating mode.

I turn up after lunch at Marina Aikido, wary of combat but determined to get a workout. I show Rita my bruises. She agrees I shouldn't fight.

'Just *katas* today and the rest of the week,' she instructs. 'Keep it slow. Concentrate on form.'

I appreciate that she doesn't ask whether I've been battered by a lover. After class I describe the attack, and how, once on the ground, with my attacker on my back, I was powerless against his fists.

Rita demonstrates some *randori* moves I might have made. 'Create a whirlwind,' she says. But once thrown, she agrees, I could do little but take the beating. Except, of course, if my legs were free below the knee, in which case I could have kicked back against the base of my attacker's spine.

Right! Why didn't I think of that? But then I remember: there were three of them, the second holding down my legs, the third my arms. In fact, I should never have fallen, and think the only reason I did was out of fear of damage to my camera . . . which they took anyway.

'Next time, don't try and protect it,' Rita advises. 'Use it as a weapon, a ball and chain. Merge with it. Let your energy flow into it. Remember, Kay, a camera can be replaced.' She lightly touches a bruise on my cheek. 'Shattered bones take time to mend.'

Walking home, on Union Street, I'm attracted by a poster in the window of a children's bookstore. RAINBOWS! it proclaims, and then: COLOR!COLOR!COLOR! Numerous books for kids are on display, all having the word 'color' in their titles. *Colors, Naming Colors, Know The Colors, Colors Everywhere* . . .

I study the window for a time, then enter the store. A friendly smile from the proprietress. I pick up one of the color books, leaf through. There are photographs of farm animals and swatches in the margins, which I assume match the colors of the animals.

A second book contains plastic overlays enabling a child to create secondary colors by mixing primaries. Familiar words leap from the pages: yellow, magenta, cyan . . . all Greek to me.

A third book also bears color swatches, along with exotic words: plum, mint, crimson, poppy, absinthe, azure, robin's-egg blue, aquamarine. The names of the colors dazzle me: hyacinth, lilac, quince, saffron. I savor the sounds: salmon, indigo, mocha, flax, ocher, Pompeian red, burnt sienna.

There's a vast world here of which I have no optical knowledge. But I can dream, extrapolate, for there are words listed for the shades I do know and see. The whites, for instance, composed of all other colors: antimony, bismuth, oyster, ivory, zinc, Dutch, Chinese. The grays: charcoal, dove, gunmetal, mouse, pearl, plumbago. And, my favorites, the blacks or achromatics: bone, aniline, ink, Japan, raven, soot and slate.

So, yes, I decide, though there is an unknown universe here there is also one I can distinguish quite well. The spectrum I know, the one of tones light and dark, is to me exquisite. I may not see the rainbow or know autumnal colors, but let no one say I cannot revel in the beauties of the world.

Hilly loves Joel's contact code: 'Secret codes, secret rings – brings back my tomboy days.'

We're sitting in a corner of The Duchess. Hilly's idea; she figures no cop will follow her into a dyke bar. It's smoky and noisy, but this time I don't mind. Now that we're acquainted there's no special need for quiet.

'In my family,' she reminds me, 'I was the only girl, born between two boys. My brothers were my buddies. We'd fight and scrap. Now one's a T-man, one's a G-man and I'm a city dick. So, see, Kay, the contest still goes on. I wanna zoom past them. I wanna be family champ.'

There's a special pungency in the air here, women oozing desire. I notice Hilly twitching. This hot-house atmosphere turns her on.

'Check her out.' She gestures toward a short-haired brunette standing at the bar. Her biceps are ringed by a coiled snake tattoo, her midriff is bare, she wears nothing but clingy Lycra shorts and a black leather halter bra. '*Hot*, huh!'

I shrug.

'Gimme a break, Kay! Girl goes to the trouble of making herself yummy like that, you can't just *not* respond.'

I shrug again. 'What can I do, Hilly? I'm just a vanilla square.'

'Hey, the culture's queer! Get with it, babe!'

'Yeah . . . now about that stuff you brought me?'

She nods, unfurls her copy of the *Bay Area News*, extracts a sheaf of photocopy paper. 'I couldn't get your dad's personnel file. That's held too close. And since he's retired it's over in dead-records anyway, which means it's basically in a vault.' She taps the papers. 'What I *do* have is the confidential IAD report on the Sipple fiasco – Waincroft, Hayes, Puccio, Vasquez, and, of course, your pop.'

I hold out my hand. She passes the bundle.

'Not pretty reading, Kay.'

'Life's not pretty either.' I thank her, tell her to expect a call from

Joel. 'You'll like him,' I tell her. 'He's a '67 vintage hippy turned serious.'

She grins. 'Sure you don't wanna stay, meet some of my buds?'

'Thanks anyway, Hilly, but I've got a date with a man.'

'Ouch!' she says. And then, an afterthought: 'Woof!'

The Buena Vista is one of my favorite drinking holes, even if it's too often thronged with tourists. Something about the joint at the bottom of Hyde and Beach, where the Hyde Street cable car ends, that brings back happy memories of Art Institute days, meeting friends here on Sunday mornings, throwing back Irish coffees while arguing about sex and art. I like the neon sign outside, the way the letters are formed, the long bar with its tiled base, the bottles arrayed before the long beveled mirror. I like the ceiling fans and the earthy waitresses and the handsome bartender dressed in crisp white mess jacket. Best of all I like the alcoholic coffee.

Sasha is waiting for me, occupying a round wood table by the window. I haven't seen him since the night he took care of me at St Francis Memorial, when I was morphined up.

Checking him out I decide he still looks good, with his dark skin, brilliant black hair and large lustrous liquid eyes. A lady's man, the nurses called him. It's pretty obvious why. It's his alluring smile, so charming and seductive. Also, I assume, so false.

'You're looking good, Kay,' he comments as I sit down. He reaches over, removes my shades, peers at the bruises around my eyes. He touches one lightly.

'What do you want me to do next?' I ask. 'Open my mouth and say "aaahhh"?'

'Not unless you're prepared to strip to the waist,' he warns. 'I want to check your rib cage.' Again he touches me. 'Tender?'

'A little.'

He grins. 'I'll be tender too.'

Quite the jocular fellow is Dr C. Patel, though I must say I like his accent.

'You talk like a Brit. How come?'

'Because I am,' he says. 'Born and raised over there. My parents came from India, but I'm a British subject . . . though most true blue Brits consider me a wog.'

'What's that?'

'A person of color. What you Americans call a nigger. Or "one of our little brown brothers" when you want to show how sensitive you are.'

'Are you bitter, Sasha?'

'Actually, no. I love it here. Home of the Free, Land of the Brave. I especially like American women.' He shows me a grin so charming it could light the world. 'And of course you yanks have the best medical practice in the world.'

I find it difficult not to like him. He's polished, smart, has a fast mouth . . . and always those gorgeous liquid eyes toward which any girl in her right mind would crawl through splintered glass.

'Tell me something,' he says suddenly. 'Who *is* Kay Farrow?'

I laugh. 'My life story?'

'A few high points will do.'

I offer him a few high points. While I do he gazes into my eyes as if smitten by every word.

'Enough about me,' I say. 'Your turn now. You can start by explaining your interesting first name.'

'My actual name's Clarence. They started calling me Sasha in school.'

'How come?'

He smiles. 'Because I wanted them to. I was reading the great Russian novels at the time and fell in love with the name. Something moody about it, also romantic.' He gazes at me. 'Tell me, Kay – do you like to dance?'

'I'm a crummy dancer,' I say.

'I'm sure you could improve.'

'Under your tutelage?'

'Why not?'

'I think I'll wait until my rib cage heals.' I smile at him. 'There's something you don't know about me yet.'

'Tell me.'

'I don't own a single dress.'

He laughs. 'Jeans girl! Terrific! You do own shorts?'

'Numerous pairs.'

'I love shorts and slacks, close-fitting garb.' He wets his lips.

'You know, Sasha – I just realized something.'

'What's that?'

'We're flirting, both of us. And flirting's against my principles.'

'Mercy!' he says.

'This is fun, but I gotta go.' I stand. 'Please let me pay my share.'

'Absolutely not. And I'm very sorry you're leaving – just as we were starting to get on.'

I wait while he takes care of the check, then permit him to escort me up the hill. Hyde Street is steep between Bay and Chestnut. By the time we reach the top of crooked Lombard, we're both slightly out of breath.

He makes his move just inside the front alcove of my building. As we kiss, I feel like a college girl getting smooched in the doorway of her dorm. He tastes good. Must be the Irish coffee. Then I hear myself sigh. He presses upon me. I feel his hardness . . . and then myself becoming wet. He presses harder until I'm flat against the granite portal wall, brings his mouth to my ear, licks it, whispers, 'I want to make love to you, Kay.'

I move my hands so that they embrace his butt, pull him closer. 'I'd like that too,' I whisper dreamily.

The night passes quickly. Sasha is tender. I relinquish my aggressive manner, lie back, yield, let him fill me, have his way. I'd have thought he'd be a selfish lover. He surprises me. Unlike a prototypal lady's man, he's caring, solicitous, attentive to my every pleasure and need.

I love his dark silken skin, the fine texture of it, its taste. I ravish him with my mouth, lick him everywhere. Then he licks me and I explode. Sweet explosion! Always with a new lover I pray that colors will show themselves, little splinters, sparks, showering off the fireworks of my rapture. Tonight they come, not the colors the rest of the world sees so easily, but colors of my imagination, colors of singers, painters, poets: cinnabar, wine-dark vermilion, carnelian, aerugo, chrome primrose, bistre, jonquil, jouvence, piccolopasso, tartrazine, solferino, roccellin. The colors of Veronese, Matisse, Vincent Van Gogh (who may have been dyschromatopsic). The colors of the passionate unfurling flower of my labia. The colors of orgasm. The colors of love. All the secret colors of my inner penetrated self . . . for though we are all born colorblind, we each have within us the ability to someday see the hues.

He leaves me shortly after 3:30 a.m. He must, he tells me, get back to his room at the hospital, for he is on call beginning at 4:00. After he dresses, he leans over me, then kneels to kiss my breasts.

'Wonderful to be with you, Kay. I hope this isn't going to be a one-off like you said.'

I look up at him. 'I don't understand you, Sasha. You're Don Juan. One-offs are your stock and trade.'

He laughs. 'How sorely you've misjudged me!'

'I did have fun,' I admit.

'Can I see you again tonight?'

I groan. 'Let's wait a couple days. But don't worry, I doubt my ardor will cool.'

I awaken late. The sun's burning in. I put on shades, go to the window, wave naked to the goggle-eyed house painter working on the building across the street. I think of something the artist Willem de Kooning once said: that he dreamt of creating a painting that would contain all the colors of the world. Such too is a dream of mine: to partake of an act of love so vivid with colors I will never afterwards miss them in my daily life.

In the bathroom I inspect my body. My bruises are fading. The smudges are fainter. If I could see colors, I would note that they're turning from blue to beige. This morning there are new marks on me, strawberry-shaped love-bites. They decorate the front of one shoulder, and there are two big ones on my collarbone.

I stretch, feel luxurious, tensions relieved. Sex is great and I've forsworn it too long. Last night I relearned something I seemed to have forgotten along the way – that there are other men besides the Judge who can make my body sing.

I take a shower, put on my robe, sit down to read the papers I got from Hilly. The Internal Affairs Division report on the Robbie Sipple attack echoes every smear I found in back issues of the *Chronicle* and the *Examiner*.

Dad was right: clearly the report was leaked. Inept, incompetent – the only pejoratives lacking are the *ad hominems*: dummies, dunces, dolts, chumps, buffoons. But the report is all the more scathing for the absence of insults, calling into question the professionalism of the officers involved. Sergeant Lucius Waincroft takes particular abuse for 'the shocking breakdown in the command structure that led to this debacle'. And Patrolman Jack Farrow, as the officer first on the scene, is held accountable for his 'abysmal failure to collect and preserve vital evidence which, even at cursory viewing, was clearly relevant to a widely known ongoing investigation of a series of capital crimes'.

Poor Dad! But there are ambiguities in the report which escaped the newspapers, hints and phrases that make me take notice. The possibility, for instance, of a conspiracy among the incompetents, dismissed as being improbable, yet considered nonetheless:

'. . . despite these conclusions, the Division Committee cannot wholly exclude several other potential explanations of the debacle: (a) one or more officers sought to conceal the mishandling of evidence by themselves and/or their colleagues, by deliberately destroying and/or mislaying the discovered materials; (b) one or more of the officers returned to the crime-scene after it was clear, and deliberately removed the discovered materials for reasons of their own.'

Translation: A screw-up and then a cover-up, or, worse, the evidence was deliberately lost because it implicated someone inside SFPD.

Another ambiguity concerns the behavior of Inspector Jonathan Topper Hale in his meeting with the patrolmen and sergeant prior to the assignment of the matter to IAD:

'. . . Hale's abuse intimidated the officers, leaving them with little choice but to remain silent lest their careers in the Department be further jeopardized. In accordance with good management practice, Hale should have cajoled these officers into remembering clearly what transpired, rather than berating them for compromising his own opportunities to solve the case. In this matter, at least, Hale appears to have overstepped, showing more concern for personal aggrandizement than the recovery of the missing evidence. The Committee points out that this is just the sort of abuse of command authority that can occur when an investigator becomes too closely identified with a high-profile case . . .'

Translation: Hale scared the shit out of everyone, making them disinclined to help lest in return they be hung out to dry.

I also note the Committee's confidential personal evaluations of the officers:

'Waincroft: out of his depth, has no business holding a supervisory position. Recommend immediate demotion with incentives to retire.

'Hayes: less than middling officer long past his prime. Retirement to be actively encouraged.

'Puccio: sloppiest of the bunch, apparently ignorant of police norms and procedures. Recommend dismissal.

'Vasquez: sharp, helpful, contrite, the officer we deem least likely to have been responsible. Recommend mild punishment. This officer should be allowed a future with the Department.

'Farrow: a decent, experienced officer who, perhaps by chance, has had a less than stellar career. Since Waincroft was in command, we remain mystified by his insistence on taking responsibility for the loss. Because he seems less than fully committed to police work, retirement to be actively encouraged.'

I walk down the slope to Polk, purchase a micro tape-recorder and cartridges at Radio Shack, then stop at a gourmet store to buy a variety of organic fruits and vegetables and a loaf of City Stone Ground bread. I carry my bag of groceries back up to the walkway on the Larkin side of Sterling Park, ostentatiously leave it on the same bench where I left the beribboned styrofoam box two days ago. As before I pirouette, knowing my savior, Drake, is watching from somewhere in the bush.

At home I eat an apple, then go to work, taking down every print, clipping, appointment slip and note pinned to my cork office wall. With the cork clean, I proceed to pin up photographs relevant to Tim's death, seeking some sort of order that will clarify the complexities by which I'm feeling overwhelmed.

A cluster of pictures of Tim go up first, casual shots I took of him on the Gulch, plus the nude of him doing the handstand, and my favorite, the glamor shot on Angel Island.

Following these I lay out my two main sequences, the one on Willow Alley where his head and limbs were found, the other, the ground in Wildcat Canyon.

Above and below these sequences I place several of the police crime-scene photos Hilly supplied, and at the end of the row, a shot I took on the boat when we let Tim's ashes go.

I stand back for an overview. *There he is*, I think, in all the startling beauty and vitality of his life, and savage uncomeliness and stillness of his death.

On a separate section of cork I arrange a sequence that profiles the Gulch, street shots and portraits of several of the regulars – Crawf, Slick, Remo, Alyson, Doreen, a few others, and the one of Knob and his acolytes I took in The Werewolf bar. Above them I post shots I surreptitiously took of various unidentified prowling johns, and, connected to these, but in a cluster all its own, the sequence of Marcus Crane at the gate of his and Sarah Lashaw's home.

In still another area I pin up pictures of the detectives, Shanley and Hilly Lentz, as well as my new comrade-in-arms, Joel Glickman. Nearby I arrange a sequence on the original T case, centered around the photo I took of Dad in front of City Stone Ground, surrounded by pictures I photocopied off of library microfilm of the other Sipple cops, plus the excellent press photo of Inspector Jonathan Topper Hale leaving the Hall of Justice the day of his disgrace.

On the opposite wall I pin up parallel sequences of Tim's studio when Crawf and I first visited it, and its chaotic state when I later returned to pack up his stuff. Back near the idyllic portraits, I tack up one of David deGeoffroy, one of the façade of Tim's mail drop, and also (the only non-photo in my show) the unidentified key I found tucked in the molding of Tim's flat.

Above the shot of Dad, I place one I made of Mom when I was at the Art Institute and first took up photography. Finally, for no reason I can think of, I add one of the detached self-portraits I shot of myself last week. Then I stand back again to see what I have wrought.

Things are connected, that much is clear, but no over-arching pattern emerges, no theme that ties everything together.

Two torso cases fifteen years apart, similar in some respects, different in others: the recent victim (I'm trying to think of Tim objectively now) has a history in which cutting played a part. I move closer to the wall, examine my before-and-after shots of his studio. I am, I realize, the only person with such pictures; except for me and Crawf, no one, including the cops, knows what the place looked like before it was tossed. I search the photos for crucial differences, objects which might have been removed. The big Angel Island print of Tim is gone; I noticed that before. Also, the curious sorting of the clothing. But where *is* his address book, assuming he had one – and what street-hustler doesn't? Where *are* the personal things – family photos, letters, passport, birth certificate? Where, for that matter, are items I know he possessed, such as the decks of cards he used for his card tricks and the balls he carried in his backpack which he juggled on the ferry to Sausalito?

I don't see any of this stuff in either set of photos, but then such items would most likely have been stowed away. When Crawf and I were there we didn't make a search, and since, according to Shanley, such items didn't turn up, it seems safe to assume whoever tossed the place carried them off. But why?

There's something else that occurs to me as I study these photographs – the fact that the person who did the tossing entered with a key. So . . . someone had a key to Tim's studio, and, I note, my eyes falling upon the key I found, he had a key to someone else's flat as well.

Too great a leap? I don't think so. The key hidden in his molding didn't fit his door, but it matches his door key in design. A key to another apartment, perhaps one in the same building? The apparition I saw the day I moved his stuff – was that Ariane, having just left the building, heading off for a stroll?

I'm excited. Laying out my pictures, seeking visual connections, has led me to this fascinating thought. And, I realize, I would never have come up with it if I hadn't intercepted David's letter and heard his Magician's Tale.

I pull out a blank white sheet of processed photographic printing paper, one of several I use for focusing when I make a print. With a grease pencil I inscribe the word ARIANE, then pin the sheet up between my photos of David and of Tim. She, I decide, is the missing piece . . . and there are other pieces missing as well: the link between the two cases, if indeed there is one, and the links between Marcus Crane and Knob and Tim.

Sasha calls me from the hospital. In the background I hear the sounds of the ER including those implausibly placid public address announcements by which surgeons are summoned to patch up horrendous wounds.

'I'm thinking about you,' Sasha says.

'Nice thoughts?'

'Better than nice.' He lowers his voice. 'Highly desiring.'

'Yes, I hear you're quite the lady's man,' I tell him.

'I used to be. Not anymore.'

'Is this a recent change, Sasha?'

'Since last night.'

'You're sure it's not just lust?'

'Oh, Kay – why so cynical?'

'All right,' I relent. 'You can come over tonight. Truth is, I'm highly desiring myself.'

I walk over to Van Ness, but the sunlight's so brilliant I decide to take a bus down to Market. From there I walk to Tim's building on Mission, enter the lobby, inspect the names on the register.

Perkins; Nakamura; Pannella/Rosenfeld; Lovsey; Swink; Yaegger; Sowards; two blanks – a typical San Francisco mix. Deciding to bring the number of vacancies to three, I pry out the black plastic strip for Lovsey.

On a hunch, I ring the buzzers opposite the blanks, apartments 303 and 500. No responses back. I climb the stairs, find the door to 303, knock, then try the key from Tim's molding. It slips into the keyhole but doesn't turn and is difficult to extract. But in the door to 500, at the very top of the stairs, the key turns easily and opens the lock.

I enter. Suddenly, I'm lost in a snow storm. The apartment, with its dazzling white walls and gleaming white floor, is so harshly lit, such a stark container of blazing light, that the rods in my retinas are instantly saturated.

I shut my eyes lest I go blind, fumble for my darkest shades, put them on. Then, slowly, I open my eyes. But even with the shades I'm lost in a blizzard. I shut down again, feel my way to the windows, grope for the venetian blinds, pull them closed. This time, though the room's still treacherously alive, I can see enough to understand that it's not light from the windows that's been blinding me but from a skylight that tents the room. I spot a pair of hanging ropes secured to a cleat on the wall, go to the cleat, untie the ropes, haul as hard as I can. Slowly a large drape rises to cover the glass. When I'm finished, ropes again secured, the room, though still well lit, is bearable at last.

It's a fine space, bigger than Tim's, and, with its high slanted ceiling and skylight, perfect for an artist. But it would be the worst possible studio for me. So much light would kill my vision.

I pace about. I'm impressed by the condition of the place, the way everything's freshly painted, kitchen appliances shiny and perfectly flush with counters and cabinets, and the new white tiles in the bathroom joined by immaculate white grout. Hard to believe I'm in the same grungy building, not in some new high-rise near Opera Plaza. Someone's renovated this flat, and I can't believe it's landlord Murray Paulus, so annoyed Tim didn't give him notice prior to being killed. Yes, someone spent a lot of money fixing this place up, someone who either is about to move in or has recently moved out.

The buzzer sounds. At first I'm nonplussed. I'm a trespasser, have no right to be here. But, in fact, I realize, since the place is empty I can't be accused of being a robber. I can claim I was looking for an apartment, noted the vacancy on the lobby register, climbed the stairs and found the door unlocked.

Better, I decide, to answer than have someone come up and find me hiding. I go to the wall, press the responder, then open the door a crack.

Footsteps in the stairwell. A woman's heeled shoes and gait. I've never found the stairwell so quiet, then recall that on other visits I heard operatic arias echoing down.

The steps approach. The person is one floor below. I tense as an attractive young woman comes into view. She's beautifully dressed in cashmere sweater and skirt, wears earrings and a necklace with a Celtic cross as pendant. She sees me too, approaches, smiles.

'Hi!' she says.

'Hi yourself.'

'I was looking for—' Her voice falters.

'Yes?'

'For her, you know, but, like – hello! – I see she isn't here.' She peers about, wide-eyed, taking in the emptiness. 'Least not anymore,' she adds.

I shrug to indicate I find the former resident's absence obvious.

'When was the last time you saw her?' I inquire.

'Oh, well, you know . . .' She smiles again, embarrassed. 'Not too long ago, I guess.' She ponders. 'Maybe, four, five weeks, something like that.'

She's young, nineteen or twenty, and her jewelry and Rolex tell me she's well off. But there's something about her that belies the upper-middle class suburban look. I check out her shoes. They're high-style fetishistic – black and chrome ankle bondage straps, imbedded steel tips and modified-for-daywear stiletto heels.

'How 'bout you?' she asks. 'I mean – were you looking for her too?' I nod. 'How long since *you*'ve seen her?'

I shrug again. 'A while, I guess.'

'Well . . .'

'Yes, well . . .'

She puts out her hand. 'I'm Courtney Hill.'

I put out mine. 'Kay Farrow.' We shake.

She squints at me. 'Kay? Have I seen you around?'

'Maybe,' I say. And then: 'Since she's moved, I guess there's no point standing here.' I look at her. 'Shall we escort each other down?'

I close the door. It clicks shut. When I try it again it's locked. 'Looks like she really cleaned out,' Courtney observes as we descend. She giggles. 'Lock, stock and barrel.'

I giggle too, though I don't quite get the joke . . . unless Courtney means to mock the cliché.

'How did you meet her?' she asks.

I shrug. 'Just around, I guess.'

'Yeah,' she nods, 'like so many. I met her at HardCandy. Of course I'd *heard* about her. Everyone has. Then one night someone pointed her out. I took one look, said to myself: "What an incredible slut!"' Courtney glances at me. I smile and nod. 'I'd never seen anything like her. Way she moved, came on. And the response she got! Like she was God's gift to us, you know.' I nod again. 'Like – *wow*!'

In the lobby I point out that there's a blank space opposite the buzzer for apartment 500.

'She kept it blank, least when I met her,' Courtney says. Then she giggles. 'I mean what was she going to put in there anyway. "Love Goddess"? "Amoretto"?'

Amoretto. The word sears my brain. I feel my cheeks flush, my hands burn, as Courtney and I part on the sidewalk. *The Amazing Amoretto*: the name David deGeoffroy devised for Ariane when he contemplated devoting himself full-time to her career.

Apartment 500, I now know, was occupied by Ariane Lovsey. David was right, she *was* close. In fact, I realize, I may have only just missed her.

NINE

I WANT TO FIND her now . . . if only to mourn with her and tell her where her brother's ashes were scattered. But I want far more: I want to know the secrets, how the twins survived after they ran away, their whole story, everything. Also I want to see this creature who so closely resembles Tim. I long to photograph her face.

Courtney Hill has given me a lead: HardCandy. I know the place though I've never been inside. Along with Eros and ATF, it's one of the cutting-edge SoMa clubs where hip young people go to dance, score, indulge fantasies of decadence.

On my way home I plot my moves. I'll ask Sasha to take me, or turn up on my own and ask for Amoretto, or show around a photograph of Tim and ask if anyone's seen a woman with his face.

I pause outside my building, then walk into Sterling Park. I want to check if my bag of groceries is still on the bench. It's not. In its place I find a piece of torn brown paper bearing Drake's *billet-doux*: 'Thanks again'. This time the signature's a simple 'D'.

My phone is ringing as I come through the door. I'm still thinking about Ariane as I pick up. The woman's voice is East Coast and refined. She tells me her name is Marjorie Wilson, and, before I can ask how I can help, she identifies herself as Sarah Lashaw's assistant.

I sit down. I'm not expecting this. Have my provocations finally forced forth some fruit?

'Sarah is extremely interested in your work,' Marjorie gushes. 'She wants very much to meet you. There's a project she'd like to discuss.'

'What kind of project?'

'A photographic one, I imagine.'

'Commissioned photographs?'

An awkward laugh. 'It would be best to discuss that with her, don't you think?'

Since Lashaw's my suitor, I decide to have some fun. 'I gotta tell you, Ms Wilson, I think there may be a misunderstanding here.'

'I assure you she's a great admirer.'

'That's nice, but the fact is I no longer do commissioned work.'

Another laugh. 'Oh, I think she understands that, Ms Farrow. I did the research on you and I can assure you I was thorough.' Pause. 'Do you ever get up to St Helena?'

'Not often.' In truth, I realize, it's probably been a couple of years.

'Sarah's asked me to invite you for lunch tomorrow. If that's not inconvenient.'

'Tomorrow . . .' I stall to clear my head. 'Don't know. I don't own a car.'

'That won't be a problem. Our driver will pick you up and have you back in town by dark.' A little pause. 'Shall we say in front of your place tomorrow, 11:00 a.m.?'

I think a moment. No one in her right mind declines an invitation to lunch with Sarah Lashaw. As for the 'project' it's hard to imagine it doesn't concern the photos I took of Crane.

'That'll be fine,' I tell her. 'How should I dress?'

'Oh, you know – country. We're all pretty casual around here.'

I'm freshly bathed, wrapped only in a kimono, staring at the city through my telescope when Sasha buzzes from downstairs. It's nearly midnight. I ring him in, then tilt the telescope up. It wouldn't do for him to find me snooping on the Judge.

He comes bearing gifts, a bouquet of roses in one hand, a split of iced champagne in the other.

'Is this courtship, Sasha?' I ask as I dodge into my kitchen to scrounge a pair of flutes.

'I'm a romantic,' he answers from the other room. 'Perhaps the last one,' he adds as I return glasses in hand.

I kiss him. I'm flattered, grateful too. It's been a long time since a man came to me with flowers and drink. Sasha's lips taste faintly of mint mouthwash. So thoughtful, handsome, hygienic! What more could a girl want?

He pops the cork with precision, spilling nary a drop. We sit and sip. He tells me he's had an easy night – no knife or gunshot wounds, two falls, one heart attack, one not-serious stroke, a couple of broken arms.

'Sounds like bliss,' I say.

He gazes at me. His eyes are incredible. I could easily get lost in eyes like his. I imagine many women have.

'Do you ever do the club scene?' I ask him.

'There's a latino one I like. Venceremos in the Mission.'

'How 'bout HardCandy?'

He smiles. 'I hear it's wild.'

'Been there?'

'Once,' he admits. 'My date insisted.'

'Well, one night soon I'm going to insist too.'

His eyes enlarge, he grins. I've surprised him . . . which is good. Now he's wondering if I do drugs, triad sex, or, God help him, S&M. Yes, poor Sasha, I can see, is falling ever deeper into lust. I set down my glass, take his hand, lead him into my bedroom, appropriately lit for another night of love.

I not only don't have clothing I consider 'country', I'm not even sure what kind that is. Also I'm angry at myself for inquiring as to the proper dress as if I care whether I blend in or not. Since I'll be damned if I'll pander to Sarah Lashaw, I squeeze into a pair of jeans, pull on a pair of cowboy boots, don my leather jacket, then thread the jeans with my only concession to fashion, a turquoise and silver concha belt I bought last winter in Santa Fe.

A dark Mercedes pulls up promptly at 11:00 a.m. The driver is female; her name is Brit. She speaks with a Scottish brogue, is polite, formal, wears a sharply tailored black suit, white shirt, black necktie, black chauffeur's cap with shiny brim.

I feel almost kinky as I settle into the back seat, luxuriating against the butter-soft upholstery. Still, remembering that someone up North wants something from me, I vow not to allow myself to feel flattered.

The drive is uneventful . . . or perhaps so smooth and comfortable it lulls me into a reverie. After we cross the Golden Gate, I close my eyes and remember the feel of Sasha, his hairless silken chest and lovely satiny ass. I spent a lot of time riding his dark thighs last night, staring into the deep dark pools of his eyes. Even the condom he used felt sleek. All his moves were perfect. My South Asian Lothario!

There's something magical about the Napa Valley, particularly in autumn after the grape harvest when the vines stand clean and bare. The air is fresh, the sky clear, the hills glint beneath the sun. It's paradise, a Northern Californian Eden. As we roll through the vineyards, I have trouble imagining this land could be more beautiful in color.

Before St Helena, we cross over to the Silverado Trail, then wind through the hills. At one point, just past the sign for a vineyard named Stag's Leap, I'm amazed to see a magnificent full-antlered flesh-and-blood stag literally leap across the road.

A mile further we turn into a track between stone columns, then start to climb. We circle the hill, at the top reach a straight and formal alley of eucalyptus. At the end I spot the stone and clapboard house, scene of the lavish picnic depicted in *House & Garden*.

The house is beautiful, serene, perfect in its proportions, grand but not at all ostentatious. Its façade speaks of that mythical protective place called 'home' where no unpleasantness intrudes – a place of inviolate security one can always return to, a fortress against the harshnesses of the world.

If one in ten thousand of us comes from a home like this I'd be much surprised. No rancor here, no parents quarreling over money, no dirty dishes in the sink, crumbs in the toaster, dust balls beneath the beds. Here the linens are changed daily, no one uses a bath towel twice, one is enveloped by the aromas of the garden, the tinkle of wind-chimes, the babbling of a country brook.

Even as the car rounds the circle that ends the drive, I squirm at the smugness of it all. Casual indeed! In this dreamhouse, I suspect, the look of every nook and cranny will be calculated for maximum effect.

Marjorie Wilson is waiting for me. She's not the efficient gray-banged type I expect, rather a clone of Brit the chauffeur – young, poised, well put together. It takes her but an instant to size me up.

'Brit was fast today. Sarah's still at her tennis lesson. Why don't we go down to the courts? We can wait there while she finishes up, or, if you prefer, I'll show you the pool. We've all shapes and sizes of swimsuits if you'd care to take a dip.'

I opt for the courts. We stroll through the front hall of the house, then into a perfectly proportioned living room decorated to the nines. A vase of fresh-cut flowers sits on every table. The huge stone fireplace is loaded with perfectly arranged white birch logs. We pass through a set of brass-hinged French doors to a flagstone terrace that runs the length of the house. From here the views are extraordinary, embracing the Valley from Oakville to Calistoga, a crazy-quilt of vineyards between two rows of wild-growth hills.

A clay tennis court is situated fifty yards below the terrace. Marjorie guides me down to a shaded area furnished with cushioned wicker. Here, waiting on a table, is a perfect frosted pitcher of fresh lemonade. She pours me a glass while I watch Sarah Lashaw play out her steely heart against her coach.

She's a powerful player – I see that at once. She has a merciless serve, a mean two-fisted backhand, a somewhat weaker forehand yet plenty strong enough. She's dressed for exertion in a plain white V-neck T-shirt, white cotton shorts, white socks with tassels and immaculate white tennis shoes. She wears one of those sunshades that consist of a bill supported simply by a band, thus showing off her locks of frosted hair. Her face and forearms are glazed as she runs about retrieving every shot her shirtless muscular trainer pounds to her across the net.

She's also, I quickly learn, a woman who doesn't like to lose.

'Well, cock-a-doodle-doo, Roy!' she hoots, when, at the end of a sustained volley, her trainer smashes a shot between her legs.

'Too fast for you?' he taunts.

'Never too fast, you wart!'

I glance at Marjorie. She meets my eyes and shrugs, as if to acknowledge that, indeed, Mrs Lashaw sometimes does get riled while indulging in stressful sport.

I quickly gain the impression of an undercurrent between Lashaw and Roy. He's in his mid twenties while she's probably fifty-five, but he shows her no deference or respect. On the contrary, he seems to enjoy flaunting his superior power while showing off his well-developed chest. Rather than playing the roles of employer and trainer they behave like lovers engaged in a stylized fight. *Yes!* her tennis game would seem to say, *you're bigger and stronger than me, but I can take whatever you dish out and smack it right back in your face!*

'Deuce!' Roy calls out the score, then sets up to serve.

Whish! His shot aces by her. *Swish!* She swings at it even though it's passed.

'Pee-yoo!' she exclaims, as Roy announces they're at set point.

I raise my camera, start shooting as they play the point back and forth, alternating shots down the line and cross-court, forcing one another from side to side. Suddenly Roy breaks the rally by rushing the net.

'Ho ho!' Lashaw shouts.

But he bats back her returns until he wears her down, then he tips the ball across and watches, amused, as she rushes and stumbles in a fruitless effort to snag it back.

'Game, set, match!' Roy savors the words, as Sarah pulls herself up off the clay.

She brushes the dust from her hips, turns to him and crows: 'You'll pay for this later, Roy-boy.'

Spotting me, she turns her back on him.

'Kay Farrow! How great to meet you!'

I gaze into the fabled and (so I've been told) violet eyes. She extends both hands as if I'm a dear old friend. When I take hold, she pulls me against her hard warm moist body so I can feel her extraordinary power.

Roy rates no further attention, not even an introduction, as Sarah, with Marjorie two paces behind, walks me back up to the house.

'We've lots to talk about,' she says. 'Just give me ten minutes to shower and change, then we'll sit down to lunch.'

The feast is served on the terrace on a table laid with a hand-embroidered cloth and gorgeous hand-painted ceramic plates. Conventional pleasantries and San Francisco gossip accompany scallops and crab over angel-hair pasta, garden-fresh mesclun, raspberry sorbet, accompanied by a local Chardonnay.

After the meal Marjorie excuses herself. Sarah leans forward as soon as we're alone.

'It's terrific to get to know you, Kay. I've long admired your work. Your show at Zeitgeist last year, those poor battered women, their eyes so proud – it really knocked me out.'

An extremely handsome woman, she looks ten or fifteen years younger than her age. She's dressed in a prairie skirt and dark silk blouse. I try to imagine her wearing emeralds. To me, I believe, they would show as a bright mid-gray, slightly darker than her eyes.

'Marjorie says you had me researched.'

Sarah smiles. 'You don't believe I saw your show?'

'Did you?' I ask, meeting her eyes.

'Check the gallery guest book,' she says merrily. 'You'll see.'

A good response. I'm also flattered . . . though I promised myself I wouldn't be. But how could my brand of art connect to anything in her life? I reach into my camera bag, flick my little tape-recorder on.

'Why did you invite me?' I ask.

She stares directly at me. When she grins engaging crow's-feet form around her eyes.

'I'd like to buy some of your pictures, Kay. Negatives as well as prints.'

I shake my head. 'I don't sell negatives. No photographer does. You must know that.'

'I do, but in this case there'd be no need to keep them. It would be a condition of the sale, based on appropriate compensation, that the pictures would never be reproduced.'

I can't believe she's being so brazen. Is she desperate or testing me for weakness?

'I'm not a blackmailer, Sarah. I don't take pictures of people to sell them back.'

'Of course not! I didn't mean to suggest—'

'But you did. You implied I can be bought. I can't. So if it's my pictures of your husband you want, neither prints nor negatives are for sale.'

She fixes me with a fierce withering gaze, like the one she directed at Roy on the tennis court. It's not the charming grin of the society page she's showing now, but her true face, the one that announces its owner gets what she wants. It's a face I'd like to photograph so much I reach beside my chair for my camera. I pick it up, start to bring it to my eye, when I feel her hand upon my wrist.

'No pictures,' she says quietly in a tone all the more frightening for being so certain and still. She tightens her grip. My wrist begins to hurt. Our eyes lock.

'Take your hand off me,' I demand.

She flashes the society page grin. 'Of course, my dear.' She lets go. 'No need to get testy.'

I lower my camera. 'I won't take pictures of you without permission, not here in your house. But outside you're fair game just like everybody else. You're a public figure, as is Mr Crane, especially when he cruises Polk Gulch in his Mercedes looking to rent himself a piece of male ass.'

'Fine,' she grins, 'that's just fine. Got it all out of your system now?'

'Most of it,' I say. 'How 'bout you?'

'I'm doing fine too.'

'Good.'

'Let's talk straight.'

'Yes, let's. Why did you ask me here? Surely you didn't think you could buy me off.'

She nods. She wants me to understand she's impressed, that she respects my guts for standing up to her even in her own rigorously controlled milieu.

'My husband has a complicated nature,' she explains. 'He has his desires as I have mine. Neither of us has ever done anything to intentionally harm another person. If we stray sometimes, make mistakes, then our transgressions are only the faults of passion and of love.' She pauses. 'Sometimes by error people get hurt. Whenever that happens we try to set things right. That might involve some form of payment to alleviate the injury. Of course there are wounds that money cannot salve, though in my experience a significant cash payment can go quite a way when coupled with a sincere expression of remorse. As you know, Kay, we all have our longings and desires. This world we live in is a difficult place. We can only do our very best not to make it worse.'

It is as pretty a speech as I have heard, and, delivered so frankly, calmly, without a waver of the eyes, contrived to soften even the harshest critic's heart. But my wrist, still smarting from her grasp, tells me this is a woman who will use any means, sweet or brutal, to get her way. So I take a moment to analyze what she's said, ferret out its rotten core. It doesn't take me long: *Our transgressions are only the faults of passion and of love.* Oh, yes! We only wound in the names of eros and amour! Never out of selfish lust, never because the flesh of another is for us but fodder! We buy bodies and if the fragile souls within should sometimes break, it is but the flaw in our carnality all humans share.

'The hormone defense,' I mutter.

She turns indignant. '*What?*'

'Everyone has his peccadilloes. But see, Sarah, I take pictures. I don't judge.'

'Then what good, may I ask, do your pictures do?'

'You said my *Transgressions* show knocked you out.'

'Surely you don't intend—'

'I'll tell you what I intend. A friend of mine, a street-hustler, was killed. Savagely, brutally, without pity, most likely out of lust. Perhaps to someone like yourself a person who does that sort of work deserves whatever he gets. I don't see it that way. Anyhow, before he was killed I recorded his life on film, and that meant also documenting the life of the street where he worked. Your husband appears in a number of my shots soliciting minors for sex. He's well known on Polk Gulch. He cruises around there in his fancy car. He's what the street kids call a chickenhawk, which means he preys on underage boys. That's not a mere "fault of love", Sarah – that's a criminal offense. As you undoubtedly know, I trapped him with my camera the other day. The shots are great. At first he preens, tries to laugh me off, but in the end he looks like a cornered rat. Okay, what do I intend to do with those pictures? Right now I've no idea. If they're relevant to the murder of my friend, I'll publish them. If not . . . well, I may just publish them anyway. I probably wouldn't feel this way if, a few hours after our shoot, I hadn't been jumped from behind in the little park in front of my house. One of the men who jumped me (he also stole my best camera) is someone I've seen acting as flesh merchant for Mr Crane. By the way, when your husband's out cruising he doesn't wear his toupee. I guess he thinks that's a good disguise. But still, for some reason, he likes to flaunt his car. Cars, as you know, bear license plates. So, you see, it wasn't hard to track him down.'

'That's it?'

'Pretty much.'

The indignation in her eyes cannot be described. She is utterly, irrevocably outraged.

'It would appear there's no dealing with you.'

I shrug. 'Not on the terms you're used to.'

'What terms then?'

I hand her my card. 'Tell Mr Crane there's no need to hide behind your skirts. Tell him to get in touch, we'll have a talk, and, depending on how it goes, I'll see what I can do.' I glance at my watch, show concern, suggest it's time for me to leave. 'You can also tell him I want my Contax back . . . if, by chance, he knows where it is.'

On the drive back to the city I sit in the front seat beside Brit. She's stiff, monosyllabic, until I ask her about the tennis trainer, Roy. 'Oh, he's a lad, Roy is,' Brit says, amused.

'Does he live at the house?'

'Has his own suite above the garage.'

'Pretty sexy guy. He and Mrs Lashaw – are they, you know— ?'

'I'm no gossip, ma'am.'

But from her grin it would appear Sarah and Roy play all sorts of games.

Back home, agitated, I phone Sasha at the hospital, persuade him I'm too tired for a visit, and suggest, in recompense, that we do HardCandy Friday night.

'Like a real date?' he asks.

'You got it, Sasha.'

'Can we dress up?'

'The whole nine yards!' I promise.

I try to calm myself by meditating for a while, but I'm still too hyped by my day in the country. What should have been a pastoral interlude turned into a nightmare. In the process I've made a powerful enemy.

Feeling the need to regroup, I grab my camera and head out for the Gulch. But I'm careful as I cross Sterling Park. Even with Drake watching out for me, I have no wish to be sand-bagged again.

Tonight the Gulch is sweet, the air warm, the regulars posing in their usual places. I find Doreen lingering at the corner of Polk and Bush.

'Missing you, Bug,' she says.

I tell her I've been trying to sort things out.

'Story of my life.' She laughs. 'Good luck!'

On Hemlock I spot Slick posing with a hustler I barely know, the one they call Sho, because, Tim told me, he's three-quarters Shoshone indian. Sho is handsome, grave, with dark skin, long shoulder-length black hair parted in the middle and lovely quasi-Asian eyes.

'I hear you take pictures,' he says when we're introduced. 'I need some headshots, 8x10s, to get my modeling career off the ground.'

I tell him I don't do glamor shots, but I'll be happy to shoot some outdoor candids if he thinks they'd help. We agree to meet the following afternoon at 5. Just then a big Jaguar pulls up. The boys, nervous, move toward it.

'Gotta go, Bug. This is our date,' Slick says.

I watch as they climb into the back seat, one dark, the other albino, hired for the evening to do God-knows-what. It takes all my self-restraint to keep from taking pictures, but tonight I don't want to get anyone upset.

I walk for a while, stopping to schmooze with acquaintances, trying to regain my fascination with this tawdry strip. But though the territory is familiar an important person is missing. I feel like a widow returning to a city where a great romance was born, hoping to find the same beauty in the streets, finding instead only piercing loneliness.

Knob is standing beside the door of an all-male video shop near Sutter, thumbs hitched casually in his belt. He's grinning at me, the grin of a cougar awaiting the nightly prowl of a yearling deer. 'Will I pounce or won't I?' his grin seems to ask. And, since I'm not feeling particularly yearling-like this evening, I dare to stop and meet his eyes.

'Still stomping the Gulch, Bug?'

'Any reason I shouldn't?'

'Figured you'd gotten enough by now. Don't want to gild the lily, do we?'

What the hell is he talking about? Have Lashaw & Crane already put out another contract?

'Amoretto,' I say. I don't know why; the name just springs into my head.

'Yeah, what about her?' Knob replies coolly.

I laugh, continue on my way, flabbergasted by his response. He didn't say 'Who?' or 'What?' or 'Fuck off!' He said 'What about her?' – which means he knows who she is.

Joel Glickman calls at 11 to say he's seen Hilly.

'She made me meet her at this western bar. She was the only woman there and I was the only straight guy. She said we were safer there than anyplace else. She says she meets you at The Duchess.'

I laugh. 'What'd you think of her?'

'Friendly, smart, straightforward enough . . . until experience proves otherwise.'

'Is she on to something?'

'Too early, kiddo. With these case-in-progress deals it's barely one in five. Remember, this isn't a whistle-blow. She's got a theory. Maybe she's right, maybe not.'

'But it's worth a shot?'

'Definitely.' Joel pauses. 'I want to see Hale.'

Jonathan Topper Hale: how I'd love to photograph him! 'Didn't he retire South?'

'Uh-uh, he's still in the area. Lives in Oakland. And, from what I hear, is still obsessed with Torsos.'

'Does he know about Tim Lovsey?'

'I hope not. I want to be the one to tell him.' Joel pauses again. 'Wanna come along?'

Friday evening. When Sasha rings from downstairs I'm still dolling myself up. Maybe 'dolling' isn't quite the right word, more like garnishing myself. I've applied several stick-on tattoos to my upper arms, the black New Age calligraphic kind. I've also painted my lips with black lipstick (if I'd used red it would appear black to me). My leather pants are secured by my concha belt. Now I'm snapping on a leather bracelet with chrome points. I buzz Sasha in, then return to self-adornment. I'm wearing a black lace bra, but can't find anything that looks good on top.

Sasha is even more decorous. No longer in his serious young physician mode, he wears a tight black muscle shirt, black Spandex pants, a chain link belt that hangs loose about his hips, and a black leather motor-cycle cap embellished by another length of chain.

We preen for each other, then get down to business – how best to drape my torso. Sasha thinks the bra is all I need.

'Underwear as outerwear,' he says, 'that's the hot new look.'

Actually it's a style that's five years old, but being unfashionable doesn't bother me; I only wish to be desired.

'Want me to go bare belly?' I ask.

'Why not? Half the women at these clubs do.'

'I don't know . . . I think I'll feel naked.'

'Let me decorate you then.'

I follow his instructions, remove my bra, then sit backwards astride a chair. He sits behind me and begins applying more temporary tattoos to my back. When he's done, he escorts me into the bathroom where I have mirrors on opposite walls. Together we inspect his handiwork. I look like a Kandinsky from behind.

'Very futuristic,' Sasha remarks.

Fine! I'll wear just the bra, my embellished skin taking the place of fabric. But Sasha has brought me a gift, a black leather collar with spiky points. He puts it on me lovingly as we both face the mirror. I like it. It matches my bracelet, says I'm kinky, and, at the same time: 'Don't get too close, my throat's inviolate.'

HardCandy like most SoMa clubs, is housed in a former warehouse. There's something ominous about a stark windowless building on a dark empty street at night. There are piles of glossy trash bags up and down the block, and a homeless man huddled beside a grocery cart on the further side. A dozen snazzy motor-cycles are lined up neatly beneath the lone street lamp, while luxury cars of various makes are parked along the curb.

No sign designates the club, just a neon strip (Sasha informs me it's violet) that outlines the door. A short line of bizarrely made-up and festooned wanna-get-ins clings to the warehouse wall. I take a place at the end of the line while Sasha goes to its head to negotiate.

He returns to fetch me. The bouncer, a hairy guy in leather vest, doesn't crack a smile as he lets us in. Meantime the wanna-get-ins glare at us with hate.

'How'd you swing it?' I whisper to Sasha.

'Fifty bucks,' he whispers.

Ouch! We walk down a narrow, dark, oppressively low-ceilinged corridor until we come to a door padded with tufted leather. Suddenly it opens and music, heavy metal punk, smacks us like a blow across the face.

We step forward, the door closes behind, then, through a confusion of cries, flashing lights, air thick with the aroma of sweat and pot, we make our entrance into Hades.

Punked-out hair styles, half-nude bodies, glistening writhing flesh – HardCandy has it all. Perhaps I'm too old, staid, insufficiently coked up, but this kind of Bacchanalian extravaganza only hurts my ears. I'm not offended by it, rather I'm bored. But far be it for me to pass judgement. There are worthy people, I know, for whom the late-night scene is a narcotic, an aphrodisiac, a cheat against the drudgery of daily life. A night at HardCandy is a way to meet a lover, score dope, dance away excess energy and angst. It's a place to indulge all one's most decadent exhibitionistic and voyeuristic fantasies. Bottom line: it's our era's stylized version of that great and eternal human enterprise, the orgy.

On Sasha's advice I've left my camera at home; the taking of photographs and/or videos is forbidden here. Thus, being denied my usual means of response, I have no choice but to step out on to the floor and join the debauch.

Sasha, not surprisingly, is a fantastic dancer. He boogies so well I look good just following his lead. About the time I break a sweat, I feel the approval of others as they grant us extra space. We use it to get into a kind of twist-shag routine. When Sasha starts scissoring his fingers, I do the same.

Gaining the impression we're being discussed, I tune-in to snippets of conversation taking place around.

'Great dancer,' a female comments.

'She's not half-bad herself.'

'Good tats on that back.'

'Dig the collar.'

'See them before?'

'Uh uh. But I like what I see.'

'Fresh meat. Let's try and link up.'

Sasha whirls me away, then separates again as we go into a series of retro-50s moves. The music pounds. Sweat runs off my body. I worry my tattoos will wash away. Then I decide to just go with the rush. Soon, feeling the intoxicating effect of rhythmic movement, I yield to the self-obliterating energy all around. *Let me become animal*, I will, and, willing it, feel it start to happen.

We're sitting with four other people at a table on the balcony above the dance floor sipping vodka and giggling at the goings-on in the passion pit below. We don't know the quartet we're with, but they know one another and are putting out feelers they'd like us to join their circle. Proper names, professions, backgrounds – such information is not exchanged. Here it's how you look, dress, dance, present yourself. In the stripped-down ambience of HardCandy, what you see is what you get.

I decide to drop a bombshell. I make my eyes large, then pronounce the magic word: 'Amoretto?'

Heads turn. Lips curl into smiles. Attention is deliciously paid.

'Seen her lately?' a woman asks. Her eyes are made up like a raccoon's.

Heads shake.

'She's like disappeared,' the other female says. This one's hair is arranged into spikes that rival the ones on my collar.

'You ought to say "it". Like – "*it* disappeared",' says the young man to my right, who sports heavily gelled silver hair.

The response to that is such wild mirth I'm led to believe he's spouted a witty line.

'Friend of mine,' it's Spikey Hair speaking again, 'she went with "it" one time. Says all of a sudden she-he-it started plucking coins from her cunt.'

'That's nothing!' Raccoon Eyes says. 'This gay guy I know tells me she-he-it plucked them from his ass!'

Much tittering over that. Seems everyone has a story. The other male in the group, whose left eyebrow and ear bear multiple piercings, offers as how, since he's actually been to bed with the creature, he's the only one at the table who can authoritatively describe her/his/its genitalia.

'Okay, Kit,' Silver-Gel taunts, 'let us in on the big secret.'

Pierced Guy offers an enigmatic smile. 'Amoretto's like one of those, you know, magical goddesses – she can change sex even while you fuck.'

'I heard that too,' says Spikey Hair. 'You go to bed with a hen, wake up with a rooster.'

'Like she does you with a strap-on?' Raccoon Eyes asks.

'No way!' Pierced Guy is adamant. 'The cock's for real.'

'Well, you ought to know!' Silver-Gel elbows Pierced Guy in the ribs.

By this time Sasha is giving me a look. He leans over, whispers: 'Who the hell are we talking about?'

I want to know more. 'Could it've been twins?' I ask.

Pierced Guy screws up his face, spreads his hands. 'Wish I knew,' he says. 'I was just too stoned to notice.'

I take Sasha's hand, tell the others we're going back down to the pit. They're a little hurt, taking our departure as rejection, but I must rescue Sasha, who is, after all, a mere lady's man. These bisexual kids we've been hanging with play in an entirely different league.

'Were you talking about someone human?' Sasha asks me on the stairs.

'Just some club-scene person I want to meet.'

'Pulling coins out of pussies and asses. Weird!'

Poor Sasha! He knows all about the insides of people's bodies, but perhaps not so much about their fantasies.

The music here is too percussive, the lyrics to the songs screamed too loud. We've only been here an hour and a half, and already I feel burnt-out. Sasha's proven his skills on the dance floor. Now I'm ready to go home.

Outside, I ask the bouncer if Amoretto's been around.

'Not lately,' he says in an ultra-serious tone that tells me he'll provide no more information. But on the way back to my apartment in Sasha's BMW, I consider the fact that when we sat down with strangers, they all knew who I was talking about. One even claimed to have spent the night with her. Knob also knew who she was. So, it would seem that Ariane is notorious in town, at least within a certain set, a fact of which I, in my isolated artist's life on the hill, have until this evening been unaware.

Back at my place, Sasha and I strip one another of kinky attire, then fall into bed. Though it would be my preference to apply rubbing alcohol and sponge off my tattoos, Sasha wants me to keep them on.

'I like you encrusted,' he tells me, perhaps not the most romantic words to escape his sultry lips. But he's been good to me tonight, taken me where I wanted to go, so now it's my turn to give him a ride.

In the morning, still half-deaf from the heavy metal assault, I pace about my apartment trying to collect my thoughts.

What do I know?

One, that Ariane lived in Tim's building.

Two, that she most likely moved out within the past week.

Three, that living so close, in possession of each other's keys, they surely saw each other a lot . . . yet Tim never let on that she existed.

Four, that just as he hustled on the Gulch, she had her own hustle going at the clubs.

Five, they seemed to have played an erotic variation on David deGeoffroy's Zamantha Illusion, Ariane going to bed with someone then switching places with Tim, thus freaking the new bed-mate out.

Six, it would seem Ariane deliberately cultivated a bizarre reputation among club people as some sort of gender-bending mistress
of legerdemain.

Seven, Ariane and Tim stole fifty thousand dollars from David,
and Tim boasted to me he had fifty thousand stashed – which has
never turned up.

Eight, it's clear that Tim's hints there was a woman in his life I'd
want to photograph were references to his twin, Ariane.

Nine, the day Tim was killed, when he set up a meeting with me,
he sounded as if he was scared.

Ten, Ariane's apparent lack of interest in recovering her brother's
body and subsequent disappearance suggests she, too, is scared,
perhaps of meeting the same fate.

But what good does all this analysis do me? None . . . unless I
can locate the girl. From the moment I heard of her I've wanted
to meet her. Now I feel I must.

I look up Courtney Hill in the city phone directory. No listing. For
all I know she's from down the Peninsula, East Bay or Marin. She's
so young she probably still lives at home with her parents. Unless,
of course, she's in college somewhere . . . in which case I might be
able to find her.

I make a few quick calls: San Francisco State, Stanford, University
of California at Berkeley. I'm prepared to make many more, but I
luck out at UC, where, I discover, a Ms Courtney Dayton Hill is
indeed registered as an undergraduate.

I leave a message at her dorm, then walk down to Marina Aikido
for class. Today my workout partner is Flora, a Filipino diplomat's
wife. We practice fiercely, throw one another well, blend energy, get
into the flow. When we're finished we realize we've been watched.
After we bow, the class applauds.

At noon Courtney returns my call, says she just returned to dump
her books and found my message. She recalls our encounter very
well and was hoping she'd see me again. Yes, she'd be happy to get
together and talk about Amoretto. We agree to meet that night at
Kabul, an Afghan restaurant in Berkeley.

A little before 5 I walk over to the Gulch for my photo-session
date with the hustler, Sho. He's so beautiful this evening I'm nearly
swept away. His hair's parted to the side, his eyes glisten, he wears a
black T-shirt that goes perfectly with his dark skin. We walk down

to Fort Mason where I pose him on the lawn overlooking the piers. Wind off the Bay blows his hair across his face. I'm touched by his gestures as he brushes it off. I shoot out a roll, then tell him I have to go. Walking home, thinking of Tim, my eyes tear up.

I take the Cable Car down to the end of Powell, there board the BART train for East Bay. The ride underwater is smooth and hushed. Emerging at downtown Berkeley station, I walk swiftly to Telegraph Avenue, where I'm caught up in a swirl of student pedestrians, aggressive street peddlers, panhandlers and hostile handicapped people speeding around too fast in motorized wheelchairs. The smell here's the universal aroma of an off-campus street – cigarette smoke, coffee, frying grease going bad.

First to arrive at Kabul, I take a table facing the door. The lighting's dim, the furnishings sparse, the aroma sensuous: Eastern spices and roasting lamb. Most of the other diners are students. The prices for the specials, posted on a blackboard, strike me as ridiculously cheap.

Courtney shows up fifteen minutes later looking more like a student than on the day we met. She wears the same expensive wristwatch and Celtic cross pendant, but tonight she's shod in Nikes and dressed in a CAL sweatshirt and jeans frayed at the knees.

'Hi!' She's spunkier than before, in appearance at least more innocent. We exchange backgrounds. She's from Santa Barbara, her father's an attorney, mother a psychotherapist. She went to a private day school, applied to Stanford and Yale, was pleasantly surprised to be accepted at Cal.

'It's very competitive,' she says, 'but the kids are great – especially if you get along with Asian-Americans. And of course my dad is happy since tuition's practically free.'

She's majoring in Rhetoric, which she knows is useless, unless, of course, she wants to make a career in academia, which, she assures me, touching the cross around her neck, she does not. She likes sports, is a member of the women's junior varsity tennis squad, active, too, in the Gay, Lesbian and Bisexual Students' Association – which is how, she tells me, she found herself in the crowd that hangs around HardCandy on weekends. She's smart, I discover, cheerful, off-beat, socially courageous, and impressed by people with strong personal style. This, she explains, was why she was so attracted to Amoretto, but also, of course, because of the woman's aura of sluttishness and mystery.

'Was it the same with you?' she asks.

'Actually not,' I say. 'I was attracted to her brother.'

She smiles knowingly. 'Her animus. I never met him, though I heard the talk. There're people who think he doesn't exist, that she really changes sex. Isn't that like – totally *weird*?'

I agree.

'No question she's got her macho side. "Watch out! I'm packing!" Such a turn-on, least for me. But mostly she's quiet, barely says a word. She kinda leads you in with her eyes. In my crowd it's a rite of passage to go to bed with her.'

'Which is how you knew the studio?'

She nods, looks at me wistfully. 'I'd really like to see her again.'

'To sleep with her?'

Courtney shrugs. 'Sure, if that works out. But actually just to get to know her better. She's just so fascinating, yet so . . . you know . . . mysterious.'

'You say she doesn't talk that much?'

'I found her secretive. When I asked how she learned to do magic she smiled like I was crazy to ask. She wouldn't tell me where she comes from, her real name, anything. She either smiled or changed the subject or did something to . . . you know, my *body*.' Courtney grins. 'She had all this incredible apparatus up there. I mean some of that stuff was huge. I can't imagine how she moved it out.'

When I ask exactly what apparatus she's referring to, Courtney giggles.

'You know, those stocks and that incredible wheel! God! Just seeing it made me weak in the knees!'

I recall her little joke when we met, the one about the studio being cleaned out 'lock, stock and barrel'. Now that it makes sense, I laugh along with her.

'Was there any kind of . . . arrangement?' I ask timidly.

'Like what?'

'You said she provides this rite of passage. What does she get out of it?'

Courtney gives me a quizzical look. 'Pleasure, I hope!'

'Nothing else?'

'You mean like . . . money?' I nod. 'How well do you know her, Kay?'

I can see I've upset her, she's wary of answering more queries. Since I seem to have fallen in her estimation, I decide to tell her the truth.

She listens intently as I describe how Amoretto's brother was a Polk Gulch hustler and how he was savagely murdered. I tell her that Tim lived in the same building as Ariane, that they were fraternal twins who as children were part of a magician's troupe. Since Tim hustled for tricks, I hope Courtney will forgive me for asking if Ariane did the same.

'Okay, now I see. Sure, you had to wonder about that.' She pauses. 'I've heard she charges a lot for scenes. But I gotta tell you,' she peers into my eyes, 'she didn't ask me for a cent.'

Time to wrap things up. I ask if she'll let me know if she sees Amoretto again or hears anything new about her. I explain that I want to tell her what I did with Tim's remains and talk to her about her twin brother whom I loved.

Courtney agrees. In front of the restaurant we embrace. Then she walks back to her dorm and I to Berkeley station.

TEN

I'M SITTING IN THE passenger seat of Joel's vintage VW beetle. We're crossing the Bay Bridge on our way to see retired Inspector Jonathan Topper Hale.

'If he's not listed, how did you find him?' I ask Joel.

'Professional secret.' Joel's smile is smug, but it doesn't take. He's too open, too generous, at least with friends. The toughness comes out when he thinks someone's covering up.

'Okay, kiddo, here's how. When Hale resigned a lawyer friend of his, Denis Roquelle, issued a statement. It's been fifteen years but he's still in practice . . . so I called him up.'

Joel, I remind myself, is always thorough.

His car amuses me. Its sides are battered from years of street parking. Foam rubber dice hang from the rear-view mirror. There's a picture of Ice-Goddess Kirstin taped to the steering wheel. The back seat's covered with a tangle of old jogging shoes and empty soda cans. Joel calls this bug 'Melvin'. Generally it's a pain when a person insists on naming his car, but with Joel I'm in a forgiving mood. He's a true-blue former love-child; his hippie-days credentials are impeccable. In the aristocracy of Bay Area social movement people, Joel is nothing less than a prince.

We follow heavy truck traffic on to 580, exit at Grand Avenue, swing around Merritt Lake. Joel hands me a map of Oakland, tells me to navigate. It takes me a couple of minutes to orient myself. Meantime, by instinct, he finds the street.

It's straight and shady in a grid of other straight shady streets, the houses lined up, each in a different style, on identically sized lots. This is older white middle-class Oakland, a neighborhood for retired cops, teachers, civil servants. Here hedges are trimmed, lawns are well kept, each façade conceals a backyard barbecue and deck.

'Not what I expected,' Joel says, as he stops in front of 4123.

I gaze at the house. 'What did you expect?'

He shrugs. 'Maybe something gothic with a turret.'

In fact it's a 50s era split-level with a rusting netless basketball hoop installed over the garage. The front windows are all draped and the shades have been pulled upstairs.

We get out, Joel pats Melvin's fender, then we follow the walk to the front stoop.

The door chimes are off-key. After a while a gray-haired woman in print house-dress peers at us through the side-light. Apparently satisfied, she unlatches the door.

'He's expecting you,' she says in a monotone. 'In his den.'

She leads us through several dark rooms, ritually opening and shutting the doors as we pass through. The kitchen is dark and smells of burnt toast. She opens another door, shows us the basement stairs, gestures for us to descend.

Joel and I exchange looks and start down. The stairwell's dim. At the bottom we pass a lavatory, furnace room, malodorous laundry area, arriving finally at a wood-panel door. Joel signals me to turn on my tape-recorder. He knocks. A moment passes, the door opens and we find ourselves face to face with Hale.

I wouldn't have recognized him on the street. He bears little resemblance to the stocky, authoritative man whose face glared out of the *Examiner* fifteen years ago. In that photograph he had clear eyes, thick black hair, a bushy black mustache. The man facing us now is gaunt, his hair is white and his mustache droops on either side of his mouth. His flesh has the pasty look of a person who rarely ventures outdoors. The famous detective, at his prime when he resigned, has cruelly aged.

'Come in.' His voice is gruff, but I note wiliness in his eyes. 'Glickman. Miss Farrow.' No 'Ms' from Inspector Hale; he's strictly a Ma'am-Miss-Mrs-type guy. As he and Joel feel one another out, I make a quick study of the room. At first glance it appears ordinary, a den outfitted with recycled office furniture, books, framed nostalgia photographs, clippings and awards. But after a minute I feel claustrophobic, and then it occurs to me that the room is not only windowless but also cramped. There's too much in here, too many old clippings clustered on the walls, too many books jammed into the bookcases, too many moldy boxes of files strewn upon the threadbare rug. And, too, it seems ill proportioned, depth insufficient to width. Perhaps, I think, it's a metaphor for Hale's mind.

'. . . Kay, here, will be doing the photos,' Joel says. Hale, seated behind his desk, examines me carefully. 'Some of the places where the torsos were found as they appear today. A portrait of you too, we hope.'

Joel pauses, waiting for Hale to agree. But Hale is searching my eyes.

'The other principals too.' Joel pauses. 'Including Steele, if we can find him.'

'Oh, you'll find him,' Hale says. 'Poke around in the garbage somewhere. Just be careful when a rattlesnake crawls out.'

If Joel's mention of the reporter who exposed Hale is meant to rile him, it works. He squints and starts to knock his knees, causing his desk to shake.

'You're his daughter, aren't you?' Hale's eyes bore into mine.

'My father's Jack Farrow, if that's what you mean.' Hale nods. 'Is that going to be a problem, Inspector?'

'How is old Jack?' Then, before I can respond: 'Still baking bread up on Clement?'

'You know about that?'

'I know a lot of things.' Hale's eyes turn cunning. 'I keep track of them all.'

'Who?' Joel asks.

'Everyone connected to it.'

'It?'

'The T case, what d'you think?'

Joel smiles. 'Roquelle says you're still interested in it.'

'Interested? Consumed is more like it.'

No obfuscation here. In a few choice words Hale has let us know why he agreed to meet.

'So,' Joel says, 'after all these years, what've you found out?'

'Maybe we'll get to that,' Hale says. 'First, I want to know why? What brings you to me now?'

'It seemed a good time to do a follow-up.'

Hale shakes his head. 'Follow-ups appear on anniversaries. There're no T-case anniversaries coming up.'

'All right, Inspector – there's a new case,' Joel confides. 'I'm going to tell you about it, but I expect something in return.'

For the first time since we've met, Hale cracks a smile. 'I show you mine, you show me yours – I remember how it goes.' He turns to me. 'Tell me something, young lady – do you think your dad's the one fumbled the evidence that night?'

'I've no idea,' I say. 'What do you think?'

'I think it was someone else. And I think your dad knows who.'

Nothing I can reply to that. I spread my hands expecting more. Hale winks at me then turns back to Joel. 'Let's start by establishing some ground rules,' he says.

I listen as they hammer out an arrangement, defining 'background only' and 'off the record', talking of 'embargoes' and 'trial balloons'. Hale is shrewd and his voice, at first so gruff, now takes on a more melodious tone. Perhaps he doesn't do much talking these days; his wife didn't strike me as much of a talk-and-listen type. Or perhaps he's energized by the chance to fence with a bright reporter once again. It's been years since anyone's asked his views, but he hasn't lost his press skills, the ones that led to his idolization as 'San Francisco's smartest cop'.

'Okay,' says Joel, 'we got rules, let's play.'

Guy-talk! I'm amused. Joel's the least jocklike man I know. He prides himself on not following sports, on not even knowing the names of local pro teams. But he's such a chameleon he'll say anything to build rapport. He tells Hale about Tim, the discovery of his limbs and head on Hemlock, his torso in Wildcat Canyon. Hale acts mildly interested, not fascinated as we'd hoped.

Joel describes the marks: '. . . the number seven. Tribal arabesques on his back, not tattooed but applied with paint. So, you see, there're similarities and differences. And of course fifteen years.'

Hale smiles. 'Who's the investigating officer?' When Joel names Shanley, Hale doesn't react. 'Lots of new faces downtown. You'd think the man would have gotten in touch.' He shakes his head. 'They've no idea what I've been up to all this time. Nobody does. Except Alice.' He points upstairs.

'Tell us, Inspector – what have you been up to?' Joel asks, trying to flatter out a revelation.

'Investigating,' Hale says. 'I'll show you.'

He turns to me, winks again, the crafty wink of a man about to amaze. Then he stands, turns to the bookcase on the wall behind his desk, reaches forward and . . . behold! The bookcase parts in the middle to reveal another room of equal size behind. Now I understand why the office seemed so cramped – Hale divided the original space in half. I also understand why he insisted on dealing with us formally from behind his desk: he needed to guard his secret space.

As he beckons us into this den-within-the-den, I try to catch Joel's eye. But he's focused on the display inside, three walls covered with a complicated chart that puts to shame my own wall display at home. This is a real detective's flow-chart: drawings, photos, maps, names, documents and queries connected by a network of strings tracking various investigative lines. Listening to Hale explain, I learn that the strings are of different colors – white tracking the chronological line, yellow the methodological, blue the evidentiary and red the psychological. In addition there are hundreds of thumb-tacked cards bearing references to undisplayed material and research notes.

Hale picks up a pointer, starts to talk. It takes him nearly an hour to bring us up to speed. His presentation is brilliant, his command of the case dazzling. I'm struck too by the fluid way he speaks, weaving each thread with the others into a fully organized design.

'This,' he concludes with a sweeping gesture, 'is the case as explored by SFPD. What I have shown you is everything they've got.' He smiles, drops his pointer to his side. 'But not everything *I've* got,' he adds.

It's then that I take Hale's picture. He glares at me, surprised. As I take another, I feel his anger rise, prepare to take a third, and am almost disappointed when unexpectedly he grins. I think a truth he knew as a cop has suddenly come back, one my father once revealed and which I never forgot: an arrested person who tries to cover his face inevitably looks more guilty than one who faces the press with head held high.

'Sorry,' I tell him, 'I couldn't resist.'

'No harm done.'

'None intended.'

'But please, Miss Farrow, warn me before you shoot again.'

I agree, not only because I'm a guest in his home, but because I know any pictures I may take later are unlikely to surpass what I have just caught: the retired detective, mad and smug in his secret knowledge, surrounded by a chart that perfectly expresses his obsession.

Having done what I was brought along to do, I put my camera aside and listen. Hale, in exchange for what Joel has told him, reveals two facets of his own investigation, making sure we understand there's plenty more he's keeping to himself.

'First, victimology. We know the identities of only two of the original victims: Gary Kendall and Robbie Sipple. Kendall's the one who had the gall bladder operation and Sipple's the one,' Hale glances at me, 'rescued by your dad. Everyone knows what they had in common. Besides a certain physical look, which they shared with the other four, they'd sleep with anything in pants.'

Hale, I note, doesn't wince the way Dad did when he mentioned that all the T-case victims were gay. I'm surprised since Hale's of the generation of homophobic cops whose attitudes long stigmatized SFPD.

'No one except me went the extra mile to dig up more, not just what they shared in terms of looks, age, orientation, but also what they were actually like, the way they carried themselves. Both were what's called "cute" – not girlish necessarily, but good-looking and—'

'Androgynous?' I ask.

Hale nods. 'So by extrapolation we can assume the other four were probably the same.' He leans on his pointer. 'Maybe not all that important, you say.'

Joel looks up. 'We're not saying that.'

'True . . . but others did, the ones took charge after I left. In fact it *is* important, because cute's a special type, and not the most common around. Macho muscle, leather, preppy, poof, bear, queen – there're all these types of which cute is merely one. And, like any kind of tribe, each has its hang-outs and dating styles. Take The Gryphon, the bar where Sipple was picked up – that's known as a cute boy's pub. While I was still lead detective we covered it pretty well. Had Kendall ever been in there? Any regulars over the years who recently stopped coming in? The handsome, thirtyish guy who picked Sipple up – anyone seen him there before? No, no and no . . . but that was just one bar. So a year after I resigned, when it was obvious the official investigation was going nowhere fast. I worked up a list of cute boy spots around the city and started checking them out one by one.

'Sometimes I had trouble along the way. I'd been on TV a lot, people recognized me, many knew that I'd been hounded out of the Department. "What do you want, Hale? We don't have to talk to you – you're not a cop anymore." But I kept at it, kept smiling and talking, till I made the right connections. Ended up with my own private intelligence net. Pretty sweet, huh?'

Actually I have some difficulty imagining this crusty old man haunting a bunch of gay bars. Still I admire him for his persistence, even as I'm appalled by his lack of self-knowledge. 'Hounded out' seems a pretty tame phrase; 'found out' would be more accurate. But then, I remember, intimate self-knowledge is not a pre-requisite for being a cop.

Hale tells us how, over time, he came to view three individuals as suspects. One had a particular fondness for tattoos, another had a medical background, which meant training in dissection, the third had neither tattoo nor butchering experience, but was definitely handsome and twice Hale followed him to The Gryphon where he picked up and took home cute young Robbie Sipple types.

Over the years Hale gave up on the handsome man; interviews with his pick-ups convinced him he was sane and gentle. The doctor died of AIDS in 1988, which left him with the tattoo freak.

'He was legendary in the tattoo underground,' Hale tells us. 'Then around the time of the Sipple incident, he just cold dropped out. Wasn't seen again. People said he moved away.' Hale shrugs. 'I've got his prints. I hope someday to make a match.'

Which brings him, he says, to the second area he's willing to discuss – the missing evidence from Sipple's basement flat.

'When I was in charge I pulled the files of every man there that night, cops and paramedics alike. No matter what anyone says I never thought that evidence was lost.'

'Way I heard it,' I tell him, 'you called the cops in and told them they were assholes.'

Hale smiles. 'Which doesn't mean I thought they were. One of them took that material, and at least one other knows who did.'

'You're talking cover-up,' Joel says.

'Conspiracy's more like it.'

'Conspiracy to do what?'

'Obstruct justice. What other damn kind of conspiracy could it be?'

Not only Hale's words, but the gleam in his eyes tells me we're in paranoid country now, a murky land full of fogs and mists, where shadowy figures with nefarious aims scheme to thwart the honorable process of The Law. Frame-ups, hidden relationships, secret agendas are at work. Sometimes, of course, the mist parts, the fog lifts, and then, for an instant, you catch a glimpse of the master plot. Conspiracies are never simple. To penetrate one you must be as devious and sly as the conspirators. And sometimes, of course, a cigar is just a cigar, or, as in the case of Torsos, incompetent cops are merely incompetent cops.

'If someone covered up,' Joel says, 'there had to be a reason.'

Again a gleam in the eye accompanied by a knowing nod and the sweet tight-lipped smile of the insider.

'You're saying a cop did these killings?'

Hale shrugs. 'You said it, not me.'

'Come on, Inspector,' Joel goads, 'tell us what you think?'

'What I think isn't important. Only what I can prove.'

I recall Hilly's notion, that only an insider on the T case could have known how to mark Tim's body.

'Seems to me,' I tell him, 'you've got conflicting theories: a tattoo freak into cute young men who suddenly dropped out, and a cop who got rid of evidence because maybe it implicated himself.'

This time the nod's even more knowing, the tight-lipped smile verging on a smirk.

'Let's just say that what may appear conflicting to you, can, upon investigation, be resolved.'

The way Hale bites off these final words tells us he'll have no more to say. He leads us from his inner chamber back into his office. Closing the bookcase doors, he turns to me.

'I've been to see your dad.'

He lightly drops this news, perhaps knowing it will fall upon me like a bomb.

'Several times. He's always cordial. Makes a damn good loaf of bread.' Hale nods toward the ceiling. 'Alice says it's the best bread other side of the Bay.'

'What did you see him about?' I ask, trying to keep my voice level, disguise the feelings roiling within.

'The bondage hood. He had a good look at it. I thought he might remember how it was made. He was helpful, made some sketches, even accompanied me to a couple custom leather shops where we looked at hoods with similar features.'

So strange, I think, Dad didn't mention this . . . but then I had a feeling after our lunch that he'd left a great deal out.

'Earlier you said you thought he knew who lost the evidence.'

Hale grins. 'Did I say "lost"?'

His coy little smiles annoy me, but I refrain from displaying irritation. Instead, feigning loss of interest, I turn my attention back to Joel. Hale's a control-freak, a trait that undoubtedly served him well as he moved up the ladder at SFPD. One thing, I know, a control-freak can't abide is the notion he no longer dominates the room.

I figure Joel, being intuitive, will understand what I'm up to. But he still has questions of his own.

'What about the new case?' he asks.

'Copycat,' Hale snaps.

'A copycat's got to know what to copy."

'The body painting? We had tattoo experts in. Word on the designs got around.'

'So why did the killer use paint this time, and not tattoo?'

'Tattooing's difficult. You have to have tools and technique.'

'Is it really so difficult, Inspector? Convicts do it without special tools. There're books that tell you how.'

'It takes time.'

'The new killer had time enough to cut the man up.'

'We looked into that. An experienced butcher can cut up a human being in less than half an hour.'

'Then why the number seven?'

'An attempt to divert attention.'

'Is that really what you think? If tattooing's so crucial to your theory—'

'Who says it is?'

'Excuse me – didn't you say so?'

'There're things I said and a lot I didn't. You came here with something interesting so I returned the favor.'

Joel shrugs. 'Then perhaps the real story isn't the old unsolved case. It's the retired cop who refuses to give up.'

'How you play it's up to you,' Hale says . . . but I can tell he's pleased.

Ending on a note of mild flattery – that's Joel's technique. He's not the sort to go for broke in one interview, risking refusal when he requests a second. Rather he's the methodical journalist who comes back again and again building trust while each time subtly prying out a little more.

Out on the street, away from Hale's oppressive basement, I breathe in then deeply exhale. The air here may not be so heady, but at least it's clear. The air down in paranoid country was thick and close.

We get back into Melvin. I study Hale's house as we pull away. It may not be gothic, may lack a turret, but there's something sinister about a split-level on a sunny day with all the shades pulled and drapes drawn tight.

Joel doesn't speak until we're back on the Freeway.

'You know, kiddo – whenever I'm with someone like that I find myself drawn in. But once I get away and think about what he said it always starts sounding dumb.'

'Hale creates a force field,' I say. 'Inside it we're his prisoners.'

'Catch the smell in that kitchen?'

'Old Alice hates him. She burns his toast.'

Joel laughs. 'Takes an expert to burn toast, toasters being more or less infallible. Still, I wonder—' Joel strokes his goatee.

'What?'

'Why he did it?'

'The letters?'

Joel nods. 'He had everything going for him, was at the peak of his career. Then he threw it all away for nothing.'

'The old Greek formula for tragedy,' I suggest. 'Arrogant pride, a reckless act . . . then nemesis.'

'Like he willed his own downfall.'

'He was a detective, Joel. He knew typewriters leave a signature, yet he went ahead and used his own. Perhaps unconsciously he wanted to fall off the high wire. Couldn't take the pressure. Better to work the T case alone from a secret basement room than face his people everyday knowing sooner or later he'd have to admit he couldn't solve it.'

Joel shakes his head. 'Too rich for me, kiddo. Think of his disgrace – getting caught writing letters praising himself, ending his career as a laughingstock.'

'But what if he does solve it? Then who has the last laugh?'

'Don't kid yourself. It's been fifteen years. How the hell's he going to solve it now?'

JOEL DROPS ME AT Third near the new Museum Of Modern Art. I walk up Howard Street to the sharply angled doorway of Zeitgeist Gallery.

Zeitgeist presents itself as a showcase for young cutting-edge photographers. In LA it would be one of many; here it stands alone. The pristine white floor, white walls and ceiling erector-set lights gives it a drop-dead New York look.

The current show is of new work by Clury Bowen, huge color prints of masses of entwined yarn which, needless to say, I fail to appreciate. I may be the most conservative artist on the Zeitgeist roster, being more of a photojournalist than the kind of photographer who sets up scenes. The closest I came to that was in my *Watcher* series, for which I dressed a store mannequin in trench coat and fedora then posed him in shadowy doorways along the Tenderloin. Shooting from behind this 'watcher' my pictures of raw street life were imbued with a noirish quality people liked. I sold many more *Watcher* prints than prints from *Transgressions*.

I find Zeitgeist owner, Caroline Gifford, in her office off the gallery floor, bent over a lightbox studying transparencies. We smooch air. Caroline's dark hair is so thick it forms a cave around her face. She's plump, maternal, her eyes soft and mellow.

'Sorry I missed Clury's opening,' I lie. 'That *Guardian* review was mean.' Caroline winces. 'I'm here to show solidarity.'

'Sweet, Kay. Clury'll be thrilled!'

In fact, like most artists I know, I'm as guilty of *schadenfreude* as the next. Also I don't get it about Clury's work. Why photograph the yarn? Why not just hang it directly on the wall?

Caroline and I spend a few minutes dishing art gossip, who got a grant, who didn't, who made a big sale, the sad tale of the local sculptor whose entire New York show went unsold. This gives me a chance to ask about various prominent Bay Area collectors, which in turn enables me to drop the name Sarah Lashaw. Caroline mentions she's been in the gallery several times.

'My show?' I ask.

'Not the opening. I'd remember. But maybe later on.' Caroline grins. 'There's a reason you're asking, Kay?'

I nod. 'She had me over for lunch, boasted she'd seen the show, made a big point about having signed the book.'

'Easy enough to check.'

Caroline sends her assistant scurrying to the storage room to fetch the *Transgressions* guestbook from the files. The girl, blotchy-faced and bony, returns with a spiral-bound filler, the kind Caroline inserts into the handmade leather portfolio she keeps with her price-lists on the gallery desk.

Caroline opens it, starts reeling off the names of prominent local citizens – CEOs, socialites, successful venture capitalists. Caroline, in addition to her excellent eye, is a genius at cultivating collectors. She sees herself as a cultural ambassadress committed to ending visual arts provincialism in San Francisco. Photographs, she exhorts her wealthy friends, are art, and, isn't it great, they're also cheap!

'Ta ta!' Caroline shows me the signature: SARAH LASHAW, ST HELENA. 'Now own up – she wants to buy your work?'

'She tried to. I refused.'

'*Kay*! Get real! If you can get some of your pictures on to *her* walls, we'll have a real breakthrough!'

'Forget it,' I tell her. 'What she wants to buy she wouldn't dare expose.'

I taxi to City Stone Ground. Dad's out, but expected back soon. While I wait I hang out with the jovial Russian staff, and enjoy the great aroma, far less intense now than during baking time, but still, for me, ambrosia.

Tamara, a stout, middle-aged Georgian woman, wants me to persuade Dad to put in a special oven so she can make her native crackling flat bread.

'They will sell, Kay. I promise. Like how does Jack say? Hot cakes. No?'

I take some pictures of the crew. A few late shoppers appear. When the last of the day's bread is sold, Peter, Dad's second, posts a sign, SORRY, NO MORE BREAD on the door.

A few minutes later Dad appears. He's pleased to find me. I get a big hug, the staff gets thanks, he sends them home, locks up, then we walk together to his apartment.

He moved here a year after Mom took her life. He couldn't bear to stay on in the house where she had shot herself. He found a two-bedroom flat in a four-story rent-controlled building on Cherry Street, the second bedroom permanently reserved, he said, for me. In fact, having already flown the nest, I never once slept there. A few years later, after City Stone Ground started bringing in money, Dad bought the building, waited patiently for the resident families to move out, renovated the flats and is now a proud live-in landlord.

We sip vodka in the bay of his living room overlooking the pines of the Presidio. The room has a spare masculine look – huge TV, leather maroon recliners with seats worn smooth. No trace here of Dad's longtime girlfriend, Phyllis Sorenson. I've never understood whether they sleep here or at her place. Phyllis, a real estate top-producer, is fifteen years younger than Dad, an aggressive dyed-blonde painted-nails divorcee. She finds me scruffy; I find her over-groomed. We don't get along too well.

'I saw Hale this morning.'

I drop the bomb just as Dad settles in. I watch him carefully. As expected, he twitches his neck against his collar.

'Joel Glickman – you remember Joel, Dad?' He twitches again. 'He set the interview up. Hale lives over in Oakland. His wife keeps the drapes pulled during the day. Whenever she leaves a room she shuts the door. His den, down in the cellar, is set up like a T-case temple.'

'Jesus!'

'He told me he's been to see you several times.' Dad nods. 'When we had *dim sum* the other day, you didn't mention you'd made up.'

Dad sniffs. 'That what he says we've done?'

'He says you've been helpful to him, especially on the bondage hood.'

'Helpful doesn't mean we're friends.' Dad shuts his eyes. 'Hale's a nut.'

'A smart nut,' I correct. 'Sly, canny, the kind who can solve a tough case.'

'Oh, he was good. In his prime, probably the best. But it's been a long time since he slipped.'

'He's still obsessed with Torsos.'

'I'm not surprised . . . since it ruined him.'

'He thinks you know who took that hood from Sipple's.'

Dad sniffs again. 'Any chance, did he mention the taker's name?'
I shake my head. 'Easy to make an accusation, Kay. A little harder
to prove it.'

'You don't deny it.'

'That's what you want?'

Again he twitches as if to free his neck from a too-tight collar.
It's a familiar gesture, one I remember well from my childhood.
He'd do it whenever he got upset. I wonder if he does it now
because, entangled in a subterfuge, he imagines his neck caught in
a noose.

'Investigating me, are you?'

'I'm investigating the brutal murder of my friend. And since the T
case is connected and you were part of that . . . well, your name keeps
coming up.' I meet his eyes. 'Please, Dad – I need your help.'

He drinks down half his glass, sets it on the floor.

'Take it from an old cop – there's not a chance in hell the person
who did in Tim is the original T killer.'

'They say he knows things only cops knew at the time.'

'There were lots of cops and it's been lots of years.' He looks at
me. 'You want to know who lost that hood? Talk to the people who
were there that night. Maybe now someone'll admit it.'

'Waincroft, Hayes, Puccio, Vasquez.'

His eyes widen. He's stunned I know their names.

'Still see any of them?'

'Rusty sees Vasquez sometimes. He's the only one of us survived
in the department. He's a lieutenant now, some kind of division
chief. Truth is, I try to avoid them.'

'Still bitter?'

'It hurt to be driven out.'

'You weren't dismissed.'

He shakes his head. 'They made retirement the only option.
Funny thing – I never much liked being a cop, but I didn't like
being forced to give it up.' He smiles. 'Even though it was probably
the best thing could've happened to me, I wanted to make the
decision in my own sweet time.'

I know it's time to leave, that if I stay any longer we'll get into
something neither of us can deal with. But as much as I want to

go I can't. Rather I feel compelled to bring up the issue that, being unspoken so many years, makes us both uncomfortable.

He broaches it first. 'The other day, I told you I thought the end of my police career pushed your mother to—' He pauses. 'I imagine you've been giving that some thought?'

I admit to him that I have.

'I shouldn't have said it. Regretted it soon as I did. See, Kay – I'm convinced sooner or later she would have killed herself. I'm certain it had nothing to do with me.'

'Oh, Dad! Don't you see?'

'See what, darlin'? Tell me.'

'The *way* she did it, like a ruined cop. It's as if she did it *instead* of you – like she thought maybe you might do it, so to keep you from doing it she did it herself.'

'That's crazy!' He's twitching continuously now. His eyes, I notice, are moist. 'I wasn't corrupt! I wasn't disgraced! I had no damn' reason to eat my gun.'

''Course not! But what if *she* thought so? You said she was depressed. Maybe she did it as an act of love, thinking if she did then you wouldn't have to. In that way, you see, she did it *for* you.'

He shakes his head. He can't stand hearing this. He gets up, starts pacing the room, flicks on the TV, snaps it off. I feel terrible. I've pushed him too far, broken our contract of silence.

'Jesus, Kay! I've tried not to think about it. People kill themselves – that's part of life. It's been hard enough to live with that without having to wonder why.'

I make my voice gentle. 'You have to deal with it. It'll always haunt you otherwise.'

'But what you're saying, that she did it so I wouldn't – that's a heavy load to carry, darlin'. A very heavy load.'

I have had to carry it too, I remind him. To be the daughter of a suicide is to have one leg kicked out from under you. You teeter, unsure of who you are and whether a gene of self-destruction isn't at work somewhere inside.

'Listen, Dad, I've got to ask you this. You're the best organized, most reliable man I know. How come you didn't secure that evidence or make sure it was secured by someone else?'

He throws up his hands. 'Back to that! Give me a break, darlin'. Even the best players sometimes drop the ball. Remember, I'd just brought a guy back to life. I lost my concentration, screwed up. I'd never forgive myself if someone else got killed. Thank God the killings stopped. Maybe the perp freaked, realizing how close he'd come. Or . . .' He hesitates. There's a dreamy look in his eyes.

'What?'

'Just something that's crossed my mind over the years. Pretty ridiculous, if you want to know.'

'Tell me.'

'Maybe the guy who tied up Sipple had nothing to do with the T case. It was a coincidence. Or maybe,' he smiles at the notion, 'the whole Sipple thing was just a plant.'

It's dark when I leave. Outside I feel as I did after visiting Hale: relieved to be in the open air.

I stop at a discount pharmacy on Sacramento, phone Joel at home, tell him I think we ought to see the four other cops who were there the night the Sipple evidence was lost. Joel says he's been the thinking the same thing. 'But why only four?' he asks.

'Because I just saw the fifth,' I tell him. 'I'm still shaking from the encounter.'

'Calm yourself, kiddo.'

'How can I? He's my dad.'

I recount the conversation. It helps to share the pain. When I come to Dad's last words, the possibility Sipple wasn't connected or a plant, Joel points out how interesting it is the way both Hale and Dad dummy up when trying to explain the loss.

Walking up Hyde to my building, I spot someone lingering in the shrubbery that demarcates the Alice Marble Tennis Courts. No danger – I'm on the sidewalk and the hedge here is extremely thick. I pause beneath a streetlight and peer into the darkness. Silence as I scan the bushes searching out the eyes of the voyeur. A rustling of branches, then a face appears amidst the leaves.

'What're you doing there, Drake?'

'Waiting for you to come home safe.'

He stares at me then disappears. I hear him as he retreats into the shadows and the brush.

In the elevator, ascending to my floor, I wonder how much Drake knows about me, whether he's aware of Sasha's late-night visits. Is he infatuated with me or merely my self-appointed guardian? In either case, I resolve, I must remember to draw my blinds.

I fall asleep around eleven, only to be awakened after midnight by the delicate touch of Sasha's hand upon my breast. I've given him my key, urged him to sneak in on me, throw himself upon me, take me harshly like a beast. He acknowledges my fantasy but says he can't bring himself to fulfill it. Too fine a gentleman is Dr C. Patel. Even so I like his style of lovemaking – slow, thoughtful, ever so chivalrous.

I don't open my eyes, instead present myself to him half somnambulant, moaning beneath his expert ministrations. He leaves me hours later as stealthily as he came, his sandalwood smell upon my body, the delicious taste of him upon my lips.

In the morning my mailbox yields a letter addressed to Tim, forwarded by Gordon from MAIL FROM HOME. It's postmarked San Francisco with no return address. I open it, find a note handwritten on the stationery of The Sultan's Tent, a posh boutique hotel near Alamo Square. The handwriting's familiar. Then I remember the postcard from Florence:

> *Gorgeous One:*
> *In town at last! Am here in my usual room awaiting your silken presence. I shall sing for four nights and then be ready for play. Please stay abstinent from the time you receive this. On the night of the seventeenth, present yourself here at 9:00 p.m., announce yourself as 'Carlo' . . . and violate me!*
> *Your devoted*
> *J*
>
> *P.S. I know I can count on your fine discretion!*

I dig out the old postcard. It was signed Jerome. I pull my *Chronicle* out of the wastebasket, open it to the arts section, check the listings. This week the San Francisco Opera is presenting *Tristan und Isolde*. Among the scheduled singers: the American Wagnerian tenor, Jerome Tattinger.

I spend the morning developing and printing the roll I shot of Sho. With his sharp, triangular chin and modeled Native American features, he's got the looks to make it as a model. I select two of the images, one full-face, the other a strong profile with the wind raising his hair. I make him twenty prints of each, laborious work, but I want him to succeed, find a way to make a living so he'll no longer have to work the Gulch.

I try writing a note to Jerome Tattinger, something I can safely leave for him at the Opera box-office. After three attempts I realize that nothing I can put on paper will be discreet yet clear enough to gain me an audience. There is, of course, an alternative: I can show up at The Sultan's Tent in place of Tim. Though not especially crazy about the idea, I don't rule it out.

Joel calls, excited. Hilly has left chalk marks signalling she wants a meet. According to our contact code, three-way meetings are to take place at 10 p.m. at The Rough Rider bar the evening following the day the marks are left.

After dinner I walk down to the Gulch looking for Sho to give him his headshots. I don't find him, instead come upon Slick in the classic one-foot-against-the-wall hustler's stance, which, suggesting loneliness, is so seductive.

Since he and Sho are buddies, I hand him the prints.

'Can I look at them, Bug?' When I nod he opens the envelope, gazes at the first shot and gasps. 'You really make people pretty,' he says, lightly touching his white eyebrows. He looks at me, then primps . . . as if I'm a mirror. 'Could you make me pretty too?'

'You're already pretty.'

'Yeah, like pretty . . . weird.'

As someone who squinted a lot and couldn't see colors, I have no trouble imagining the kind of abuse Slick took as a kid. 'Pink Eyes!' 'Colorless!' The taunts were probably worse since to be albino is to wear one's affliction on one's face. Achromatopsia, at least, is a hidden malady.

I invite him for coffee. We walk a block to Roy's, the grungy place Crawf and I went after Shanley showed me Tim's head.

I ask Slick about his date with Sho and the man in the big Jaguar who picked them up.

'Guy's fussy, fussy.' Slick pauses. 'Tim used to go with him. I won't see him alone, tell you that.'

'Because he's dangerous?'

Slick shrugs. 'Any of Tim's old johns – I'm real careful now.' He shows a sickly smile. 'Don't wanna die.'

Yeah . . . but suddenly I'm angry with Tim. So many things he didn't tell me, so many sides he didn't show – world-class opera singers, johns in Jaguars, a boyhood in a magician's troupe, a strange twin sister into bizarre sex for pay. I still want desperately to find out who killed him, yet now, I wonder, did he really view me as a friend? I think he did, yet he held back so much . . . and that wounds me still.

When I arrive at The Rough Rider, I find Joel alone nursing a beer, looking awkward in a new ill-fitting glossy black jacket.

I slip in beside him, peck his cheek, then check out the jacket . . . which, it turns out, isn't made of leather.

'Vinyl! Oh, Joel!'

'Looks good, huh?'

'No. And it doesn't feel good either. Where'd you get it?'

'Discount place. Eighty-nine ninety-five.'

'Figures. Why'd you bother?'

'I don't want to look out of place.'

I peer around. The joint is filled with tough-looking leathermen in motor-cycle jackets with close-cropped hair and beards. Poor Joel! A Pulitzer Prize, two decades as an investigative journalist, and he's still too cheap to buy himself a proper San Francisco disguise.

'Take it off before Hilly gets here,' I advise, 'unless you want her to take you for a dork.'

Joel barely has his jacket off and stuffed behind his back when Hilly shows up in tight jeans and body-molded vest.

'Hi, guys!'

Tonight she's wired, less interested in flaunting her orientation than providing us with information. 'First thing yesterday morning we have a meeting in Captain's Charbeau's office. Shanley, me and a Lieutenant Vasquez from vice crimes.'

'Luis Cruz Vasquez?' I ask.

Hilly nods. 'Himself. So okay, the guys are talking. Being the junior detective in the room, I stay quiet. Shanley brings everyone up to speed, which is basically we got zilch, he's pursuing a john-did-it theory and I'm still working on connections to the old T case. At that point you'd think Vasquez would mention *his* connection . . . but he doesn't. Meantime Charbeau's getting antsy. After a couple minutes – this is why I signalled you guys – Charbeau says, like out of thin air: "Why're we gangbanging this so hard?"

'We all look at him surprised. Shanley goes: "What do you mean?" "What I mean," Charbeau says, "it's just another cocksucker killing, right?" I go: "'*Scuse me!*" They all turn to me with these Oh–we-forgot-*she*-was-in-the-room! expressions.'

I find myself liking this direct, indignant Hilly more than the canny ambitious woman I've been dealing with.

'Charbeau's black, tough as hell. Now he realizes he's offended me. He starts to back-pedal. "Vice crimes wants to help out. They know the hustlers and johns. Lieutenant Vasquez asked to sit in on account of the gay felony prostitution angle." Figuring that's enough to keep me from filing a grievance, Charbeau adjourns the meeting.

'Immediately Vasquez takes off down the hall, me chasing after. "Hey! Lieutenant, Lieutenant Vasquez, sir! Please, sir, a precious moment of your time." I finally catch him at the elevators. He glares at me, annoyed. "Yeah, detective, what's on your mind?" "Just this, sir—" I sputter. "I know you were there the night Sipple was attacked and I was wondering if you had any thoughts you'd like to pass on. Like who beside Hale's task-force knew the details of the T killer's MO?'

'Vasquez, he's six one, stares down at me like I'm some kind of bug. "Why don't you move your fanny back to the squad room, detective, before I have a talk with your Captain?" Just then the elevator opens, he steps in, stares straight ahead like I don't exist and pushes the button for the executive floor.'

It's a good vignette, Joel says, atmospheric too, but, he tells Hilly, it doesn't prove there's any kind of cover-up. A hustler homicide is bound to annoy the Homicide Division chief, if only because such cases are rarely solved. As for Vasquez, it's understandable he doesn't want to be reminded of what was undoubtedly the nadir of his career.

'Still,' I point out, 'he came to the meeting. If he wasn't interested why did he bother?'

'I don't know,' Hilly says, 'but I'll tell you this – if he'd used just two more words, like "*wiggle* your *juicy* fanny back to the squad room," I'd have brought him up on a sex harassment charge.'

After Hilly leaves, Joel, uncomfortable in the bar, offers to drive me home. In the car we discuss Hilly's story. He says she was right to call for a meeting; any documentation police are dragging their feet only makes the Gulch story better.

Then, since we're going to be speaking to Vasquez, we discuss whether to reveal how much we know.

'Can't,' Joel says. 'Minute we do he'll know Hilly's the leak. He'll tell the others, they'll all be wary of her and Charbeau'll pull her off the case.'

'So what do we do – act like we *don't* know he's aware?'

'Absolutely!' Joel smiles. 'I'd love it if he lied.'

We plan the interviews: I'll do the taping; Joel'll make the calls and set them up. After he drops me, I spend a couple of minutes walking the perimeter of Sterling Park trying to catch a glimpse of Drake. No sign of him, so I enter my building, take the elevator up. The moment I step into the little vestibule on my floor, I realize something's wrong.

My door, which I always lock, is open an inch. I move toward it cautiously, and, hearing nothing, push it open all the way. When I turn on my foyer lights I discover the lock's been jimmied. Then, peering inside, I see the mess.

Books and papers are scattered on the floor. All my living-room furniture's up-ended. My telescope is broken like someone stamped hard on the tube. And there's a foul smell in the room. It takes me a moment to locate the source: a pile of excrement in the center of the rug left by the invaders to show me their contempt.

I quickly check the other rooms. Nothing broken in the kitchen, but in my bedroom all the contents of my closets and drawers have been pulled out, ripped up and strewn. My underwear is in tatters, several pieces festoon my bedside lamp. My mattress has been gouged with a knife, my bedding ripped. In the bathroom I find my toilet clogged with condoms and tampons from the cupboard.

Sick in my gut, I check out my office. It's been hit the worst. My computer discs are gone, my computer screen is smashed, the keys of my keyboard have been pried loose and one of my screwdrivers has been jammed into the disk drive. My flat files have also been rifled, prints torn up then piled on my light table where they've been covered with some sort of tar. The flow-chart I constructed has been ripped from the walls; all the pinned-up photographs are gone. In their place horrible words have been spray-painted on to the cork: DIE!CUNT!DIE!; DIE STINKING BITCH. One of my self portraits lies on the floor, eyes viciously cut from my face.

I rush to the darkroom. My enlarger's been vandalized, my enlarging lenses are missing, but the door of my negative safe is still intact. The one roll of negatives I was working with, the roll I shot of Sho, lies scrambled in the sink.

More insults spray-painted in here: SUCK ME WHORE; EAT SHIT & DIE; FUCKING CUNT EAT SHIT. The intruders' message is clear: we're brutal; we've violated you; to us your art is trash; our threats are sexual; our scatological attack is but a warning; next time we'll rip your body as we ripped your underwear.

I return to the living room, face the windows, cry out to the city, howl out my rage. I yell a few times, then, hands shaking, dial 911. Trying to keep my voice level, I tell the operator what's happened. She advises me not to touch anything and wait downstairs if I'm afraid. Officers, she kindly assures me, are already on their way.

Still standing at my window amidst the debris, I look out at San Francisco. It appears so calm, still, beautiful behind the glass. The Bay, too, is still, reflecting the moon. Traffic on the bridges moves like molten metal. The Alcatraz light sweeps my face, paints my walls, moves on. Feeling frightened, alone, terribly vulnerable, I suddenly yearn for my father's embrace. Then, resolving to be strong, I decide that first thing in the morning I'll go out and buy myself a gun.

TWELVE

KIM COATES AND DAVID Choy, a pair of good San Francisco cops, show up eight minutes later. Both in their twenties, one black, the other Chinese, they arrive while I'm still photographing the damage.

They analyze the means of entry (Kim: 'Hate to tell you this, Ms Farrow – your front door lock is crap') and the pattern of destruction (David: 'Probable reason they didn't break dishes is fear of alerting the neighbors'). Apparently the only decent lock I have is the one on my negative safe, bought to protect against fire, not burglary.

Andy Lamott, landlord and resident manager, is the next to appear. He and his brother inherited the building; Andy now occupies the penthouse floor. He's a dignified, sweet-natured guy in his forties, not above performing such menial chores as shining the brass in the elevator cab and sweeping the sidewalk out front. Awakened by the rumpus, he appears in jacket and tie to apologize for my ordeal. Building security, he promises, will be immediately upgraded. He'll install a closed-circuit TV system, the motion-activated kind, to videotape all entrances and exits. And first thing in the morning he'll put a new security lock and alarm on my door.

'My brother and I, Ms Farrow, are very proud of our building and equally proud of our distinguished tenants.'

Such gallantry!

Sasha, turning up at midnight for fun and games, spots the patrol car out front. Storming in like a knight-on-white-charger, he's relieved to find me safe. He assists as, with Kim's and David's permission, I scrape the shit off the living-room rug. Then he flips my mattress and makes up the bed with fresh linen, while I gather up torn clothing, underwear, ruined prints and broken equipment into garbage bags. When Sasha's finished with the bed, he finds a can of touch-up paint in the kitchen and sets to work painting over the graffiti.

By this time the cops are finished. Kim tells me I'll be hearing from a detective in the morning.

'We take sexual threats of this kind very seriously,' she says.

As soon as they're gone, I collapse into Sasha's arms.

'Soon, Kay,' he says, wiping away my tears, 'this ugliness will pass as water runs through sand.'

Sasha, I decide, would make a terrific psychiatrist. I resolve to steer him toward this specialty away from his current preference, gynecology.

In the morning there's a sympathy note from the elderly couple who live downstairs. If this had happened in New York, I doubt anyone would have shown concern, but here in San Francisco we observe the old-fashioned niceties.

To forestall the intervention of another detective, I report the invasion to Hilly. And since it's legitimate police business, I phone her directly at the Hall of Justice.

She agrees there's an almost certain connection to the beating provoked by my follow-up on Tim's murder. Then Shanley comes on the line.

'Cowardly little shits!' he says when I repeat the story. He promises I won't have to deal with a new detective; he'll have my case attached to Tim's. 'We told you to leave the investigating to us. Lay off now, Kay. Trust us to do our job.'

My next call's to Dad at City Stone Ground. He's horrified but quick to dissuade me from acquiring a gun.

'A threat mean as that, darlin' – of course you take it seriously. But with a good lock they won't get in again. Packing a gun – that's different, that's taking it to another level. You'll need a permit, and, if it's going to do you any good, a firearm combat-training course. You're better off living defensively for a while – staying off dark streets, and, when you go out, being sure to watch your back.' Good advice, but I'm not so enamored of his next suggestion, echoing Shanley's, that I leave the matter to the cops.

'I'm not playing Nancy Drew here,' I remind him. 'I'm a photographer working on a project.'

'Pretty dangerous project, sounds like to me.'

'Yes, dangerous,' I agree, 'but have you ever known me to chicken out?'

A brief pause while Dad thinks that over. 'Never, darlin' – I'm proud to say.'

'I'm going to keep on doing what I've been doing,' I tell him, 'and we'll just have to see what they do next.'

Mid-morning I contemplate walking down to Polk to buy a selection of organic fruits and vegetables for Drake. Then I decide that would look too much like a bribe. This isn't a game, I remind myself, and Drake's not a pet.

I repair empty-handed to 'our' bench in Sterling Park, take a seat and wait for him to show.

I sit there undisturbed for twenty minutes, straight-backed and apprehensive so he knows I'm waiting for him, not just resting my bones. From the excitement last night he's certain to know what happened and he may know a good deal more. So why is he keeping me waiting like this? Is he timid, afraid of getting involved? Or is he afraid I'll be angry with him for inadequately guarding my home?

I pass the time thinking about George Sterling, poet of the city for whom this park was named. There are San Franciscans who still call him 'our Baudelaire' because of his famous couplet: 'The blue-eyed vampire, sated at her feast/Smiles bloodily against the leprous moon'. Born just after the Civil War, he was a great pal of Jack London and Ambrose Bierce. The latter wrote him: 'You shall be the poet of the skies, the prophet of the suns'. For years he was a local romantic literary figure. Theodore Dreiser described him as hovering over the city 'like a burnished black holy ghost'. In 1926, in his room at the Bohemian Club, he killed himself, like so many in his circle, with cyanide.

I hear a branch snap behind me.

'That you, Drake?'

'It's me.' From his voice I can tell he's close, just a few yards behind the bench. I don't turn for fear of scaring him off.

'Want to sit with me a while?'

He takes a seat at the opposite end, leaving an empty space between us. Knowing he's eyes-shy, I glance quickly at him, then away.

'I looked for you when I came home last night.'

'I saw you.'

'But you didn't show yourself.' No response. 'You know what I found upstairs?'

'They did bad things.'

'Yes, Drake. They tore up my place, ripped my clothes, ruined my computer. They wrote awful things on the walls. Threatening things.' Again, no response. 'Did you see them?'

He whispers: 'Yes.'

'Want to tell me who they were?'

This time, when he doesn't answer, I turn to engage him. He's staring out across the path toward a clump of leptospermum trees whose thick exposed roots undulate like serpents.

'Help me, Drake. Please.'

He bites on his lip. The sun glints off his hair. 'No cops,' he says.

'No cops. Just you and me. I have to know so I can protect myself. You understand, don't you?'

Silence, then: 'I went to college, Kay.'

For a moment I'm puzzled, then I understand. I'm talking to him like he's a child, stupid and uneducated. He wants me to know he's not.

'Chemistry major,' he adds. 'I didn't graduate. Too much stress. But I got good grades.' He sighs. 'Maybe someday I'll go back and finish.'

'Which college?'

'Reed,' he says casually.

I believe him. He could be a brilliant boy, high-strung, mentally disturbed but with an IQ in the stratosphere. The streets of Berkeley are filled with emotional cripples, clever kids who somehow got off-track. So why not also the Hermit of Sterling Park?

Time now to let him talk. I've made my plea; I can only hope he'll tell me what he knows. Meantime we engage in neighborhood gossip, not the kind I'd be likely to hear from anyone else, rather Drake's own odd angle on people as viewed through the prism of his madness.

'The white-haired lady with the schnauzer,' he says, 'the one who talks to her dog all the time?'

I nod.

'I've heard what she says to him. She talks about current events. She'll say "The situation in Russia is grave, isn't it, Leopold?" That's the dog's name. And then she'll wait for him to reply. He doesn't of course, but she pretends he does. Then she'll say, "I'm not sure I agree with that view, Leopold. There's an economic aspect I think you've overlooked." She'll talk to him like that for a whole hour, walking him around the park. Then she'll stop right in the middle of the conversation. "Go on, Leo! Go on, boy! Make poopy for Mommy! Make good poopy now!"' Drake turns to me. 'See, she calls him Leopold when they're talking like intellectuals, but just plain Leo when she remembers he's a dog.'

Drake continues with tales of other Russian Hill eccentrics. Our neighborhood has its share. Some of his vignettes are sad, others charming, all reflect his off-beat view. Suddenly he claps his forehead. He looks at me, then away.

'Three of them. It was dark. I'm not sure, Kay, but I think the same ones beat you up. One waited across the street. He had a phone. The other two went in carrying bags. Then I saw beams in your rooms.'

'Beams?'

'From flashlights, beams criss-crossing in the dark. They were there ten minutes. When they came out the three of them crossed here . . . and out this way.' Drake gestures toward the steep steps that lead down to Larkin.

'Did they pass close?'

'Maybe twenty feet.'

'Did you recognize them?'

Drake ponders. 'One of them. I've seen him here a couple of times. He comes into the park, watches your place. He never sees me.'

'How do you know he watches my place?'

'I figured that out last night.'

'Can you describe him?'

'Stocky, muscular.' Drake combs his fingers through his scraggly beard. 'Buzz cut, goatee. He's not a nice man.'

You sure got that right! I think.

'Did he go upstairs?'

Drake shakes his head. 'He was the one with the phone.'

'If I showed you some pictures, do you think you could pick the men out?'

Drake smiles. 'Like the police?'

'But not for them, Drake. Just for me, okay?'

'I'll try.'

'That would be a big help.'

'You're my friend,' he declares.

I reach across the bench, take his hand. 'I have to go. I've still got a lot to do.'

He pulls his hand away. 'One thing?' His voice sounds urgent. 'The . . . mmmmman who cccccomes.'

The stutter is new to me. Feeling his tension, I try to relax him with a smile.

'What man?'

'The dark one who comes to see you very late.'

'That's Sasha.'

'Is he your bbbboy ffffriend?'

'Well,' I smile, 'come to think of it, I guess he is.'

Drake smiles sweetly, apparently relieved the dark man is not a stalker. But leaving him, I realize he's not only my secret admirer but also a kind of stalker himself.

Returning home I find Andy installing my new lock and alarm. His handyman is in the bathroom unplugging my toilet with a plumber's snake. Inspired by these efforts, I go to work. My first call is to the Kavakian Carpet Cleaning Company to arrange a pick up and steam-cleaning of my rug. Then I call Beds Unlimited and order a new queen-size mattress.

I call my favorite photographic supply house, order a new Beseler 45MXT enlarger with Aristo cold light head, 50mm and 75mm Rodenstock enlarging lenses, a new grain focusing scope and twenty boxes of assorted printing papers – all to be shipped by next-day air. I consider ordering a new Contax G1 but decide to put that off. Perhaps my stolen camera will turn up; meantime I'll keep working with the Nikon.

A new computer can wait; a telescope cannot. I phone Omega Optics and order a new Celestron. Now, with my credit card nearly maxed out, all I need are undies. I slip on a pair of shades and take the Hyde Street cable car downtown. At Nordstrom I go mad in the lingerie department, a first for me since I usually buy underwear at discount. On my way home, clutching my purchases, the cable car rattling up the hill, I realize my real work lies ahead – making hundreds of new prints to replace the ones destroyed. But no matter. There is satisfaction that my negatives, my capital, escaped unscathed.

*　　*　　*

Sasha's managed to switch night duty with another resident and will be by in an hour to pick me up. Since he was so sweet last night, I decide to please him. I apply lipstick and eyelash liner, put on a black silk blouse and pants over my sexy new black lace bra and panties, and slip on black pumps instead of boots. 'Kay!' he exclaims when he arrives. 'You're all dressed up for a date.'

'Right,' I tell him, kissing him on the lips. 'A one hundred percent wowie-zowie date. Our first!'

He takes me to Eden Roc, a dinner club on Nob Hill. We make our entrance descending a curved staircase lit by Deco period sconces. The tablecloths are damask, the waiters wear tuxedos and there's a separate snack menu featuring luxury foods – smoked salmon, foie gras, varieties of caviar. Entertainment is provided by Sheila Hudson, an old-time torch singer, belting out classic world-weary tunes: 'When My Baby Left Me'; 'I Get a Kick Out of You'.

Sasha says he's amazed at my manner, that I seem almost serene.

I tell him I am. 'Being beaten up then invaded – it's been bad, but not as bad as I'd have thought. I coped, survived, and here I am. I don't know why, but I'm feeling good.'

'You're a brave girl, Kay.'

'You can say that after you've seen me cry?'

'Nothing wrong with shedding a tear or two. I occasionally shed a few myself.'

'You?' I gaze into his deep liquid eyes, eyes that never fail to move me. 'What could possibly make you weep?'

Sasha smiles. 'Lots of things – homesickness, missing my mother, my sisters. Also the miseries of the world, people who starve, patients I try to save and then must watch as they die. Then all the little rudenesses, incivilities, petty meannesses and cruelties of life. Human viciousness . . . as reflected in those awful writings on your walls. I had to paint them over, Kay – I couldn't bear leaving them there to poison your eyes.' He smiles again. 'I know what you're thinking: "My hard little brown lover – he's perhaps not so tough as I thought. He's a" – how did Humphrey Bogart put it in that film – "a sentimentalist?" Maybe I am. It's not the worst insult, is it?'

I'm impressed, moved. 'I think I'd call you a humanist, Sasha.'

'Ah!' He smiles. 'I like that even better!'

'I think I misjudged you.'

'I believe you did.' He gazes at me. 'So tell me, how *did* you judge me until tonight?'

A tricky question. I have to be careful. 'I found you charming.' He nods. 'Extraordinarily handsome.' He bows. 'Vain.' He smiles. 'Sexy.' He demurs.

'But—?'

'But perhaps also a little . . . superficial.'

He grins. 'Better than empty.'

'You aren't either, Sasha. You're quite marvelous. You know it, and now I know it too.'

He leans forward. 'Tell me, Kay – do you think perhaps you might come to love me one day? Can you give me some small hope for that?'

I don't know what to say, so take the easy path. 'Let's talk about it next spring,' I suggest. 'Meantime, see how things go.'

A little later, Sasha again makes me see colors, rockets that shoot up, explode, branch out, shoot, explode and branch again until the blackness is flooded with brilliant sparks to which I add imaginary hues: jasper, henna, garnet, honey, beet red, blood red, blush . . .

'I fear for you,' he whispers against my neck. 'I want to protect you from all the dangers.'

God! This gorgeous man's not only a sentimental humanist, he's a real old-fashioned romantic! Lucky me, writhing in his arms. What was it he called himself – my hard little brown lover? How about my silken-fleshed South Asian prince who licks me with his silver tongue and prongs me with his golden cock? My salty dusky Gujarati doctor who plays me like a flute, makes my body arch, fills my head with lovely rainbows?

In the morning, as soon as my new gear arrives, I set to work in the darkroom making prints. Not fine prints for exhibition, just legible images so I can again lay out my project on the wall. But first I create a mini Rogues' Gallery of Polk Gulch hustlers for Drake, all the usual suspects plus Tim, Crawf, Slick, Remo, and, of course, Marcus Crane. When I'm done I separate out my suspects, then place them at random in the pack.

I work like a demon through the afternoon, stopping only to munch fruit. A little after 7:00 p.m., losing concentration, I decide to knock off for the day. In the middle of my shower, I suddenly realize today is the seventeenth. Tonight at 9 Tim's devoted J will be expecting him at The Sultan's Tent.

Should I or should I not attend the gentleman? I can make decent arguments either way. As I towel off I decide. Curiosity demands I go . . . and I know I'll despise myself for cowardice if I don't.

The Sultan's Tent has been carved out of the old Demoine Mansion, a Moorish fantasy of domes, arches, minarets, built at the turn-of-the-century by an eccentric sugar baron. Situated on a cul-de-sac off Alamo Square, it dominates the surrounding Victorians.

Heavily damaged in the 1906 earthquake, it was converted into a rooming house in the 30s. After decades of neglect, it was boarded up in the 80s after being declared uninhabitable by city authorities. Five years ago a pair of smart entrepreneurs bought it cheap then spent a fortune on renovation. Regilding the domes, retiling the minarets, they turned it into a luxurious boutique hotel catering to visiting soloists, singers and conductors in town to perform with the San Francisco Opera and Symphony.

Dressed in my usual tough-girl garb, Nikon around my neck, I enter the main courtyard through an arch. At once the sounds of the street are replaced by the rustle of leaves, tinkle of wind-chimes, murmur of running water. I'm in an ersatz Moorish garden planted with palms and aromatic plants. At its center is a marble fountain feeding a rectangular pool stocked with lily pads and carp.

Octagonal lanterns of perforated metal shed soft light upon the paths. I follow one to a terrace where two women in evening gowns sit on a swing couch conversing softly while puffing on attenuated cigarettes.

Seeing what looks to be a lounge, I pass through another arch, enter a domed room carpeted with overlapping Persian rugs. At the opposite side I find the reception desk. A clock above shows the time.

'How may I help you?' asks the snooty clerk. He wears a dark blazer bearing the hotel monogram, sports a blond pompadour and manicured nails.

'Jerome Tattinger, please.'

'You have an appointment?' I nod. He looks me over skeptically. 'Whom shall I announce to Mr Tattinger?'

'Tell him Carlo is here.'

'*Carlo?*' He raises one eyebrow.

'You got it.' I stare him down.

Snooty shrugs, picks up a phone, announces my arrival. 'Very good, sir!' Snooty hangs up, shows me a leer. 'He'll see you in his room . . . Carlo.'

'Which room?'

'Mr T *only* stays in our Seraglio Suite. Two flights up the curving staircase,' he gestures, 'then through the red door surrounded by cherubs.'

The red door looks black to me, but the cluster of cherubs gives me confidence. I pull a rope, hear the tinkle of a bell, then a warm bellow: 'Enter, Gorgeous One!'

I take a deep breath and walk in. The first room, an oval, is dimly lit. Silk tenting covers the ceiling and cascades down the walls.

'In here! The sanctum sanctorum.'

I cross the oval and peer into a second smaller room, dark and also tented. A plump middle-aged male lies naked on the bed, face-down, rump up, legs spread, supported by pillows.

'Please . . . I can't wait . . . violate me, Gorgeous One!' he begs, twitching his butt. 'Afterwards we'll talk and drink.'

Petrified I remain in the doorway. I can't make out his face.

'Damnit, boy! What're you waiting for?'

'Tim's dead,' I murmur.

Tattinger freezes. Then he flops on to his back. 'I don't – another game—' He sees me, screams, frantically covers himself with bedding. 'I thought you were – Oh, God!' He spots my camera. 'Please, no pictures. *Please!*'

'No pictures,' I promise. 'I mean you no harm. I was his friend. I found your note in his mail. I wanted to write you but was afraid someone would see the letter. So I came myself. I didn't mean to scare you. Really.'

He peers at me. He's holding bedding to his chin. 'Come closer, girl. Let me see your face.'

I approach, curious to see his as well.

'Sit here on the side of the bed.'

I sit.

His hair is thin on top, his face puffy, his jowls thick. Neither ugly nor particularly good-looking, I might take him for a banker if it weren't for the compelling quality of his voice.

'Your name?' I tell him. 'Do you know mine?' I nod. 'You truly wish me no harm?' I nod again. 'You gave me quite a start, young lady.' The words roll from him. 'Actually, when I heard your voice I thought you were someone else.'

'Another woman?' He nods. 'Amoretto?'

He smiles. 'So you know her. Why didn't *she* come tonight?'

'She doesn't go out much these days.'

'I see.' He squints at me. 'Tell me what happened . . . if you can.'

As I tell him how Tim was killed and my commitment to discovering by whom, tears start pulsing from his eyes. I like him immediately for this display, also his shamelessness at being caught butt-in-the-air.

'Let me hold you, dear.' He reaches for me.

Without thinking I lay beside him. Immediately he wraps me in his arms. I feel his strength, then his body tremble as he sobs against my hair. Soon I'm sobbing too. I feel as I did with David deGeoffroy, relieved to be with someone with whom I can share my grief. It doesn't matter to me that Jerome Tattinger most likely met Tim on the street. All that matters is that he loved him enough that now, hearing he is no longer in the world, he weeps.

We lie this way for several minutes, soothing each other until finally we lie still.

'He was so beautiful. It hurts me to think of his body broken. You know, my dear, I sometimes imagine him when I sing: his face, the curve of his lips, those incredible eyes. His comeliness has been an inspiration to me. As it will continue to be. Something so special about that boy . . .'

I wait in the oval living room while he splashes water on his face. When he rejoins me he's wearing a dark silk dressing gown and monogrammed slippers, carrying a bottle of chilled Champagne.

'A toast to his memory?'

I nod. He wraps the bottle in a napkin, pops the cork and pours us each a glass.

'Dear Tim, wherever you are, may you always have good cheer.' He clinks his glass against mine, then drains it off.

'I'm a not-especially-attractive fifty-eight-year-old man,' he confesses. 'Nevertheless, I like to think he held me in some esteem. Oh, I paid him for his services and we played all kinds of nasty games. I would grovel before him, beseech him to hurt me.' He laughs. 'He often did. But still there was something deep between us, something money can't buy.' He refills his glass. 'Intimacy, my dear. You see, in my foolish self-indulgent life I've lain with many boys, but with very few have I felt such trust.'

I like listening to him. He is, I understand, a world-class singer renowned as much for his dramatic abilities as for the warm, sonorous timbre of his voice. To listen to him is to harken to him, for his voice is like a magnet.

He tells me he is on the road nearly the whole year long, fulfilling engagements in opera houses around the world. In each city he has a favorite hotel, usually a favorite suite, and in most a favorite boy he has selected after numerous try-outs and escapades.

'In Milano there's Roberto. In Paris . . . Jean-Louis. Hans in Vienna, Roger in London, Dick in New York. But the one I loved best was my beloved Tim, he of the green eyes and what I call the *ephebe*'s girdle. He had such a slim, hard, pale, hairless body, you know – such a big heart, such a tender touch . . .'

Ephebe: the Greek word for adolescent male, the very word I used to describe Tim to myself. Hearing Jerome employ it I share with him my conception of Tim as a gentle warrior of the city, perhaps doomed to being a sacrificial victim of its lust.

He loves my concept. It appeals, he tells me, to his Wagnerian taste for mysticism, melodrama, archetypes. Within half an hour he finishes off the rest of the Champagne, then retreats to his sanctum sanctorum to fetch another bottle from the minibar.

'So you met Amoretto?' I ask when he returns.

He raises his eyebrows, grins fiendishly. 'I did indeed!'

'She, Tim and you— ?'

'Yes, my dear. And, if you'll allow me, the word for what we did is . . . *partouze*. Oh, I know – on the vulgar street they call it a "sandwich", in the suburbs a "threesome". The mathematical types, I believe, say "three-way". I much prefer the French word. Listen to it again: *Part-ouze* . . .' He enunciates slowly, drawing out each syllable. 'Delicious the way it almost imitates the slippery sucky sounds one makes. So delightful, wicked, sinfully carnal and hedonistic.' He burps. 'Actually, I rather enjoyed the ordeal – which is not to say I'd want to partake again.'

'It was Tim's idea?'

'Oh, yes! Innocent little me – I would *never* have thought of *that*!' He grins, a mock expression of lechery. 'He said he had this twin, which made me very excited. Then he mentioned the twin was a she, which caused a certain deflation, shall-we-say. But when I finally saw them together, how much alike they looked, and discovered how incredibly kinky she was . . . well, all I can tell you is that afterwards I knew I'd had an – experience.'

'And the two of them – with each other— ?'

'That, my dear, was the best part! Brother-and-sister! Like Tristan and Isolde. The depravity of it! The absolutely scrumptious degenerate depravity!' He scowls. 'Cost me a damn' fortune too. A scene like that, you know, doesn't come cheap.'

Jerome, intoxicated, is growing woozy, and I'm feeling hurt, for the dumbest reason too. I've discovered that Tim and Ariane did little numbers together for pay, and it pains me that in his copious confessions Tim never said a word. But then, I think, how could he? How would he have broached it? Perhaps he felt that such a confidence would cost him my respect. If so, how wrong he was. I would have loved him all the better for his openness.

I help Jerome to his bed where he sprawls upon his back. In the process his dressing gown slips open to reveal flaccid genitalia between pale hairy thighs. Immediately he begins to snore. Nothing musical about him now. I glance at his bureau where I notice the score for *Tannhäuser*, a lavish gold wristwatch, a fine leather breast pocket wallet, assorted coins and ten fresh new one-hundred-dollar bills perfectly aligned. This money, I assume, was intended for Tim in return for a night of delicious violation. Ah, well . . . Soon, I expect, Jerome will find himself a new companion here.

I tiptoe out, close the door, descend the curving stairs. As the reception desk, Snooty wide-eyes me as I pass.

'Lovely time with Mr T?' he snickers.

Perhaps he expects a tip. I walk by him without breaking my stride.

'Goodnight, *Carlo*,' he sneers.

I sleep poorly. Is it because I'm afraid of another invasion? I think rather it's because Sasha's on duty and cannot be here with me tonight.

The time's coming, I know, when I must sort out my feelings for him. Unfair, to allow him to love me so earnestly without giving him something substantial in return. When we first started going out, I viewed him as a terrific companion with whom to share laughs, good talk, great meals, great sex. Then, somewhere along the line, my feelings began to change. Now I see him in a deeper way. Yes, I believe I could love him. So why didn't I tell him so at Eden Roc?

In the middle of the night I get out of bed, go to the living room, unpack my new telescope, set it up on the old tripod and aim it at the Judge's terrace across the way.

No lights on over there. It's far too late. He always retires early on weekday nights. Still, I use it to explore his terrace, the pots of geraniums, the porch furniture, the three-legged grill on which we used to cook, the round table and tightly woven straw café chairs where we sat when we ate outdoors.

I recall a birthday dinner I prepared for him, a ragout of lobster tails and a simple salad accompanied by my father's bread. Champagne. A tiny cake I bought at an Italian sweets shop in North Beach. One candle only to represent the day ... but, lest we forget, fifty-four silver stars I picked up at a paper store enclosed with my birthday letter so that they spilled upon him when he opened it up.

Stardust, he called those fluttering glittering stars. And then he kissed me. That was the last birthday we celebrated. I think I knew then that though I loved him with all my heart, he merely enjoyed my company ... and the pain of that revelation is with me still. He's fifty-six now. It's been nearly two years since we've spoken or met. I've seen him, of course, quite a few times – from here through a lens, with his friends, a new lover or two, or just lying in his swimsuit on his chaise on a Sunday afternoon, taking the sun while reading a brief.

They say that those who are abused become abusers in turn, that those upon whom suffering is inflicted will inevitably inflict it upon another even to a greater degree. This, I'm told, is a basic tenet of psychology – that we will do unto others as they have done unto us. Now, standing here spying on the Judge's empty terrace, I take no pleasure in the notion that Sasha may be harboring a love for me which, in his mind at least, I do not return.

I spend most of the morning working in the darkroom, then go out a little after 11 with my pack of mug shots to the bench in Sterling Park.

Again Drake keeps me waiting. Perhaps he's testing my patience, hoping I'll give up and leave. Undoubtedly he's watching me; to watch is his profession. But though he loves me in his strange way and sees himself as my protector, identifying my violators frightens him too much.

Sympathy enables me to wait him out. While I do I imagine the silent war raging in his head: his every anti-social instinct telling him not to get involved, while his voyeur's love demands he do the gallant thing. Which side will win, the self-sufficient hermit or the love-sick knight? By remaining on the bench, I force the issue. He must come to me or quit this park, his home.

Finally he shows up. The noon church bells have rung, a distant work whistle has sounded . . . and he must see by the still way I sit that I will stay here if necessary the entire day.

'Kay.'

His whisper startles me, seeming to issue from behind my back. Drake has the ability of a Native American tracker to emerge silently from the woods. He can, I believe, stand within yards of people without them even suspecting that he's there.

'Drake.' I softly pat the seat beside me. But, just as before, he perches at the far end of the bench.

'Sorry I'm late,' he says. 'I've been nervous.'

'I understand.' One of his feet, crossed over the other, is shaking. 'I brought the pictures,' I tell him, 'but you don't have to look at them. Your choice.'

'I want to help you,' he says. 'I'm scared, that's all.'

'I promise you'll never have to talk to the cops, or testify in court, or attend a police line-up, or do anything beyond telling me honestly what you know.'

I turn to him in time to catch his nod. How fragile he is, I think. Perhaps he suffers from some mild form of autism, not so serious as to warrant being hospitalized, but painful enough so that encounters of any sort fill him with severe anxiety, even dread.

'Are you ready or should we put it off? I can come back later, if you want?'

'Let's do it now.'

I nod, set my little stack of mug shots face-down between us on the bench. 'What I'd like you to do, Drake, is pick up the pack, turn it over and slowly look at each picture in turn. If you recognize any of the three men you saw that night, set those pictures aside. But look at them all. You might not recognize any, or perhaps just one. That's fine. Don't try and please me – just tell the truth.'

With interpersonal skills like these, I think, I should have become a cop. Except I'm not sure I've been all that skillful until Drake finally picks the photos up. Then I recall how in my adolescence I actually toyed with the notion of law enforcement work. Dad told me gently I could do many things in life, but, being colorblind, not that.

I decide not to watch Drake as he examines the faces, believing the less pressure I exert the more conscientiously he'll perform. Instead I listen to the sounds of the park, the thunk of tennis balls on the courts above, singing birds, whispering grasses, the wind fluttering the leaves. The sound of the city is present too, muffled traffic, the faint ring and clatter of the Hyde Street cable car a block away, muted sounds from off the water, a special blend I've heard nowhere else. Every city, I believe, has its din. The din of San Francisco is music to my ears.

It's a quirky town of alleys, stairways, culs-de-sac, funny little houses clinging to the sides of hills, some built on stilts. Gulls wheel above the Embarcadero. Ferries criss-cross the Bay churning trails of wake. Someone once said that this is a city that looks as if it were built by gods. In fact it was built by innumerable eccentrics, which accounts for its special combination of grandeur and charm.

'Kay.'

I turn back to Drake. The pack of photos is just where I left it on the bench. He is staring out, as he did the other day, across the gravel park path toward the pines.

Seeing that he has set no photos aside, I feel deflated. Either none of my suspects is guilty or Drake is incapable of singling them out.

'Hungry?' I ask. 'Want me to get you some food?'

He turns to me. 'Aren't you going to ask?'

'What?'

'Did I see them?'

'Did you, Drake?' I ask softly.

He nods. 'All three. You'll find their pictures on the bottom.'

He stands as I reach for the photos. I pick the pack up, turn it over, and at that moment he slips away. Suddenly I'm alone and he's gone . . . like a phantom who was never here.

THIRTEEN

KNOB AND HIS ACOLYTES: the photos Drake pulled do not surprise me. Yet ambushing me at night in the park is one thing; not that hard to get away with. But breaking into and vandalizing my apartment – whatever possessed them to take such a risk?

As I walk home I think the matter over. It couldn't be our little run-in at The Werewolf; that was street stuff, bluster. Which brings me back to my theory they were paid to do it. Considering that their attacks occurred after my confrontation with Crane and my rebuff of Sarah Lashaw, I return to the notion that Crane and Lashaw ordered me hit.

Fine! At least now I know whom I'm dealing with. And I'm prepared to take this escalation as proof Crane's got something serious to hide. Knob's a street-hustler, the acolytes are punks, but Marcus Crane is acting like a man in trouble . . . and I doubt that his fear of me is over a few fuzzy photographs showing him soliciting on the Gulch. Entering my building, I glance at the video security camera. The lens is small but it gives me comfort. Upstairs, when I turn my key in my new lock, there's a sweet sound as the bolt is thrown. I shut the door behind me and disarm the alarm. If I fail to do so within fifteen seconds a siren will start to shriek.

I go immediately to my darkroom, pull negatives of the shots I took of Crane in front of his house, print up the whole series on 8x10 paper, squeegee the prints, pin them up and look closely at his face.

Is this the face of a killer? Perhaps in the final shot. But is it also the face of a man who could cut his victim into pieces in Wildcat Canyon, paint up the torso, then haul the head and limbs back downtown?

I have doubts. Crane's too suave, his car's too nice; he's not the type to sully himself. Sure, he'd plunder a person's body, use him without qualm – but would he take pleasure in the blood, eroticize the butchery? I don't think so. Still, I must not forget, he is my enemy.

Joel calls. He's been phoning around trying to locate the four cops.

'We can't see Hayes – he's been dead five years. Classic gun-in-the-mouth cop suicide.'

Even as I wince, I understand Joel has forgotten about my mother.

'Waincroft,' he continues. 'lives down in Santa Cruz. Night watchman at the pier amusement park. I finally got hold of him. Sounded like he does a lot of drinking. Says he wants to think it over before submitting to an interview.'

From cop Sergeant to night watchman – what a fall!

'Puccio's another story. You know Giordano's in North Beach?'

'Pizza and pasta joint. Great calamari salad.'

'It's his mom's place. He's the maître d'. Invited us over tomorrow for a late lunch after the crowd thins out.'

'What about Vasquez?'

'Since he's still a cop, his interview'll have to be cleared through SFPD Public Affairs.'

I tell Joel about the break-in, Drake's ID of the perps, my hunch that Knob and his boys are working for Crane.

'I'm worried about you, kiddo.'

'I can take care of myself.'

'Maybe . . . but, admit it, so far you haven't done too good a job.'

He's right, which pisses me off. 'So tell me, Joel – what would *you* do if three guys jumped you then broke into your house?'

'Well,' he says, 'I guess I'd put in a new lock, then sign up for a martial arts class.'

I print up my shots of Knob and his flunkies on polycontrast, quick-dry them with my hair drier, place them in an envelope with my 8x10s of Crane, walk down to Marina Aikido, take a class and shower. Afterwards I use the pay phone to call Maddy. She says it's okay to come over, so I walk on to her place on Alhambra.

She looks particularly fragile today, but I know better than to inquire after her health. Still I'm touched when, in the hallway, she takes hold of my arm. After we're seated on her couch, I notice the translucence of her skin, the thinness of her wrists, the delicacy of the cords that protrude from her neck. Her eyes, on the other hand, are sharp as ever.

'You look good, Kay,' she says, 'strong, confident. But you've been having trouble.'

How well she knows me.

'That's why I've come.'

She glances at my envelope. I open it, pull the photos, spread them out. 'Not proof sheets this time, just prints.'

Unlike other teachers I've had, slop prints don't bother Maddy. Technical stuff, she knows, can be taught by anyone. She concerns herself with how her students see.

'These are grab shots of hostile models,' she says. 'A couple are very good. This one—' she picks up the shot I took of Knob and his boys at The Werewolf, '—and this—' she chooses the last in my series on Crane, the one in which he appears about to break. 'But you've done a lot of work like this, Kay. You've learned how and you do it well. You shoot them straight and refuse to flinch.' She looks at me, questioning. 'But you didn't come to hear that. There's something else.'

I ask her if she'll look closely at the pictures and tell me what they say to her about the people.

'I know this isn't what you usually do, Maddy, but you're so perceptive . . . and I need some good advice.'

She waves her hand to shush me, resumes studying the prints. I watch her as she peers at their faces. I wonder why I have come to her for this when I could have easily shown the shots to Rita Reese. Rita is also shrewd about people; she could tell me whether Knob and Crane are truly dangerous. But Maddy is the only person I know who has come to her understanding of the world through black and white photography.

'This man—' she is studying my Crane series, '—at first he doesn't know what to make of you. You confuse him, threaten him. He's accustomed to masking himself and at first he does it well. Quickly he comes to hate you. I'm sorry to tell you – his hate goes deep. It fills him. He is a man who can hate easily. Beneath his mask, you see, he's a man who hates himself.'

She turns to me, shows her most sibylline smile. 'Yes, your pictures are like stories.' She pats me on the knee. 'Proof of their power.' She picks up the shots of Knob. 'Not much here. He buys, sells, trades. One of your hustlers, I suppose, though there's something that separates him from others you've shown me. He's older, harder, tougher. He's got a vicious streak.'

She picks up The Werewolf shot. 'Here he looks different. He wants to show you his scorn, but like the first man he's afraid.' She looks at me. 'You know how, after we hurt people, we study them closely to see how deeply we have cut?' She taps her forefinger against Knob's face. 'That's how he's looking at you here. But he doesn't find what he wants. Instead he sees strength – which surprises and awes him. Yes, he's afraid of you, Kay. And he will hurt you again if he can.'

I feel sweat break out in my armpits.

'The two with him?' I ask.

'Kids.'

'So you don't think they're bad?'

'Only in a gang. Then they'd pile on. But alone,' she shakes her head, 'they're cowards.'

The sky is dark by the time I reach The Hampshire Arms. The grunge on its granite façade is lost in shadow. The same lackadaisical gum-chewing kid with bad skin is sitting behind the desk. He's the opposite of Snooty at The Sultan's Tent. There they guard their guests; here they regard them as whores and all their visitors as johns. Doreen's in, Alyson's out. Doreen invites me up, but, as usual, begs me first to walk around the block while she cleans up. When, finally, I present myself, the room is, also as usual, *not* cleaned up and redolent with booze.

Doreen sits at the dresser in a camisole applying eye make-up. I notice a tightly curled jockstrap at her feet.

'Hey, Bug!' She pecks my cheek, then lightly strokes my arm. 'Great biceps, dearie. Get some tats, spike up your hair, pierce your brows, go punk.'

I sit on the bed, watch her skillful moves as she wields her eyelash brush.

'Business is off. Soon the holidays'll come, then the short cold days of winter. What I need now is a new john, dearie – someone handsome and flush who'll take me to Hawaii.'

'I hope you find him, Doreen.'

'Don't know.' She shrugs. 'Either I'm losing my looks, or the pickins are gittin' slim.'

I show her my Werewolf photograph.

'Yeah, Knob and his flunkies. They don't look pleased.'

She turns back to the mirror.

'The flunkies – do they have names?'

'Price and Pride. Frick and Frack.' She shrugs. 'One on the right's Tommy, one on the left – they call him Boat.'

'Boat?'

'Uh-huh.' Doreen draws her eyebrows with an economy of motion that would do any girl proud. 'I once asked him about that. He said his given name is Bato, which means something like "Hey, kid!" in Serbo-Croat. His family lived in France, and the kids there starting calling him *Bateau*. Later, when he moved to the States, that got translated into Boat.'

'How old is he?'

'Fifteen tops. Jailbait. Tough on the outside, mushy as caramel underneath. It's that sweet candy part, dearie, that they like. Ass-skin soft as a baby's, the puniest patch of body hair and cock hard as a spike.'

'Knob and his flunkies – what's the deal there?'

'Come on! You know! He rents them out, high prices too. Ever notice how he protects them, barely lets them out of his sight? He's their mom, they're his pussies . . . and, come to think of it, the most valuable commodity on the Gulch.'

She finishes up her eyes, turns to face me, cocks her head. 'Why so interested, dearie?'

'The three of them beat me up. And that's not the half of it.' I tell her about the break-in, the things they wrote on my walls. The sexual insults shock her.

'Positive they did all that?'

'I've got a witness.'

'What're you going to do?'

'Still thinking about it.'

'Want some advice?'

I shrug.

'Leave it alone, Bug. Whatever hard feelings Knob had toward you, they're over now that he's put you down. But raise the stakes and he could do you serious harm. There're rumors about him, dearie – and none of them are nice.'

I thank her for her counsel, but don't commit either way. In fact, I have a plan, but need more information before deciding whether it'll work.

'Tommy and Boat – any difference between them?'

'One's got lighter hair, but that's not what you mean.' Doreen ponders. 'Boat's softer than Tommy, more naive. Tommy's more your smart-ass type, Boat's more your run-away kid.'

'Thanks, Doreen.'

She looks into my eyes. 'Think about what Mama told you, dearie – don't mess with Knob. He's the kind who'll squirt you with lighter fluid, toss in a match, watch you burn, lick his lips and walk off whistling a merry tune.'

Knowing my new hotel-quality mattress has arrived, Sasha comes to me at midnight with a bouquet of irises, pocket full of ace bandages, twinkle in his liquid eyes and devilish plan.

Lovingly he ties my wrists to the bedposts, spreads my thighs, ties them back to the handles of the box-spring, then produces a feather with which he tickles my parts. I giggle and squirm, thrash and laugh, my nipples swell, I go creamy until all I can think of in this rapture is requital.

'Please, please, please . . .' I moan. But sweet dark Sasha enjoys inflicting pleasure. I writhe until I reach a point beyond endurance. Finally my lover comes upon me to deliver me from desire. I cry out, tremble, give myself up. I want to draw out every quantum of his passion, employ him to help me mount crest after crest of pleasure. And so I do until at last I arch, then fall back released.

It takes a long time for the vibrato in me to subside. Meantime Sasha, who smells as usual of sandalwood, whispers to me the erotic secrets of multi-armed Hindu deities and their consorts, fleshly means, he promises, we will use to join together and pierce our earthly prison.

'Insights! Revelations! Orgasms like bolts of lightning!'

'Sounds great,' I tell him, burying my face in his shoulder. 'I'm crazy about you. You know that, don't you?'

I feel him quiver with delight.

Then, as an afterthought: 'Next time, Doctor, I'm tying *you*!'

They have a wood-fired oven at Giordano's, the kind that fills the restaurant with an aroma of wood smoke and baking pizza crust.

The walls here bear a sooty patina, there are plain wood tables, creaky old chairs, a long bar frequented by local characters and an array of framed and inscribed photographs of movie stars and famous figures from the worlds of sports and California politics.

Joel and I are sitting with Enrico ('Call me Ricky') Puccio in the proprietor's booth opposite the cash register near the door. From here Ricky can greet his friends as they pass in and out. He's a short, stout, balding guy in his fifties, dressed in dark trousers, white shirt with french cuffs, and flamboyant tie. He doesn't look like an ex-cop, rather like what he is – an ebullient, happy, hospitable host at a very busy dining spot, adept at greeting guests.

I glance around. Though it's past 2:30, most of the tables still are filled – tourists, people from the financial district, local store owners, North Beach regulars. There's a plate of olives in olive oil on every table, a basket of bread sticks and a bottle of wine from the Giordano family winery. The pastas and calamari salad here are famous. Another house specialty is the antipasto plate of fresh mozzarella with tomatoes, basil and roasted red pepper. But in the end it's the pizza that brings them in – the best pizza in town.

Ricky has stood to shake hands with a man I recognize, a lawyer friend of the Judge. When he rejoins us, he apologizes.

'Room'll clear out soon. Now eat and drink. When things settle down, we'll talk.'

This suits me. I'm dying of hunger. But Joel is unhappy. He likes focused interviews. Today he's at the mercy of an extravert.

I recall the evaluation of Puccio in the confidential Internal Affairs report: 'Sloppiest of the bunch, apparently ignorant of police norms and procedures'. *Well*, I think, *Ricky may have acted sloppy and dumb back then, but he runs a sharp operation now.*

Shortly after 3, he joins us in a buoyant mood. I switch on my tape-recorder.

'What can I tell you, guys?' he asks. Then, before Joel can reply, he touches my arm. 'Give my best regards to your pop, Kay. Tell him to come in sometime and that his money's no good here. Tell him I like to feed old pals.'

'As I told you,' Joel says, 'we're doing a piece on the T case. And that, of course, includes Sipple.'

Ricky stares at Joel then pops up, this time to speak to an elderly woman in the back.

Joel shakes his head. 'He doesn't want to talk.'

'Why's he seeing us?'

'Wants us to like him.'

'Do we?'

'Not yet,' Joel says.

Ricky returns scratching his head. 'Sipple, Sipple – oh, yeah!' He beams. 'Nearly forgot about that. Now why'd you bring it up? There's good things in this life like weddings and graduations, and there's crap like Sipple you want to forget happened. Know what I mean?'

But soon we get to it. Ricky's too loquacious, can't abide the silence that follows. So he starts off on a riff accompanied by an array of gestures and expressions sufficient to mime his feelings to the world.

'They called us buffoons! Know what that means to an Italian? Got any friggin' idea? Clowns, fools – it's what we yell at the politicians when they march them off to jail for graft. So don't be so sure we were all that stupid. Maybe we weren't stupid at all.' Again Ricky touches my arm. 'You know your pop, Kay. You know how smart he is. If he was stupid that night, then that was about the only time he was – right?' He shakes his head vigorously. 'Maybe we were a few good cops doing a dirty job best we could.' He shows a secretive grin. 'Maybe there was a lot more that happened back then than met the eye . . .'

He doesn't tell us what that might have been. Rather he retells the story we already know, but from an insider's point of view. All the while there's a look of complicity in his eyes that implies we share a secret about the matter, which, by mutual consent, none of us will broach.

'Now let's take a look at who was there that night, all right? I'm talking about the sworn officers, no one else.' Ricky takes a lick at his thumb, sticks it up.

'First we got Wainy Waincroft, straight arrow Sergeant, last of the true blue-flame believers. You don't make Sarge being an asshole, least not in good old SFPD. Sure, old Wainy had a temper, he could knock a guy around it came to that. Busted a few heads in his time, no doubt of it. Not a college man, no . . . but few in those times were. Ragged around the edges – you betcha! But stupid?' Ricky shakes his head. 'I never heard anyone call Wainy stupid. Not until Hale, that is.'

He prongs his forefinger.

'Next you got Billy Hayes. Squirrelish little guy, eyes like a rodent, but shiny, hear what I'm saying? Shiny little eyes, not dull. Billy was a boxer. Did you know? Was City Golden Gloves finalist in the bantam-weight division, thought about turning pro, went into the cops instead. Boxed for us a while as a welterweight. Was Potrero Station champ a couple years. Coached kids in the Activities League and they loved him for it. Sweetest little guy, Billy. Best hand-eye coordination you ever saw. He could pack one helluva wallop. So was he dumb?' Ricky shrugs. 'Good clean record. Never lost any evidence, made his share of collars, but then boxers act like dummies sometimes, all that bobbin' and weavin', you know – all those punches to the head. Softens up your brain, they say – though funny no one ever noticed any softening in Billy till Inspector Jonathan Topper Hale – let's call him "Halo" since that's what he puts around his head! – yeah, not till the old Halo himself brought it up.'

Ricky sticks up his middle finger.

'Jack Farrow. Truly kingly man. Worked bunko five–six years in Chinatown with Rusty Quinn, made more collars there than the Chink cops worked with 'em. Learned the lingo, built up a network, ended up with an army of deep throats up Stockton, down Grant. You didn't mess with old Jack. Sweet guy, but not one to take any crap. They say he could swing a nightstick good as anyone in Central. Course when they transferred him to Park Station, maybe he turned slow and dumb. Funny thing though – no one I ever spoke to noticed it.'

His ring finger rises.

'Me? Better let someone else tell you. My ma, the old stove out back – she taught me never toot my own horn.'

Ricky raises his pinky.

'Which leaves us with Louie Vasquez, number five. Kind of odd man out, his being Hispanic and the way he approached the job. Now the squawk on Louie was that he acted real bright, going to college at night, betterin' himself, all spit and polish, shoes shined like mirrors. But the deeper squawk, the locker room skinny, was that Louie was an intriguer. Not too big on swingin' the stick, not Louie. More the gabby type. Yack, yack, yack. But when the shit hit the fan, they said, old Louie, he was more'n likely to take off on those bright shiny shoes of his.'

Ricky places his hand flat down on the table, fingers spread as far as they will go. His nails, I note, are beautifully groomed, but his hand is quivering, the knuckles losing color as he presses down hard with his palm.

'Five guys,' Ricky says, 'Wainy, Billy, Jack, Ricky and Louie – and suddenly they all go stupid. Find important evidence in a capital case but don't recognize it as such. Lose said evidence because no one takes care to follow SOP. Five guys, competent guys, tankin' on the job. But funny, isn't it that those five, all bright enough, all with good records, suddenly go flat all together? Like there's this contagious disease, know what I mean? This disease that strikes them all at once. And suddenly they're – what? – bunglers, screw-ups, buffoons. Yeah, I *do* think it's funny. Matter of fact, I wake up sometimes middle of the night and laugh so hard my wife gets mad. "You dreamin' comedy again, Ricky?" she steams, kicking me in the shins. "Shut up, *paisan*, you'll wake Ma and the kids." But it's still so friggin' funny I gotta bury my head in the pillow to stifle the guffaws.'

Joel and I sit gaping. The riff is finished. Ricky, knowing his performance has been splendid, rises in the manner of a grand seigneur. ''Scuse me now, guys. Gotta consult with Ma out back. Your lunch is on the house. No tips neither. Your money's no good here – least not today!'

Later, outside on busy Columbus Avenue, I turn to Joel.

'Do you like him better now?'

'Actually, I do,' Joel says. 'He's got a way about him. The way he talks – it warms you up.'

I walk through the labyrinth of narrow lanes that adjoin the financial district, short little streets lined with old low brick buildings which now house galleries and antique stores, specialty book shops, elegant architects' and attorneys' offices. Jackson Square, Gold Street, Balance, Hotaling, Gibb, Ils Lane – the core of what's left of the once-infamous Barbary Coast.

The late-afternoon light down here is sweet, shadows are long, you can hear your footsteps as they ring off the cobblestones. I wander here as I allow Ricky's words to float through my head seeking to net some secret from the depths . . . a secret which floats so close I almost feel I can touch it, but which always, just as it comes within my grasp, slips elusively away.

*   *   *

I find myself thinking a lot about Ariane Lovsey. From what I've discovered this woman is so powerful and strange as to make the other players I've met in this pursuit seem but ordinary folk. David deGeoffroy, Jonathan Topper Hale, Jerome Tattinger, Sarah Lashaw – I've met vivid personalities, all bigger than life, spoken with them, entered their orbits. But the one who exerts the strongest force field is Ariane, Amoretto, the one I've never seen.

I'm spending nearly all my time in the darkroom now, printing out my negatives, assembling my pictures into some sort of visual order. Perhaps, I think, in the rarefied details of the photographs, the shadows, backgrounds, the very grain of the film, I will discover the hidden pattern that I seek.

I've always loved darkroom work, employing my minimalist palette of blacks and whites. I feel safe here, protected by the solid walls and door, eyes comfortable in the gloom where my vision is at its best. So much easier to work in dim confined space with paper, film and chemicals than to go outdoors with a camera and confront the inconsistencies of natural light. And too, I know, cowardly. It was Maddy who, three years ago, told me to get out and walk the streets.

'You want to photograph people, Kay? Go out and smell them. Get that close. Smell developer and acetic acid and you'll stay a studio photographer. Smell people and you'll start becoming a photojournalist.'

Finally, mid-afternoon, three days after our lunch with Ricky, Joel calls to rescue me from my cell.

'We're going down to Santa Cruz. Waincroft's agreed to talk.'

We take Route 1 along the coast; it's the slow way, but it's beautiful and will give us time to unwind and talk. We pass the seal rock beaches, turn south, and a little north of San Pedro Point pass some serious surfers riding awesome waves. After Half Moon Bay there's barely any traffic, just miles of empty road running along the coast, rocky portions alternating with State beaches named for the creeks that run down to them from the hills. There's heavy fog here, the road snakes and I feel good sitting next to Joel, breathing the thick salty darkening air. Better, I think, to chug along with him in Melvin than to recline against the butter-soft seats in the back of Sarah Lashaw's chauffeured limo.

'I haven't spoken to a soul since we lunched with Ricky,' I tell him. 'Thanks for rescuing me. I've been talking to myself.'

'Not a bad person to talk with,' Joel says. 'Any thoughts on that lunch?'

'His five-finger exercise – it haunts me still.'

'Join the club.'

'He must've told us something. By any chance, did you figure out what?'

Joel shakes his head. 'It was more of a mood thing, like they were all smart guys, suddenly they all went slack and that's really funny, except it isn't. But I keep thinking there's another level.'

'Me too.'

What I don't tell him is that the real reason I locked myself in my darkroom for three full days was so I wouldn't run over to City Stone Ground, corner Dad and try to coax out an explanation.

The Santa Cruz Beach Boardwalk is the last beachside amusement park in California. Tattered, tacky, tawdry but proud, it dominates the bay, attracting kids and old folks nostalgic for those pre-Disney days when a roller-coaster, carny music and cotton candy were all you needed to instill the blend of forced humor and melancholy summed up in the hollow word 'amusement'.

In my Art Institute days I did my share of picture-taking here, roaming the boardwalk on weekends, catching images of the last hippies as they lurched stoned beneath signs depicting clowns with riotous smiles. Easy juxtapositions, art school stuff, but that was a time when nearly everything I saw through the viewfinder caught my eye. Busted windows, abandoned gas station pumps, feral street cats, overflowing trash barrels beneath thrashing palms – I would show Californians what they passed every day but didn't see, filtered through the fine artist's prism of my eye.

I soon got over it, learned the difference between picture-taking and photography. Still, I know, sometimes an amateur will catch an image by accident so strong a pro could shoot a hundred rolls and still not equal it. Whenever I see a photograph like that I wonder again about what I'm doing. Which is why I need Maddy to coach me and keep me on my path.

Joel and I are standing outside a run-down paddy bar called The Brogue two blocks back from the boardwalk on a street lined with raunchy motels. The gaunt and haggard man standing before us does not resemble the Lucius D. Waincroft I've been expecting. Time, I know, always takes its toll; Hale, I recall, looked far different than in his photographs. But the face of the Wainy now facing us is totally unlike the proud stubborn Sergeant's face that appeared in the row of mug-shot photos published in the *Chronicle* under the headline BUFFOONS. This man has rotten teeth, unshaven cheeks, burst capillaries streaking his nose. His eyes are milky, the left one twitching as he leers. When he bends toward me, I want to turn my back; instead I bow my head, forcing him to plant his kiss upon my hair.

'Do ye not know me, Kay? What a fine woman you've become!' His breath reeks of cheap booze and rum-soaked cigars. But now those milky eyes are filled with merriment. 'Remember Uncle Wainy? I've known ye since you were a wee girl.'

I have only the vaguest memory of him from childhood, being presented to him by Dad at cop picnics and sporting events. We used to attend those kinds of affairs before my mother turned agoraphobic, the first step in the decline that culminated in her suicide.

He studies me. 'You've got your ma's sweet eyes, Kay. You truly do. Fine gal, Carlotta. I miss her . . . as I'm sure Jack and you must do. Most likely you think of her every day.' He chucks my chin. 'You've become an artist, I hear.'

'Photographer.'

'Yeah, sure, but that's an artist too, I understand.'

As he turns to Joel the neon sign of The Brogue casts a shaft of light across his face – red light, I assume, though to me it appears as a glowing black bar. A dark uniform with some sort of security service patch on the shoulders hangs upon Wainy's emaciated frame.

I step back to take his picture. He poses grandly, Napoleon-style, hand thrust deep inside his shirt. A heavy gun belt from which dangle the tools of his trade – field radio, flashlight, nightstick, holstered automatic – droops below his waist.

Flash! Whap! I catch an image: The Ruined Cop.

'Five to seven,' he says, 'time to go to work. Hope the two of you don't mind walking along with me. That way we can talk while I do my job.'

As he leads us down to the waterfront, he explains that after Labor Day the amusement park is closed except on weekends. But that doesn't stop all sorts of riffraff from trying to force their way in from the beach.

At the gate he introduces us to another uniformed guard.

'Just going to show these young people the place, you don't mind, Mac,' Wainy says.

The gate-keeper shrugs. We pass through the office, Wainy pulls his card, sticks it into a time-clock, returns it to its slot, picks up his watchman's key, clips it to a chain attached to his belt, then motions us out to the kennel area where he attaches a leash to the collar of an elderly black Rottweiler, whom, he tells us cheerily, the guards have nicknamed 'Crud'.

'Come on, Crudder. Come on, boy,' he addresses the creature in a sing-song. 'Another night, another dollar, doggie – off to make our rounds . . .'

Soon we're walking along a spooky row of shuttered booths, dimly lit by occasional security lamps and the glow of streetlights beyond the fence. In season the booths here, faded signs tell me, offer soda, burritos, franks and taffy, or provide places where you can win a kewpie by virtue of your marksmanship or by defeating an expert at guessing your weight and age. There are booths that sell horror masks, magic tricks, poo-poo pillows, where you can be photographed beside cardboard cut-outs of Bogie, Elvis, Marilyn, Reagan or the Pope. But tonight everything's closed down, the only sounds in this nightscape Crud's panting and the echoes of our steps upon the wooden walk.

'Hale! Seen him, have you?' Wainy hoots, his chuckles resounding along the corridor of shuttered shacks. 'He came down a few times. Asked me to open up. Ha! I wouldn't say a word, sent him packing. Last time he begged me. "Please, Wainy, *pleeeeease*." Didn't mind seeing him grovel, I tell you. "No," I said, "I'd rather die a ghastly death than tell *you* anything, you no-good bastard son of a bitch." That was about a year ago. I think he got the idea. Hasn't been back any rate.'

'What did he think you could tell him?' Joel asks.

'Where we stashed the evidence – what else?'

'*Did* you stash it?'

'Ha! That's what Hale thinks. Gotta a bug up his arse. Bug's been nibbling at his 'rhoids since the day it happened. Hated me 'cause I wouldn't take a polygraph. "Now why should I take it?" I asked him. My lawyer told me: "Don't even think about it, Wainy. They're going to bounce you out, let 'em. But don't give 'em ammo they can use to shoot you down." Good advice so I hushed up, never told 'em a thing. Then they tried to take my pension. Was in and out of court five years over that. Case was settled in the end, though not so well for me. Which is why I'm doing this damn' job here. Isn't half bad actually. Pays for the booze and smokes at least.'

He yanks on the leash. 'Damnit, Crudder! Stop scamperin', you stupid mutt!'

But Crud, though old and overweight, pulls Wainy along faster than he wants to walk, forcing him to angle back like a thin man marching in the face of a ferocious wind.

'These hounds're damn near useless,' he says. 'Still, the company insists we use 'em. They think big black dogs scare off invaders. Theory is kids who try and get in here from the beach side will hear the dogs and think twice. Ratfuck! Kids don't give a damn. They're wearin' wetsuits anyway. They just stick some sleeping potion in hotdogs, throw them at the mutts, the mutts gobble them, next thing you know they're lyin' on their backs snorin' like there's no tomorrow.'

The sight of Wainy trying to control Crud inspires me to take another picture. I step away to catch him in profile tilted backwards as he fights the irresistible canine force.

'Poor Billy!' Wainy exclaims over the suicide of Billy Hayes. 'After the cops he tried all kinds of work. Not like your pop, Kay – who could always make one helluva loaf. Billy didn't know nothin 'cept boxing and law enforcement. He took up coachin', tried to develop a couple kids, but soon as he'd find a prospect some sweet-talkin' manager'd steal the kid from under his nose. So old Billy finally threw it in. Won't say I haven't thought occasionally of doing the same. Only reason I haven't is . . . curiosity. I'm always wonderin' what's going to happen next. Never find out, will I, if I chow down my gun?'

We enter the roller-coaster perimeter. Wainy uses his watchman's key to open the gate. Inside, the wood and steel structure looms above us like the skeleton of an enormous dinosaur.

'Couple of us here the other night,' Wainy says, 'caught ourselves one real live intruder.' His milky eyes go cold. 'Crud and the other fella's dog cornered him, then we surrounded him and beat him. Bloody pulp when we got done.'

Wainy heehaws then shows a leer that chills my blood. Does he think Joel and I will admire him for this? Is he trying to psych us, or doesn't he give a damn? Probably the latter, I decide. He's a wasted man living in an enclosed world of booze, mean memories and the beat we're walking with him now.

'Won't be able to work much longer,' he says, a propos of nothing. 'Got lung cancer. Eatin' me up inside. That's why I'm so thin.' He turns his head, spits. 'Wainy's never been a squealer, and I ain't startin' now. So you won't get nothin' out of me, not even on my deathbed you won't.'

I glance at Joel in time to see his eyes catch fire.

'You're saying there *is* something to be gotten out of you?' he asks.

Wainy lets out with a crazed laugh. 'You bet there is, friend!'

'Come on, Wainy,' I plead. 'Tell us. Who'll be hurt by it now?'

'Your dad for one. Why don't you ask him, Kay, see what he's got to say?'

'About what?'

'What'd you think, girl? *It*. Hear me? What the hell else we talking about? What're we doing, for Christ's sake? What'd you come down here for? Not to pay your goddamn' respects. I know that. You came to ask 'bout the same thing Hale, that wheedling bastard, tried to sweet-talk an answer to. *IT!* Stinkin' *IT*. That stupid bag of – ha! Give the man a kewpie doll, Harry! – that bag of ever-lovin' shit-eatin' fuck-all *ev-eye-dense!*'

Though Joel keeps at him, plugging him with questions, Wainy's done answering for the night. He goes silent on us, leading us back toward the security gate, mumbling something about having to feed Crud his dinner.

'I'm not used to walking these boards with visitors,' he mutters.

'Saying you know where that evidence is, Wainy?' Joel asks again.

But Wainy doesn't reply. He's finished with us, can't wait to see our backs. I try and stall him by asking him to pose again. He obliges but the humor of his Napoleon stance is lacking, as is the pathos when he was being dragged forward by Crud. Now he just stands there, blank, dejected, grim.

Then I get an idea.

'Take off your shirt,' I tell him.

'Kidding me, Kay?'

'Uh-uh. Strip. I want to see some skin.'

He hoots, but even so strips to the waist, handing off Crud to Joel.

'Great!' I tell him, focusing. 'Now put the gun belt back on. That's right, the way it was. Just let it hang there. Yeah!'

Flash Whap! Flash Whap!

'Now do something, Wainy! Give me a show!'

He thinks a moment, perplexed. Then he gets a notion. He starts whistling, some sort of Irish ditty, then starts moving, raising his feet, pumping his arms, hopping.

Whap! Whap! Whap! Whap! Whap! I can't believe my luck. The man's dancing an Irish jig right there in the middle of the deserted amusement park. He's got the ribs of a concentration camp survivor and the expression of a lecher, and still he high-steps, while Crud, incredulous, sits on his haunches watching his mad master dance. My motor-drive hums, my flash strobes the night as I freeze him in absurd postures against the stanchions and girders behind. I shoot till he's exhausted, wheezes, coughs, finally bends forward to let the drool run free.

'How you like them beans, girl?' he demands, crouched over, expectorating on to the boardwalk.

I like them very much, I tell him. And, to myself, I give a title to what I'm sure will be a remarkable series: 'Wainy's Last Hurrah'.

At the gate he bids us a sweet farewell.

'Kind of you to drive down and see me,' he says to Joel. They shake hands, then Wainy turns to me, looks deep into my eyes.

'You're a grand-looking gal, Kay,' he says. 'Carlotta's eyes too. Such lovely music she could play. Break your heart with it she could. So beautiful it was to see her fingers rise and fall, the delicate way she caressed the keys. Be well and happy, that's what I wish for ye, Kay. I do.'

And with that, teary-eyed, he kisses me in the center of my forehead, then turns away.

'Come on, Crudder boy. Time to chow down, doggie.'

He strolls with the big black dog back toward the kennel while we stare after him from the other side of the gate.

Joel and I barely speak on our way north, the fast way this time, the one that mounts the hills, picks up Route 280 west of San Jose, then follows the freeway up the peninsula.

'This is getting interesting, Kay. I'm thinking – maybe Hale was right.'

I don't respond because I know what he means – Hale's theory that there was some kind of obstruction of justice conspiracy in which Dad played a part. I really don't want to think about that. For one thing it strikes me as implausible. It was Dad, after all, who suggested we talk to the other cops. Why do that if he had something to hide?

'My father's the most honest man I know,' I tell Joel. 'All he's interested in is baking honest loaves of bread.'

'Kay!' Joel sputters. 'I wasn't – didn't mean—'

But of course we both know what he meant.

'Let's talk to Vasquez,' I suggest. 'Then, if you still want to interview Dad, I'll set it up.'

San Francisco sparkles as we approach it from the back; I always think of the front of the city as the water side. The lit towers of the financial district stand like totems against the sky. A few minutes later, as we drive past the low buildings of SoMa, a distant growl of motorcycles rends the tranquil night.

This is reality, I think, thankful to be home. Wainy's world, so dark and menacing, frightened me more than I realized.

Joel drives me up Russian Hill through residential streets. I'm glad he doesn't choose Polk or Van Ness – I need quiet now, have no desire to pass through the Gulch.

'I'll never forget the sight of that old man,' Joel says, 'whistling and dancing on the boards. He knows he's a goner, but still he danced till he dropped.' Joel turns to me. 'A dance of death, do you think?'

'Or a dance of courage.'

I ask him to drop me a block from my building. After he stops the car he takes my hand.

'Are you willing to follow this all the way, Kay – no matter where the trail leads? Because if you're not, that's fine. Just say the word. If you don't want to go on, I'll understand.'

I shake my head. 'I'll go all the way with you, Joel. But thanks for giving me the choice.'

He kisses me. I get out, cross Hyde then saunter along the hedge looking to see if Drake is watching me from within the park.

'Kay!'

His whisper cuts to my ears. I follow the sound until I see him standing in thick foliage beside the trunk of a Monterey pine.

'Thanks for waiting up for me.'

'Will the Doc be coming by tonight?'

I shake my head, and, as I do, note Drake's relief.

Later, upstairs, safe in my flat, staring out at the Bay, I can still feel the press of Wainy's lips upon my forehead and the power of his scrutiny as he peered into my eyes.

Joel phones at noon. I take his call in the darkroom where I'm working up prints of Wainy dancing his jig in the night.

'I spoke to SFPD Public Affairs. There'll be no sanctioned interviews with Vasquez on the T case or anything else.'

'His decision or theirs?'

'Both, I expect.'

'What do we do now?'

'Ambush-interview him tonight when he gets home.'

By five we're set up, sitting in Melvin, on the opposite side of Valley Street from Vasquez' 1930s period house. The street is lined with nice well-kept homes set side-by-side on small well-tended lots. The Noe Valley is known for its excellent climate, warmer and far less foggy than Russian Hill. A neighborhood of affluent young marrieds, yuppies, conservative gays, it costs plenty to buy a home here. Vasquez, whom Joel tells me is married with three kids, appears to be doing well.

I'm nervous sitting here, loaded camera and micro tape-recorder in my hands, scrunched up in this uncomfortable little car. Especially as time passes, the sky darkens, and there is as yet no sign of our quarry.

'What if he doesn't show?' I ask Joel.

'We'll wait till seven. If he doesn't turn up, we'll come back in the morning, try and catch him then.'

'I'm wondering – is it really all that smart to surprise a cop? What if he thinks we're threatening him and pulls his gun?'

'I'll identify us as press right away.' He shows me his police press pass. 'Flash this in his face.'

'And if he walks by?'

'Whatever he does he'll give us a look.'

'Which is when I'm supposed to take his picture?'

'You got it, kiddo. Now sit back, keep your powder dry.'

Still I'm worried. What can Vasquez possibly tell us in a situation like this, in full view of his neighbors, with his family hovering just behind the door? Joel says we're here to show commitment to our story, and, if Vasquez gives us a 'no comment', to put it squarely on the record. Still I'm nervous. I wonder how Dad would handle it. If Vasquez is smart, I think, he'll smile, invite us in, offer us Cokes, tell us he's sorry but under orders not to talk, then send us home with sincere regrets. And if he isn't smart, if we unnerve him? Then, I think, God save us from his wrath.

He turns up finally, just about the time I'm thinking he won't, parks his car, a new silver Taurus, in his driveway.

Joel touches my arm. 'Go get him, kiddo!'

He's out his side before I can open my door. After that I move fast, nearly tripping as I cross the street, all the while struggling to keep up with Joel and intersect with Vasquez before he reaches his front stoop.

He feels ambushed all right. He stops to peer at us, alarmed. He's blocky and tall. I understand why Hilly felt intimidated. He has a head of thick black hair, wears heavy black-rimmed glasses, stands erect like a military man on parade.

'Joel Glickman, *Bay Area News*!' Joel speaks so fast the words run together.

'You were told – no interviews.'

Vasquez starts up the front steps. I focus my camera ready to catch him when he turns.

'We've already talked to Hale, Ricky, Wainy and Jack,' Joel says. 'Only fair you get a chance to tell your side.'

Vasquez wheels, furious.

Whap! My strobe glints off his glasses.

'Bastards!' The word comes out of him in a hiss.

'What's the problem, Lieutenant? We're going to write about this whether you cooperate or not.'

'You're scum! Get out!'

Whap! Whap! Got him twice more!

'"Journalist scum".' Joel scribbles in his notebook. 'Sir, can we quote you on that?'

Vasquez squints at me. 'Who're you?'

'She's—'

I wave Joel off. 'Kay Farrow, Jack Farrow's daughter.'

Vasquez stares hard at me like he's photographing me with his eyes.

'Your dad ought to spank your behind,' he whispers with an

intensity that makes me tremble. Then he mounts the last two steps, enters his house and slams the door.

'He's bad,' I tell Joel.

We're sitting in a bar on Church Street, the nearest one to Vasquez' house. I'm still shaking from the confrontation. Joel's trying to calm me down.

'I know what he said degraded you, Kay. But put it in context. How'd you feel if someone stuck a flash camera in your face?'

'I'm not talking about being degraded.'

'What is it then?'

'He's a bad cop.'

'Come on! He's head of felony prostitution. How bad can he be?'

'I don't care what he's head of,' I say. 'I've known cops all my life. I know what they're like. He's got bad cop's eyes. Hale, Ricky and Wainy didn't. They were only nuts.'

Joel spreads his hands. 'I'll give it a couple days, write him a note, see if he's changed his mind about an interview.'

'He won't answer. Then you'll want to talk to Dad?'

Joel meets my eyes. 'Don't you think I should, kiddo?'

THE TIME HAS COME to see the Judge. It's been nearly two years since we've exchanged a word. My only sight of him has been through the lens of my telescope. As far as I know he has not seen me.

I receive the summons mid-morning. The phone rings, I pick it up, hear his voice. No secretary or clerk on first to announce the call, just that voice flowing from the receiver like rich warm honey. Hearing it, my heart speeds up.

'I've missed you, Kay.'

It's the composed, rational, mellifluous voice that becalms all passion, melts all rage. A touch of cheer in it too. Today he's at his best, not judicial, stentorian or pompous. I hear the voice of the man I loved, the man who loved me then betrayed me without even understanding how he had.

'I need your wisdom,' he says. 'I'd like to see you, tomorrow evening if possible. But if you don't feel up to it, or would rather postpone . . . of course I understand.'

He wants *my* wisdom! Sweet Jesus!

He was always good at this, making me feel special, singled out from the multitude. To tell me I am among those few to whom he would turn for counsel is to make me feel exalted.

We make a date. I will come to his home at six tomorrow for a drink. He would make it for tonight if it weren't for the County Trial Attorneys Roast or some such affair.

'Justice, remember, Kay, is also politics,' he reminds me.

'Yes, I remember,' I tell him . . . and think: *You taught me so much.*

I have trouble concentrating on Sasha when he comes – for this is the night I am to tie *him* up. *Rope-trick, rope-trick* – the word keeps flashing through my brain. I seem to be getting things mixed up: my sex life, bondage, trickery, David deGeoffroy and his magic show. Am I so confused I feel tied in knots? Or am I merely haunted by the image of a shower of dismembered limbs?

Thankfully I recover my concentration. Then Sasha and I start having fun. Wanting my bindings to be symbolic, I toss the ropes aside.

'I'm not going to tie you,' I tell him. 'Tonight your shackles shall be composed of will.' He loves the discipline of the exercise, revels in it, thrashing and squirming as I gnaw. When he can't stand it anymore, dares to remove his wrists from the headboard, I admonish him ('Naughty, naughty!'), place his hands back where they belong, and recommence the torturous raptures I'm inflicting upon his dusty flesh.

'You're terrible, Kay. Wicked!'

How can I not adore a man who calls me that?

'Yes, a love witch!'

I lap at the precise spot where he relishes it most and can endure it least.

'Lord Vishnu, save me!'

It's an act, but such a delightful one. We finally break down into giggles.

Normally I care nothing about clothes, but here I am before the mirror nervously trying combinations. Should I go as funky urban artist? The Judge used to like that look. How about stylish fashion photographer? That's how I was dressed the first time we met. Ingenue, the kid he fell for? I can probably put together a schoolgirl's outfit if I try.

I'm disgusted with myself for being so indecisive, though I know this is how people behave when they're dressing to meet an old lover for a drink. We want to make ourselves as attractive as possible in the hope that he/she will feel a twinge of regret. Could the Judge be worrying about his wardrobe too? No, not him; he's too confident and mature.

I finally decide on my 'fine dining' outfit: black silk pants and blouse, black pumps, concha belt, silver earrings plus my liquid silver necklace from Santa Fe. I look good, I think, checking myself out before I leave. Actually it's hard for me to dress badly since everything I own now is black, white or gray. Something I learned the hard way after years of making a fool of myself choosing clashing colors and wearing mismatched socks.

Darkness comes early these late-autumn days. I take a Union Street bus up to Grant. When I get off it's just six o'clock. Thinking it better not to arrive on time, I kill five minutes in an antique store then meander north via Lombard toward his building on Telegraph Hill, catching the aroma of wild fennel and resin from the conifers and Monterey cypresses that surround Coit Tower.

The Judge's condo comprises the fourth floor and penthouse of a gray stone building, its façade broken by finely detailed bays.

Ascending I notice lush new carpeting on the stairs. My pulse, I note, is steady. Pausing at the third-floor landing I take the measure of my sangfroid. No gloss on my forehead, no trembling in my limbs. Excellent! Even though I feel vulnerable (this being one of those few occasions when I've chosen to go out without my camera) I also feel strong. He's waiting for me in his doorway. Sparkling eyes, cleft chin, sleek combed-back hair. His neck is perhaps a bit more leathery than before, but that's appropriate for an ex-Marine. The gray zone in his hair has expanded up his temples, but that only adds to the clubman appeal. He wears a dark blazer, chevron tie, striped shirt with pure white collar. Perfectly creased slacks, glowing shoes . . . he's the very image of a Man of Distinction stepping out of a Scotch whisky ad.

'Kay!'

He gently pulls me to him, kisses me lightly on the lips.

'Been too long. So great to see you.' He stands back. 'You're looking great too!'

Dare I blush!

We take the spiral staircase up to the penthouse. The large Japanese plum blossom screen still adorns one wall, the Khmer bronze stands safe in its niche. The Judge, a collector of Far Eastern antiquities, heads the accession committee at the Museum of Asian Art.

He uncorks a bottle of Napa Valley Cabernet, pours us each a glass, then slides open the terrace doors. I step out, go immediately to the railing. He follows, stands beside me. The sky is black, the air clear, horizon broken by the elegant outline of the Golden Gate Bridge, its traffic flowing like a distant molten river in the night.

We stand in silence. I search Russian Hill, find my building, then the window through which I regularly aim my telescope. In his living room I noticed a small spotting scope on a tripod. I wonder: does he use it to snoop on me?

'The view hasn't changed,' I say. 'The air here's sweet as ever.'

'Have you?' he asks. I turn to him. 'Changed?'

'I hope so.' I peer at him. 'How about you?'

He gives the matter judicial consideration. 'I hope so too.' Then gently: 'Do you have a lover, Kay?' A little taken aback, I admit that I do. He nods wistfully. 'Lucky guy.'

'What are you telling me?' I ask.

'What I told you on the phone – that I've missed you. I loved you dearly, Kay. I'm sure I always will.'

Not knowing how to respond, I merely nod. 'Do you ever look over at my place?' I ask. 'I look over here all the time.'

He smiles, shakes his head. 'I try not to indulge myself. Better to steer clear of might-have-beens.' He smiles again. 'But if occasionally my eyes do fall upon your windows, I always tip my hat . . . even when I'm not wearing one.' He raises his hand to eye level to show me how he does it.

We go back inside. I sit down. He refills my glass, takes a seat on the opposing couch.

'Tell me what you've been up to?' he asks in a manner so sweet and avuncular I let down my guard.

I tell him about my investigations into the old T case, my worries about Dad, that he may have been involved in something illegal. The Judge listens intently as I speak. At one point he gets up to turn on the exquisite Japanese lanterns that line the room.

I lean forward. 'If it turns out there was obstruction of justice and Dad was involved . . . I guess what I'm asking is – can what I'm doing get him in trouble?'

Manicured fingers stroke the square cleft chin. 'You're asking a legal question, Kay. I'm not your lawyer. I'm a federal judge.'

'But surely you can tell me the law.'

'I can . . . but should I? Is that really what you need from me tonight?' He pauses. 'I think you need another kind of counsel. You want to know whether you should go ahead, no matter what the risk. Not the legal risk, but the risk to your integrity. Personal integrity's very important to you – I remember that.'

'I was brought up to believe it's the most important thing about a person.'

'Which is why I—' He smiles. 'But I already told you.'

*Which is why I loved you . . . Is that what he doesn't want to say
again?*

'Nearly every lesson Dad taught had to do with truth and honor.
There was one . . .' I tell The Judge the story, a bedside tale from
my youth:

A man was sent out upon a treasure hunt, the kind where you
find a note that gives clues to the position of the next note, etc,
until finally you locate the treasure. In Dad's story the hunt takes
up most of the hero's life. He is told that when he finds the treasure
he will discover 'the most valuable thing in all the world'.

The man travels the globe, works out the clues, finds note after
note, and after twenty years ends up less than a mile from where
he started out. The last clue takes him to a rock, beneath which,
he's been promised, he will find the treasure.

He lifts the rock, digs beneath it, down five feet, ten, fifteen, but
finds nothing. Feeling he's been tricked, he flings himself upon the
ground. Then he notices that something's been carved on the
bottom of the rock. Excited, he adjusts it to catch the light. There
are five letters inscribed: T-R-U-T-H. Truly 'the most valuable thing
in all the world'.

The Judge laughs. 'Your dad's great. That's a terrific story. And
I think in it you may find your answer too. You were taught that
seeking the truth is a life-time's work. I think you must pursue it
now no matter how the chips may fall.'

He's good tonight, the Judge is. I always thought he'd have made
a great teacher. Now that he's shown me my answer lies within my
query, I'm reminded of something similar Maddy once said: 'We
take pictures to discover what we can't see, the truth invisible to
our naked eyes.'

'You make it sound so simple,' I tell him.

He smiles. 'Most solutions are. Still I think you should consult
a lawyer. I can give you several names. There may be some way
of handling this whereby, depending on the outcome, the damage
won't be too great.'

I thank him. We fall into silence. I'm waiting for him to tell me
why he called. When he doesn't, I ask: 'That business about needing
my wisdom – you were joking, of course.'

He smiles again. 'Perhaps wisdom wasn't the right word. Compassion – that's closer to what I meant.'

More silence.

'I don't understand.'

He looks slightly nervous now. 'You're involved in something, Kay – something you may have misunderstood.'

I tighten. 'If this is about—'

'Please!' He raises his hand. 'No names. We can only speak of this if we don't use names. Agreed?'

I stare at him. 'If that's how you want it.' I take a deep breath. 'What have I misunderstood?'

'It's not so simple . . .'

'Most solutions are,' I remind him.

He looks grim. I think: This may be the only time I've seen him at a loss for words.

'Sometimes people engage in acts,' he says, 'acts that may strike others as wrong, immoral, but which are not as they appear. I mean, who among us has the right— ?' He smiles. 'Pretty funny, I guess, coming from a judge. What I'm getting at, Kay, is . . . well, suppose someone takes a benign interest in a class of deprived young people who are living in a way we can't even imagine . . .'

'*Benign?*'

'You're smirking. Have I said something wrong?'

'I don't mean to smirk, but what you're saying is absurd.'

'Look, I know what you think, but, believe me, you've got it wrong. It's a matter of preferences, nothing more.'

'Just preferences? Are you sure?'

'People like that, prominent people, don't relish having their private lives spread out for all to see. So, sometimes, they'll act in a self-protective manner, which, if you look at it from their point of view, makes perfect sense.'

'Just self-protective – is that really what you think?'

'Wait a minute, please.'

'No, you wait.' I stand. 'I can't believe this, can't believe it. We're not talking about the same people. We *can't* be. If you'd only come out straight and say their names.'

He shakes his head.

'Right . . .' I move to the bronze Khmer figure, stare into its expressionless face. 'You're the one's got it wrong.' I wheel, face him. 'I've been beaten! My life's been threatened! Do you know that? Did they tell you *that?*'

He stares at me. 'If that's true—'

'It is.'

'Then my advice is go to the DA's people, tell them your story, leave it in their hands.'

'I can't do that yet. I've got no proof.'

A thin smile. Now he must feel he has the upper hand. 'That could mean there's nothing to be proven.'

'There's plenty.'

'Then let the justice system take its course. For your own safety, Kay, stop playing Private Eye.'

I nod, walk over to the plum blossom screen, note the austere elegance of the design.

'I guess I don't really like that advice,' I tell him.

He's surprised. 'It's good counsel.'

'"Playing Private Eye" – for me this is not a game.'

'I didn't mean to diminish—'

'I'm a photojournalist. A terrible crime's been committed. I'm investigating it. It's the subject of my book.' I turn to him. 'In your eyes I guess I'm still the pretty little art student with the too-big camera around her neck.'

'I didn't mean to make you angry.'

'Who says I am? Though I admit the last time we met I was.'

'Because I had a meaningless fling with someone who meant nothing to me?'

'Because you made *me* feel meaningless. You still don't understand.'

'You left me. I got my punishment.'

'I got mine too . . . because I missed you more than I like to say.'

'Look, Kay, I never claimed to be a paragon.' He shakes his head. 'I'm human, flesh and blood, with frailties like everyone else. You held me to a standard I couldn't meet. That was your verdict. Painful as it was, I had to accept it.'

'Which is why I forgave you,' I tell him, though his comments remind me so strongly of Sarah Lashaw's mea culpa, I feel sick. 'The person you showed me wasn't the person I wanted to be with, so for me it had to end. And, admit it – you were starting to get tired of me anyway. I wasn't getting younger. Yet you gave me so much that for all my anger I still treasured you in my heart.'

God! I didn't come here to say all this. What kind of damn' hole am I digging for myself?

'Listen,' I tell him, 'a few moments ago you shushed me. That hurt. I want to discuss this thing up front. I want to tell you my side of it. Then I want your advice.'

He looks scared. 'Don't!'

I stare at him. 'You mean that?' When he nods, I nod back casually, my heart sinking inside.

He relaxes, smiles. We talk about our careers. I ask him if there's still a possibility he may move up to the Appellate Court.

'There's a chance I may move even higher,' he says smoothly. 'For obvious reasons I can't say more.'

I nod. I'm satisfied. He has disappointed me, perhaps as I hoped he would. He has failed my integrity test, placed ambition above loyalty, making it possible for me to feel released. No longer need I long for him, wonder which pretty young woman he has lately seduced. And if he should manage to earn the high judicial appointment he seeks, I will hold close my knowledge that his rectitude's a sham.

'Have you ever been compromised?' I ask him boldly.

He stares at me as if I'm mad. 'What kind of awful question is that?'

I meet his eyes. 'Sorry. I just wondered, in view of what you've said. I mean, these people are your friends, you're in their circle. They're wealthy. They have political clout. Perhaps they checked around, found out we were once lovers, so they decided to approach you, persuade you to intervene.'

'Act as a conciliator in a dispute between friends. Nothing wrong with that.'

'No, except they lied to you, tried to use you. I'd think that would make you mad. But it doesn't seem to have had any effect, which tells me you believe their phony story – whatever it is.'

'I don't take sides, Kay.'

'That's right, you're a judge. And Justice is also politics.'

Choking back tears, I quickly descend the spiral stairs. He follows, but before he can reach me I let myself out then rush down to the street.

Now there are things I must do. I order a taxi from a pay phone, tell the driver to take me to the Castro.

In the Safeway on Market, I buy a box of chalk, walk over to the mailbox on Collingwood and 18th, leave the mark that will tell Hilly I seek a meeting at 8 the following night. Exhilarated at having set things in motion, I drop into a burrito joint for dinner. Then I taxi home, change clothes, grab my camera and go out again on foot to stalk the Gulch.

The fog has suddenly rushed in from the ocean causing particles of water to accumulate on window screens. But despite the mist, the Gulch tonight seems especially alive, hustlers posing awaiting clients – who appear to be in scant supply.

I spot Sho beside the Korean Bar-B-Q in classic stance, one leg bent so his foot is pressed against the building wall. I sidle up to him, ask what's going on.

'Police sweep,' he says. 'Scared off the johns. Usually takes a couple days for things to settle down.'

I take up a position beside him, position my foot the same way, breathe in the cooking smells, enjoy the feel of the concrete wall against my back. Checking out the parade emerging and disappearing into inky mist, I sense an abundance of energy, hunger, testosterone.

I turn to him. I'm fascinated by the triangular shape of his face and the way it's framed by his long center-parted hair.

'Tell me, Sho – did you ever go out with the bald guy, the one drives the Mercedes coupé?'

He squints, asks why I'm asking.

'Just curious,' I tell him. 'What's his scene about?'

Sho smiles. 'Can't tell you that, Bug.'

'Hustler's secret?'

'You'd probably—' He screws up his face.

'—throw up? You think I'm that naive?'

He shuffles awkwardly. 'It's just – it's hard to explain to a woman.'

'Believe me, there's nothing I haven't heard about and little I haven't seen.'

He shuffles again. 'Rain probably told you.'

I don't reveal how pleased I am to receive this confirmation that Tim knew Crane.

'I hear he can be mean,' Sho finally says. 'Depends on his mood. Different strokes for different folks. Never messed with me. Probably knew if he did I'd bust his nose.'

So much for a 'benign interest'.

I'm content to leave it at that, but there's more Sho has to say.

'Rumor is he bashed a couple kids. Pissed everybody off. Some of the guys got together, agreed they wouldn't go out with him anymore. But, you know, there's no way to enforce something like that out here. Anyway, I'm sure he still finds what he's looking for, young and sweet. What he likes to do with them – I couldn't say.'

'Knob rents him his boys, doesn't he? Tommy and Boat?'

Sho is surprised I possess such sensitive information.

'You're wired pretty good, Bug.'

'Knob put you with him?'

Sho shuffles, shakes his head. 'There're things I just can't say.'

'Tim used to tell me stuff.'

'Yeah . . . look what happened to him.'

'You think he got offed because he talked too much?'

Now it's Sho's turn to shrug. 'You don't mess with Knob and make a living on the Gulch,' he says.

I thank him, saunter off into the gloom, chewing on this new bit of information. So Knob is king here, rules with a merciless hand. Tim never told me that, but then he was a free-lance, and, in Sho's words – look what happened to him.

I join the parade, searching for Knob, but don't spot him on the street. Perhaps he's in one of the bars, doing a deal in the back of someone's car, or, unpleasant thought, tracking me even as I seek him out. I stop a couple of times, turn abruptly in the hope of catching sight of him behind. But the gloom's so thick I doubt I'd see him even if he were trailing me at fifty feet.

I ask myself: what makes me so important to Knob? For all I know he administers beatings twice a week. But then I'm the only one here who carries a camera, a device that can document meetings between people who would deny they ever met.

Back home, setting down my camera, I realize I didn't take a single shot. An odd event, but then it's been a strange evening all around.

Approaching my telescope, I swing the tube from its usual position, trained on the penthouse of the Judge. I don't even bother to check the viewfinder to see if he's standing outside brooding over our final words. Rather I pick the whole apparatus up and move it to the bay window of the dining room. The view from here is only a smidgen different, but the new position will remind me I'll be taking a new perspective from now on.

The phone rings. I pick up.

'I'm in a pay phone.' It's Hilly. She doesn't identify herself. 'Got your message. I'll be there.' She clicks off.

I smile; I do enjoy this cloak-and-dagger stuff, so perhaps the Judge was right. In a sense I *am* playing Private Eye . . . but then it no longer matters what he thinks.

Ariane: I dream of her, this woman I have never seen. I may have lost Tim, but it gives me hope that his twin, whom I'm convinced I will one day find, still walks the earth.

In the morning I wait around until 11, then set out for Clement Street. I want to arrive just after the baking and Dad's prime business hours, yet catch him before he goes out on errands.

He's standing outside City Stone Ground when I arrive, talking to one of his suppliers. I study him as I wait: a huge friendly bear of a man in a white apron with smears of flour on his forearms and cheeks.

The staff is friendly. Everyone greets me. 'Hi ya, Kay!'

'Hi!'

Tamara brings me coffee and a slice of panettone. Peter stops to show me the new narrow crusty baguette. Kids, he tells me, love these long thin loaves; they pretend they're swords, fight duels with them.

Dad gives me a great hug. 'Wanna have lunch?' he asks. 'Chinese?'

I shake my head, suggest since it's a beautiful day, we pack a picnic and take it into the park.

He thinks that's a great idea, strips off his apron, goes to the refrigerator, extracts a half bottle of rosé, packs two narrow baguettes into a canvas bag, then leads me down Clement two blocks to a Russian deli, where he purchases napkins, pickles, hard-boiled eggs, a little container of blackberry and green coriander sauce, and a cold flattened Tabaka-style chicken which he orders cut up.

With these gastronomic treasures, we walk into the Presidio, find an empty picnic table overlooking the golf course and sit down to feast.

We make small-talk for a while. He knows I've come for a reason, but for now we pretend we're on a pleasant father-daughter outing in the woods.

I ask after Phyllis. He tells me she's made a huge sale in Pacific Heights.

'Sold a floor of that fancy ocher building on Washington.'

'Don't know it, Dad. Remember, I don't see colors.'

He winces. The moment the words escape my lips I'm angry at myself for being bitchy.

'Sorry,' I tell him. 'That wasn't necessary. I had no right. You, who helped me more than anyone . . .'

He places his hand on mine. 'I'm a fool to have forgotten, darlin'.' He smiles. 'It's the building next to the big Spreckels house.'

'Sure, I know it.' ·

'Sold it for two million eight. She'll split six percent – net eighty-four thou'. Not bad.'

I can tell he's not really excited by this; he repeats it by rote, as if straight from Phyllis Sorenson's lips.

'Phyl says she wants to blow some of it on a Christmas trip. She's got Hawaii in mind. When I told her I always spend my holidays with you, she said she'll invite you and her daughters along.'

I can imagine how much fun that's going to be – Christmas in some big beach-front hotel beholden to a woman I can barely stand, along with her two college-age daughters whom, having met only once, I hoped never to see again.

'Actually, Dad, I'm not sure that's such a good idea.'

He laughs. 'That's what I told her. So it's off.'

'How're the two of you getting along these days?'

'So so,' he says. 'Actually, I think we're getting kind of tired of each other, wanna know the truth.'

I nod respectfully, not sure I'm happy about that. Though I don't care for Phyllis, I hate to think of Dad companionless.

'We went to see them,' I say.

He looks up; he's nibbling on a Russian pickle. 'If you don't mind my asking, darlin' – just who is "we" and who is "them"?'

'We is me and Joel. Them is Ricky, Wainy and Vasquez. Billy Hayes is dead.'

He nods.

'You didn't mention that the other day.'

'I didn't much feel like describing how it happened.'

I nod to show him I understand. 'Anyway, Vasquez refused to talk.'

'Figures.'

'Ricky and Wainy, on the other hand, they talked a lot.'

Dad dips a piece of chicken into the blackberry sauce, places it in his mouth. He's so calm, so thoroughly at ease, I wonder if I'm on to something after all. 'They went off on riffs, the two of them. Lots of words but the underlying meaning wasn't clear.' Again Dad smiles. 'Still, thinking it over, I decoded some of it. You know, what they call the subtext.'

'I believe I've heard that word, on public television.'

'You're hilarious, Dad!'

He grins. 'Humor, they say, can sometimes leaven the load.'

I'm grateful he wants to lighten up. At least this time he isn't twisting his neck against his collar.

'What I got out of it is more like a theory. Because, you see, though they were drinking and talking crazy, they were also careful about what they said. Maybe they thought we were recording them.' I pause. 'In fact, I was.'

'So, you got a theory, darlin', share it, why don't you?'

I lay it out for him, first Ricky's numerous references to each cop's propensity for violence.

'Billy Hayes's boxing skills, a hint that Vasquez might be cowardly. Wainy, he said, busted a few heads in his time. What he said about you is you could swing a nightstick good as anyone in Central Command.'

'And himself?'

'He didn't say.'

'Ricky knew how to be a brute.'

'So that leaves us with a gang of five cops, four with tempers, capable of beating people up.'

'That's good.' Dad smiles. 'I'm impressed. Go on.'

'Ricky also made a point about how none of you were clumsy or dumb, none of you the type to bungle evidence. Yet somehow, by some mysterious process, you all seemed to become afflicted at the same time with this "lose-the-evidence disease".'

Dad laughs. 'Disease – I like that. Kind of sums it up.'

'What're you telling me?'

'Just listenin', darlin'. You're the one doing the tellin'.'

I boil down Wainy's ravings. 'First he boasted about how he and a fellow guard in Santa Cruz beat an amusement park intruder to pulp a few nights before. Then he claimed to be harboring a secret about Sipple, which, if he told it, could hurt people including you.' Dad doesn't blink. 'Finally he admitted this secret concerned the location of what he referred to as "that bag of ever-lovin' shit-eatin' fuck-all ev-eye-dense".'

'So, darlin', what'd you make of all that?'

'That Wainy's still got a violent temper and that the Sipple evidence wasn't neglectfully lost, but stashed.'

'Putting that together with what Ricky told you, you come up with a pretty grim picture, right?'

'Jesus, Dad! Do I have to spell it out?'

'Only if you want to, darlin'.'

'You could put it together for me, couldn't you?'

'I could,' he says. 'Let me think about it a little first.'

Suddenly I realize that what he's just said is about as far as I've been prepared to hear him go. Anything more and I'm not sure I can take it; anything less and I'll leave with the feeling he's a liar.

'That was a load of crap you handed me the other day,' I tell him. 'About the guy who tied up Sipple maybe not even being the T killer. Or – what was your other theory? That maybe the whole Sipple incident was a plant – whatever that was supposed to mean.'

Dad stares at me, not blinking.

'*Why?*'

'Why what, darlin'?'

'Why'd you try and mislead me?'

'If I did, you can be sure I had my reasons.' He pauses. 'Know something?' He smiles. 'That I didn't succeed only makes me proud of you. Prouder than ever!'

I study him. He's showing me the face of a parent whose kid has just won a trophy. I realize he actually *is* proud his deception failed.

I want to scream: What's going on? I turn to him. He's staring into my eyes.

'*What,*' I ask him, '*what the ever-loving hell did the five of you guys do?*'

FIFTEEN

EVEN FROM THE FIRST moment Jack knew.

That wasn't what he told Hale of course. He admitted nothing, played stupid, figuring that was his only way out of the jam. Still, he maintained, he knew from the first moment he walked in, and so did the others when they arrived . . . but damned if any of them would admit it.

Soon as his eyes took in the scene – the nude kid bound, the tattoo equipment – he *knew*. He recognized the tattoo stuff because he and Rusty Quinn had worked bunko in Chinatown, and he'd been in a lot of tattoo parlors over those years. But it really wasn't that or anything else he consciously added up that told him this was a failed T killing. Rather it was the smell, the way the whole place stank of craziness and homicide.

First task, he knew, was save the kid . . . if he wasn't already dead. But even as he moved in to wrestle the black leather hood off his head, his eyes probed the edges of the room to make sure the T killer wasn't still there. He wasn't. The room had an empty feel to it, yet there was this feeling of menace too, something strong, powerful, that stank of hatred, cruelty, blood splashed and spilled, bones broken, tissue rent. There was a real smell too, the smell of an exotic brand of soap, sweet and spicy all at once, with something added to it, something unexpected, dark and black, and he knew what it was – the dark stifling smell of licorice.

He got the hood off, saved the kid, worrying even as he did that he'd pick up something awful from his mouth. Not HIV, for no one knew about AIDS back them, but something vile like gonorrhea or syphilis the kid was nurturing in the warm wet swamp-pit of his throat, acquired from giving blow-jobs at the baths or whatever they did in there – Jack didn't like to think too much about stuff like that.

Yet, despite his fear, he breathed for the kid, became his lungs until he felt him respond. Then he felt as good as he had in the twenty years he'd been on the force – because the best times for him had never been stopping a suspect or making a collar or sitting in a courtroom when a jury came in with a verdict. The good, the heady times were helping people, doing such small fine deeds as assisting a mother to find her lost child in the crowds on Stockton, or persuading some girl with dirty hair and scabs on her arms to get herself into detox before she caught pneumonia and died there on the Haight. This time it was saving this kid's life, because he hadn't the slightest doubt that if he'd walked up the hill instead of run, or taken his time about searching the flat before wrestling off the hood, the boy, who now lay before him spitting and puking, would be dead.

Maggie, the middle-aged landlady from upstairs, was watching from the basement doorway horrified. Maybe it was the kid's nudity or the choking and vomiting or just that something so sordid was taking place in her house. Whatever, he ordered her back upstairs to call for an ambulance and extra cops, and then, when she was gone, took the kid's head in his lap, mopped his face, told him he was going to be okay and asked who had tied him up.

The kid couldn't speak too well. He was in the twilight limbo state of a person who'd just crossed the line back from death. But he did manage to croak out a word that sounded like it was maybe a person's name, something like 'Skelton', Jack thought, though he wasn't sure, and the kid was looking so distant and terrified, he decided to let it rest a while.

Then it occurred to him there'd be no chance to pursue it, for the whole thing would soon be out of his hands. The T case was the biggest game in town, was, as everyone in the Department knew, the exclusive no-intruders-allowed province of the elite investigative unit headed by the city's top cop and press favorite, Inspector Jonathan Topper Hale.

Billy Hayes was the first to show. The two of them always got along, so when Billy entered in that fighter's crouch he invariably used when he set foot in a room, as if entering a ring for a bout, Jack didn't say a word, just waited, curious how Billy would react. He wasn't surprised when Billy shot his bright blue little fighter's eyes around, took everything in, sniffed the air, blinked and said: 'Bad, Jack. *Bad!*'

What was bad about it? Jack wanted to know. But before he could ask, Billy came out with it himself:

'It's the smell, ain't it – like you sniff sometimes around a gym when one fighter's beat up on another too hard, the murderous smell the trainers call "the stink".'

Billy checked the kid's pulse, then Jack pointed out what the perp had left behind – the hood with its elaborate trussings, so sinister and black, fraught with hazard, pungent with his victim's vomit and sweat; the tattoo gear, old stuff, crude, acquired most likely third or fourth hand, and the sooty smell that came out of the jar of black tattooing ink; the hypodermic syringe lying on the wooden stool, full of some colorless viscous fluid with a cotton swab tucked carefully beneath its tip; finally that thing you couldn't see, the aroma lingering over everything, strong enough to cut through the smell of the vomit and the ink, the sweet/acrid licorice scent of the soap.

They sniffed it together without speaking, trying to track it to its source. It took them straight back to the kid, the skin of his torso though not his head or arms or legs. That's when Jack went into the bathroom to sniff at the soap in the depression of the sink. Nothing there so he stuck his head through the greasy plastic shower curtain into the rusted sheet metal stall, and this time he got a heavy hit. But the bar in the soap-dish was ordinary without a trace of the cloying odor, so he came back out, knelt beside the kid, said: 'He washed you up first, didn't he – with his own soap too?'

The kid's eyes were glazed. He was done puking, but his pulse was still racing hard. The kid stared up at him, then gulped and nodded, and Jack felt the rush of having psyched a problem out, the kind of surge he figured a detective probably got every day but which was sweet and rare to him.

Just then the paramedics burst in. They took over the way they always do like everything is life-and-death, gave the kid oxygen, placed him on a gurney, covered him with a blanket and wheeled him out.

When they were gone Billy looked straight at Jack, fire in his squinty little eyes, then configured the forefingers of both hands so they formed a 'T'.

Jack nodded, Billy smiled, and next thing Wainy and Ricky arrived, trailed shortly afterwards by Luis Vasquez.

Wainy was half-drunk and so was Ricky; they'd been hitting bars around lower Fillmore when they got the call. But soused as they were, they got real quiet when they walked in, smelled the smell, felt the vibes, sensed the solemnity between Billy and Jack.

No one touched the evidence or handed it around . . . though that was the story they would later tell. They were too smart, too experienced to do a damnfool thing like that. Rather they circled in, discussed it, then Wainy pulled out his leather-covered flask, took a snort, passed it around, and everyone, except Vasquez, took a snort as well.

They knew what they had: the first break in the biggest case of the decade, hard evidence, stuff the T killer had actually touched. And they knew soon as they called it in they'd be pushed straight out. Their names wouldn't appear in the papers. Though there might be some mention of patrolmen who'd stumbled into a scene then dutifully turned it over to detectives, it would be Hale and his people who would be named and quoted and praised. There was nothing they could do about that and it rankled them hard, for to stumble into a crime scene like this, a scene so alive, filled with still-hot-from-the-perp's-hands evidence – this was what a good cop lived for, a chance to be a great cop, solve a big and gruesome case. And they knew soon as they called it in they'd be back to being plain patrol cops like before.

They stood around a while bemoaning their lot, griping about the injustice of it. They took more snorts from Wainy's flask. When they finished it off Wainy went out to his car to retrieve the full bottle of Jack Daniel's he had stashed beneath his seat. When he came back his face was pink – he'd been hit by an inspiration. They didn't have to call the task force, he said, least not right away. If they wanted they had a few hours cushion time to pursue the T case on their own. They were five smart cops, experienced cops who knew their way around the city, right? So here they were, standing in this Aladdin's cave of evidence. Was there any reason they couldn't solve this thing, track down the T killer, emerge as heroes and at the same time drive Hale and his crew of strut-around detectives nuts?

The bottle went around again, and by the time it made three circuits they were raring to go.

'So now let's take a little look-see here at what we got,' Wainy said.

First there was the hood. Billy slipped on a pair of latex gloves and picked it up. They looked at the clasps. Solid stainless steel, not the cheap chrome stuff you usually see. The hood, butter-soft, had that smoky leathery smell. The sewing and riveting had been done by hand. No store tag inside. Made-to-order, had to be.

But if you knew a little about made-to-order S&M gear, you knew the guys who fit and cut and riveted the stuff were proud of their work. Most of them had a private mark they put inside, their initials or some kind of signature. Since there was nothing in this hood, that could mean it had been made by the T killer himself.

The tattoo gear didn't tell them much. Old and most likely untraceable. But the ink could be traced. There was the manufacturer's name and a batch number right on the jar. A good phone detective could track that down in an hour. The syringe was a job for the Crime Lab boys. They could tell what kind of juice was in it and lift the prints.

So how the hell were the five of them going to track this friggin' killer? Things were bleak, the bottle made another pass. When it reached Wainy again, he took a deep draught, and, when he lowered his head, showed a canny smile.

'Hey,' he said, 'let's face it, we're not detectives, we don't work phones, lift prints, do lab analysis, we can't compete. But I say we got our own area of expertise – we know what real people do. We're patrolmen, so I say forget the detective crap and take a look at this from our angle, the real life street side we know better'n anyone else.'

That got them going. Even Vasquez got caught up in it. Wainy had set them on the track, they all had things to say, but finally it was Jack who laid it out.

It wasn't all that complicated when you looked at it, he said. Here was all this evidence left behind by a guy in a big hurry to get away. This guy, call him the T killer, had to be scared shitless, because now, for the first time after five perfect homicides, he was in a real predicament. All kinds of stuff that could be traced back to him was sitting here in this cellar. He had to know that if the right cops got hold of it, he might as well as turn himself in. Whether that happened would depend on a number of circumstances such as whether Robbie Sipple survived. But whatever the outcome, he owed it to himself to do his damnedest to get his stuff back. If he was lucky and the cops who'd gone in were as stupid as they looked . . . then, maybe, there was a small chance he could retrieve it and get away clean. In which case, even though he'd goofed, his chances of escape would be astronomically enhanced. So, figuring it was that or the gas chamber, he just *had* to take the shot.

'Sure,' Billy said, 'that's what I'd do. I'd wait around till after we all leave, then break in and hope to hell that stuff is still here to take back.'

Wainy and Ricky went along. Then, for the first time, Vasquez spoke up.

'If he's smart,' Vasquez said, 'he's still in the neighborhood, walking around, keeping an eye on the house. If a bunch of squad cars show up, he knows he's fucked. But if he sees us who came in go out again, he might just figure he's got a chance.'

So where's he watching from? they asked one another.

'Could be he's got a car parked up the street,' Ricky said. 'Or just out pacing, walking the sidewalk, circling the block, maybe with a dog to give him cover.'

The rest of them didn't think the dog idea made sense – a killer doesn't usually bring along a dog when he's going to snuff a guy. Still, they agreed, he could be out there walking, or circling in his car, or just parked like Ricky said. Problem was how to bait him, make him think all of them had left. Would he know how many of them had originally gone in? Not likely – the five of them arrived at four different times, then the paramedics showed, so even if he'd been watching, he probably couldn't have kept track.

'What we gotta do,' Wainy said, 'is four of us exit together like we're all done here for the night. One of us stays behind, in the closet or lav, radio on, ready to call if anyone comes in. Meantime the four of us hover a block or so away, say down on Waller or up on Carl Street. Then, when our buddy here gives the word, we all rush the hell back, grab the guy and shake the shit outa him till he spills.'

Of course everyone of them said he was best qualified to stay. Wainy and Billy meant it, Ricky and Jack played along, Vasquez didn't mean it at all. The way it ended up they drew straws and Billy won.

He'd be fine, he said, when Wainy asked if he didn't want company. He had his billy club, gun, deadly-weapon fists, and, best of all, the element of surprise. If the T killer returned it would be because he was sure he had a chance, not because he suspected a trap. All Billy had to do was pounce the guy, cuff him, kick him couple times in the gut to subdue him, then wait for his pals to show up, which shouldn't take them more than half a minute.

Wainy and Ricky were the actors. They made the best show out on the street, up-ending the bottle, wiping their mouths on their sleeves, saying 'good night, sleep tight, see you in the morning', that kind of crap. Vasquez and Jack played it straight, mumbling stuff like 'drive careful now, give my love to Sue, thanks for another cruddy night on the job'. Lots of glad-handing, arm-across-the-shoulder man-to-man cop garbage, then Wainy and Ricky stumbled into Wainy's car, while Vasquez and Jack casually wove their way down the street, and then up a block, where they took up positions inside an all-night grocery, radios on, waiting for Billy's call.

Was an hour and a half before it came. When it did it was quick and shrill, interrupted by static and firecracker sounds: 'Son of a . . . he's here! Fuckin' dipshit! Hurry, guys! *Shit! Take this, asshole!*'

Jack was rounding the corner of Frederick and Clayton when he saw Wainy's car pull in front of the house. Vasquez, he thought, was trailing, the way he had all evening, like he was calculating just how far he wanted to go in this thing. But Jack wasn't thinking about Vasquez just then. Seeing Wainy and Ricky rush down the outside steps to the flat, he ran fast as he could so he wouldn't be last one in to help.

Billy, as it turned out, didn't need any help. It was dim in there, no lights, just the barest amount of illumination coming through the high cellar window from the street, but it was light enough for them to see Billy had the guy down on the floor, was kicking the shit out of him, right foot, left foot, right, left! Like he was dancing, skipping rope, doing him in the belly, kidneys, ribs, spine. And the guy – he was good-sized, a lot bigger than Billy, who had always been a lean welterweight – was moaning and writhing there the way Robbie Sipple had done just a couple hours before.

That, anyhow, was how it struck Jack: poetic justice, he thought, lungs still aching from the run. One guy nearly kills another, and now he's down there on the same floor nearly getting killed himself.

It was Wainy finally pulled Billy off, which wasn't so easy, Billy being in auto kick-him mode. Then Jack got down with the guy, turned him over as Ricky switched on the lights, so they could all get a good look at him for the first time.

What hit him first was the sweet/acrid licorice smell of the soap. But the guy was no sweet beauty anymore. He was a mess, nose cracked, one eye hanging out, teeth splintered, struggling to breathe, with some kind of awful stinkin' ooze trickling out of his mouth.

Jack looked up at Billy. 'Jesus, what the hell did you do to him?'

'I dunno. Cracked him couple times with the stick, then smacked him around.'

'Shit! The guy's losing it. He'll die on us we don't get him help quick.'

Silence. Then Ricky spoke, almost in a whisper: 'We can't get him help – you know that, Jack.'

Which was true. No need to discuss it. They all knew it perfectly well. Whoever this guy was, T killer or not, if he died on them they'd all go down too. Not just Billy but all five of them; they knew the law, knew they were all accessories. They'd been parties to a conspiracy, the kind of cop conspiracy gets prosecuted hard: five rogue cops going against the rules, getting drunk, taking the law into their own hands. Moreover they'd held back material evidence in a capital case. They could get ten years for that, maybe twenty . . . unless, of course, they could come up with a story that would float.

A lot of booze had been consumed that night, but not one of them felt intoxicated then. The guy on the floor, whoever he was, was gasping out his life, and they all knew they'd better think up something fast or forget about having futures.

It was then that Vasquez emerged. The earlier portion of the evening he'd been the reluctant one, the outsider, non-drinker, the one none of them knew very well. He'd only walked in because he'd heard the call for officers and happened to be close at the time. He'd gone along with everything quietly, but now that they had trouble he took charge.

First thing, he instructed, they had to get the guy out of there fast, dead or alive, along with all the evidence. They needed to restore things to the way they'd been an hour and a half before, when they'd all pretended to leave. In the new version Billy didn't stay behind, he left with them, then they split up on the street and each went his separate way. No hanging around, no ruckus, no beating up the suspect. They all just went home, their only crime forgetting to bag, seal and log-in the evidence.

The landlady had told Jack she was going to take sleeping pills, so it was doubtful she'd heard a thing. The street had been deserted, no one out there watching them come and go. At worst, Vasquez said, there might be some dispute about what time they left, and, of course, complaints that they'd bungled the crime scene. But everything would turn out when Robbie Sipple described the guy and Hale and his people searched him out. When they couldn't find him they'd assume he ran away after retrieving the incriminating evidence.

Not bad, Wainy said, when Vasquez finished. But what do we do with the guy?

Jack, who'd been kneeling beside him, checked his pulse, looked up at them and shook his head.

Deep-six him, Vasquez said. Dump him in the Bay and get rid of the evidence somewhere else. It'll work, he said, it'll be like the guy knew he was doomed, so he went and jumped off the fuckin' GG Bridge. So now let's get to it, he said, get him the hell out of here before someone happens along.

No need to discuss it. It was a decent plan, and their futures were at stake. But when they stripped the guy preparatory to wrapping him in one of Sipple's blankets, they couldn't believe what they found.

His body was covered with bizarre tattoos of a type none of them had ever seen: arm bones tattooed on his arms, leg bones on his legs, rib bones over his ribs, all in a brilliant raucous red. Just like a skeleton, Billy said, and then Jack remembered what Robbie had mumbled when he'd asked who'd tied him up. 'Skelton', he'd thought he'd heard, but the word surely must have been 'skeleton'. It was a man with tattooed red bones all over his body, Skeleton-man, who'd done this awful thing. Which meant this dead man before them really *was* the T killer and that made Jack feel good. They hadn't killed some innocent guy, one of Sipple's friends who happened to wander in. No, thank God! They'd gotten the killer. Against all odds they'd planned and sprung a perfect trap.

The fog: Jack remembered how thick and cold it was by the time they reached the Presidio gate. There'd been no mist on the Haight, but when they got over to the Bay they found themselves in a swirl of it, so cold and damp it chilled him to the bone. Here they were, five cops, stinking of booze, cramped into Wainy's crummy car, driving wildly through the fog-bound forests of the Presidio, with a naked serial killer's body wrapped up inside the trunk.

It was crazy, Jack knew, but he couldn't think of an alternative. One thing to lose important evidence, another to beat a suspect to death. And it wouldn't matter that Skeleton-man actually *was* the T killer; in fact that probably made things worse. A suspect in a high-profile murder case, Hale in charge, then five rogue cops catch him and act as judge, jury and executioner – they'd never be forgiven. So he just breathed in the cold wet air, so close and thick he could chew it almost, and prayed they'd be able to get rid of Skeleton-man, and then all get home safe without being caught.

They were headed for Fort Point just below the Bridge, the spot where, in Hitchcock's *Vertigo*, Kim Novak leaps into the Bay. The Fort itself, that time of night, wasn't visible till they reached its base, and even there the bridge girders above were mostly lost in the fog that surged through the Golden Gate like billows of black smoke.

Wainy backed his car up to the sea wall; he and Billy got out, opened the trunk, and with Ricky's help carried Skeleton-man to the chain fence, each rusty link bigger than a man's hand. They carried him over, then on to the black boulders of the breakwater. Here they unwrapped him then lowered him into the waves, lapping and roiling like thick black oil. They watched as he floated off into the fog. The tide would carry him beneath the Bridge, either into the shipping lanes or against the south tower barrier. Eventually he'd be washed ashore, probably somewhere on the Marin side. Naked, strangely tattooed, with no accompanying ID – the Coast Guard would figure him for a jumper. There was some talk then about whether they ought to leave his clothes up on the bridge in a neat pile the way jumpers sometimes do as a final farewell to the world. Vasquez agreed that might make for a nice touch, but said they couldn't take the risk.

On the way back through the fog, they worked out their story. The point, Vasquez kept reminding them, was to keep it simple and as close as possible to actual events. Everything straight up till 10:30 p.m. Minimum amount of fabrication after that. It'd be okay, he said, if their stories differed slightly since cops' stories often do. But the essential points must be the same. If just one of them stumbled, he could bring the rest of them down.

It was then that Jack offered to take the greater share of the blame for forgetting to remove and preserve the evidence. He'd been first on the scene, he should have closed it down. He told them he'd long wanted out of SFPD and so was willing to take the fall.

Back at Park Station, in the parking lot, Jack, realizing they'd yet to go through Skeleton-man's clothes, asked the others whether they didn't wonder who he was.

'Not me,' Wainy said.

'Me neither.' Ricky shook his head.

Vasquez turned away. Billy shrugged. It was Billy, they'd agreed, who would get rid of the clothing and evidence.

'And don't tell us what you did with them neither,' Wainy instructed just before they all split up.

Jack intended to go straight home, but was too tightly wound. He needed some kind of transition and knew where he could find it – an ear into which he could confess his sins, a mouth from which absolution would flow.

He and Rusty had worked Chinatown five years, bunko most of that time, narcotics, too, for a while. Best beat in the city, people said, if you were smart and knew how to work it.

So maybe he and Rusty weren't so smart, or simply lacked desire. Corruption didn't suit them; they were interested in other things. For Rusty that meant getting laid, for Jack understanding how Chinatown worked. So even as they patrolled together, each pursued his interest in his own way.

Rusty befriended a string of gorgeous Asian prostitutes who took good care of him at the special Chinatown price for friends. Who could blame them? Wasn't Rusty's fault those beauties were turned on by a hairy Caucasian cop.

Jack learned some Cantonese then started making friends, up and down Stockton, Grant, Jackson, Washington, the alleys – Ross, Pontiac, Stark, Old Chinatown – narrow dead-end streets where when you passed you could hear the slap of mahjong pieces against wood, and where, in cellars and on the upper floors, whore houses, opium dens and gambling parlors were installed.

The partners got along well, in time became best friends. So that night when Jack felt his springs about to bust, it was natural he search Rusty out in half a dozen hang-outs he frequented late at night.

He found him finally at Choi's Triple-X, a nudie-cutie live-action cabaret at the eastern end of Chinatown. Out in front of Choi's a busty sloe-eyed hawker-girl was leashed to a pagoda-shaped stanchion, enabling her to act as a warm-bodied gatepost without fear of being carried off by rowdy passersby.

There was a stripper worked here, one Becky Yee, who at the time possessed Rusty's heart. Jack found his old partner in her dressing room, holding one of her yellow silk stage garments to his mustache.

Sensing at once that Jack was in trouble, Rusty guided him to a beer joint around the corner. Immediately Jack began spilling out the evening's events, Rusty nodding, consoling, giving Jack succor to face his demons.

'A purely innocent occurrence,' was how Rusty described Skeleton-man's demise. 'No harm intended. Could've happened to anyone, Jack.'

'Yeah, but we all knew Billy was violent,' Jack said. 'We shouldn't have let him stay.'

'We're *all* fuckin' violent,' Rusty countered. 'Anyway it's not killing the guy that'll bring you trouble. No jury'll convict you for that. Vasquez steered you wrong. It's covering up, lying about it. If Hale smells a rat he'll be all over you. He'll follow you all to the ends of the earth . . . and then on to your graves.'

Rusty's advice was terse: once you take the coverup route, you can't consider turning back. You brave it out, lie and bluster, hope your story holds and none of your buddies breaks. The code of silence, he said, should get you through, and if no one IDs the body, or, better, doesn't connect it to Sipple, the odds of things working out are probably four to one. What Jack ought to do now, he said, was go home, take a shower, get a good night's sleep. The next couple of days were going to be rough, so the better rested he was, the greater his chances of getting by Hale.

But there was something else Jack wanted to discuss: who the T killer was. They'd killed a man. It didn't seem decent not to know his name.

'You got his clothes, check them out.'

Jack explained that Billy took them. 'Look, I'm no detective,' Jack said. 'I don't know where to begin.'

Rusty knew: 'Start with the car. Walk the streets up there, chalk the tires, let a couple days pass and see which cars don't move. Then run their plates. I doubt he parked more'n a block or two away.'

*　　*　　*

When he finally got home, he found Carlotta asleep, but when he came out of the shower she was sitting up in bed.

'Nice evening with tootsie-baby?' she inquired. She had a way of hissing the word, which was why, Jack supposed, she used it instead of 'girlfriend' or 'lover'.

There was no tootsie-baby, of course. They both knew that. It was just a little joke between them whenever he came home late. But tonight he wasn't in a joking mood, was too sloshed, wrapped up in his troubles. So he made a mistake, forgot to humor her, mumbled something about finding the quip stale.

She settled back under the covers, face creased with hurt. 'Sometimes you're a real bastard, Jack.'

'Sure,' he acknowledged, 'sometimes a damned unhappy one too.'

Silence while he pulled on a fresh pair of boxers. He was going to slip into bed beside her, when she issued her retort:

'One of these days soon I'll stick my head in the oven. Or jump off the GG Bridge. Then maybe you'll look back and regret the hurtful things you said . . .'

The mention of the Bridge at that particular moment came close to pushing him over the edge. It was one o'clock in the morning, he'd saved one man's life, then been party to the killing of another. He was exhausted, but he didn't care – he wasn't going to lie down beside her now. Instead he went downstairs to the kitchen and set to work making a perfect, honest, truth-telling loaf of bread. He dozed while the dough rose, then fired up the oven and baked it off. When it came out it was beautiful – soft and chewy at its center with a gently shattering crust.

Though he wasn't due on duty till 4 p.m. the following day, he planned to go early to the Haight and start marking parked cars like Rusty said. But just as he was preparing to leave the house, he got a call from Wainy. They were wanted down at the Hall of Justice right away.

When he arrived he ran into the other four along with Mercurio, the Park Station commander. Sipple had dropped dead a couple hours before, of a heart attack the doctors said. Meantime Hale's team had spotted the case, gone over to the crime scene and found a mess. Now they wanted the evidence Wainy had reported on the forms, and, when he couldn't produce it, all hell broke loose.

First they were distributed among five small interrogation cubicles and left alone to stew. During that time Jack thought about Sipple – how exhilarated he'd felt after saving the kid's life and how miserable now that all his efforts had been for naught. Then Mercurio came in and told him how serious the matter was. This was the T case and somebody'd better remember something fast or heavy discipline would be meted out.

Next a two-man team of detectives, T-case investigators, hard jaws and flinty eyes, came in. Jack had to tell them his story three separate times, more time passed, then he and the others were herded into a conference room, seated opposite the entire T case task-force. The detectives glared at them. Mercurio, arms folded, stood against the wall. Minutes passed then Hale entered. Jack, who only knew him from appearances on TV, found his eyes frighteningly pale. Hale didn't bother to introduce himself, just started to talk.

He didn't shout at them or scream, yet every word came dripping with contempt. As the task-force glowered, and Mercurio shook his head, the five of them endured the dressing-down. They had royally fucked up, and now because of that more innocent people would likely be killed. They had disgraced their shields, which they no longer deserved to wear, were meager examples of cops, everything an SFPD cop shouldn't be – stupid, clumsy, weak, inept, unreliable, undependable, totally unfit. If it were up to Hale he'd nail their hides to the front of the Hall, signs saying DICKHEAD hanging around their necks. Fortunately for them their fates were in other hands. But he'd taken this opportunity to express the task-force's scorn, hoping they would do the honorable thing and resign. He held no hatred for them, merely pity. At that he left the room, followed by his detectives. When everyone had gone, Mercurio informed them they were dismissed then left them without a glance.

For Jack that half-hour was the most humiliating of his life. The others, he guessed, felt the same. Billy sat low in his seat. There were tears in Ricky's eyes. Wainy looked broken – a functioning alcoholic, his whole life revolved around being a cop. Only Vasquez appeared unmoved. He was completing college at night, people said. Glancing at him after the dressing-down, Jack detected a frightening sang-froid.

They didn't speak as they filed out of the building. Word on what had happened quickly spread. Reporters clustered around peppering them with questions, peering at them in that curious way one stares at people in disgrace. They ran a gauntlet of cops, attorneys, handcuffed criminals, all stripping them with mocking eyes. Jack was trembling when he reached his car. Safe inside, he leaned over his steering wheel and wept.

Back at Park Station he was informed by his sergeant he'd been reassigned to desk duty pending a hearing. No way now could he risk going up to Frederick Street and placing chalk marks on the tires of parked cars. Too many task-force people milling around, too much visibility, too many questions he wouldn't be able to answer if he were seen. The only thing to do was sit at the bare desk, stare at the wall, put in the hours, then go home to his wounded, troubled wife.

She was on psychiatric leave from her job as school music teacher; she'd broken down too many times in class. When he'd come home he'd usually find her at her piano, either sitting morose and still, or else struggling with the Schubert B-flat sonata, a piece that wandered and ruminated in ways she could never resolve so that she constantly became lost within it, repeating sections over and over for hours at a time. It was, Jack felt, the saddest piece of music he ever heard, and, in her hands, so tearful it filled the house with gloom.

He tried to counter this darkness with the aroma of baking bread. He baked some magnificent loaves over those weeks, bread-making his only respite from Carlotta's melancholy and the forces crushing him down. Every day he waited for Skeleton-man to show up, searching the papers for one of those one-paragraph items about an unidentified jumper washed to shore. Nothing.

At work he daily checked the missing persons lists, looking closely at reports that mentioned tattoos. There were no such reports.

What had happened? Had Skeleton-man drifted out to sea, been devoured by ocean beasts, torn to pieces against the rocks? Had he no lover, parents, siblings, friends, no one who missed him and declared him missing? Had he existed at all? That his body never turned up gave the whole experience the hallucinatory quality of dream.

The summer passed. He, Wainy and the others avoided one another. When they'd meet by accident, they'd nod grimly and move on. All appeared broken except for Vasquez, who, strangely, seemed to gain strength from the debacle.

The next few months Jack and Carlotta rarely spoke, he lost

in wonderment at the sour way his life had turned, she mired ever deeper in depression. Their friends avoided them. It wasn't his disgrace, Jack understood, but the aura he and Carlotta cast. Carrying themselves like broken souls they had become exemplars of despair.

When the IA Report was leaked, Jack didn't waste time. He didn't like leaving in disgrace, but was determined to get out fast. He borrowed some money from his brother-in-law, arranged a bank-loan for the rest and that September opened the City Stone Ground Bakery on upper Clement Street.

After the first day of business, exhilarated at last to be doing what he loved, he came home to find Carlotta slumped limply over the foot end of their bed. She had lain down, thrust her head back till it was upside down, stuck his spare revolver in her mouth and fired. Death for her had been instantaneous. But, perhaps the opposite of her intention, guilt over what she'd done would haunt him the rest of his life.

Years passed. The memory of that night of rescue and murder would fade, though the recollection of certain tactile impressions – the licorice smell of the soap, the thickness of the fog, the oiliness of the water – remained intense. And what could never fade was the image of Carlotta that faced him when he returned that first night from the bakery – the bizarre position of her head, the glassy stare in her eyes, the garbled agony of her mouth. Sometimes, early in the morning, when he worked dough in his hands, Jack would take a few moments to sculpt human features. Then as he mashed the dough back into a loaf shape, he would re-create the distortion of her face.

It was seven years before Hale approached him for the first time, late one afternoon walking nonchalantly into the bakery, purchasing a baguette, smiling slightly when Jack, handing him his change, recognized his face. This was a different Hale than the man who'd berated them down at the Hall that awful afternoon. He was a thin man now, his mustache was gray, his eyes and hair had lost their luster.

'How you doin', Jack?'

At first he was anxious; Rusty, after all, had warned him Hale would pursue them to their graves. And then, with Hale so amiable, he wondered if he'd stopped by to make amends. When he discovered what Hale wanted, he was shocked and horrified: the man was still working the T case on his own and had come to ask for help.

Thus began the series of annual visits that always set Jack on edge – Hale in his you-and-I-are-now-equals mode, stopping in to discuss the details of the hood. One year he asked Jack to make a drawing of it from memory, another year had him accompany him on a tour of custom leather shops. Word got back that Hale was also making unannounced visits on the others. Wainy said he enjoyed these encounters for the opportunity to play Hale for a fool. Ricky Puccio laughed them off, Billy Hayes found himself rattled. As for Vasquez, he was still in the Department, climbing steadily up the ladder. None of them knew whether Hale had taken to dropping in on him, but Jack doubted it. There was something about Vasquez that caused people to want to stay clear.

There was a cat-and-mouse aspect to Hale's visits, a message in his congeniality. His thin smile announced: 'I know about the conspiracy, I know more than you think.'

Because the meetings were so widely spaced, they appeared to be made without pressure. But Hale's apparent lack of urgency became a form of pressure in itself. It was as if he was saying: 'I have all the time in the world to get to the bottom of what you did. Sooner or later one of you'll break. Till then I'll be coming around.'

One autumn day, ten years after Sipple, Billy Hayes wandered in. Jack's greeting was guarded, but Billy pretended he didn't notice. He asked Jack if he had time to talk. They strolled up Clement, past the little Asian groceries and hole-in-the-wall restaurants, then over to quieter California Street where there was a neighborhood bar Billy knew.

Here they talked about this and that, what each had been doing, Jack's success with the bakery, Billy's troubles as boxing trainer and promoter. Then Billy steered the conversation around to the event that had changed their lives – the accidental death of Skeleton-man and the puzzle of who he was.

Billy mentioned Hale's visits, how unnerving he found them, as if Hale already knew everything that had happened and was just waiting for one of them to spill. He said he'd been tempted several times to dig up the garbage bag containing Skeleton-man's clothing and the other evidence he'd hurriedly buried behind his garage, then throw the stuff into the ocean to be rid of it once and for all. He'd even, he admitted, prepared to excavate by the rear foundation wall several times, but each time lost his nerve before his shovel hit the dirt. It was as if, Billy said, so long as that sack remained in the ground, the whole haunting nightmare would stay on hold. But if he should ever bring it up, no matter his purpose, the consequences could not be foreseen.

Three weeks later Billy shot himself. It was Hale's visits, Jack was certain, that drove him to it. That, Jack believed, was what Hale wanted from them all: either give up the evidence, tell the story straight, or eat your guns – your choice.

A month later, Jack drove out to where Billy had lived on Railroad Avenue in South San Francisco. He told himself he wanted to see how Debbie Hayes, Billy's widow, was doing. But when he arrived he didn't get out of his car. Instead he paused in front of the house then circled the block to locate the rear of the garage, set on a weed-choked strip that lined a dusty stretch of track. He stared at the garage for a while, a flat-roofed structure built of cinder blocks, then drove back home.

It bothered him that he knew where the stuff was hidden. He hadn't wanted that information, but back at the bar Billy had casually let it slip. Or perhaps not so casually, Jack thought – perhaps Billy had come by with the sole purpose of telling because he already had his suicide planned and wanted to pass on the burden first.

Whatever Billy's intent, Jack realized, he was now back in the nightmare. He not only knew what had happened, but now also where the evidence could be found. Evidence that would not only resolve the T case, lead to the identification of the T killer and satisfy Hale, but that would also ruin people's lives, not least of all his own.

Or was he wrong?

That's what he wondered now that Kay had pried the story out of him. If she'd been right when she speculated that Carlotta had shot herself to lift from him the burden of his guilt, then perhaps Billy had killed himself for a similar reason – to take on responsibility for the awful act in which they'd all played a part.

But if that were true then why hadn't Billy left a note addressed to Hale, confessing everything, telling where the stuff was stashed?

Carlotta hadn't left a note either.

So the truth was that in both cases Jack didn't know, and, further, there was no way he could ever find out.

SIXTEEN

THE SHADOWS OF THE pines are long now, striping the close-cut grass. There's a chill in the air, a breeze from off the Bay that makes me cross my arms and huddle in my sweater.

Dad gazes past me . . . at a pair of golfers. I look at them too. One stands, hands on hips, while his companion prepares to swing. With the stroke the iron blade of the club catches the sun transmitting a flash. Instinctively I blink . . . too late to save my rods from saturation. Several seconds later, when my vision clears, I find Dad searching my eyes.

'It rips my heart when the light hurts you,' he says.

A great love for him wells up. I need to hold him close. I step behind him, wrap his massive torso, press my chest against his vast broad back.

I can feel him shudder. Through his cotton shirt the tips of my fingers detect the beating of his heart. He was always my supporter, builder of my confidence, telling me I could do anything I set my mind to. Yes, he taught me, I had a handicap, but not one that need hold me back. If I loved the night, that's when he'd take me out for walks, tell me stories, teach me to ride a bicycle. If the midday sun blinded me, he would play catch with me at twilight, take me to the beach at dusk, teach me to swim against the sunset.

'She must have been so wounded.' He's speaking now of Mom. 'She wouldn't have done it otherwise.'

'And angry,' I say. 'Most likely at herself.'

He shakes his head. 'At me.'

I don't understand it and never expect to. Who can comprehend her parents' marriage? All I know is that to kill oneself one must be possessed by an enormous rage. My heart goes out to both of them – to her for her ferocious anger, to him for all the ravages wrought by guilt.

'I meant what I said, Kay.' I wait for him to explain. 'So proud you didn't give up. I tried to confuse you. I didn't want you to know. But deep inside I hoped you'd figure it out.'

'You taught me the importance of truth,' I remind him. 'So you see, I couldn't flinch.'

I walk him back to his bakery. At the door we embrace. Then I walk down to Arguello and catch the #33 bus. It follows a singular route, along the rim of Golden Gate Park, meanders through the Haight and the hills north of Twin Peaks, finally depositing me at the corner of Castro and 18th, the intersection known as Hibernia Beach.

It's magic time when I arrive, the sky still darkening, my favorite hour in the city. The Castro is alive, people going rapidly about their affairs while others linger against the sides of buildings or sit on benches observing the passing scene. An urgent young man with an AIDS petition gently importunes me. A smiling young woman, hair like straw, offers me condoms from a basket.

Autumn chill has not discouraged the exposure of flesh. Here skin is always king. Tank-tops abound, bare arms exhibit tattoos, hair glows, eyes glisten, men and women alike wear shorts to display attractive legs. Still too early for my meeting with Hilly, I decide to float with the crowd. As I walk pairs of eyes meet mine, lock in, then release me with a smile. This is the way here and most of the time these street gazes are more ironic than lewd, gazes of what-might-have-been, wistful admiration exchanged. For a moment our lives cross, we esteem one another's beauty, then move on. The world turns, the clocks advance, yet for an instant we pause to acknowledge we share the earth and that each of us lives under the tyranny of his desire.

I think of Dad's strange intersections that night fifteen years ago – breathing the breath of life into Robbie Sipple, kneeling beside Skeleton-man, feeling his life ebb away. Did Dad commit a crime? Did any of them beside Billy? Yes, of course, and I cannot condone what they did. But, with the possible exception of Vasquez, I forgive them. They've been punished enough.

I pause at a pay phone, dial Joel. Ice-Goddess Kirstin answers.

'You are very missible here,' she says in her Swedish-accented sing-song. Does she mean I'm missed, admissible or merely miserable? Before I can ask she turns the phone over to Joel.

'We need to talk. I know where the Sipple stuff is stashed.'

I can feel his excitement through the wire. 'Your dad?'

'He told me everything. We can break the T case, Joel, but we have to protect him and the others by blaming it all on Billy Hayes. He didn't tell me to do that, but it's the only way. He didn't even say dig it up or don't, just told me what happened and where it's buried.' I pause, out of breath.

'Can you come over?'

'I'm meeting Hilly in half an hour. I'll drop by soon as we're finished.'

Hilly looks sloppy tonight, eyes tired, hair wild, not gelled. She's wearing a faded Grateful Dead T-shirt and grungy fatigues. I'm pleased she didn't dress hot.

We attract no attention in our corner of The Duchess; it's clear we're not here to play. The loud scene swirling around us is fun. I enjoy the spectacle of funky women on the make. It's only the smoke I dislike, but then Hilly explains that here a cigarette dangling from a (preferably bee-stung) lip is considered a luscious come-on.

'I'm beat,' she informs me, applying her beer bottle to her brow. 'Shanley gives me shit, Charbeau gives me shit. I'm on to something, but those oafs don't see it. It's a crappy life, Kay, being a cop.'

'Want to tell me about it?'

'Not especially.' She peers at me. 'You called this meet. What's up?'

I wonder why she's being secretive. Is she irritated with me or just feeling testy?

'There's a pimp on the Gulch they call Knob,' I tell her. 'Don't ask me his real name – I've no idea. He wheels and deals, acts as middleman for underage hustlers. He hangs out with two kids, Tommy and Boat, runaways who think he's God.'

'So?'

'They're the three beat me up in the park. Last week the kids vandalized my place while Knob stood look-out downstairs.'

'Great! Swear out a complaint. I'll pick 'em up.'

I explain why she can't, that my only witness is a park hermit terrified of the police. He won't testify and would be ineffective if he did.

'So what's the connection to Tim Lovsey?'

'Someone put Knob up to it, wanted me scared off. Why do that if he isn't the killer?'

'How do you know someone put Knob up to it?'

'Just a hunch. But I think there's a soft spot – the runaways. I hear the one called Boat is mushy. If you pick him up for soliciting, get him alone, put on pressure, there's a chance he'll break. So I was thinking – suppose you squeeze him, turn him against Tommy, then turn the two of them on Knob. With two witnesses ready to testify against him, maybe Knob'll say who ordered me hit.'

She studies me. 'You got it all figured out.'

'Just a suggestion, Hilly.'

'You think like a cop.'

'Is that a compliment?'

She smiles, sips some beer. 'You're talking about entrapment. That's tricky business. There're all sorts of niceties – coercion, legal representation, "fruit of the poisoned tree". And it gets trickier when you're dealing with juveniles.' She pauses. 'This Knob – tell me more about him.'

I tell her what I heard from Doreen and Sho, that Knob's ruthless and in effect rules the Gulch.

She nods. 'Probably got a record. Too bad you don't know his name.'

I show her the photo I took of him at The Werewolf. She examines it.

'Looks like he's been around.'

'I could go through the mug books.'

'That's slow and a lot of times doesn't work. Prints are better. I can run them through AFIS, do a national screening.'

'You want Knob's fingerprints? We'll get 'em!'

She brightens up, we bring our heads close, quickly hatch a plan. After a while the butch bartender appears with another round of beers. An anonymous person has sent them over.

'She doesn't want to be pointed out,' the butch informs us, squinting down one eye, raising the corresponding nostril. 'Said to say you guys look very friendly so she thought she'd act friendly too.'

Joel owns a run-down Victorian on Roosevelt Park Hill, not far from where Sipple lived in the upper Haight. The place has what realtors call 'good bones' plus a fine rear-window view across the city to China Basin. A dusty granddaddy palm, centerpiece of a jungle, obscures the front of the house. Making my way beneath it, traipsing through a mesh of vines, I nearly trip over an abandoned rake. Joel, no surprise, is not big on domestic up-keep. A feral cat scoots beneath the stoop, gazes up at me, meows.

I notice a mezuzah beside the door. Ice-Goddess opens up. Her long hair is parted in the center; her large Nordic eyes sparkle with spirituality. Joel found this willowy young blonde shortly after Rachel Glickman dumped him, a week after their second daughter left home for college. Rachel, dark, homely, serious and brilliant, is a tenured Professor of Sociology at San Francisco State. Kirstin, fair, beautiful, bright only in the wattage of her smile, makes fabric collages and reads runes for pay.

'Hi, Kay!' she moos.

We embrace.

'Am I still missible?' I ask.

She stands back, perplexed. 'Golly, I hope not!'

So . . . whatever she was trying to tell me earlier will remain a mystery to us both.

She leads me to Joel's office in the attic, a clone of his cubicle at the *Bay Area News*. No Pulitzer certificate here but a similar decor – cartoons posted on the walls, dog-eared books jammed top first into shelves, a chaos of clippings, manuscripts, articles-in-progress, an old manual Underwood on the desk. Joel claims to despise computers.

He listens, fascinated, as I recount Dad's saga. When I'm finished he reminds me of one of my exchanges with Hale.

'You pointed out he had conflicting theories,' Joel says. 'Remember what he said?'

I think back. 'Something like . . . once you understand what happened the theories no longer conflict.'

Joel nods. 'A tattoo-freak cute-boy T killer and a cop who gets rid of unwelcome evidence. Two separate crimes. Which means Hale more or less figured it out. Amazing!'

Joel's right: it *is* amazing. Hale's statement, so cryptic at the time, now makes sense. So, I ask, does this mean we're going to tell him where the stuff is buried?

Joel muses. 'Obsessed old detective, forced out of his job, works the case fifteen years, finally finds missing evidence. Eureka! The old T case is solved!'

'It's a good story, but I don't like it, Joel.'

'Neither do I.' He starts to pace. 'Hale's a paranoid and paranoids are dangerous. He won't buy that Billy Hayes did it all alone. He'll want to string up everyone . . . including your dad.' He pauses. 'Which leaves us with Hilly. All she wants is glory. She's got no axe to grind so we can probably make a deal with her up-front.'

'We could just let it go, couldn't we?' I ask.

A knock on the door. Kirstin appears with a pot of herbal tea and three hand-painted Scandinavian cups.

'I am thinking your thirsts would use a good quenching,' she says.

Joel smiles, the sweet my-heart-is-touched grin of an indulgent father whose daughter is showing off her goodness. Kirstin, I understand, is what he's always wanted: a shiksa innocent who reminds him of his time on the Haight – heroic days and nights of good dope, dumb talk and endless sex with doped-out girls wearing flowers in their stringy hair.

Kirstin pours the tea, settles on a hassock, exposes milky thighs. She sips, then, a propos of nothing, announces she and Joel have decided to make a baby. I turn to Joel; he glows with pride. Sure, it figures – he could use a second crack at youth. I've seen plenty of gray-haired men like him trotting around supermarkets with papooses on their backs filling grocery carts with baby chow and Pampers.

He turns to me. 'Could you bear to let it go?'

There's a side of me, I recognize, that could, that would just as soon leave buried evidence in the ground, especially as I now know that the T case has nothing to do with Tim. But there's another part of me that can't stand the notion of leaving things incomplete, that, like Dad, wants to know who Skeleton-man was.

'On what basis could Hilly get a warrant to dig?' I ask.

Joel smiles. 'Tip from a confidential informant – you and me, kiddo. Not all that farfetched. She's investigating the T-case angle on the Tim Lovsey homicide. She starts asking around about the old case. Someone calls, tells her where the evidence is buried. She goes to a judge, says her source is reliable. Judge scowls . . . but lets her dig.'

Kirstin's tea tastes of bitter herbs. I can barely stomach it, but Joel sips as if it's ambrosia. I suddenly wonder if Kirstin holds him in thrall with more than sex, with spells and secret potions.

'What about Debbie Hayes, Billy's widow?'

'I doubt she knows anything and even if she does she won't make a fuss. She's getting Billy's pension. She won't want to screw that up.'

'So Billy goes down as the bad guy?'

Joel shrugs. 'In a major sense he was.'

Kirstin, following our dialogue like a spectator at a tennis match, doesn't have a clue as to what we're talking about. Still I sense she's hurt at being ignored. When I turn to thank her for the tea, she flashes me a grateful smile.

'If it all works out,' Joel says, 'we'll be handing Hilly fame beyond her dreams.'

'And if that encourages her to get to the bottom of who killed Tim, she'll deserve it,' I reply.

I've no idea where Drake gets his food; the groceries I leave for him couldn't sustain a child. Where does he find the water he needs – to drink, bathe, launder his clothes? Where does he sleep when it's cold, store his covers when it rains, go to the toilet, shampoo his hair? When he ventures out of Sterling Park where does he go? How can he survive in a wood the size of half a city block?

The homeless, I understand, have survival strategies, holes and caches, stocks of booty. Some get by collecting aluminum cans, others barter, still others find saleable treasure scrounging trash. There are soup kitchens in church basements, shelters offering toilets and hot showers, and the urban parks where they reside can be gold mines to those who know how to live off the detritus of a wealthy town.

I sit with Drake side by side on a bench, he, as always, perched as far from me as he can get. Filled with feelings yet unable to form attachments, he likes me at a distance, even loves me in his way, but up close I frighten him, am too solid, too real. Better a fantasy woman glimpsed at night through a window from afar, than a live palpable female person seated in broad daylight three feet away.

The trees break up the sunlight, scatter it upon his face. We talk about his future. He hopes to go back to school one day, resume the study of chemistry. He's from Oregon, misses the rain. His favorite color is green. He has a sister. Photochemistry is interesting. Do I use Kodak Dektol? Do I believe someone really wants me dead?

His non-sequiturs touch me.

'Do you think someone does?' I ask.

He turns away, nods. 'I do,' he says gravely. 'But he will have to kill me first.'

*   *   *

We're cruising slowly along Polk in Hilly's old Volvo, the kind that in California seems to last forever. Hilly is driving, I'm in the passenger seat, an actor named Rob Mathews is in back.

Rob's in his forties, well groomed, dressed tonight like an affluent dentist. I met him a few years ago when I did some fashion photography for his wife, an ad exec. He's a member of the company at Berkeley Rep specializing in middle-aged character roles. He's intrigued, he tells me, by the proposed gig.

'Never played a chickenhawk before,' he says, stroking his mustache. 'But how tough can it be? I like girls in their twenties, so why not boys in their teens?'

Hilly guffaws.

Rob leans forward. He's eager, wants to internalize the role. 'How should I behave? Timid or bold?'

'Either way,' I tell him. 'Some guys are cocky, most are scared. They know if they get caught they'll lose everything, job, wife, kids. You gotta be obsessed to take the risk.'

Rob understands.

'There he is.' I point out Knob as we cruise by. He's standing alone in his usual spot between Bush and Sutter, back propped against a wall beside an all-male video store.

'Looks mean,' Rob says.

'*Is* mean,' I tell him. I slink down in my seat in case Knob looks up.

Hilly asks Rob if he wants her to make another pass. Rob says that isn't necessary, he saw Knob clear enough. Hilly drives two blocks, turns the corner, cuts over to Larkin, stops.

'What's my best lead-in?'

I turn to Rob. He's cool. In his shoes I'd have the jitters. I advise: 'Tell Knob you hear he's the man to see. He'll probably pretend he doesn't know what you're talking about. If he asks who steered you to him, just say "a friend". If he insists on a name tell him you can't give it up, it's a matter of personal honor. He'll laugh . . . but that'll build his confidence. Offer to buy him a drink.'

Hilly hands him an envelope. 'The photos inside are sterile. Hand them to him discreetly at the bar. Tell him this is the type of kid you want – young, long hair, smooth. Since you don't want him to think he's being set up, make a big point that for legal reasons you don't want a kid under eighteen. What you want is someone who *looks* underage. Can he fix you up?'

'Great! But what if he does?'

'He won't. Not tonight. Too risky,' Hilly says. 'You'll have to see him two or three times before he'll agree to do business. Show him you understand this, that you came by to get acquainted, build trust. The important thing is to get his prints on the photos. Don't worry if you touch them. We'll eliminate yours, go for what's left.'

Rob nods, gets out of the car. Hilly and I wish him luck then take off. We've agreed to meet him in an hour at the Buena Vista. We drive for a time, threading through the Tenderloin. It's a weekday night; people are hanging out. The hotels down here don't rate neon signs. You can see the stains on the window shades even from the street.

'Jesus, what a gutter!' Hilly says.

'I don't know, it doesn't seem all that bad.'

She glances at me. 'Yeah, you can say that. You live up on Russian. No whores or homeless up there. The air's sweet. You got a pretty view. Every once in a while you come down, take a few pictures, then go back up. That's fine, Kay. But reality's down here where it stinks full-time.'

'Ah,' I say, 'the cynical cop!'

'You bet!' She bites her lip.

I'm annoyed. I don't like being patronized. I decide to smack her back.

'Of course *you* don't slum around,' I tell her. 'With your cozy flat in the Castro, your cat, your life-style, your hot dyke bars. Give me a break, Hilly. I take a few pictures, you make a few arrests – after which we both go home. Frankly, I don't see the difference.'

She chews on that as we run a gauntlet of addicts clustered around the door to a Cambodian restaurant.

'You're right. I'm feeling mean tonight. Sorry to take it out on you.'

'What's the matter?'

'The job. Believe me, I could tell you a few things.'

'Please do,' I urge her.

Again she bites her lip. Then it comes, the torrent. Charbeau, she tells me, has been riding her. Last week he called her in, told her she wasn't cutting it. When she asked what was wrong he said it wasn't her work, it was the way she strutted around. 'I got nothing against female detectives,' he told her, 'fact I think they're great.

What I can't stand is anyone, male or female, who fucks me up with a colleague.'

She knew immediately he was talking about Vasquez. 'You don't mess with a guy like that,' Charbeau told her. 'Whatever you think of him, you don't talk to him the way you did.'

I ask if this goes back to the incident by the elevators.

Hilly shakes her head. 'Something else. He blew up when I asked him about the soap.'

She pulls into a bus stop, cuts the engine. Though I've no idea what she's going to say, I feel my pulse speed up.

'There's stuff I didn't tell you,' she says. 'I first noticed it out at Wildcat Canyon after Shanley sent you home. Timothy's torso had been washed with a very strong type of medicinal soap, so strong you could still smell it on him in the rain. Sweet and peppery. Like licorice.'

The word sends a tremor across my chest.

'We decided to keep it quiet. Might turn out to be important. Then, when I went through the T-case file, naturally I looked for references. Nothing until I got to Sipple. Remember, he wasn't carved, he died in the hospital of a heart attack. But a couple of the cops who found him – Hayes and your dad – mentioned a strong smelling soap. So I got this weird idea: here we got a copycat T-killer homicide with several things out of whack – paint instead of tattoos, a big number "seven" lest we miss the point, and the torso washed with scented soap . . . which resembled what happened to Sipple, but to no one else. Remember what I was looking for? Insiders who knew the T killer's MO. But here we got this similarity to Sipple, but not to any of the rest. So I start thinking maybe the leak didn't come from the T-case task force, but from someone who was just in on Sipple. Then's when I went to see Vasquez. Maybe he'd have an idea or two, maybe he wouldn't, but I wanted him to know he hadn't intimidated me when he told me to move my fanny in the hall.'

Now I'm shaking. Could Hilly be right? What if Tim was killed by one of the five? Since it couldn't be Hayes or Dad, that leaves just three – Wainy, Ricky, Vasquez.

'The lieutenant tells me to close the door, doesn't invite me to sit. He stares at me very cold. I guess the asshole thinks I've come to apologize. He hears me out. When I'm done, he keeps staring at me like there must be more. I stare right back. No way am I going to blink. So our little staring contest goes on a while, then he asks if I'm an ambitious cop. Sure, I tell him, I'm ambitious . . . to clear my cases just like everyone else. I'm investigating a homicide and I've come to him for help. If he doesn't choose to assist, fine, I'll go on about my work.'

Hilly smiles. 'I wasn't sure I had the balls to stand up to the guy. Now I'm wondering if standing up to him was so smart.'

'Why?'

'Something scary about him. Way he looks at you, like he's looking through you, through your eyes into your brain.'

Vasquez. Suddenly my Crane theory doesn't look so neat. I prodded Crane, threatened to ruin his reputation, so why wouldn't he want me beaten and my photographic files destroyed? But that doesn't prove he was Tim's killer. How could he have known about the soap?

Vasquez knew. And then I remember something else, that Vasquez is in charge of felony prostitution. He could have known Tim. He could even have killed him. *But why would Vasquez do that? It doesn't make sense.*

Hilly's still talking. Meantime my head's swelling with heat.

'. . . word on the lieutenant is he takes protection money, that he's got deals going all over town. On Polk Gulch, here in the Tenderloin, on Capp Street in the Mission, the real bottom of the barrel.' She peers at me. 'You're looking queazy, Kay. You all right?'

'Migraine,' I lie. In fact, I feel as though the top of my head's about to blow off.

'Anyhow, makes you wonder, Charbeau standing up for a guy like that, while I'm just trying to do my job.' She shrugs, glances at her watch. 'What d'you say we head over to the Buena Vista, scope out Rob?'

We find him standing at the bar, enjoying a Scotch, displaying a victor's smile. No need to ask whether he got Knob's prints; he not only got them, he never touched the pictures himself, just handed the envelope to Knob, watched as he went through them, waited until he replaced them, then took the treasured envelope back.

'Not a bad guy once you get to know him,' Rob says. 'Brute type, but with a certain savage charm.'

Hilly excuses herself; she wants to rush the photos to the

fingerprint lab. I pick up the tab for Rob's drinks, then buy him dinner.

'You won't have to see Knob again,' I assure him.

'I'm thrilled, Kay. Frankly, I was scared.'

'I never would have known,' I tell him.

Rob beams. 'Must mean I'm a good actor,' he says.

Sasha spends the night. It's been days since we've seen each other. He's been on duty and I've been busy exploring the oddly connected trails of my life. Tim, Dad, Mom, the Judge, Ariane . . . Knob, Crane, Vasquez . . . and perhaps other strands to which I may be too close or which I'm too blind to see.

Sasha, as it happens, bathes with perfumed soap, which imbues his skin with the aroma of sandalwood. I ask him why he likes it.

'Don't you?' he asks.

'Of course. Just curious why you chose it.'

'Actually, I never much liked scented toiletries,' he says. We're lying side-by-side naked in my bed, in contact from our shoulders to our calves. 'Shaving soaps, men's fragrances, lotions. People give them as gifts. Usually I take one sniff then pass the stuff on. But one day . . .' He stops. 'This is embarrassing.'

I nudge him. 'Go on!'

'A lady I was seeing—'

'Lady?'

'She was. But so as not to offend you, we'll call her a woman. Anyway, I was staying over one night.'

'As you're accustomed to do.'

He nods. 'And in the morning when I took a shower and used her soap it was scented with sandalwood and I liked it very much. So, though I never saw this lady – this woman – again—'

'As was also your custom.'

He laughs. 'Although we stopped seeing one another, having failed to fall in love, I did in fact fall in love with her bath soap . . . and have been using it ever since.'

'Great story, Sasha!'

'Glad you like it, Kay. And I hope someday you too will look back and recall receiving a similar gift from me – a scent sniffed, a dish tasted, perhaps some little trick I've taught.'

'Bed trick?'

'Wouldn't that be fine?'

'You're a great lover, Sasha. You know you are. I've learned a lot from you. Felt, you know, special things. I hope we're going to have a future together.'

'We will,' he says, firmly.

I turn, plant my elbow, prop my head on my fist, so I can look straight into his dreamy eyes.

'Here's my secret, Sasha. I'm speaking seriously now. My fondest wish is to see colors. And, surprise! Some nights with you I actually do. Oh, not real colors, of course. Sadly, that's not possible. But the equivalent, the *sense* of colors. It's hard to explain.'

'I love what you're saying.'

'It's like a flowering. Objects take on a different dimension. There's an unexpected depth, a richness . . . which is what I've always thought colors must endow. I dream more vivid dreams, see more brilliantly. The light opens up, hues are revealed.'

I turn to lie on my back, stare up at the ceiling. 'You see, I have ways of knowing colors – from music, passages in Wagner, Berlioz, Scriabin, Debussy, Rimsky-Korsakov. From literature too – the greens in Walt Whitman, golds and yellows in Gerard Manley Hopkins, Conrad's reds and blues. I also know colors from the great painters. I look at the paintings and imagine . . . Poussin's blue, Degas's green, Van Gogh's yellow, Rembrandt's brown.'

He leans over me to kiss my eyes.

'My mom was a music teacher,' I continue. 'She tried to teach me colors via correspondences with sounds – the chromatic scale, orchestral color, how harmony could be thought of as a kind of color-mixing too. We'd listen to records. She'd make analogies between the sounds of the different instruments and the intensities of different hues. The yellow sounds of the clarinets, violets of the oboes, reds of the trumpets. Crimson flutes. Dark blue cellos. Aquamarine violas. Pure blue violins. We'd spend hours listening. I tried to memorize the correspondences. The keys too. She told me D-Major was purple, D-Minor was tawny, A-Major was green. In the end, unfortunately, her lessons didn't take. She was so disappointed I didn't have a good ear. Later she took my artistic ambitions as rejection. Music, you see, was such a perfect medium for a colorblind girl. She thought I went to art school just to spite her. She was wrong, of course. I found my way there, discovered black and white photography, a way of making pictures in which the line and shape take precedence over the field.'

I turn back to him. 'Still, I wish I could have pleased her, Sasha. At least learned from her, learned the colors.'

'You're not blind, Kay.'

'Not at all. My whole life's about seeing – looking, peering, selecting, creating images. And, who knows? If I *could* see colors, most likely my colors wouldn't be the same as yours. Scientists say it can take but the slightest difference in a chromosome, a single amino acid, to change the way a person perceives a hue. But never mind! I'm talking about the colors I *do* see. Sometimes I see them in my mind via sound and touch and smell, but the best time for me, the time I see them most beautifully, is when the two of us make love. All of which is my way of telling you, Sasha, that this woman already has a story to tell, for she has already received your gift. And – need I add? – still longs for more . . .'

Mid-morning I phone Dad: 'You okay?'

'Sure, darlin'. You?'

'I'm doing good.'

'Glad to hear it. What we talked about – that was bound to hurt.'

'It cleared the air. Thanks for sharing it with me.' I pause. 'We'll probably try and dig up the evidence now. Unless you object?'

A long pause. 'Go ahead.'

'You're sure?'

'Do what you have to do.'

'Billy can take the rap. Joel says his widow won't be hurt.'

'Poor Billy!'

'Poor you! But don't worry – we won't throw you to the wolves. Not Ricky or Wainy either. No guarantees for Vasquez.'

'A word of advice, darlin'.'

'Please?'

'Go for it, but watch out for Vasquez. He plays dirty, a dirty game.'

The phone rings. It's Caroline Gifford at Zeitgeist.

'You won't believe this, Kay. I just got off a call from Sarah Lashaw. Says she wants to buy thirty or so prints, a representative selection of your work. Wants to come by tomorrow, make choices.' Caroline pauses. 'Isn't that fab?'

'No, sorry, Caroline, it's not.'

'Hey, girlfriend, this is business! You can't refuse a serious buyer. We're talking twenty-five, thirty thousand dollars here.'

'I understand, but, see, Lashaw isn't buying, she's bribing, and I'm not in the bribe-taking business. Trust me on this?'

A silence. 'Oh, I trust you all right. But I gotta tell you, Kay – sometimes it really hurts.'

I keep thinking of Ariane: where is she now? To what extent was she involved in Tim's death? I've talked to David deGeoffroy twice since Tim's funeral, and each time he asks after her with special tenderness. I'm still convinced I haven't heard the whole story from him and will only learn the rest from her . . . if I'm fortunate enough to find her.

I think about the Lovsey twins going through adolescence on their own, and then the forces that must have driven them to work the street. I think of their deft hands and brilliant minds, their interchangeability, androgyny and charm, their love of juggling, tumbling, pulling coins and scarfs out of orifices, most of all of the bravery with which they faced the world. They never allowed themselves to feel degraded no matter the disdain in which their work was held. Magician-nighthawk purveyors of lust, gorgeous, sensuous objects of desire, they entered the dark subconscious of the city, maintaining their dignity in the face of all its sleaze and scorn.

I enter an old-fashioned professional building on lower Market, the kind with a cage elevator and echoing lobby. An elderly attendant with dragon breath operates the apparatus. The cage jerks and trembles its way up, depositing me on the eighth floor after numerous false stops.

The corridor here is lined with doors with bubble-glass panels bearing the names of tenants. Aromas ooze out of open transoms – mouthwash from the waiting room of Lawrence Fisher, DDS; cigar smoke from the suite of Courter & Lee, Admiralty Insurers; stale coffee and pizza from the hole-in-the-wall workplace of Susan Marzik & Associates, Private Investigations. But from my destination, the law office of J. F. Judd, Esq., Criminal Defense, there is no smell, no essence, no odor at all.

The receptionist, a middle-aged battle-axe with a bitter mouth, gives me the once-over as she snatches away my card. Five minutes later a squat bald man with canny eyes waddles out to greet me.

'Hi! I'm Judd,' he says, escorting me to his office. 'Thanks for dropping by.'

'You were expecting me?'

He gestures me to the client chair. 'I figure you came to settle Lovsey's account.'

I examine him as he sits behind his desk. Late-thirties, flashy tie, flabby jowls, grossly overweight.

'That's not why I'm here,' I tell him.

'Look, the client's deceased. I'm open to settlement.'

I'm not prepared for this, but what the hell? I offer him two hundred dollars.

While Judd thinks it over, I peer around. His office is a den of files, law books, briefs, and, on the walls, satiric Daumier barrister car-toons. He is, I quickly understand, small-time. No big murder cases here, just penny ante stuff – drug possession, solicitation, petty theft.

When I turn back he's studying my face.

'Beaten up, weren't you?'

Jesus! 'Does it still show?'

He shakes his head. 'Not at all.'

'Then how— ?'

'Tim told me. Wanted me to nail the son-of-a-bitch. I told him I'm a defense attorney, not a prosecutor, his friend should go to the cops. That was the last time we spoke. A day or two later he was killed.' Judd shrugs and shakes his head.

Suddenly I feel heat rising from my chest, the same sensation I felt when Hilly told me about Vasquez. *Ariane – it had to be! But who beat her and why?* Knowing I must anchor myself, I think of Rita's admonishment in aikido class: 'Find your center, Kay. Root yourself.'

'It wasn't me he was talking about.'

'You said—'

'I was beaten afterwards.' Judd raises his eyebrows. 'Do you remember exactly what Tim said?'

Judd neither nods nor shakes his head, just continues to stare, waiting for me to explain.

'The night he was killed we were supposed to meet. He wanted my advice. He was upset, scared. Maybe what he told you had to do with what he was going to tell me.'

Judd turns away. 'Attorney-client privilege extends after death.'

'But you already told me some of it. I'm just asking for the details.'

He widens his eyes, body language for 'What's in it for me?' I understand him perfectly: for chump change Attorney Judd would sell his soul.

I make him an offer: 'I'll settle Tim's account.'

'In full?'

I nod. 'Providing you tell me everything.'

In fact, twelve hundred fifty bucks will empty out my bank account. But then, I remember, I just turned down a fortune from Sarah Lashaw. I reach into my camera bag, whip out my checkbook, turn on my micro tape-recorder at the same time. I write Judd a check, show it to him, then pull it back.

He smiles. 'You wouldn't stiff me now, would you, Ms Farrow?'

'Is that what you're used to – getting stiffed?'

'Unhappily, yes.'

'You'll get this when you tell me everything, from the first time you met Tim Lovsey to the last time you spoke.'

He studies me a moment, swivels around in his chair, starts to talk. It isn't an uninteresting story. Tim was picked up on Polk Gulch, got into a car, took a hundred bucks to receive a blow-job from an undercover cop. A second after Tim accepted the money, the cop put him under arrest. Then it was off to the Hall of Justice, with a little conversation en route. What Tim needed, the cop advised, was a good lawyer to settle his case. When Tim said he didn't know any lawyers, the cop recommended Judd, then stopped so Tim could phone him from a booth. 'Police officer scam,' Judd explains. 'Arrest a guy, tell him he needs a lawyer, steer him to one who knows how to deal. Everyone's protected – the cop gets paid off, the lawyer gets his fee, the arrestee gets his freedom and can't claim later he was solicited for a bribe.'

'How much?'

'In this case five hundred. I negotiated it down from a grand.'

'For which you billed him twelve-fifty.'

'Of which my cut was seven-fifty. A fair fee, believe me. I was called out of bed.'

'You're saying Tim never paid you?'

Judd shrugs. 'He was a hustler. What d'you expect?'

I don't believe him. He wouldn't have listened to Tim's story about the beaten girl if he hadn't already been paid. I very much want to ask the arresting officer's name, but decide to hold off till I hear the rest.

'No jail, no bail, no court appearance,' Judd continues. 'The matter was privately settled. Then, like I mentioned, last month Tim calls me about this girl, says she's been badly beaten up. He's pissed, wants me to represent her, bring criminal charges against the guy, sue him, the works. When I tell him I don't do that kind of work, he says he'll find someone who does. Next thing I read in the newspaper he's been killed.'

'Did he say who beat the girl?'

Judd shakes his head.

'I think he did,' I tell him. 'And when you heard the name you got scared.'

'Think whatever you like, Missy. Twelve-fifty only buys so much.'

Missy! What an asshole! 'Well, you got me there, Mr Judd,' I tell him. 'For me twelve-fifty's a stretch.' I search his eyes. 'It was a rich man beat the girl, wasn't it?'

Judd shrugs. Does he know I'm bluffing? Did he sell the news of his client's intentions and by so doing get Tim killed? Is he such a cheap piece of crud that even after collecting on that, he sent the bill for twelve-fifty figuring he could squeeze it out of Tim's estate?

'You're not going to tell me. I understand. At least give me the name of the cop.'

Judd smiles. 'Too sweet a deal. I'm not about to mess that up.'

'Fine.' I stand. 'Then you don't get paid.' I tear up my check, sprinkle the pieces on his desk.

He opens his center drawer, brushes the pieces into it. 'You're a welsher, Missy, but your check taped back together'll be enough to persuade a small claims judge.'

'Fuck you! You're the one welshed. And now I'm going to fry your ass.'

'What're you talking about?'

'Friend of mine, an investigative journalist, is going to turn you inside out – bank accounts, every case you ever tried or settled, who your friends are, which ones are cops. A sleazebag like you – something's bound to turn up. By the time we're done with you, you'll be disbarred.'

'You can't prove a thing!'

I hold up my tape-recorder. 'I think I can." I start toward the door.

'Hey! Wait! We can work this out.'

I turn. He's up now, menacing, coming around the side of his desk.

'Gimme that tape!'

I laugh. He lunges at me. I grasp his wrist, turn, throw him across the room. He crashes into his filing cabinet. When he rises I note that his forehead's cut.

'*Bitch!*'

'Have to do better than that, fatso.'

He lunges again. This time I knifehand the side of his neck, then backfist him across the nose. He crumples to the floor. I stare down at him. He looks pathetic. I take his picture twice.

A knock on the door. It's Battle-axe. 'Everything all right, Mr Judd?'

'Yeah, go back to work.' He glares up at me. 'I'll get you for assault.'

'God, you're dumb!' I show him the recorder again. 'It's still running. You attacked me. I defended myself. It's all on tape.'

He touches his nose, winces. His eyes go meek. 'What do you want?'

'Names. The rich man who beat up the girl, the cop who took the bribe.'

'They'll kill me if I tell.'

'Who's "they"?'

'Listen, please—'

'*You* listen! You've been stupid. When I walked in here I didn't know about a beating. I just wanted to know who arrested Tim. You could have refused, written off your twelve-fifty, sent me on my way. Instead you got greedy, showed off, as much as admitted you sold Tim out. Now it's time to get smart. You've got my card. Tell me what I want to know or take what's coming to you. You got three days.'

As I leave old Battle-axe gives me the evil eye.

'Your boss needs help. Got bandages?' I ask. I bring my face close. 'Does he often attack women? You really should speak to him about that.'

Sasha wants us to spend Thanksgiving at an inn in the wine country or perhaps south in Pebble Beach or on Big Sur. The idea is to luxuriate – sleep late, make love on crisp linen sheets, eat breakfast in bed, bathe in a hot tub, take long romantic walks in the vineyards or on the beach. It sounds great. I give him my blessing. Three hours later he calls back. We'll have to spend the holiday in the city; every luxury place in Northern California's booked.

Not to worry, I tell him. My idea of a perfect Thanksgiving is to catch a movie, hit Chinatown for a platter of grilled salt-and-pepper shrimp, walk home holding hands, make love, snuggle close then fall asleep.

I stop at the Farmer's Market on the Embarcadero, peruse the produce, buy a bag of clementines which have just come into season. Due to my achromatopsia, eggplants and tomatoes appear the same shade, namely black. But colorblindness, I feel, has its advantages, forcing me, unable to make quick decisions based on colors, to look carefully at shapes. Yes, it is the shapes of things, their forms not their fields, that reach my eye. Colorblindness has taught me to look steadily, view the world, discern.

Tonight, playing with my telescope, studiously avoiding the terrace of the Judge, I reacquaint myself with my neighbors, then sweep the city searching for points of interest.

Alcatraz, the forbidding rock, fills my eye-piece. Then the apex of Coit Tower, and several office buildings downtown outlined in lights for the holidays. But, as always, it's the smaller structures of North Beach and Telegraph Hill that engage me, variegated cubes arrayed, stacked, fitting together like pieces in an intricate, superbly constructed puzzle. Doors, windows, street lamps, houses, stores, churches, playgrounds, schools – the variety and complexity of shapes is music to my eyes.

I realize that what I love best about San Francisco, and have rarely found anyplace else, is that here all these forms and shapes add up to something I can grasp. Each piece, each part, fits together to make the whole. The city is a unity, and now I wish that the mysteries that taunt me, the maze of photos pinned to my office wall, will come clear as well.

In the morning I leave half my clementines on the bench for

Drake, whom I haven't seen in two days. An hour later, when I go out again and cruise the spot, I find my package gone. I only hope it was Drake who took it, not some other denizen of Russian Hill. Since he has declared himself, as much as promised to protect me with his life, I figure the least I owe him is decent nourishment.

I meet Joel at the *Bay Area News*, then we saunter over to The Transcendental Café for lunch. The late-autumn light catches the varnished Tarot cards that paper the wall, creating a reflective sheen. The resident swami sits at his usual table reading the fortune of a boy with tresses.

I fill Joel in on what Hilly told me about Vasquez and the scented soap, then play him the tape of my exchange with Judd.

After listening to the noise of our fight, he gazes at me with mock awe.

'Gosh, Kay – you really *do* beat guys up!'

But he's confused about the rest, not clear on the identity of Tim's beaten friend. I tell him about Ariane, David deGeoffroy, the Zamantha Illusion, the twins' heist of deGeoffroy's savings, Ariane's strange identity as Amoretto, the key hidden in Tim's molding, and how I met Courtney Hill in Ariane's vacated flat.

'Damnit!' he exclaims when I'm finished. 'Why didn't you tell me this before?'

'It didn't seem relevant and I didn't want to distract you. Then, yesterday, I realized it may have been the reason Tim was killed.'

Joel nods. 'What about Vasquez?'

'Suppose he was the cop who picked Tim up?'

'A lieutenant, commander of the felony prostitution squad?'

'Why not? He's got a nice house. I'm sure he can use some extra cash. Suppose he freelances after hours? Cops run scams all the time.'

'Actually, now that I think about it, it's a good one too. Vasquez knows the streets, knows the pick-up lines. Boys and girls – he goes after them all. They take his cash, he's got them cold. He doesn't even have to have sex with them if he doesn't want to. Just make the deal, fork over, snap on the cuffs.'

'How can we be sure?'

'That'll be hard. But since both Hilly and your dad say he's dirty there's probably something there. Let me ask around, see what I can find.'

'When do you want to tip off Hilly on the buried treasure?'

'Soon. Keep working with her, Kay. As for Judd,' Joel smiles, 'that was a pretty good bluff – your friend the investigative journalist. Only trouble is . . . it would take me months.'

'I think Judd'll call.'

'I think so too. But be careful, kiddo. Knock a guy around, humiliate him like you did, you may end up facing a mad dog.'

Hilly and I meet again at The Duchess. Tonight her hair is beautifully slicked back. She's glowing with triumph. She's got a match on Knob's prints.

'Your friend's a bad boy, Kay. Up to his ears in shit.' She pulls out a computer print-out, reads off a list of names:

'Raymond Crogan, aka Ray Crow, aka Ray "Crow Bar", aka Ray "Knob" Krell. Arrests go back to his teens – stealing, pandering, soliciting, battery, attempted vehicular homicide . . . a few more. Get this: two California felony convictions, the first for burglary, two-year sentence, fourteen months served, the second for felonious assault upon a police officer – five years sentenced and served at Pelican Bay.' Hilly looks up at me. 'Bottom line, under California three-strikes law he's vulnerable.'

'Meaning— ?'

'Beating up on you and stealing your camera was a big mistake. If a DA can prove it to a jury, he'll get twenty-five to life.'

How marvelous! I think, and then. How strange that Knob would take such a chance. Which may explain why he pulled the pillowcase over my head and sent his boys up to my flat while he stood look-out below. He must have been paid a great deal of money to take chances like that. Knob may be many things, but he isn't stupid . . . and to risk life in prison to settle a score would be stupid beyond belief.

Hilly agrees. 'Hiring out kids for sex is a felony too, and he does that every night. Which makes it even more risky. Unless—' She grins.

'What?'

'He's got protection.'

Something about the smile on her face tells me she's tasting blood. What better vindication, after all, than to nail Vasquez for taking bribes? 'What're you going to do about it?' I ask, hoping to taunt her into action.

'I like your idea of hauling in Knob's boys, breaking them, turning them into witnesses. Trouble is . . . if I take this to Charbeau, he'll shoot me down or put Shanley in charge. And if I try it without authorization, I'll get shit-canned even if it works.'

She ponders. 'Thanksgiving's coming up. Shanley and Charbeau'll both be out of town. I was going to drive down to LA, spend the holiday with my folks, but now I got a better idea.' She squints. 'With everyone away I'll have the field to myself. If I handle things right, it could be over before anyone gets back.'

7:00 P.M., THANKSGIVING NIGHT. A chill in the air. Mist clings to the streetlights while buoy bells and mournful foghorns float up to me from the Bay. I'm standing still and alert in the strip of park between Larkin and Hyde at the base of Russian Hill. The old clock tower at Ghirardelli Square is barely visible through the vapor.

I've chosen this location and also the hour, insisting the meeting take place after dark. Judd argued for Fort Mason Park in daytime, but I took a hard-line, figuring that anything he wanted would not be good for me.

I wait under cover of a small grove of olive trees a hundred feet back from the street, beautiful ancient, gnarled specimens with thick black twisted trunks. Beneath these boughs the air smells good, sweet and loamy. And from here I can watch for Judd's approach.

The fog is heavy, the place is dark and isolated, there are no pedestrians, and, this being a holiday, traffic is sparse. But I'm not worried. Having already physically defeated Judd, I have the psychological advantage. Moreover, in darkness my vision is far superior to his, and tonight, unlike the night I was sandbagged in Sterling Park, I'm on guard.

I know this territory well, traverse it regularly. Although a good two hundred feet below the summit of the hill, it is but three blocks from my building. I often walk down here via the Larkin steps, guided by the anise scent of wild fennel that grows so luxuriantly in the city. Anise, of course, is an olfactory cousin of licorice, that haunting aroma Dad smelled on Skeleton-man's body.

A mid-size Toyota approaches, slows, speeds away. Three minutes later it reappears. This time it pulls into a parking space on Bay, then hovers, lights and engine on. I tense; this must be him, the timing is right and the behavior appropriately peculiar. A minute passes, the driver cuts his engine, waits a few seconds, douses his lights and gets out.

I recognize him immediately, the aggressive waddle, extended paunch. He's even carrying an over-stuffed briefcase the way a harassed lawyer should. I watch from my hiding place as he peers about, then paces back and forth never straying far from his vehicle. Several times he stops, checks his watch, looks toward me and the trees above. Finally, nervously, he goes to the benches where I told him to wait, chooses one and sits, cradling his briefcase in his arms. I peer around to be sure no one's lurking. I search the shadows beneath surrounding trees for human forms. I scan the crest behind, the flat fenced-off reservoir above, finally the backs of the buildings behind me on Chestnut Street where several large windows are dimly lit.

No uncommon movements, visible confederates, nothing extra-ordinary or out of place. This is a dog-walking area, but tonight the haze has confined evening strollers to residential streets. The only sound, beside the buoys and foghorns, is the erratic rumbling of the cable beneath the tracks on Hyde.

I stoop, step out from beneath the boughs, straighten up, stand still, scan my surroundings again. Judd, back to me, sits quietly on his bench. I'm eager to go to him, but hold myself back. Five minutes more, I decide, to be certain he's alone. Then I'll approach him from behind.

Judd moves as if to turn. 'Don't!' I order. I hear the same labored breathing I heard in his office after I knocked him down. 'Let's make this quick,' I snap. 'Give me the names.'

'Yeah, and what do I get?' he asks, his voice whiny, shrill. 'You hand over the tape, how do I know you didn't make a copy?'

'You don't. Which is why I won't be handing over the tape.'

'*What?*' He's outraged. It comes back to me now – how much I dislike him. 'I thought we had a deal.' Again he starts to turn.

I place my hand on his sweaty pate, feel revulsion at the touch. 'Face front! We *do* have a deal. You give me the names, you don't get disbarred.' He squirms beneath my palm. 'Of course I've copied the tape,' I tell him, 'deposited it with friends . . . as I have all the incriminating photographs I took since I started delving into this vipers' nest.'

'Why should I trust you, Missy?'

How I loathe that word! Sensing he's stalling, I turn, check the trees behind, see nothing, focus again on the back of his head.

'My deal expires in twenty seconds. Talk or I'm walking away.'

'You can't!'

'I am!' I retreat a step.

'*Wait!*'

'*Talk!*'

'Sure.' Suddenly he turns, a light flashes and I go blind.

An extremely brilliant lamp, a strobe, has been fired point-blank at my face. Instinctively I start running up the hill, feeling my way blindly, scrambling, grasping desperately at gravel and weeds.

I open my eyes, see nothing, but hear someone climbing behind. Propelled by terror, I rush on as, slowly, my vision clears. At the top of the ridge, I turn and look down. I have but a split-second to glimpse the scene below before lights flash again, twice this time, from two different points. Again blinded, I turn and rush forward, colliding with a fence.

I know where I am, at the fenced perimeter of the old underground Francisco Street reservoir, closed off by the Water Department because the roof is weak. I turn right, run along the fence, brushing one hand against the metal. There are at least two people chasing me and both have strobes. If I trip and fall, they'll overtake me. I must out-run them even though I can't see. If I can keep from looking back, I'll gradually regain my sight. But if I turn to face them they will strobe me again, and then I'll be at their mercy.

The air's chilly but I sweat as I stumble along the path. I can see now, better every second, can also hear my pursuers' steps. Not Judd, I'm certain; he's a waddler, couldn't move this fast. Who are these people? Where did they come from? Then it hits me: they must have been hiding in Judd's car. He hid his strobe in his briefcase, fired it at me, then they got out with strobes of their own and chased me up the hill.

I scramble back down toward the olive trees, choose one, hit the ground, crawl on my belly beneath the branches until I reach the trunk. So long as they can fire off strobes, I don't have a chance. If I turn to fight, they'll blind me; if I try to hide, they have lamps to find me out.

I hear them now moving in the darkness. They know I'm in the grove. I catch a glimpse of one. He's holding a cell phone to his ear. They're conferring, coordinating their search. In a minute one of them will spot me. If I'm to survive I must move fast, regain my advantage – superior vision at night.

I choose the one closest. In silhouette he looks familiar, but even with my sight restored I can't make out his face. I crouch, ready to rush him, waiting for him to turn his back. Rita said: 'Use your camera as a ball-and-chain. Merge with it.' I wrap the strap of my Nikon around my hand until there's but a foot of slack.

He steps closer, stops and stares. Now he's just fifteen feet away. When he turns, I charge. He hears me, raises his strobe. Swinging my camera I knock it from his hands. On the reverse swing, I smack him in the side of the head. He goes down. I stamp hard on the strobe, hear the lens and bulb crack beneath my shoe. He groans, moves. I kick him, then hear a shout. His colleague is charging at me from below. I turn just in time to avoid another burst of light, dash back up the hill, stumbling on my own shadow as the strobe flashes again and again like a hot lash against my back.

Ping! Something nicks the earth beside me. *Ping!Ping!* Two more nicks, closer. Must be bullets! I scurry along the north-south reservoir fence, prepared to rush up Larkin steps.

Suddenly another figure rises before me. I turn. Behind me the man with the gun is gaining fast. Cornered! I rush the new man, am about to strike him with my camera, stop just as the strobe behind me fires off. The light reveals Drake, illuminated like a ghost, his face chalk-white and flat. Confused, I drop my camera. Drake pulls me to him, pivots, pushes me down, then through an opening at the bottom of the fence.

We race across the asphalt. I'm terrified. I know the reason this area is fenced, the weakness of the roof, can feel it cave beneath my feet.

'We can't cross here!' I tell him. 'We'll fall through.'

Drake whispers: 'Stay with me. You'll be safe.'

He guides me to a wooden walkway that angles across the asphalt. I glance back, spot our pursuer wriggling beneath the fence.

Drake lifts up a flap of asphalt, pulls up boards, throws them aside.

'Down,' he orders.

'Into the water?'

'It's empty. Go down, Kay. Feel for the ladder.'

Ping!Ping! More shots! I find a footing on the ladder, scamper down, several times feeling Drake's heels as they scuff my head. Just as I reach the bottom, the silhouette of our pursuer appears in the hatch above. I jump for the floor. Drake leaps too, then yanks the ladder from the opening. It crashes down raising a cloud of dust. I turn away and choke.

It's black down here, the floor is covered with debris and muck, there are pillars at regular intervals, the ceiling is twenty-five feet high, and the smell is of old iron, rust and rot. Drake guides me toward the Hyde Street side. The man in the hatch opening is firing his strobe, trying to find us in the gloom. I flatten myself behind a pillar, draw in my legs, freeze. My vision has grown keen; I don't relish the thought of losing it. I shade my eyes, then peer around taking care not to look directly at the strobe.

This reservoir, I recall, was built in the last century. For years there's been talk of making it safe, retrofitting it to withstand a magnitude-8 quake. Meantime it's been sitting here, a vast subterranean space, forest of old columns supporting a crumbling roof, dusty, unused, uninhabited by anything except rodents and an occasional vagrant.

In the distance I spot another ladder leading up to a second hatch. Our pursuer apparently sees it too, for he and his strobe disappear from the opening. I hear his footsteps on the roof. I whisper to Drake we must pull the second ladder down. Drake brings his finger to his lips. The ceiling creaks. He grins.

The groan of wood under strain. Splintering, then a scream as a huge piece of roof crashes down. An explosion of dust. I turn away. When I look back up the night sky's visible. The man pursuing us has fallen through. When the echoes die, I hear his cries in the darkness, like the whining of an injured dog.

To approach or not? I hold Drake back; the man may still have his gun. 'Is there another way out?'

Drake nods, starts crawling. I crawl after him through the dust toward the sound of traffic on Hyde. By the time we reach the reservoir wall, the moans of our fallen pursuer have grown faint. Suddenly there's a roar as a cable car ascends. I think of myself with Sasha, just a few weeks ago, walking up this hill which I am now beneath, en route to our first kiss at my door.

Drake motions toward rungs built into the wall. He climbs, I follow, until we are at the top, parallel with the slanting sidewalk. We swing ourselves up, Drake pushes out a section of grillework, then we crawl out between close-fitting struts. At last in the open, I gulp fresh inky fog.

'You saved my life, Drake.' He's stunned when I take his face in my hands, plant a chaste kiss on his cheek. I feel him withdraw. When we were in danger there was contact; he grasped me, pushed and pulled me to safety. Now that we're safe, he retreats back into his solitude.

He lowers his eyes. 'I am always watching out for you, Kay.'

'I know.' I gesture toward the reservoir. 'He's still down there. I've got to call the cops.'

He nods sadly.

'You won't stay?'

He shakes his head. 'Be careful. The other one—'

'I'll be careful.' I touch his hand. 'Thanks.'

He re-enters the park. I watch as he skits along the reservoir fence toward Larkin, disappears in the fog. He will climb back up to Sterling Park, I know, hole up again among the trees and shrubs and from there gaze up at my window. I wish that one time at least we could hug one another, but I know this is something my secret watchman of the woods will not permit.

I walk up to Chestnut, find a pay phone. My finger trembles as I punch in Hilly's number. Thank God she's home! Excited, she hears me out. When I'm done she says: 'I'm on my way.' I replace the phone, venture carefully back toward my vantage point among the olive trees, noting that Judd's car is no longer on the street.

I'm looking for the other man, the one I hit in the head. There was something familiar about the way he moved I couldn't place. No trace of him now, but I do find my Nikon and the strobe I smashed. To my amazement Dad's old camera still works; beneath the black exterior it's solid brass.

I pick up the broken strobe, examine it. Brand-new. Judd brought them here expressly to blind and kill me. How did they know I'm photophobic? I look down at my hands; they're still shaking. I drop the strobe in the dust.

I feel no pity for the man I struck or the one lying at the bottom of the reservoir. I have no doubt that if they'd caught me, they'd have heaved me through that very roof.

Three squad cars pull up, then Hilly in her Volvo. I tell her about Judd. A minute later a police rescue unit arrives followed by an ambulance. Hilly joins them. I watch through the fog as men and women with flashlights go to the reservoir, peer down through the hole. A crew arrives with a portable block and tackle. Another crew sets up a generator and lights. Rescue workers descend. I start taking pictures, hear the crackle of police radios, watch as the injured body of my pursuer is hoisted up.

He's placed on a stretcher, rushed down to the ambulance. Hilly walks to where I'm standing. She's carrying another broken strobe and a 22 automatic in a zip-lock bag. There's some kind of attachment on the barrel. Hilly tells me it's a silencer.

'It's Vasquez,' she says. 'He can't move. Lots of broken bones.' She stares at me, smiles, shakes her head. 'Can you believe it, Kay – chief of felony prostitution shooting at an unarmed woman with an illegally silenced gun! Jesus hot fuckin' dog!'

I tell her why I'm not surprised, that I suspected he was Judd's partner in the scam.

She tells me Vasquez is crying for his lawyer, that she's sent a team to find Judd and arrest him, also put out a call to all hospital ERs to look out for the man I hit.

'There's plenty of blood,' she tells me. 'Looks like you whacked him good.'

'I'm thrilled.'

'Seen him before, Kay?'

'I think so. Can't remember where.'

'It'll come to you.' She steps closer, smiles again. 'Last night I checked Knob's record at Pelican Bay. They try and train the boys up there, teach them a trade so they can find work when they get out. Guess what? His job was in the kitchen, apprentice meat-cutter.' She curls her lip. 'They say near the end he got pretty good.' She pauses. 'I'm going to pick him up. Wanna come along?'

As we drive over the top of Russian Hill, followed by two squad cars each containing a team of uniformed cops, I catch glimpses through lit windows of cheerful domestic scenes, families clustered in comfortable living rooms relaxing after Thanksgiving dinner. Down on Polk it's a different story, lonely singles sitting in all-night Chinese restaurants staring at their food. In doorways the homeless lie like broken dolls, while the addicts in the alleys peer at us with haunted eyes.

After Bush Street we come upon hustlers. Hilly says she's surprised to see them out. I tell her what I learned from Tim, that around holidays business is always good, the streets filled with lonely johns, married men seeking rough-trade, obsessed chickenhawks yearning for sweet boy-love in the night.

We spot Knob, standing with Tommy and Boat beside the door of The Werewolf. Hilly drives a block, pulls over, confers with the cops in the squad cars, returns to talk to me. The cops, she says, will scoop up all three, separate them, run the kids down to the Hall of Justice, place them in cubicles. She'll take Knob in her car on a longer, slower ride around the city. Certain he'll ask for a lawyer, she wants to talk to him informally first. I can't come along, but I'm welcome to meet her later at the Hall.

'Aren't you afraid to be alone with him?' I ask.

Hilly grins. 'He's already done one five-year stretch for felonious assault. I kinda doubt he wants to go back for life.'

I walk home, shower, change and then, in an attempt to stop my hands from shaking, clean my camera and reload. The shaking's so bad I can barely get the fresh film aligned.

Calm yourself. Find your center, Kay.

I go to my office, look down through the window at Sterling Park. Drake's down there, I know, possibly, this very moment, gazing up at me.

I phone for a cab. On my way out the door, it suddenly comes to me – the identity of the third man with the strobe.

I return to my office, check the photos pinned to the cork. Yes, now I'm certain – it was Sarah Lashaw's lover and tennis coach, the man I know as Roy.

The receptionist at the Hall of Justice phones for Hilly. She comes down to meet me, glow of triumph on her face. I sign in, a guard hangs a VISITOR'S ID around my neck, Hilly escorts me back up to the homicide division.

I tell her about Roy. She beams. 'It fits. The house of cards is falling fast.'

In her office she instructs the duty detective to call the Lashaw house in St Helena, get the full name of the resident tennis coach. Then she takes me into a viewing room.

The cubicle on the other side of the one-way glass is small, oppressive like a cell. I think: Maybe this is the one where the T-case detectives worked over Dad. Knob faces us. He doesn't look like King of the Gulch tonight. His eyes are puffy; there are bruises on his cheeks.

I turn to Hilly. 'What d'you do to him?'

She grins. 'Explained a few facts of life. Like whatever happened he was going down, the only question being whether he'd get life or lethal injection.'

'Okay if I take his picture?'

'Be my guest.'

As I trip the shutter, I think I see him wince.

'He's in recovery,' Hilly says. 'That's normal after a confession. Come on, I'll show you the videotape.'

She escorts me to another room equipped with TV monitor and VCR, gestures me to a chair, slaps in a tape, fast-forwards it, stops.

'Here's the good part,' she says, restarting the tape at normal speed.

I lean forward. This, I feel, is a moment I ought to savor.

Knob, sobbing, desperate: 'I *swear* I didn't kill him!'

Hilly's voice, sympathetic, calm: 'But you know who did?'

Knob, crying, insistent: 'Wasn't me!'

'But you did *something*, right?'

A moan, a nod: 'Helped clean up, that's all.'

'Clean up? What does that mean?'

'He was dead. I did some cutting. I *swear* – he was already dead.'

Hilly freezes the frame.

She has things to do, leaves me alone to watch the rest of the tape. I stare spellbound as Knob tells how Crane became his most important client, the huge amounts of money Crane paid him to procure boys:

'He kept wanting them younger, prettier. I broke my ass trying to please the guy. Then he met Rain, liked him . . . which wasn't good for me. See, Rain worked freelance. He wouldn't cut me in.'

'You hated Rain for that?' Hilly asks.

Knob winces, shakes his head. 'Wasn't personal. Business, that's all it was. He stole my best client. It's tough out there.'

'Tough?'

'I had expenses. I was paying out big to Vasquez.'

'For what?'

'Protection. If I didn't pay, he'd run me off the street.'

'You the only one who paid him?'

'No, everyone does. He knows everything going on, names of all the important johns, who pays how much and what they get for it. He knows Crane, takes money from him too. Knew Rain. When Crane got in trouble with Rain, he was there to help.'

'What kind of trouble?' Hilly asks.

'Rain stopped seeing the john.'

'Dropped him?'

Knob nods.

'Why?'

Knob shakes his head. 'Didn't like the way Crane kept crowding him, I guess.'

'You said Crane paid big.'

'He did, but Rain didn't care. Last month he comes to me, asks me to find Crane someone else. "Get the guy off my back, I'll give you a split," he says. So then we were friends again.'

'What happened?'

'Beginning of October, when Rain stopped seeing him, Crane started talking crazy. One night he tells me since he can't have Rain he wants the next best thing. I try to fix him up for a three-way with Tommy and Boat, but this isn't what he's got in mind. Turns out he wants Rain's twin, the girl.'

Amoretto! I marvel at how her story keeps getting entwined with this. And certainly it makes sense: if Crane couldn't have Tim, he'd have his androgynous twin, Ariane. Boy, girl – small difference if the game was about possession.

Knob requires little prompting now. Studying his face, expressionless eyes, listening to his matter-of-fact tone, I'm mesmerized as much as repelled. I even think I catch a glimmer of relief. Cool and amoral as he is, Knob isn't a pure sociopath, just a Catholic boy gone bad carrying a burden of guilt. To confess to Hilly is to seek absolution, a first step toward redemption. She wants so much to understand him; he tries so hard to make her understand. After all, he keeps insisting, he didn't kill anyone, just helped clean up . . . and was thus but a bystander to the drama.

'Scene with the girl didn't work out. Way I heard, got nasty too. I think that was Crane's plan – belt the girl around, get Rain mad. Then Rain'd *have* to come see him.' Knob laughs. 'Oh, Rain got mad all right. Real mad. Said he was going to go after the guy, report him, sue his ass. I told him "Don't do that!" It's the number one rule on the street. You don't tell on these guys. They got too much to lose – family, reputation, whatever. You threaten them, try and blackmail, they're as likely to kill you as pay you off.

'Not that Crane had the guts to kill anybody. Least I didn't think he did. More like he'd hire someone do the job. There're plenty of guys on the Gulch, addicts and what-not, they'll do anything you pay 'em enough.'

But Knob had underrated Crane, who, as it turned out, *was* quite capable of killing Tim. Knob didn't know what happened, only that Crane came to him and Vasquez afterwards with twenty-five thousand cash each to clean up and cover up the killing.

Right away Knob knew what to do – cut Tim up and dispose of the pieces. Then Vasquez got the bright idea of tying the Homicide Division up in knots. He'd wash Tim's torso with licorice-scented soap, then apply designs and the number '7' to make it look like a copycat T killing. Knob, figuring the head and limbs would never be found, bagged and dropped them into an alley dumpster. Vasquez, hoping the tricked-up torso *would* be found, ditched it in open sight in Wildcat Canyon.

'So, see, I didn't kill anyone,' Knob says, pleading for sympathy. 'I'm bad, but not that bad. Like I said – the kid was dead. Guy offers you a bundle to clean up, what would you do? Huh?'

Hilly reappears to tell me Crane and Roy have just been picked up at Sarah Lashaw's San Francisco house. I'm impressed with the way she's handling things. Without a supervisor to slow her down, she's moved decisively. Now with Crane under arrest, I have to agree that, yes, the house of cards is falling fast.

'The way it comes down,' she says, 'Vasquez and Knob were accessories after the fact. They'll both get life sentences for that. Crane'll get the needle, Roy and Judd'll do time for trying to kill you. It's all over now except for the trials.'

I shake my head. The riddle is solved. Now that I know the story all the pieces fit: Crane, the Chickenhawk, kills Tim to shut him up; Knob, the Butcher, cuts up Tim's body; Vasquez, the Bad Cop, ornaments Tim's torso to confuse the investigation.

But why did Crane have to kill Tim? Why not just pay him off? I think I know. Crane, I believe, tried to pay, but Tim refused his money. Ariane, his beloved twin, had been brutally beaten; no amount would stop him from bringing Crane down.

*   *   *

In the morning Joel and I attend the arraignments. The courtroom is packed with squabbling lawyers, bored cops, irritable bailiffs, terrified spouses, some with infants in their arms. Judge Helen Lesser, gray-haired and gaunt, presides.

The players perform like robots, each accused person approaching the bar with counsel, listening to then answering the charge, followed by a brisk argument over bail, a quick decision by the judge, a stroke of the gavel, then a rapid march-off to the wings. We sit through a string of minor cases: pick-pockets, prostitutes, shop-lifters, persons accused of peddling without a licence. At one point Hilly approaches with an attractive young Asian-American woman whom she introduces as Assistant DA Patricia Chu. Pat Chu, Hilly tells us, will be prosecuting the Lovsey defendants. We shake hands, Pat returns to her table, Hilly whispers: 'She's young but one of the best.'

The clerk calls Luis Vasquez.

One Laurence Granby steps forward, former police officer, now shiny-suited defense attorney specializing in the representation of accused cops. His client, he tells Judge Lesser, cannot appear, being presently in the hospital recovering from a fall. He presents papers allowing him to plead in his stead.

The charges are read: attempted homicide; corruption; obstruction of justice; accessory-after-the-fact to murder. Granby tells the judge that his client pleads innocent. Mr Vasquez, he argues, being a sworn law enforcement officer with strong ties to the community, should, upon his recovery, be released without bond.

Pat Chu, with just the slightest hint of a snarl, argues for confinement. Judge Lesser agrees, orders Vasquez transferred to the jail ward at Cal Med. 'Next!' she tells her clerk.

J. F. Judd appears, accompanied by his former law partner, a rumpled old-timer named Jeremiah Waldroon. The charges: false representation; solicitation of corruption; conspiracy to commit murder. Waldroon asks for minimum bail. Judge Lesser sternly sets bond at one hundred thousand dollars.

Raymond Krogan, aka Knob, accompanied by Public Defender Wendy Aronson, is called next. Knob pleads guilty to the charge of accessory to murder. Pat Chu informs the judge that Krogan has agreed to testify against other parties in return for being allowed to plead to a single three-strikes offense. Since there can be no bail for a three-strikes offender, Judge Lesser sets a date for the formal plea and sentencing. Knob is led away.

Next up is Peter Royal, known to me as Roy, dressed in pressed chinos and tennis shirt, head swathed in bandages. His lawyer assists him in pleading not guilty to the charge of attempted murder, then asks for bail.

'My client,' he pleads, 'is the injured party here. Truth is, the person he's accused of trying to kill, tried to kill him . . . and nearly did.'

Pat Chu explains that the victim, namely me, was acting in self-defense. She asks for two hundred thousand dollars bond. Judge Lesser agrees, smacks her gavel, asks the clerk to call the next case.

The room becomes still. This is what everyone's been waiting for. Marcus Crane, toupeed, dressed in dark grey slacks, bespoke sports jacket and Pacific-Union Club tie, walks confidently to the bar, accompanied by J. Carter Hackford, possibly the best and certainly the most expensive defense attorney in San Francisco. The charge: first degree murder.

During the reading, Crane, head held high, stares straight ahead. But scanning the courtroom I spot Sarah Lashaw. Our eyes meet. She glares raw hatred. I turn away.

Hackford argues for bond; the charge, he says is based solely on the testimony of a lying street-hustler and convicted felon. He lists various important corporate and charity boards upon which Mr Crane sits, his role as scion of one of the city's oldest, most distinguished families, the lack of any criminal record and the absurdity of the notion that such a man would attempt to flee.

Pat Chu reminds the court that this is a capital case, describes the brutality of the crime, the overwhelming evidence, and states the fact that no citizen, no matter what his station, is entitled to special privilege.

Judge Lesser agrees, remands Marcus Crane to the custody of the Sheriff's Department, to be held in jail pending a preliminary hearing.

Outside we're swarmed. TV and print reporters, photographers and videotape cameramen, press close. Even though I'm wearing shades, I hold up my hand to protect my eyes.

The questions fly at me.

'Is it true Tim Lovsey was a hustler?'

'You took photos of Crane soliciting kids, right?'

'Why'd they want to kill you, Kay?'

Keeping silent, I try to work my way through, Joel gently pushing his press colleagues aside to create a path. Suddenly the crowd parts, then deserts us. A far bigger attraction has appeared.

'Mrs Lashaw – is it true your husband's part of a ring of chickenhawks?'

'Sarah! Did you know Marcus Crane was gay?'

'How's your tennis coach involved?'

'Did you put him up to it?'

'How's it feel to be married to a child molester?'

The questions resound as Joel and I escape the crush. Out on Bryant Street, he turns to me, winks.

'You'll be on TV tonight, kiddo.'

Sasha is on duty, so I go over to Dad's on Cherry Street to watch the evening news. Since I'm more interested in his reactions than in seeing myself, I study him as he waits for my appearance. He's nervous but also rooting for me, I can tell, actually looks proud when I come on.

'Oh, boy!' he says. 'That's it, darlin'! Give it to 'em, give it to 'em good!'

Since, in the film clip, I speak not a word, it must be my silence that he likes.

'No, it's you, darlin' – your dignity, the way you move. Class! They recognize it. Now that Lashaw lady – she comes off like a tart.'

I have to smile. His vocabulary's so quaint. Tarts, fairies, tootsie-babies – such archetypes populate his mind. But if he's an old-fashioned guy, his heart is big and his integrity intact. When the news segment is over, he flicks off the set.

'So what's next, darlin'? When're you planning on digging up Billy's stuff?'

'Joel thinks we should give it a month.'

Dad nods. 'Good idea. Wait till after the holidays at least.'

Hilly, Joel, Ice-Goddess Kirstin, Sasha and I meet to celebrate the publication of Joel's front-page story in the *Bay Area News*. We assemble at the bar at Zuni, my favorite San Francisco haunt because of its food, conviviality and eccentric triangular flat-iron space. When our table is ready we ascend to the balcony. Conversation and laughter bubble up to us as we eat. This, I think, is San Francisco at its best – happy, youthful, still a little wild.

Sasha's great. Everyone likes him. But as dinner progresses, Hilly slips into a funk. When Joel asks what's the matter, she says being without a date makes her feel odd man out.

'Jeez, Hilly,' Joel says, 'now that you're famous you'll get hit on all the time.'

'Yeah,' she says, brightening. Then just as quickly she deflates: 'But then how'll I know it's me she likes and not just the true-blue image?'

A few days of euphoria, then the let-down. It's all wrapped up . . . except it's not. *Exposures*, I think, will work. I'll have a book, a coherent story with beginning, middle and end. But still there's something missing. In my anger and the passion of the chase, I forgot about my loss. Now I miss Tim terribly. His smile, eyes, beauty, the perfect planes of his face, the way he used to touch me when we talked. I long for closure, cannot find it. His twin, carrying at least some portion of his spirit, somewhere roams the earth. I know I must find her, that until I do I cannot rest.

Early-December days are clear this year, the light oblique and sharp. Hard to imagine winter rains are coming soon. In daytime it's balmy, people walk around in jogging clothes. I spot a Santa Claus standing on the corner of Mason and Sutter ringing a bell in shorts. At night the air is crisp; the city sparkles beneath the moon. I study various neighborhoods through my telescope, recalling David deGeoffroy's certainty that Ariane must be nearby. Why hasn't she come forward? Surely she knows of the arrests. She also knows who I am and how to find me, but I have no notion of where to look for her.

Joel's call awakens me from a dream. I answer groggily, brain fogged with sleep.

'Crane's dead, killed himself.'

'*What?*' My head clears fast. '*When? Where?*'

'Last night. In jail. He wasn't on suicide-watch. He was acting so cocky the jailers left him alone. Somehow he got hold of a belt, used it to make a noose, got up on a stool, secured the belt to the window bars, kicked the stool away. They're pissing blood downtown. Hackford's yelling the cops railroaded an innocent man, hounded him unto death. Lashaw was just on the air fuming with indignation. It's all the fault, she says, of a sick, obsessed girl. That's you, kiddo. And a scummy journalist – me. She named us both.'

'Jesus!'

'Don't worry. She and Hackford'll be sorry. I just got off the phone with Pat Chu. The DA's office believes in the public's right to know. They'll release details of their case this afternoon.'

At 5 I turn on my TV, watch the press conference live. Pat Chu is terrific – smooth, even-tempered, precise – and she presents a devastating brief. She's got it all, chapter and verse, even the gun used to shoot Tim, registered to Crane and found in Knob's hooch. She shows the knives Knob used to do the cutting, the wad of money he received from Crane, Crane's lease on the Washington Street pied-à-terre where he engaged in sexual acts with under-age boys. Best of all, she offers serology reports showing that traces of Tim's blood were found in the love-nest, on the carpet where he fell after he was shot, and in the drain of the bathtub where the butchering was carried out.

'The evidence,' she says, 'is overwhelming, as Mr Crane surely recognized. Naturally we deplore his suicide. We'd have much preferred to take our case to a jury. Still we must surmise that Marcus Crane took his own life to spare himself and his family a blistering defeat at trial.'

Joel asks me to join him at Crane's funeral, to be held in Grace Cathedral. I decline. I have no wish to stand outside in a vulture's pack of photographers ready to pounce when Sarah Lashaw appears.

I've had more than enough of that doomed, demented couple. Like specimen insects, they'll be pinned forever in my memory. Instead I spend those hours working quietly in my darkroom where the safety light gives off a comforting glow.

An image emerging slowly from a sheet of photographic paper immersed in developer – the magic of it stirs me still. It's the same feeling I get when I look out at the city at night. I smile at the wonder of it, the mystery.

Two weeks before Christmas, Dad again asks me to join him, Phyllis Sorenson and her daughters on their holiday trip to Honolulu. But he doesn't demur when I remind him we agreed a joint vacation wouldn't work.

'I'll miss you, darlin'.'

I tell him I'll miss him too.

'Just hate to think of you all alone.'

'I won't be alone. I'll be with Sasha.'

'That's right.' A pause. 'You know, I really *like* that boy!'

I thank him, but haven't the heart to respond that I wish I liked Phyllis as well.

In fact, Sasha, having learned his lesson at Thanksgiving, has reserved a room for us at Treetops in Big Sur. Our stay, he promises, will be 'sybaritic'. Needless to say, I can't wait.

16 December. Hilly stops by to return my Contax G1 and Zeiss 28mm lens, discovered in Knob's hooch in the Tenderloin, the little room he rented at the corner of Turk and Jones. Both are in as good shape as they were the night Knob grabbed them. I'm thrilled. I love this little camera which has served me so well, and am mystified Knob didn't try to sell it.

In fact, Hilly tells me, Knob kept everything – the pistol Crane told him to get rid of, the butcher knives he used, even Tim's clothing, wallet and keys. She thinks it's because, during the time he served in Pelican, Knob acquired convict traits – compulsive neatness, covetousness, an inability to throw anything away.

Just before she goes she slips me a transcript copy of his amended confession.

'It's got a few more details,' she says.

I place it on my bedside table, then, uncomfortable with the notion of sleeping so close to it, hide it away in a drawer.

Still it oppresses me. Why, I wonder, can't I just sit down and read the damn' thing? After all, it's an essential part of the story. If *Exposures* is to be a proper account, I must know everything that happened.

After three days I give in, take it to the living room, lie down on my couch and start to read.

Soon I'm immersed. Then I come to the part where my life intersected with the events described. The night Tim was killed, when I went out to meet him on the Gulch, I spotted Crane, whom I dubbed Baldy at the time, speaking with Knob then handing him a package I was sure contained drugs. A few seconds later, passing

Crane, I noticed he was upset, but when I asked Knob what their conversation had been about, he shrugged the encounter off.

In fact, I now learn from Knob's amended confession, it was during that brief exchange that Crane paid him to get rid of Tim's body. A few minutes after receiving the money and the key, Knob went over to Crane's Washington Street pied-à-terre, hauled Tim's body into the bathroom, placed it in the tub and commenced his grisly work.

There is fascination in madness. Crane, according to Knob, was truly mad:

'. . . I'm in the bathroom cutting. Suddenly he comes in, this weird look on his face, says he wants to keep Rain's head. I ask him, "What're you going to do with it, man? Make love to it, put it on the wall like a fuckin' trophy?" "I want it!" he says. He tries to grab it out of the tub. I slap him down. "Look," I tell him, "I got work to do, I don't need this kinda shit." Vasquez comes in, pulls him into the other room, so I get on with the job . . .'

Yeah, the job.

The Friday before Christmas I deliver my important gifts: a carry-on bag for Dad, not too imaginative but he'll need it for his trip; a handmade craftswoman's kaleidoscope for Maddy ('May you always see beauty, Maddy!'); the shell of a chambered nautilus for Rita ('For you, you hard-assed softie!'); a pad of play money for Caroline Gifford at Zeitgeist ('Next time, I promise, it'll be real!'), and a bottle of Courvoisier Extra for Rob Mathews ('With special thanks for your very special help!')

The day Sasha and I are to drive South, I prepare a holiday package for Drake: an assortment of the organic health foods he likes, plus Christmas cookies and a bottle of Italian egg liqueur. I wrap the whole thing up in foiled paper, tie it with a mix of ribbons, slip a couple of poinsettias beneath the bow, then place it on our bench.

I wait a while, hoping he'll show himself. I want to tell him how things worked out and that now I'm out of danger. He doesn't appear. He's been so elusive the last couple of weeks, I wonder if something's wrong. I take a brief walk around the park, but find no trace of him. When I return to the bench the box is gone. He's here all right; he simply chooses not to show himself. That's fine. I call out: 'Best wishes for the holidays, Drake,' then return to my apartment to pack.

*   *   *

Treetops is a dream. Our suite is a detached house set up on stilts among the redwoods to protect their roots. We have a fireplace, hot-tub, porch furnished with wicker chairs, huge bed made up with incredibly luxurious sheets arranged for perfect viewing of the Pacific.

At night we watch a cruise ship pass, lit up like a city. Then a thick fog hugs us in. In the morning we arise to find whales cavorting in the waves, blowing off fountains of spray. There's nothing to do here except eat, sleep, read, make love and receive deep Swedish-style massages from the staff.

On Christmas morning after breakfast we take a long hike through the woods. At lunch we exchange gifts: a black silk dressing gown for Sasha, a small framed Indian tantric painting of a female warrior for me.

I'm overwhelmed. The drawing is exquisite. Sasha tells me it's colored, but he thinks the effect is more powerful in black-and-white.

'How do you know?' I ask.

'I photographed it first to see.'

What a fabulous man! 'I'm crazy about you, Sasha. I chose a black robe for you because you wear white all day.'

He kisses me. We repair to our tree-house to make love. After that a long soak in our hot tub, then a double massage as we lie side by side while a pair of tender-fingered masseuses knead our flesh. This, I think, must be what 'sybaritic' means.

Before sleep, I look closely at the painting. It's less than a foot square, yet filled with energy. The woman warrior holds a sword in one hand, a shield in the other. At her feet lies a half-clad male.

I ask Sasha if there's a story to go with it. He says there're a hundred possible stories, and, to demonstrate, he'll tell me one.

'The warrior is you, Kay – powerful, indomitable, a woman of convictions, never to be trifled with. The man is your lover, me, "slain" by your fierce beauty. We've made love all night. Now we recline declaring our love – you in your warrior's crouch, female power enhanced, I at your feet drained, but in bliss.'

'Sasha,' I tell him, 'that's just wonderful.'

8 January: foggy, wintry. Hilly, 'based on information received from a confidential source', has secured a search warrant from Judge

Henry Beck to dig up the area behind Billy Hayes's widow's garage.

Debbie Hayes doesn't act surprised when we show up – Hilly, Joel and me, a van carrying two cops and three criminalists with shovels, trailed by a backhoe and driver from Public Works.

Debbie's a big blowzy middle-aged woman with a Texas twang. Hard to imagine her with Billy, the lean, fast-talking welterweight. But she doesn't object or squawk or carry on. I get the impression she's cried lots of tears in her life and more or less expects disasters.

When I ask if I can take her picture, she invites me into the house. There's a display of family photos on the spinet, no sign in them of kids. I pose her holding a photo of young Billy to her chest, in which, in head-guard and trunks, he receives his Golden Gloves award. There's an expression of longing on her face that seems to deepen as I shoot. Afterwards she stands by the window staring out at the men.

'It's nice to have a bunch of guys around again. Billy used to bring his cop-friends home. I miss those days.'

She asks me if I think it'll be all right if she takes a case of beer out to the crew, or whether she should wait until they find whatever it is they're looking for.

Dusk comes early in January. It's dark and cold by the time the trench is dug, fifteen feet wide running along the rear of the garage. The backhoe operator had to take special care not to break into the foundation.

I shiver in my jacket as the criminalists start sifting dirt. They wear miners' lights on their helmets; the beams criss-cross as they work the pit. A train passes behind the house, hissing its way south to San Jose. Neighborhood kids cluster around to watch. Not much conversation, just steady work by men anxious to finish a tough job and go home.

I keep my eyes on Hilly, wondering what she thinks, why she supposes Billy buried this stuff and to what degree she suspects Dad's involvement. We've tipped her off without telling her the entire story. In return for our tip, she's promised not to delve too deeply. As Joel puts it, she's chosen personal glory at the price of never understanding Billy's motivation. In this matter each of us has used the other: Hilly to greatly advance her career; Joel to break a terrific story; I, as best I understand myself, to preserve the symmetries; all of us to uncover the dead T killer's identity.

Photographing the scene I try to capture its starkness, the sense I have that we're digging up a grave. A couple of times people call Hilly over, but in each instance the find turns out to be a stone.

Shortly after 7 p.m., a cop near the corner of the garage holds up a black polyethylene bag knotted at the top. Hilly takes it to the van, hands it to the chief criminalist. Miraculously the plastic hasn't torn.

During the opening I fire off rapid frames. Behind me the men light cigarettes while herding against the chill.

Once the bag is opened an odor is released, earthy and, perhaps in my imagination, faintly tinged with licorice. I catch my breath as the criminalist pulls out a set of mildewed clothes, then the hypodermic, the tattooing gear, finally the awful ominous hood slippery with mold.

Hilly turns to me: 'Do you believe this, Kay? Fifteen years in the ground?' She turns to the others. 'Yes! *Yes!*' she whoops. They cheer, hug, congratulate. I photograph their faces, the pride, the gloating.

Joel sidles over. 'Big moment.'

'Absolutely,' I agree.

'How do you feel?'

'Nervous. Afraid it'll backfire on Dad.'

'Don't worry, kiddo. Hilly'll see he isn't hurt.'

'How does she explain it then?'

'An old dead cop's perversity, something like that.'

'What'll Hale think when he hears?'

Joel smiles. 'That he's been screwed. You know, by the powers that be, the forces of darkness, the conspirators. He was methodical, did everything right, more or less figured out what happened. Only trouble was . . . he didn't know where to dig.'

'Any regrets about not telling him?'

Joel shakes his head. 'I like Hilly.' His smile is sly. 'I'm going to have the best cop source in town, for years to come, I think.'

I'm spending the better part of my days in the darkroom now, marking up proof sheets, printing my selections out. Twice a week, late in the afternoon, I drop by Maddy's to show her my work. She confirms some of my decisions, questions others, but never challenges my premise. Often she'll point out a new direction, a route into the story via an alternate set of images. Guided by her counsel, I make final choices, then return to the darkroom to work up exhibition-quality prints.

Some photographers I know hire a printer, but I like printing too much to farm it out. Choosing the paper, selecting contrast, exposure time, burning and dodging – I never find the process dull. And the fact that it's slow and must be done by hand adds to the pleasure. Available-light street photography is quick; one shoots fast, guided by instinct. Making prints is more like working with traditional art materials, paint or clay or wood.

The treasure-trove discovered behind Debbie Hayes's garage yields nothing in the way of fingerprints. Perhaps Skeleton-man wore gloves or time or moisture eroded whatever prints were there. It doesn't matter; in the end it's the hood that takes hold of Hilly's mind.

Well on her way to earning Hale's old title 'San Francisco's smartest cop', she and Joel try to run it down, trekking leather store to leather store, smoothly working their way into the Bay Area leathersex community.

Hilly's lesbianism and Joel's Pulitzer Prize don't hurt, opening up doors which an ordinary team would probably not discover were there. Within days they are able to set up a meeting with several senior leather community people, ageing experts on the arcane history of their scene. I'm invited, in my role as project photographer, to document the gathering.

Our host is Chet Bellows, a vivacious, charming, grizzled survivor of gay life. White-haired, in his late sixties, decked out in leather vest and worn black leather chaps, he greets us from the window of his Folsom Street loft, when we call up to him from the street.

'Catch!' he yells, throwing down the building key in what turns out to be a knotted sock. Hilly gracefully scoops it from the air, unlocks the building door. We enter a dark lobby, ascend in a freight elevator, then, upstairs, emerge into another world. The loft is spacious, beautifully furnished with antiques, there are good paintings by Bay Area artists on the walls, and case after case exhibiting a vast eclectic collection of books.

Chet introduces us around: David, Fred, Bill, Adam and Cindy, all dressed casually in gear. No giggling here, these are serious scene leaders, 'wisepersons' Chet calls them, working on an oral history project that will document gay and lesbian leather culture as it grew and changed in San Francisco over the past thirty years.

We help ourselves to beer, then Chet introduces Hilly, who explains what she's looking for and shows the gathering what she's got. The wisepersons are fascinated by the hood, which they pass among themselves, commenting on its fine craftsmanship and design.

'Stitching reminds me of Al Jameson's work,' Cindy says. 'His fittings looked like this too.'

The hood makes another round. The men agree:

'Does look like a Jameson piece.'

'What happened to Al?'

'Died of AIDS in '83.'

'His old lover, Dan Fowler – he's still around. I saw him on line at The Castro Theatre a few weeks back.'

'Dan'd know for sure.'

'Shouldn't be hard to find him.'

Chet Bellows goes to the phone, makes a couple of calls, reaches Fowler, who says he'll be happy to come over and give us his opinion on the hood.

While we wait for him, the group reminisces about the T case and what it meant to them at the time, how they feared a backlash from a normally tolerant city on account of the awful brutality of the crimes.

'We were scared,' Cindy says. She's a friendly stout woman in her forties, short gray hair, pale eyes, beatific smile. 'Back then most folks didn't understand what we do is the opposite of sadistic murder.'

'Safe, sane and consensual,' Adam adds. 'A lot of folks still don't get it.'

As they talk I'm impressed by their gentleness, intelligence, commitment to social justice. These are bright, friendly people who hold down sophisticated jobs: Chet's a retired professor of psychology, Cindy's a midwife, Fred's a computer programmer, Adam's an industrial designer in Silicon Valley, Bill's a flight instructor and David's an attorney. I can feel the strong bonds of affection between them, forged by years together on the barricades.

'We're queer and we love it,' Chet tells us. 'We're also a despised minority. We've found the best way to confront our detractors is with solidarity, openness and shared humanity. "We're your children and you're ours" – that's the essence of our message.'

Dan Fowler arrives. A tall, thin, bespectacled, weathered-face guy in his fifties, he wears faded jeans, boots, a wrangler's jacket and carries a beaten-up attaché case.

'Oh, certainly – this is one of Al's,' he says, taking hold of the hood. 'His stitching, his fittings.' Although the police lab removed the mold, they couldn't resuscitate the leather. Still Dan fondles it. 'He always used best quality hide.'

Dan opens his case, pulls out an over-sized ledger, leafs through it. 'I kept his old design-and-order book.'

I catch Joel's eye, then we both turn to Hilly. She cranes forward as Dan stops several times to examine drawings of full-head hoods. Finally, he nods.

'Sure, here it is, order number S-H17.' He drums his forefinger on the design, hands the ledger to Hilly. '"S" is for special, "H" is for hood. This was the seventeenth special order hood Al made. It's all there – date, customer name and address.' I read the data over Hilly's shoulder: Burton Boyt Quint, 110 Moraga Street, San Francisco.

Hilly, Joel and I pile into Melvin then drive off into the cold night to view Quint's old address. I'm thrilled, Hilly is frothing, Joel is trying to stay cool but I can sense he's excited too.

It's a miracle, we all agree, that Chet Bellows's group identified the deceased leather worker, and that his surviving companion kept his order book as a memento of the man he loved.

Moraga is in the Sunset, the vast grid of residential streets south of Golden Gate Park that extends to the Pacific Ocean. It's often foggy here, perhaps the foggiest district in the city. Most of the homes are modest two-story flat-roofed cubes erected side-by-side, painted in what I'm told are pastel hues. The population now is largely Asian-American, but fifteen years ago there was more of a mix. Since Burton Boyt Quint has long since been fed to the fishes, our purpose is simply to find his building, gaze at it, take in the vibes.

It's a doll-house sort of place, simple one-story bungalow with garage on one side and narrow strip of lawn on the other. It's small, innocuous, and lonely on account of that extra bit of land on an avenue where nearly every other structure abuts its neighbors.

'Perfect place to do bad stuff,' Joel says.

Hilly squints as she peers at the house. 'Like cut guys up,' she says.

Silence. In fact, it turns out, we're all thinking the same thing: what if some of the missing heads and limbs are buried beneath that grass or walled-up in the cellar?

'You got your work cut out,' Joel tells Hilly, 'that is, if Quint's the one.'

'He's the one.' There's something prideful in her now. An enormous success is within her grasp. She can feel it, can already taste the spoils.

'What'll you do now?'

'Backtrack the name,' Hilly says, 'come up with a social security number. Check military, school, voting and car registration records. Look through old phone books and trace the ownership of the house. We know the T killer had access to a car if only to carry and dump his torsos. What happened to it? What sort of job did Quint have? When did he disappear? Who *was* this guy?'

Joel looks at me. 'There's one more thing we can tell you,' he says to Hilly, 'to help you stay on track. It's the only other thing we know and you must promise you'll never ask us how we know or reveal it to anyone.'

Hilly agrees; how could she not, since we're offering her the keys to the law enforcement treasury? Joel describes the full-body red skeleton tattoo on the T killer's arms, legs and ribs. If Hilly can turn up someone who knew Burton Boyt Quint and can recall a tattoo like that, then, Joel tells her, she's found her man.

Long days in the darkroom trying to produce expressive prints. In a book of photographs, no matter how fine the gravure process, some quality is always lost. As I work I think of my tonal fields – glove-soft grays, glistening whites, velvety blacks – as my palette. In that limited but expressive range, I feel I can convey any color that exists.

Sometimes I stop work to think about the differences between the cases: Quint and the old T case; Crane's murder of Tim. Skeleton-man's crimes, brutal and sinister as they were, contained at least some mystery and passion. But what Crane did to Tim strikes me as utterly, irredeemably evil.

Sasha warms me. After difficult days, I revel in his arrivals at night.

Then the feel of his hard dark body, silken skin, the look of his gorgeous deep liquid eyes. In bed he whispers sweet intimacies into my ear. I adore that he whispers, no matter that no one's around to overhear. It's as if we inhabit a country of our own, a dark secret country of love.

Why, I wonder, did it take me so long to come to love him? Surely not on account of any deficiency of his, Sasha being not only beautiful but wonderful as well. And, I tell myself, I must be careful not to blame the Judge. No, the fault was purely mine, my inability, my lack, something that froze up inside when Tim was killed, which only Sasha could warm and melt.

Hilly's making good progress, Joel tells me. If her investigation pans out, it'll be the crime story of the decade. Charbeau and Shanley no longer mess with her, are much too awed and scared. She's been on the fast-track since she broke the Lovsey case. It's only a matter of time, they know, before she's given a command position. Joel says she's aiming for chief of Homicide, and if she solves the T case, she may just get it . . . and more.

I drop by Cherry Street to see Dad. There's a new openness between us, has been since he made what we both now smilingly refer to as his 'confession'. He tells me he's thinking of expanding his social life, which will mean cooling things down with Phyllis. He'd like to get out more, he says, meet new people. The notion of him dating makes me smile.

Drake has disappeared. I haven't seen him in days. Twice I leave him food packages; both times they're left untouched. Has something happened to him? Is he ill? Or has he simply moved away?

I wish he'd contact me, even though I know maintaining relationships is not his forte. Just as he used to glide in and out of the shadows, so now he seems to have drifted from Sterling Park. But to what sort of life? Though he was difficult to talk to, I miss him more than I'd have thought. And a good part of my sorrow comes from the knowledge that, if he has left for good, I know no way to find him again.

Hilly has turned up a lot on Burton Boyt Quint, including the fact that he disappeared around the time Sipple was attacked.

His car, a 1979 Ford Mustang, probably stolen from the Haight, was discovered abandoned a few weeks later on Bluxome Street near the CalTrain Depot. A Streets Environment tow truck dutifully pulled it to the pound, where, after the requisite thirty days, it was auctioned off.

Quint never renewed his California driver's license or car registration. A month and a half after his disappearance, his landlord, one Kam Yong Choi, had his furniture, clothing and possessions removed from the Moraga Street house, stored them one hundred twenty days, and then, in accordance with California law, put them up for auction, the receipts to cover Quint's unpaid rent.

Quint worked in a print shop on Upper Geary. The company disposed of its old employment records long ago. But one senior worker vaguely recalls him as 'the quiet guy who one day stopped showing up'.

No one on Moraga Street remembers him, but few of the neighbors were living there fifteen years ago. Landlord Choi passed away, the house was sold by his estate, is now the property of a wealthy Vietnamese who leases it out to an immigrant Chinese family, and has neither the interest nor obligation to allow SFPD to take it apart.

Tattoos: Hilly wishes she could work that angle, round up old timers in the tattoo community the way she and Joel gathered the wisepersons of leathersex. But since she has no justification for asking about a set of red skeleton tattoos, she's at a loss how to proceed.

Joel and I take her to dinner in North Beach, persuade her that her goal of nailing the T killer's identity down one hundred percent will probably not be met. What she should do now, Joel suggests, is write a report to the Chief of Police on everything she's discovered, making a strong circumstantial case that Quint and the T killer were one and the same. And if the Department chooses not to release it, Joel will write a front page story describing Hilly's quest to solve the city's most perplexing series of unsolved crimes.

'It'll almost be better than nailing Quint,' Joel tells her. 'You'll be seen as a dedicated detective who left no stone unturned. You followed the trail as far as it went. Most people will believe Quint's the guy, and that little shadow of doubt will make the saga even better.'

Hilly mulls on that, decides she likes it. 'It really *is* better,' she says. 'Like having a new lover, when there's still a little mystery left.'

*   *   *

Judd's lawyer, Jeremiah Waldroon, makes a deal with Pat Chu: Judd will plead guilty to one count of solicitation of corruption in return for testimony against Vasquez. The agreement calls for Judd to serve two-to-six in the country club prison in Chino. In addition he'll permanently give up his right to practice law.

Peter 'Roy' Royal, on the other hand, has not yet come to terms. Pat Chu is pressuring him to implicate Sarah Lashaw, but Roy is holding out, at least for now. Pat believes Lashaw is paying Roy to take the fall.

'God knows, she can afford it,' Pat says.

The end of February brings heavy showers. The city is washed clean by days of driving rain. I find myself depressed. *Exposures*, which was going so well, has bogged down. The stream of images which, a month ago, seemed to flow, now strikes me as awkward, at times even forced. Tim's story is so complex there are times when even I get lost. I think of Mom, the last months of her life, trying over and over to play through Schubert's B-flat sonata, forever stumbling over the repeats, unable to find and play the climax.

Sasha tries to help. He suggests I get out of the house, start a new project or take time off, anything to stop staring out at the rain. I'm too isolated, he says, too wrapped up in work. I need stimulation, fun, something to make me laugh. I disagree. What I need, I think, is illumination, a flash of brilliant light.

The last day of the month, 6 p.m. Magic time is over. I'm gazing out at the dark sodden city. It's been a windy umbrella-shredding sort of day, about as miserable here as it can get.

The phone rings. Dazed, I pick up.

'Hi, Kay! It's Courtney Hill.'

The voice is familiar, but for a moment I can't place the name.

'You said if I ever heard anything about Amoretto to let you know.'

Suddenly I'm alert.

'This isn't definite . . . but then nothing about her is.' Courtney laughs. 'An ex-boyfriend of mine, part of our old HardCandy crowd, thinks he saw her down in Mexico a couple weeks ago. He was there on vacation, thought he saw her crossing the street. He called out to her, but she didn't turn. He tried to follow her but it was night and then he lost her in the gloom. He isn't positive, mind you. She looked different, he says. Older maybe. But the way she moved – if it wasn't her, he says, it could have been her twin.'

I try to steady my voice. 'Where in Mexico?'

'Resort town up in the mountains, San Miguel de Allende. Cool place, full of expatriates. You might like it, Kay. They got some kind of art school there.'

AFTER A DAWN FLIGHT from San Francisco, total chaos in the Mexico City airport, then a four-hour bus trip, I arrive finally at San Miguel. It's 5 p.m., the sun is low, the light soft: magic time has just begun. Within minutes of starting out on my first exploratory walk I understand I've arrived at some kind of paradise.

The air here, scented by flowers, is cool and dry. The hills above town are ridged with ancient stone terraces; the plains below are studded with cacti. But it's San Miguel itself that seems enchanted. Striding its steep, narrow, cobble-stone streets, I feel myself slipping into a trance-state, spellbound by the aura of old Mexico – shadowed, timeless, serene.

Through partially opened doors I catch glimpses of courtyards, hear the gurgle of fountains, smell the rich aroma of blooming plants. By the time I reach the main square, the *paseo* has already begun. Mariachi musicians, pants embellished with silver discs, play a bullfighter's march, while hundreds of young people circulate along covered sidewalks before an approving audience of elders seated in cafés.

I start taking pictures. Grave young men in tight jeans pace in one direction; smiling, beribboned girls move along in pairs in the other. It's a mating dance of quick glances, bold looks, flashing eyes. As the sun fails and the shadows lengthen, the intensity of this public courtship builds. A swarm of bats swoops into the air; a flock of cawing blackbirds settles on the tops of the pollarded laurel trees. The last rays of slanting light hit building façades, etching out details, baroque balconies, carved escutcheons, causing the walls to glow as if lit from within.

A three-legged dog limps across the *zocalo* then disappears up a narrow street. Prowling the square, I suddenly find myself face to face with a bent old man. He's a commercial street photographer, packing up his huge view-camera for the day. His portable stand, already shut, is plastered with snapshots – young couples posed stiffly before the soaring wedding-cake façade of the town cathedral.

Darkness falls, the air turns chilly, lights come on in branching iron streetlamps built like enormous candelabra. The courtship ritual reaches a peak. Bells start tolling; nuns scurry across the *zócalo* on their way to vespers. I huddle in my leather jacket, hands deep in my pockets. *Are you here, Ariane? How will I find you in this maze of angled streets, courtyards, barricaded doors?*

Setting out in the morning I devise a plan. I will explore the town block by block, resting in restaurants and cafés; after dark I'll hang out in bars and cantinas, and late at night at discos, the sort of places where, in San Francisco, Amoretto found her prey. I will give myself five days. San Miguel is small, compact. Unless Ariane is in seclusion, sooner or later our paths should cross.

Will I recognize her? I know she resembles Tim in posture and face, that her hair's the same length, that she's shorter but moves in a similar way. I recall how I mistook her on Mission Street the day I cleaned out Tim's studio. Yes, I think, if I see her I'll know her right away.

Eyes shielded by my heaviest shades, I commence my search, pausing every so often to peer into shops. The craft stores don't interest me, but I'm impressed by the multitude of galleries. According to my guidebook, San Miguel is a town obsessed by art. For years I've heard about the Instituto Allende, which attracts painters from all over the world. When I find it, I'm touched; it's small, beautifully situated. San Miguel, I understand, is a city of colors – contrasting pinks, ivories, mustards, terracottas. Most likely it's these chalk hues that draw the artists. Still I'm content with the wondrous clarity of the light. The town strikes me as the perfect place for a surprise encounter, an unexpected meeting with a lover or an enemy.

Four days without success – I'm discouraged. At dusk, seated by the *zócalo*, nursing a coffee, I despair of accomplishing my mission. Exhausted by lengthy walks and late nights spent in ear-splitting discos, I ask myself whether the time hasn't come to give it up. I'm here, after all, only because someone I don't know told someone else he *thought* he saw Ariane. Maybe he did, and she's moved on. Maybe she's here, and doesn't go out. Maybe she was never here and the sighting was a mistake. Still I'm haunted by the coincidence with Tim's remark that he would retire to San Miguel when he gave up working the Gulch.

Suddenly it comes back to me – the smile on his face when he told me he had a house picked out. I think: *That's it!* It *wasn't* just a fantasy; he and Ariane had it planned. They would come here together. Perhaps they already *owned* the house.

I struggle to recall Tim's description: church and jacaranda tree on the corner, sharp angle in a narrow street, old stone wall, carved wooden door with coat of arms above, courtyard 'dripping with bougainvillaea', pots overflowing with flowers hanging from iron balustrades.

I grow excited. This is a place I *know*, a place I've passed numerous times! I sit back, try to visualize it, then understand my error. Of course I *know* it! It's a generic description applicable to nearly every block in town. All of San Miguel looks like that! Have I yet walked down a street here that doesn't?

What to do? I ask myself how Joel would find the house, or Hilly, San Francisco's new 'smartest cop'. It's easy: go to the registry of deeds, backtrack house sales, discover if anyone named Lovsey owns property here. I know I can't do that myself, but I can hire someone who can. Excited again, I gulp down my coffee and walk swiftly back to my hotel, where, with the assistance of the phonebook, I find a single listing under the rubric *Agencias de Detectivos*: Julio Manolo Mondonado, '*especialista en investigaciones matrimoniales*'.

Sitting in his shabby office across from the railroad station, I feel like a character in a cheap Mexican film. Manolo, on the other side of the desk, is a hulk, has a thick accent, an even thicker musk-like scent, a lounge-lizard's mat of shiny black hair and a mustache so wide, bushy and black as to rival the tail of a mink. But more off-putting than his facial hair and odor is the complicated contraption of straps that criss-cross his shirt, from which an enormous black revolver protrudes. I wonder: is this what a Mexican client expects in a private eye?

'Call me Paco,' he says, with a fake grin. My new friend, I surmise, fancies himself quite the lady's man. A pale anorexic young thing, introduced as María, sits slumped beside his desk interpreting and scribbling notes as we converse.

I peer around. The windows are filthy, the Venetian blinds uneven and cracked. A dusty fan hangs lifeless from the ceiling. A huge, black, scarred, old double-door safe broods against one wall.

As I explain what I want, Paco leans back, grin fixed upon his face. When I'm finished, he sits straight again, furrows his brow, then quotes me the *gringo* price: 'A thousand dollars US.'

'That's crazy,' I tell him, standing.

'Please, not so fast. We will make you a courtesy accommodation.'

'How much?'

He strokes his chin. 'If my operative takes care of it,' he gestures toward María, 'for you, Señora, two hundred, cash up-front. A very good price for a records search. Believe me, we don't need business here.'

Still way too much, but I agree since it's a task I can't accomplish myself. Handing over the money, meeting María's submissive eyes, I smile at the notion that she's an 'operative'.

After a trek around town and a leisurely lunch, I find María waiting in the lobby of my hotel.

The moment she spots me she shakes her head. 'No owner by that name,' she says meekly. 'I am sorry.'

I thank her, turn to go upstairs when I feel her tug at my sleeve.

I turn back.

'Perhaps I can help you, Señora.' Her English, I note, is very good.

'You have an idea?'

She shrugs her narrow shoulders. 'Perhaps if you tell me your story I will think of something that can be done.' She peers into my eyes. 'No extra charge.' She pauses, then, beneath her breath: 'He is a brute.'

This remark wins me over. We adjourn to the hotel terrace where she reveals that she's a graduate of the Xultan School of Investigatory Detection in Mexico City, that her dream is someday to own her own agency in Guanajuato, and that meantime she's serving her apprenticeship with Manolo, whom she loathes.

'He is a womanizer, incompetent, ignorant, corrupt, but for now he is the cross that I must bear. He has no inkling of this, but one day soon, after I learn his secrets, I shall leave him and set up on my own. Then I shall become his rival. He will be surprised. I shall steal all his business. The beast will learn what it is to be vanquished by a woman, one who smiles sweetly while harboring rage within her heart.'

What have I stepped into here? María, waving her hand to dispel ugly thoughts, turns her attention back to me.

'At Xultan we learned that the most essential task of an investigator is to listen closely to the client. If you will kindly tell me your story, perhaps I shall hear something that will lead me to a solution.'

She's attentive to every nuance of Tim's description of the house, in the end agreeing there's insufficient detail. In response to her question about the habits of the woman I seek, I describe Ariane's expertise in stage magic and kinky sex-for-hire.

'There is no such woman here,' she says gravely.

'No commercial sex?'

'True, there is, but not like that. Also I would think that a woman who lived that kind of life would come to San Miguel to live differently.'

Certainly that's what Tim had in mind. I peer at María. I'm impressed. Perhaps I have underrated her and the Xultan School of Investigatory Detection of which she's such a proud diplomate.

'Purgation,' she says. I stare at her. 'Our subject, to begin anew, may have felt a need to purge herself.'

'There's a place for that here?'

'Not in San Miguel, but nearby at Atotonilco. Men and women at separate times make pilgrimages to the Sanctuario to cleanse themselves of sin. They stay a week. The food is simple. They sleep on stone floors, silence is required and many use *disciplinas*, little braided whips, to scourge themselves. Some wear actual crowns of thorns and approach the sanctuary on knees made bloody by sharp stones. The fascinating thing is that those who do this so enjoy it. You can see their pleasure,' María's eyes widen, 'in their eyes.'

We set off by taxi. Our journey, less than ten miles, takes us by roadside bath-houses set up beside hot mineral springs. The village of Atotonilco is small and dusty but the church is huge, looming above the plaza.

María leaves me alone in the gloomy echoing nave choked with statues and religious murals. She is off to the convent behind, photo of Tim in hand, to ask the nuns whether a foreign woman who resembles him has made pilgrimage in recent months.

Waiting, peering around the vast brooding space, I'm astounded by the many images of suffering. Saints exhibit bloody wounds; Christ figures display whip-marked backs. The paintings range in style from academic to naive, but there is one constant: an obsessive savoring of martyrdom and pain.

María returns. Yes, she says, a light-haired American, vaguely resembling Tim, did come on a woman's pilgrimage in the autumn. Though thousands have since come and gone, several nuns remember her since it's so rare for a *gringa* to come as a pilgrim, and on account of the fervor with which she practiced her devotions. At last proof Ariane has been here! And if she is starting life anew, that may explain why I haven't seen her in the discos, and why she refused to recognize Courtney Hill's friend on the street. But, I realize on the road back to San Miguel, I'm no closer now to finding her than I was before.

'I'm so sorry,' María says, when we part at my hotel. 'I wanted so much to solve this case.'

'You've helped me a lot, María.' I press a hundred dollars into her hand. She tries to return it, but I insist. 'You're on your way to becoming a fine detective. Save this, add to it and soon you'll have enough to open your own agency.'

Her smile is so brilliant it could blind.

My final afternoon in San Miguel: I walk the streets, camera in hand, trying to capture the unique flavor of the town. During magic time I sit on a bench in the *zócalo*, watch the *paseo* until the last light drains from the sky. Then I walk slowly back toward my hotel to pack, intending to depart for Mexico City on an early-morning bus.

Church and jacaranda tree on the corner. For perhaps the twentieth time I pass that combination. *Sharp angle in a narrow street.* There're so many sharp street angles here. *Pots overflowing with flowers hanging from iron balconies.* All balconies here are iron, and nearly all support overflowing pots of flowers. *Carved wooden door with coat-of-arms above.* I have seen innumerable heraldic devices in San Miguel, from the elaborate coat-of-arms on the palace of the Counts of Canal, to crude little shields dangling above tourist shops.

But suddenly I realize that there's something else I know, something important I've forgotten. I stop, stand still at the bend in the street, close my eyes to allow the memory to flow back. Not something architectural like the street and balcony and coat-of-arms, rather something subliminal from another dimension, appealing to another sense. Not visual but aural. Sound. Music – *yes!* Now I remember! Those operatic arias that flooded the stairwell in the building where the twins lived on Mission Street in San Francisco.

I hear an aria now when I strain my ears, faintly in the distance. Am I imagining? I backtrack a few steps, pause, listen, hear it again, faint still yet present. I move forward fifty feet, stop; I can no longer hear it. I walk back, pick it up again. Yes, it's real!

Slowly I circle the block. On the street behind I hear the music, faintly at first but growing in volume as I approach an old walled house. Moving carefully, trying to position myself as close as possible to the source, I finally recognize the voice and aria: Maria Callas singing '*Morrò, ma prima in grazia*' from *Un Ballo In Maschera*. It was Callas's voice too that I heard in that tenement stairwell.

I approach the door. There's a coat-of-arms above. I push it open, enter a paved courtyard, solitary fig tree at its center surrounded by fallen fruit. The stone floor is illuminated by an electrified lantern hanging from a wall. Immediately I'm suffused by the aroma of bougainvillaea. The opposite wall actually does seem to 'drip' with it. Now the music is clearly audible.

Following the sound, I move to a set of stone stairs, mount them, find myself on a covered balcony overlooking the court. The sound is full strength now, close, so very close. I approach a door, press my ear to it. It's coming from within, the room just behind.

I pause, step back, knock.

At first nothing, no reaction, no sound of approaching steps. The music, in fact, seems to increase in volume. I take in the lyrics: '*ma queste viscere, consolino i suoi baci*'— . . . let his kisses console this body.

Slowly the door opens. A slim young woman in silk robe stands poised in the doorway, a glowing room behind. She peers into my eyes, no trace of surprise on her face. Finally, slowly, she nods her head.

'I know who you are. You're Kay,' she says quietly. She smiles as if expecting me, steps back so I can enter.

For a while we simply stare at one another while the music echoes off the high curved ceiling, a dark celestial canopy studded with gleaming painted stars. The floor too is dark, the wood glossy and rich; the stucco walls are white. No pictures on them, just an old wooden crucifix at one end, a stone fireplace at the other. Embers glow in the grate.

She sits very still, as if displaying herself. A dozen thick church candles, set in holders upon the floor, send flickering shadows across her face. She has, I note, the body of a model, but I'm frightened by what I see above: Tim's features, but with something added that makes her face distinctive – ferocity in the eyes and a devouring aspect to the lips and mouth. No perfect mirror-image of her twin, she looks stronger, more savage.

'I thought one day you might turn up,' she says, 'if you cared enough . . . and since we've never met, I couldn't know.' She smiles. 'He spoke of you often. He liked you very much. I believe he even loved you in his way – which was curious, wasn't it? His way, I mean. He was so gentle.' She shakes her head. 'Not at all like me.'

She gazes into my eyes. I look away. The furnishings in the huge room are sparse – a wooden table, several colonial era chairs, nothing more.

'You look as I imagined, Kay. He described people very well. He could be funny too about people's flaws, but he never said a mocking word about you.' She pauses. 'We were lovers. I suppose you know that now.' She pauses again. 'It must have been very difficult to find me. You must be a clever person and have cared a good deal to take the trouble.'

I gasp. She speaks too casually of things that to me are monumental – Tim's and my feelings for one another, my tortured quest for him that became a search for her.

'I know,' she says, 'you must think I'm awful.' She shrugs. 'Perhaps I am. But then who isn't really – when you come down to it? Shall I turn off the music? I'm sure you have questions. If not I can't imagine why you've come.'

She moves to the stereo, flicks a switch. The great room goes silent. She pulls her chair up close so that we sit but a yard apart, places a footstool between us, rests her slippered feet upon it.

'Put yours up too,' she urges.

I shake my head. She shrugs.

'I see my words have hurt you. I only wanted to let you know how much he cared. He told me so, and how tempted he was. But for people like us, you see, abstinence is always more expressive than seduction.'

She pauses, shows me her full face in repose. She's so stunning, intense, I can't take my eyes off of her . . . and wish I could. I would like to get up now, leave. But if I do, I know she'll haunt me forever. Coming here in search of Tim, I've found someone entirely different. Yet physically she is Tim in female form. It's this contradiction that's got me so confused.

'Why didn't you claim him?' I ask.

'His body?' She tosses her head. 'Timmy and I weren't into dead bodies much. We figured once you're dead that's it. Also I was hiding. A little later I fled.' She shrugs. 'Anyhow, I heard you had things well in hand.'

'You could have called me.'

She blinks. 'I probably would have one day.'

'We scattered his ashes at sea.'

'Yes . . . that's fine.'

'David deGeoffroy came.'

She laughs. 'Oh, I'm sure!'

I can't believe how uninterested she is, am angry too at her reaction that it was okay to leave town without a word since I had taken on the bereavement duties.

'What happened,' I demand, 'between you and Tim and Crane? How did all this come about?'

She turns away, and as she does her face seems to harden even more. Still her eyes, I note, are stunningly beautiful, deep, opaque, like Tim's. I wonder: who is this woman and why do I feel so uneasy in her presence?

'. . . they called Crane "Dome" on account of his being bald, which he was too vain to show. A man hires hustlers off the street, then he's too embarrassed to take off his toupee.' She sneers. 'Pathetic! Anyhow, Dome fell hard for Timmy, which bored him no end. One thing to be desired, another to have a client who's obsessed. Dome was crowding him, would have suffocated him if Timmy had given him half a chance. Dome wanted Timmy all to himself, offered to set him up in his love-nest, make him his full-time pet. Timmy wasn't interested, didn't care about money – silly boy! He enjoyed the game too much, the hustle. Control was fine, but once they grovelled he'd get bored. Too many new bodies to explore, fantasies to fulfill. So he turned Dome down. And that, it seems, made Dome very mad.

'One day he saw Timmy with a rival, another rich guy they called "JJ" for Jaguar John – on account of how he picked up hustlers in his Jaguar. The next night Dome sought Timmy out on Polk, demanded he stop seeing JJ. Timmy laughed, told him he'd see whomever he liked, that JJ had offered to take him to Key West over Christmas . . . which was true. Dome said he'd do better than that, take him to Paris, Rome, anywhere he liked. Timmy explained that wasn't the point, JJ would take him to those cities too if he wanted . . . then let him hustle for himself. In fact, he told Dome, JJ liked to watch him do it – which, I guess, infuriated Dome even more. Though, of course, he didn't show it. According to Timmy he went all wet-eyed and limp.'

This doesn't sound like the slick Marcus Crane I observed. 'Was Crane really in love with him?' I ask.

'As much as someone like that is capable of love.'

I think back to Knob's confession, the bizarre moment when Crane tried to take Tim's head. 'What happened?'

Ariane grins. 'Dome decided he wanted to do it with us both. We charged a grand for a Zamantha – that's what we called it. I guess David told you about our old Zamantha substitution trick. A Zamantha, as you can imagine, is a sex act in which the john starts out in the arms of one and ends in the arms of the other. People liked it. It freaked them out. We liked it too. It was fun, made us giggle.'

As Ariane speaks she glances occasionally at me, but most of the time stares past me at the crucifix. She is, I feel, talking primarily to herself, recalling events that took place just months ago as if they happened in the distant past.

'There were rumors about Dome – that he was violent. Still we decided to go ahead. He'd always been correct with Timmy, and during our Zamantha he was fine. We got him hot, got him off, twisted his brain into a pretzel. Afterwards he was so grateful it made me want to puke.'

She stands, goes to the fireplace, tosses a fresh log upon the embers. Sparks fly. She gazes at them, smiles as she watches them die.

'Want a drink?' she asks. 'Joint? All of the above?' I shake my head. She shrugs. 'Excuse me while I indulge.'

She leaves the room, comes back with a snifter of cognac in one hand, a lit joint in the other, takes a short sip from the glass, a long drag from the joint, resumes her seat, smiles at me, continues with her tale:

'Few days later Dome goes to Knob, asks him to arrange a scene with me alone. You're willing to pay, you get to play, so I go up to his love nest, we start getting into it, he makes a few suggestions, some I accept, some I don't, I make a few to him, we take it a little further, and . . . suddenly he's out of control. Bam! He hits me! Bam! He socks me in the eye. I fall to the floor, then he's all over me, sitting on me, pinning back my arms, slapping me with his free hand.

'I'm not like you, Kay, not a fighter. Timmy told me you train in martial arts. Dome's big, powerful. The only way I know to get through a scene like that is go limp, take it till he tires. What I don't want to do is make it fun for him by crying out or begging him to stop. It was a while before he quit. Afterwards I lay there hurting. Then he threw a bunch of money at me and told me to get out.'

She takes a long drag from her joint.

'Back home, looking in the mirror, I was appalled. My face was a mess, both my eyes were black, my lips were all puffed up. I didn't go out much those next few days, just hunkered down at home.

'Soon as Timmy saw me he went bananas, announced the time had come for us to quit The Life. "Why do we keep doing this?" he sobbed. "We got money saved, our place down in San Miguel. We don't need this shit anymore." But first he was going to stick it to Dome, go to the cops, file charges. "He's married to this society bitch. I can ruin him," stuff like that. I told him forget it, just spread the word and no one'll touch the guy again. But Timmy was furious. He loved me, introduced me to Dome in good faith. Dome injured me. Timmy wanted revenge.'

She stands again, goes to the fireplace, takes a final drag on her joint, flicks the butt into the flames, then stands with her back to the fire.

'When I counted up the money Dome threw at me, it came to a fairly decent sum. I pointed out to Timmy that ruining Dome's reputation would hurt him, sure, but wouldn't do anything for us. On the other hand, reparation money would.

'Timmy didn't like that, said blackmail wasn't our style. I told him how silly that was seeing as how we'd done things far worse. I also reminded him that, far as the cops and public went, I wouldn't be the most sympathetic victim in town. Finally he agreed to meet with Dome, squeeze him for as much as he could get. Take Dome for a bundle – that was the plan. Then be on our way.'

She returns to her chair, sits, extends her feet toward the footstool, which, in her absence, I've been using to rest my own. My first instinct is to relinquish the space. Then, recalling David DeGeoffroy's words about her need to dominate, I move my feet just a bit. She notices, smiles slightly to herself, carefully positions hers so they're beside mine, not quite touching but close.

'I was with him when he phoned you that afternoon,' she says. 'He was going to introduce us that night. He'd told me a lot about you, your work, what you were trying to do. He'd spoken of getting us together for weeks. After you photographed him nude, he had this notion you should shoot us nude together. He wanted that, and, after I saw your photos, so did I.'

She finishes off her cognac, bends to set down the glass, then partially straightens herself so our heads are just inches apart. I occupy her attention now. She no longer looks out across the room. Rather her eyes, filled with candlelight, bore into mine.

'I thought you could take some really great shots of us. You know, shots that would show people what we were really like. No one ever saw us clear. We were either this sordid incestuous pair or this weird couple who were so much fun to fuck. There're plenty of close twin sister-brother couples, but we knew we were special, did things no one else had ever done. Our mentalist routine, for instance. There'd never been another twin sister-brother act like ours. Then, when we grew up, became sex magicians, we offered our Zamanthas, a unique experience, providing bedazzlement, genderbending rapture. We were Queen and King, God and Goddess. Who else offered anything like that?

'Sure,' she shakes her head, 'we were paid for it! After all, that was our work. But for us it was so much more. We loved the street, anonymous sex, being so hugely *desired*. We were explorers discovering new ways of leaping out of our skins – transcending, exchanging, the one becoming the other, the other the one. Sister, brother, separate yet the same. Two! One! Two again!' She snaps her fingers. 'Zamantha! Twins!'

She moans. 'It couldn't go on too long. We both recognized that, knew one day we'd burn ourselves out. But always there was our plan to come down here, start out fresh and clean.' She sniffs to mock the notion. 'We even planned to write a memoir, the story of our adventures. Perhaps a little like St Augustine's, you know.' She grins. 'A confession of all our sins.'

She leans back, eyes still locked to mine. She has me spellbound. We sit in silence for a time, then church bells start to toll. I wonder: why did she send Tim off to blackmail Crane alone? The number one rule of the street, Knob said: never threaten a john or try to blackmail him; do that and you're as likely to get killed as paid.

'I waited two hours for him that night,' I tell her. 'Finally I gave up, went home. Crawf called me early in the morning, said the cops had found—'

'Sure. His head.'

Though she winces I'm struck by her lack of emotion. 'Like the Zamantha,' she adds. 'Except this time it wasn't an illusion. The child wasn't made whole at the end.'

'How did you hear?'

'Gulch telegraph, same as you. At first, when he didn't come home, I wasn't too concerned. We both did a lot of overnights. Then, early in the morning, when I got the word, it was already all over town.' She smiles. 'I was on the landing just above when you and Crawf went into his flat. Soon as you left I went in myself.'

'It was you who cut up his bed roll.' She nods. 'What were you looking for?'

'His passport, letters, money, an album of photos of us when we were kids. I took one of your portraits too, the one he liked best, took it down, rolled it up. When I got here I had it framed.' She smiles. 'Now it's hanging over my bed.'

'I'd like to see it,' I tell her.

She brightens. 'My bed?'

'My photo above it actually. All the rest too, if that's all right?'

'Sure,' she says, 'the grand tour.'

She smiles as if to herself, flicks the stereo back on. Again the voice of Maria Callas fills the room. Explaining that the apartment occupies an entire floor of a subdivided eighteenth-century mansion, she leads me from the living room into a sumptuously proportioned dining room, then into the kitchen. Here we pause while she refreshes her cognac, and fills a snifter for me. Then on to the two studies, each furnished with day beds, to which she and Tim could retreat when one or the other desired privacy. Finally to the doorway of a large dark room with fireplace. 'The bedroom,' she announces, gesturing me in.

We enter. She lights a long match, applies it to wood set in the grate. Seconds later kindling erupts, the flames throwing our shadows upon the walls, also revealing various strange furnishings arranged like sculptures about the room – an open coffin on a platform, a sword-box big as a steamer trunk, pieces of large-scale magical apparatus, a scaffold, a guillotine, a set of pilgrim's stocks and a huge rotating wooden disk.

I'm taken aback. Looking around, I find Ariane sitting on a huge carved bed, watching me, enjoying my bewilderment. Above her head hangs my Angel Island portrait of Tim magnificently framed like an old master painting.

She tries to lure me. 'Look!' she says, flinging herself back upon the bed, pointing upwards at a skylight. 'Lie down beside me, Kay. You'll see a wonderful sight. The moon, the stars – the sky's magnificent tonight.'

But I decline, instead take a step backwards, then raise my camera to my eye.

'Oh, yes! The photographer!' she announces, amused. 'Want me to pose, strip?'

'That won't be necessary.' I prepare to shoot.

'No nudes . . . oh . . .' She feigns disappointment, then, like David deGeoffroy, starts to pose.

'How's this?' She turns on to her belly, grins like a pin-up girl. 'Or this?' She curls back a leg. 'Just tell me what you want and I'll do it. I'm like that, you know, happy to oblige.'

I ignore her, start shooting, fascinated by the strange double portrait revealed by my strobe – Ariane writhing mock-seductively on the bed beneath the photo I took of Tim bare-chested on Angel Island late last summer.

She's disappointed, I can see, wants my full attention, is annoyed at my refusal to approach. Or perhaps she understands it's the image of them together that interests me, for suddenly she gives up the pin-up poses, sits erect, rests her back against the carved backboard, draws up her knees, clasps her arms about them, then eyes me solemnly like an owl.

'This more like it?' she asks.

'Better.' I crouch to enhance the drama of the shot. *Whap!* 'Tell me something, Ariane – was it all that wise to send Tim to see Crane alone?'

'Huh?'

Whap! I shoot again, leaving my question hanging in the air.

'What're you talking about?'

As my strobe dies, I catch a flicker of anger in her eyes. 'Something Knob said when he confessed.'

'What?'

'That you should never try and blackmail a john, that's the number one rule of the street.'

Whap! Whap! Whap! I work the motor-drive to catch the astonishment on her face.

'Dome killed Timmy for love,' she says.

Whap! 'How come you're so sure?'

I feel her studying me, evaluating my gullibility. 'It's clear enough.'

Whap! 'Clear how?'

'Since he knew he'd never have Timmy again, he made sure no one else would either.'

'Oh, so that's it.' I nod. 'Then it wasn't fear of being blackmailed again and again, the worst nightmare of a john, especially when he's closeted and prominently married like Crane. So dependent too on the wealth of his wife.'

She tosses her head. 'Dome had tons of money. He could easily have paid us off.'

'So he killed Tim for love?'

She nods. 'A kind of love.'

Right, I think, *a kind of love.*

Through this colloquy, a feeling has grown in me, a suspicion so horrifying that at first I reject it as absurd. Perhaps Ariane knows what's in my head, for, as if to distract me, she suddenly exposes her torso by opening her silk robe, then re-tying the arms of the robe at her waist.

I don't comment or react, recalling Maddy's theory that by leaving a portrait subject to his/her own devices, the photographer can inevitably force a revelation. *Fine,* I think, *go ahead! Show yourself! Perform!*

'This is what you want, isn't it?' she asks, standing beside the bed so that her bared upper body is parallel with Tim's. 'I can imagine the caption too – "The Lovsey Twins: A Study In Narcissism & Incest".'

Whap!Whap!Whap!Whap!Whap! I fire away, my strobe creating such potent light that soon it floods the rods in my eyes. No matter, I continue shooting blind, my Contax automatically adjusting exposure. For me the scene has become albescent, but, in my blindness, the suspicion returns. Did she send Tim to his death? Could that be possible? What could have been her motive?

I shoot out the roll, stop, wait for my rods to clear, reload, Ariane watching me the entire time.

'Something's always bothered me,' I tell her. 'Maybe you can help me out?'

'Sure.'

'Why didn't Tim tell me about you? Even casual acquaintances knew he had a twin, but he never said a word to me and I was supposed to be his friend.'

'That hurt you?'

'Still does.'

She shrugs. 'Last fall we tried to separate. We'd tried it before, it didn't work, but still, last September, we tried again. It was just impossible, you know – needing each other so much, yet each of us wanting desperately to live his own life. Of course this time it didn't work either. A twinship like ours was too powerful, not something you can just walk out on, escape. Only death can release you.' She pauses. 'And sometimes even that won't do it. So, you see, if Timmy neglected to mention me, that was just his way, his attempt.'

As she talks on, I resume shooting, moving closer, framing her head and Tim's together, disengaging the motor-drive, taking individual shots now, seeking moments when her expression matches his, moments, too, when she shows herself as his darker half.

She's speaking about David deGeoffroy, and what she's saying doesn't jibe with his Magician's Tale. In her version, their affair went on far longer than a few weeks. Even more surprising, it was merely an after-thought, she says, to David's seduction of and affair with Tim, his primary object of desire, which started a full year before the twins escaped.

'It was like I was this little puppy dog,' she says bitterly, 'and David was throwing me a bone so I wouldn't get too jealous.'

'What about Bev?'

'What about her?'

'Did she know what was going on?'

'Why would she?'

'I thought, since she was his girlfriend, she might have picked up—'

'Girlfriend! What a hoot! Bev was his stage assistant, not his lover. David deGeoffroy's a bisexual pedophile. How pitiful he can't admit it. How contemptible!' She guffaws. 'Listen, we had no choice but to run away. As for stealing, we only took what was rightfully ours.'

Suddenly the design I thought I'd grasped changes form. Like looking through a kaleidoscope then giving it a tiny twist – inside the pieces need only shift a bit for a completely different pattern to emerge.

The link I could never grasp, between the Lovsey twins as children and what they later became, now comes clear. From child magicians performing the disconcerting Zamantha Illusion then passing the hat, they mutated to grown-up sex magicians performing Zamanthas for well-paying clients. Seduced in childhood, robbed of innocence, taught to fascinate, magic was the only way they knew to gain love, feel desired. David deGeoffroy taught them to perform sex as he had taught them to perform magic, forging a chain of shackles that would forever bind their souls.

Ariane's speaking now of their childhood, the imaginary universe they created, their fascination with magic that predated their fateful meeting with David. The best aspect of being twins, she says, was the fun of confusing others. Thus David's Zamantha Illusion was but a formal rendering of the switched-identity games they'd always played. If David hadn't entered their lives, she says, they'd probably have given up the games. But once they joined his magic show, the game became theirs for life. This, she tells me, was their glory and also their shame, their feeling that they were inseparable, caught up in a force-field which bound them so tightly existence apart became impossible.

Another turn of the kaleidoscope, another new design. *There*, I think, is Ariane's motive. Sending Tim to blackmail Crane alone, she put his life at risk. If Crane killed him she'd be free; if Tim returned, they'd both be rich.

'I still miss him terribly,' she moans, as if reading the awful thought in my mind.

'But isn't there a side of you that's also relieved?' I ask.

'*Oh, no!*' Her eyes enlarge. *Whap!* My camera, I think, will catch the truth: her lie.

'You want to know what he was really like,' she whispers. 'I can show you. You can know him through me.'

We're resting in oversize chairs on either side of the bedroom fireplace. Music from the main room wafts to us, echoing off the walls, the great voice of Maria Callas singing of the torments of love.

I'm tired now. I close my eyes. It's the cognac, I think, also my exhaustion, the fatigue that comes when a great quest ends in anticlimax. I feel myself slipping into a semi-somnambulant state, like a person hypnotized, subordinate to another's power.

'Kay . . .' Her whisper, low-pitched, seductive, enters my ear, then, like a snake, seems to twist its way into my brain.

I don't want any part of what she's offering. The truth, I recognize, is that I find her sinister. Yes, I sought her out hoping to find Tim again through her. But though I recognize there's much that's attractive about her – her strangeness, the intensity that fascinated her lovers at HardCandy, the fervor that struck the nuns at Atotonilco – still she's too hard, dark and frightening, too willful. I now see nothing of Tim in her, nothing at all.

'Come!' Her voice jars me. 'Turn-around's fair play. You had your fun, took your pictures. My turn now. Time for a little magic.' She glances at the array of magical apparatus across the room. 'Yes, I think . . . *the wheel.*'

Even as she guides me to the great wooden disk, I feel apprehension. I only play along in the hope of getting more out of her – something she's holding back yet needs to confess, the burden of guilt that required such strenuous purgation at Atotonilco. Perhaps, I think, if I let I play out her little game, she'll open up and tell me what I need to know.

So reluctantly I accompany her, don't even resist as she helps me slip out of my shirt, spread-eagles me against the rough cork surface of the disk, then binds my ankles and wrists to the imbedded steel rings. Funny, I think, how each of us has her weapon – mine my camera, hers this huge piece of magical apparatus.

After securing me, she stands back, squints critically, makes several small alterations in my position, then an adjustment that causes the wheel against which I'm pinioned to tilt back.

Suddenly feeling helpless, I try to wriggle free.

'Don't!' she advises, pressing firmly on my shoulders. 'To make this work you're going to have to keep very still.'

'What're you going to do?'

'Nothing too terrible.' She smiles. 'Actually, I think you're going to like it.' Her eyes sparkle. 'Timmy always did.'

She gazes at me, lightly brushes her hand against my cheek. 'I'm going to kiss you,' she says.

She leans forward, presses her lips against mine, even as I twist my head away. She steps back, glances at me, annoyed. I meet her eyes.

'That's not going to work, Ariane.'

'Isn't it?'

I shake my head.

'Fine!' she snaps. 'Have it your own way then.'

She reaches forward, pulls a lever, there's a mechanical sound, then the disk starts to revolve. Moments later, turning, I feel a swelling in my head. Then, in panic, I understand I'm gazing at her upside down.

'Turn it off!' I yell.

'Hush! Timmy loved the wheel. So will you.'

'I'm getting dizzy.'

'You're right, it is turning too fast. Not to worry – I'll slow you down.' She reaches forward, makes an adjustment. 'There, that's better.' I feel my rotation slow.

Pinned to this wheel, turning sluggishly before her, I feel like a captive set pitilessly upon a spit.

'You have to trust me now,' she says, stepping back. 'I never missed with him. I won't with you. At least, I'll try not to,' she adds with a smirk.

It's then that I see the knife in her hand, its blade catching light from the fire. She turns it so it flashes in my eyes. The brilliance blinds me. Then I hear it whoosh past my face.

My God! She threw it at me! She knows I know! She's going to kill me!

I blink rapidly to regain my sight. Just then a second knife plunks into the wood inches beneath my arm. I feel the wind as it passes. Then I rotate another quarter turn. She throws another knife. Then, when I'm upside down again, another.

The cork scrapes my back as I freeze against it. I'm furious, terrified. I shut my eyes, order her to stop.

She ignores me, and still the knives come, landing all around me, beside my neck, torso, outlining my legs, whistling as they pass, vibrating when they hit the wood. I open my eyes. Ariane, oblivious to my terror, is concentrating entirely on her throws. Turning before her, I am, I realize, no longer a person in her eyes, have become merely a target.

'Go ahead, scream if you like,' she says. 'For some, they say, the screaming helps.'

Understanding that's what she wants from me, to hear me scream, I resolve I'd rather die than give her the pleasure.

Whoosh!Plunk! Another knife lands, this time but an inch from my ear.

'That one was really close,' she says. 'Sometimes, I'd throw them that close to him. So close that for an instant both our hearts would stop. Afterwards, when I'd let him down, he'd be slick with sweat and his body would tremble for half an hour.'

She bites her lip and throws another. This one lands beside my hand.

'One day,' she says, 'we were working on a new ending to the routine. Our concept was great – I'd fling the usual thirty or so blades as he revolved, then, the new finale, I'd throw a trick-knife straight at his chest. It would penetrate to his heart, blood would gush and . . . blackout! The audience would go crazy, scream! We wanted so much to do it, but couldn't figure out how. So, just to see how it would look, I attached the front half of a broken knife right here.'

She approaches me, stabs her finger hard between my breasts.

'It looked so cool. Then, I remember, I found a red candle, lit it, dripped thick red wax all up and down his chest.' She traces the path of the wax upon my flesh. 'Just like blood. To see how it would look.'

Another twist of the kaleidoscope, another shift in the pattern. She is, I realize, recounting Tim's Saint Sebastian fantasy, the one he expressed the day I photographed him nude.

She steps back from me again, further than before. 'Just four more,' she warns me. 'To the four points of the compass, as we used to say.'

Whoosh!Plunk! Whoosh!Plunk! Two knives land quickly on either side of my chest. I can even feel the second graze my left breast as I turn.

Whoosh!Plunk! The third lands just above my head, cutting through my hair.

The next will be the one, I think. She'll go for my chest, my heart, the very place she stabbed me with her finger.

She lets me rotate a full turn, waits until I'm nearly upside down. Then . . . *Whoosh!Plunk!* The knife lands close up between my legs.

She leaves me to rotate several times before she shuts off the motor. When the wheel finally stops, I end up slightly off-center, dripping, dizzy, outraged.

'You did well,' she compliments me as she loosens my bonds. 'No sissy stuff, whimpers, screams. Timmy always behaved well too. Brave – manly, you know,' she sniffs.

Free at last, I shake my head to clear it, then find my shirt and put it on.

'You're angry with me?' she asks.

'Of course!'

'But, Kay – I thought you'd like it? The thrill, I mean. I was never going to hurt you, wanted to give you something to remember, that's all.'

'You presumed too much,' I tell her coldly.

She stands back. 'You don't like me, do you?'

'Not much,' I admit. 'I'm finished here. I'm leaving.'

'Please! Don't go,' she begs. She lurches toward me. I step back. She stumbles, falls.

'What did I do wrong, Kay? Tell me?'

'Why don't *you* tell me?'

'What do you mean?'

I stare down at her, hating her.

'I'm waiting,' I tell her. 'But not for long.'

She gazes up at me. Suddenly I find her pathetic. I address her with contempt.

'A few hard days at Atotonilco, maybe a half-baked confession to a priest. Lousy food, crawling around on stone floors, a few self-administered lashes of the *disciplina* – is that all it takes to purge your little soul of guilt?'

She starts to weep.

'Oh, please, Ariane – don't go sissy on me now.'

'God!' she whines. 'What do you want from me? What do you *want*?'

'Spit it out!' I tell her.

'What?' She gazes at me, eyes watery, mouth slack, her beauty now all drained away. 'That I sent Timmy to see Crane alone? Yes, that was wrong. But it was his choice too. We took a gamble and we lost. I see that now—'

'What do you see?'

'That I shouldn't have let him. He would have done whatever I wanted. I should have—'

'*What?*'

'—should have thought it through.'

'So why didn't you?'

'I don't know,' she cries, 'I don't know. I just don't know.'

'Oh, I think you do, Ariane. I think you know very well.'

She continues to stare up at me, then crumbles.

'I just wanted . . .' she moans. 'I thought . . . if I could finally be, you know . . . just be *alone*.' Her body shakes as she sobs helplessly on the floor. 'Was that so bad?'

Murder by omission. Gazing down with pity at her abject form, I wonder what will become of her, whether she'll ever free herself of guilt. I shrug, pick up my camera, make my way through the apartment, descend the stone steps, cross the courtyard, open the heavy door to the street.

Dawn has just broken. I've been up, I realize, the entire night. As I slip outside, a *burro* carrying firewood treads by escorted by a small boy wearing a huge sombrero. I walk swiftly to my hotel, shower, change clothes, pack, order a taxi, make it to the terminal just in time to catch the first bus out.

On the drive down to the plain, I ask myself if I was right to leave her like that, sobbing, so pathetic in her anguish. Is she evil? Probably, I think. Certainly she is mad and capable of evil acts. I know too there is nothing she can tell me that will further illuminate the mystery of the twins. I only hope that in the photographs I took, there will be one or two that will encapsulate their passion.

Late-winter rains batter San Francisco. This cool gray city of love turns gray indeed. Water, funneled into the streets, rushes down the hills. There is flooding, a sinkhole opens on Seacliff, a mud-slide shuts down Route 101 cutting off Marin County for a day.

My own days now are constant, spent in the darkroom producing prints. Sometimes the work goes well, more often it turns difficult, in which case I walk down to the marina, take aikido class with Rita, then walk on to Maddy's for a consultation.

Spring comes, flowers bloom, the city feels young again. An unexpected postcard arrives from Portland. The message, written in block letters, is spare, succinct:

> *HI, KAY! MOM DIED. I'M STAYING*
> *NOW WITH SIS. SEEING A SHRINK.*
> *MAYBE GOING BACK TO COLLEGE SOME*
> *DAY. MISSING YOU AND RUSSIAN HILL.*
> *HOPE ALL GOES WELL.*
>
> *DRAKE*

I'm very happy to hear from him, to learn he's in care and safe.

Hilly calls, tells me she's tired of 'jilling off', that she's now 'out there' seriously searching for a lover. Giggling, she adds that, to her immense surprise, at The Duchess at least, her new-found fame has cut no ice at all.

On Sundays Dad and I have gotten into the habit of taking long slow hikes at dusk. We vary our route, sometimes walking from Fort Mason through Crissy Field to Fort Point, other times exploring the shimmering upper forests of the Presidio, or striding along Baker Beach looking at old gun emplacements, then continuing on to Point Lobos, Lands End and the ruins of the Sutro Baths.

Today, striding the footpath between the Great Highway and the dunes, we marvel at the way the sun melts into the Pacific.

Dad mentions that Hale came by City Stone Ground on Friday, and, for the first time in years, didn't ask about the leather hood. He looked hunched and haggard, Dad says, bought a couple of baguettes, made small talk, suddenly leaned forward, whispered 'You and your daughter betrayed me', then scuttled off.

We shake our heads over that, then walk on keeping stride, relishing the moment when the sun slips away leaving only a glow behind.

'It's night now. Your time, darlin',' he says.

I look at him. There's still something unspoken, a question that's been nagging me for months. Now that it's dark I dare to pose it.

'When did Wainy see Mom play the piano?' I ask.

Dad's surprised. 'He told you he did?'

'He spoke of the beauty of her fingers as they caressed the keys, told me I have her eyes.'

'As you do, darlin'. As you do.'

'You were close friends then?'

He looks away. 'Not me and him so much.'

'Him and Mom?'

'Yeah. Sort of.'

When he turns back, I see tears in his eyes. He must think the dark conceals them; otherwise he would not have faced me. He has forgotten how well I see at night.

'I must pity the man now he's such a wreck,' Dad says. 'Back then he was handsome. Hard to believe, I know.'

What can I say? Is it any of my business, these intimate corners of my parents' lives – whom they loved, betrayed, the adulterous games they played? I don't like to think of Mom having an affair with Wainy, handsome or not, or with any other man, or Dad with another woman. But I can deal with it. I believe I've even come to love them the more for their weaknesses. Tim was flawed too, as are we all. For me now it's only the flaws that are worth photographing, not the smooth concealing masks. And so I turn back to the ocean, now just barely rimmed by the rapidly failing light.

Brave, wonderful Sasha comes to me at night, helps me to see 'colors'. On days when he's off, we draw the blinds and make love for hours. Then we go out to walk. San Francisco is a city of unexpected, suddenly revealed views. We climb and descend, always trying new routes, always delighting in the exquisite light as it hits a building or paints our shadows upon a wall.

Now, on nights when I'm alone, I never think about the Judge. Also on these warm spring nights I rarely look through my telescope. Rather I sit and gaze out with naked eyes taking in a panoramic view. The city is whole for me now; I can see my future in it. I will wander its streets, take pictures of its people, and, though never seeing its colors, will feel them and, by feeling, come to know their beauty.

Tonight, again inspecting my final photographs of the twins, the ones I took in Ariane's bedroom down in San Miguel, I view them as the key images in my book.

Exposures, I now understand, is many things at once: murder story; horror story; story of good and evil; the story of a street-hustler, his life and death; of Tim and Ariane Lovsey, the Zamantha Illusion by which they were formed and the world of illusion in which they lived. In the end it is also a story of light and shadow, black and white, and all the tones between: desire, love, fear, courage, greed and pain – the tale of my quest.